Bad Boys
Next Exit

Bad Boys
Next Exit

Shannon McKenna
Donna Kauffman
E.C. Sheedy

BRAVA

Kensington Publishing Corp.

http://www.kensingtonbooks.com

CONTENTS

MELTDOWN

Shannon McKenna

Chapter One

Jane hugged her lunch booty to her chest as she stepped out of the elevator. A mocha frappuccino, chicken and pesto on a baguette, a fresh fruit cup, and just one tiny, perfect precious jewel of a dark chocolate champagne truffle rattling around all on its lonesome in a white paper bag. She silently repeated the resolution of the day to herself; no more skipping lunch because of her frenetic boss Charlene's crisis management style. From now on she was going to take at least a few minutes to eat, and she would chew each bite properly, too, like a civilized human being. It wasn't so much to ask, considering how she busted her buns for this place.

Mona, the receptionist, held out a thick sheaf of pink message slips and rolled her eyes expressively as Jane walked by the front desk. "Charlene couldn't find you. She's freaking out. Where'd you go?"

"I have to eat." Her voice sounded guilty and defensive to her own ears, so Jane took a calming breath and smiled at Mona as she took the messages. She was in control. Dignified. And now she was going to sit down to eat lunch at her desk, as was her God-given right and privilege.

Erica, one of her coworkers, grabbed Jane's arm as she passed her cubicle. The frappuccino listed dangerously to the side. Jane barely managed to catch it in time.

"There she is, the woman of a thousand voices! Sylvie and I are fishing for marketing managers, but we've hit a wall. Would you make some of your magic calls for us, Jane?" Erica pleaded. "Pretty please? Be the spoiled southern belle. I love that character."

"Oh, no, be the English dowager duchess," Sylvia begged. "She's my favorite. That snooty old bitch always gets results."

"No floor show until after I've eaten my lunch, you guys," Jane said firmly. "Then I'll be anybody you want me to be. I promise.

OK?" She marched onward to her office, avoiding Erica's and Sylvia's imploring puppy dog eyes. She was such a hopeless sucker for guilt.

The whole headhunting firm took shameless advantage of Jane's well-honed theater skills. She could impersonate anyone, fooling the most suspicious receptionists or secretaries when it came to ferreting out the names and titles of her prey. And once they had identified the most likely executives, she and her colleagues then did their best to lure them away and place them elsewhere. For a nice, fat commission.

She was good at it. Scarily good. But first, lunch. Everyone deserved to eat, and a hardworking headhunter was no exception.

She had just settled in at her desk and raised her sandwich to her lips when Charlene burst into her office. "Jane! Finally! Where on earth were you? What's the status of the Brighton account?"

Jane put down her sandwich with a sigh. "You gave me that file forty minutes ago, Charlene. I've barely had time to read it, let alone—"

"Turn up the heat on this one, Jane!" Charlene gestured frantically. "Everything else goes to the back burner. Brighton Group just lost their general manager to Corinthian Hotels and Resorts. I want you to find a hot candidate, soon! Al Brighton just called me, and the man practically had a stroke on the phone. I want to throw him a bone. Like, now!"

"Yes, I know," Jane said patiently. "I read the file. I understand the situation, and I was just compiling a list of their main competitors. I'll start making the calls as soon as I finish eating my—"

"Start with Crowne Royale Group. Their management team rocks. Everything they touch turns to gold. And I've got the number right here. I looked it up for you. Am I a peach of a boss, or what? Go on. Call 'em."

Jane cast a longing look at her melting frappuccino. "Of course I will, as soon as I—"

"I need your killer instincts on this, Jane. Brighton will fork out two hundred thousand a year for a kick-ass general manager, and if you get lucky, Pierce and I will renegotiate your contract. Twenty-five percent of each commission, starting with this one.

You do the math. And we can even sweeten the pot by tossing in a nice, fat contribution to that youth theater group of yours, hmm? Never let it be said that Grayson and Clint don't support the arts."

Dollar signs flashed in Jane's mind. The headhunting firm took fifteen percent of the first year salary of each candidate she placed. Twenty-five percent of that sum would be hers. $7,500. If her bosses kicked in a donation on top of that—oh, boy. She would almost have a budget for the fall project for her theater troupe of at-risk neighborhood kids, the MeanStreets Playhouse. Rehearsal space, sets, props, lights, costumes, none of it came cheap. She and the other Playhouse founders were always scrambling for funding.

The Playhouse was the only thing in her life that she really gave a damn about. Being able to personally guarantee the kids' fall project . . . oh, it was tempting. Even more tempting than a melting frappuccino.

Jane exhaled slowly. "I need a strategy." She could feel her voice harden as she slipped into work mode. "I'll be a writer. I want to write a fawning feature article on their hotel, so I need a tour from the GM."

Charlene grinned in toothy triumph. "Go on. Call 'em up. I love watching our prim little Jane morph into a ruthless shark."

Jane dialed. "Crowne Royale Group," a young woman responded.

Her acting skills clicked into high gear. "My name is Jane King. I'm from *Europa Air Inflight Magazine*," she lied smoothly. "I'm writing a series of articles on luxury accommodations, and I hope to feature Crowne Royale Group. I'd like to organize a preliminary tour so I can get an idea how I want to proceed. Is your general manager available?"

"Um, actually, he's in a meeting right now," the girl said. "One sec while I check his schedule . . . oh, wait. How about today at three?"

Jane blinked. It was already almost two-thirty. It was never this easy. "Uh, that'll be fine," she said. "And I'll be meeting with . . . ?"

"The GM's name is Gary Finley," the girl told her.

Charlene beamed as Jane scribbled down directions. "Well?

Don't just sit there! It has to be destiny! Freshen up your war paint!"

"Right, boss."

Jane's dutiful smile faded as soon as the door clicked shut. She sincerely liked her flamboyant, high-maintenance employer, but she had no energy to spare for drama right now. She fished her makeup bag out of the desk, set up the mirror and stared into it with critical eyes.

Yikes. Fluorescent lights would make even a Hollywood diva look like death warmed over, she reminded herself. She'd been tossing awake, staring at the ceiling every night, and it had started to show.

She should be feeling pleased with herself. She was the best headhunter in the firm. She'd dragged in a lot of revenue for Grayson & Clint. Problem was, she was sick of the intrigue, the power games.

It had started out innocently enough. Her budding theater career had gone straight down the toilet four years ago in the wake of her disastrous affair with Dylan. She'd needed money, and a distraction. This job had provided both. She'd been edgy, angry, in the mood to jerk people around. Headhunting the way she did it was an outlet for her thwarted acting skills, and a way to crawl out of the hole that Dylan had put her in. She'd never meant it to be permanent.

She wasn't angry and edgy anymore. She was tired and lonely, and her personal life was a flinty wasteland, but hey. One problem at a time. It was a longish cab ride to the Crowne Royale Group's executive offices. No time to mope, or to eat lunch, either. She had to pop into a phone booth and emerge as the headhunter from hell.

She pulled off her glasses, and popped in her contacts. She dug out some hairpins and proceeded to twist and tuck until she had a smooth French roll. She liked the smidgen of extra height, the Gwyneth Paltrow air of restrained elegance. The brown skirt and nipped-in blazer were fine. Shimmering mocha lipstick, translucent powder to soften the freckles, a sweep of mascara, and her face was in order. She slipped her feet into the pumps that added three inches to her well-rounded five-foot-three frame, and watch out, world. She was good to go.

The job ahead of her was simple: to inveigle herself cleverly into Gary Finley's office without compromising his current job. If he looked promising, she would then persuade him that he would be better off working for Brighton Group than for Crowne Royale. Too bad she hadn't worn a low cut blouse, but no biggie. Her boobs commanded respect even when she was buttoned up to the neck. So, unfortunately, did the breadth of her hips, but it was better to accentuate the positive, right?

It was well worth jerking around a few overpaid hotel executives if it let her fund the MeanStreets kids' fall project. So what if she lied through her teeth to get past the receptionist? Big fat deal. She was a good actress, not a bad person. Maybe she should've become a spy, and used her talents for deception in the service of her country. She gazed into the mirror, affecting the steely poise of a Hollywood superspy.

"The name's Duvall," she said coolly. "Jane Duvall."

She snorted at her own goofiness, but hey. If she had to lie like a dog to make her living, she should at least try to have some fun at it.

The executive office of Crowne Royale Group was located in a side wing of the Kingsbridge Crowne Hotel. It was a former nineteenth-century timber baron's mansion in the Queen Anne district, and had been fully restored to its original splendor. Jane looked around the reception area, grudgingly impressed. Sixteen-foot ceilings. Sumptuous furniture, the kind you sink into with a grateful sigh, but need a crane to get yourself out of. Antique area rugs. Sunshine blazed through the windows, rare for a Seattle afternoon even in the summer. It lit up the rich tones of the dark, gleaming parquet. The minimalist arrangement of blush pink orchids on the receptionist's desk probably cost hundreds of dollars by itself. The place practically dripped money. Ripe for the plunder.

The only jarring note was the girl behind the desk. She was strikingly pretty, with liquid dark eyes, but her gleaming dark hair was twisted up into strange, spiky knobs over her ears. Hair sticks were stuck through, decorated with bobbing beads on springs that looked for all the world like insect antennae. Her lush mouth was painted a bright, frosty purple. "May I help you?" the girl asked politely.

"I'm here to see Gary Finley," Jane said. "I'm Jane King."

The receptionist's grin showed off a mouth full of braces. "Oh! The writer from the magazine, right?"

Ah, excellent. Jane smiled. An ingenuous receptionist was a hard-bitten headhunter's dream. "Yes. I had an appointment with—"

"With Gary, I know. I have some bad news. We had an emergency at one of the restaurants. Gary had to run off and fix it."

Jane sighed inwardly. "I see. Can I reschedule?"

A thoughtful frown tugged the receptionist's brows together. "I have a better idea," she said, her dark gaze oddly intent upon Jane's face. "I'll just have you meet with Mac. He used to be GM. He's been everything around here, from busboy on up. Who better than Mac?"

A prickle of tension ran up Jane's back. "And who is Mac?"

"Our CEO, Michael MacNamara," the receptionist said proudly. "He knows everything there is to know about this place, believe me."

It was clear from the girl's expression that Jane should be pleased and honored. It took all of Jane's iron self-control not to look aghast. The last person she wanted to chat up was the guy she was plotting to steal a key employee from. "Oh, I don't want to bother your CEO—"

"No bother! It'll do him good to remember where he came from. He gets too big for his britches sometimes." The receptionist stood, revealing a very bare and enviably flat midriff. "Come with me. I'll just put you in his office until I have a chance to tell him about you."

"Oh, no, really!" Jane said desperately. "I'd rather reschedule—"

"Don't worry! Mac is great. You'll like him. Follow me." The girl's antennae bobbed jauntily as she strode down the corridor.

Jane followed, running rapidly through her options. She could cut her losses and bolt, or she could bluff this out in the hopes of contacting Finley later. Charlene would be very unhappy if she blew this before she'd even made contact. Damn.

Oh, whatever. For the MeanStreets kids, she could spin out this charade for a few extra minutes. She was a trained actress, after all.

Wow, that purple leather miniskirt was fearless. The girl was like something out of a rock video superimposed onto an ad for luxury real estate. "Amazing hair ornaments," Jane commented.

The receptionist grinned over her shoulder. "You like them? I bought them on my lunch break. Mac's gonna have kittens."

This CEO had some problems getting respect from his subordinates, if this girl was any indication. She was awfully likeable, though, and certainly beautiful. Maybe she traded on her looks.

The girl flung open the door to a large office and gestured Jane in with a flourish. "Make yourself comfortable. Mac will be along any second. I'm Robin, by the way. Can I bring you some coffee or tea?"

"No, thank you." Jane was charmed at Robin's friendliness in spite of her awkward predicament.

Out of force of habit, she scrounged a piece of company letterhead out of the printer. She was tapping names and titles into her Palm Pilot when she heard the commotion. A furious, rumbling bass. Robin's light alto responding, protesting. The noise grew steadily closer.

". . . enough of your garbage, Robin." The words were spat out like bullets. "I'm sick of you testing my patience. Get those damn things out of your hair."

"I'm just expressing my individuality, Mac—"

"Individuality, my ass. You knew that Danny and I had a three-thirty with Carlisle and Young, and still you schedule me to baby-sit a magazine columnist? That's a job for Gary!"

"But Gary's not here! The sous chef at the Copley was having a nervous breakdown, and Gary had to go deal with it!"

"So why didn't you schedule her to come in on another day? Use your brain, for God's sake!"

Oh, dear. She'd landed smack in the middle of an internal power struggle. If there were a back door handy, she would slither out of it and to hell with Gary Finley. But there was no back door.

The voices were getting louder. Jane braced herself.

"I never claimed to be a secretary, Mac. I'm just trying to help. If you don't like how I manage your schedule, maybe you should fire me." Robin's voice was supremely unrepentant. "Go ahead. Make my day."

"Goddamn it, Robin—" The door was slapped open so hard, it crashed against the wall. Jane flinched back.

He filled the door frame. Utterly filled it. Her indrawn breath stopped in her lungs and just hung there, motionless.

He was amazing. It wasn't the perfect word, but it was the first one that stuck to him. Gorgeous was too frivolous. Handsome was too bland. His face was square and rawboned, with hollows beneath broad, jutting cheekbones. His gleaming dark hair was clipped severely short. Straight black brows, penetrating gray eyes. His features fit together so perfectly. The blunt jaw, the hooked nose, the sculpted perfection of his sensual lips. The raw force of will stamped all over his face.

She couldn't look down and examine the rest of him, because her eyes were locked with his. She got a vague sense of big, broad. Tall. Well dressed, but his clothing was subordinate to him, and therefore unnoticeable. All she really saw were those eyes. Fierce and bright. Preternaturally aware, like a timber wolf on the prowl.

His eyes moved over her body. She became very conscious of how much smaller she was. Of the bulk of his big body, blocking her exit. Her blazer felt too tight, her skirt too short. Her clothes too . . . hot.

"Hello," he said simply.

She opened her mouth, but the dry squeak that came out was audible only inside her own head. She felt so intensely female. The lace of her bra rasped against her taut nipples. Her belly pressed against the satin lining of her skirt. Her panties felt too snug.

His lips looked velvety, sensual. Merciless.

She clamped her thighs around the rush of sexual awareness— if that was what this was. She wasn't sure. This feeling had no precedent.

He appeared to have forgotten his dispute with Robin. Antennae boinged as the girl shoved him aside and poked her head around his massive shoulder. Her eyes were wide with delighted curiosity.

"Ms. King, this is Michael MacNamara," she announced. "We call him Mac. I swear, he's not usually like this. He's usually much more smooth and civilized. I bring out the worst in him. He's my big brother, you see. We have issues. But he's a really good guy."

"Ah. I understand," Jane murmured.

Robin stabbed the man's broad chest with her finger. "Be nice to her, Mac. This isn't her fault, so be mad at me, not at her."

His eyes flicked down. "Don't worry. I'm plenty mad at you." He whipped the hair sticks out of her hair. Robin squawked in outrage as knobs of gleaming hair unraveled over her face. "Get lost, shrimp," he said. "I want to talk to Ms. King in private. I promise I'll be nice to her."

"Give those back!" Robin lunged for her hair sticks, but her brother evaded her flailing arms with ease. She gave Jane a dark look. "Don't let him bully you like he does me!"

Jane blinked at her. "I, ah, can't imagine why he would."

"And watch out if he tries to sweet-talk you! First he lays on the charm, and then poof, it's the thumbscrews and the sodium pentothal!"

"Robin, you're losing it." MacNamara's voice was rigidly calm. "Remember our conversation about professionalism?"

"Screw professionalism! Give those back!"

He swept his arm backward, nudging his sister gently out the door. "We'll discuss the dress code later. Cover the phones, please."

He slammed the door and flicked the door lock shut.

The sound of the lock click sent a tingle of primitive feminine wariness through her. He froze, his hand lingering over the knob. "Sorry," he said. "It's just a reflex. I do it when I need privacy." He opened the lock with a deliberate flick of his finger. "Didn't mean to make you nervous."

"That's OK." His perceptiveness made her more nervous still.

He tossed Robin's hair sticks onto his desk. "I apologize for the circus act. My sister's going through her rebellious stage."

"Maybe you should fire her," Jane blurted. "She wants it so badly."

It was the first thing that popped into her mind, and judging from the sudden chill in his eyes, it had been the wrong thing to say.

"Thank you for sharing your opinion," he said.

She winced. "Sorry. Forget I said that." She fidgeted under his cool regard for a long, tense moment.

He relented, and a brilliant grin transformed his face, carving deep dimples into his cheeks that flanked the sexy grooves around his mouth. As if he needed dimples, on top of everything else. "Never mind," he said. "Let's try this again. Please call me Mac." He held out his hand.

Jane extended her own. She was speechless again, and he was patiently waiting for a reply. Her fingers were swallowed by his huge hand. He didn't shake it, just held it, in a warm, implacable grip.

"And you are Jane King," he prompted. "The magazine writer."

His words jolted her. Where was she going to find the presence of mind to lie to this man when she could barely speak at all? He lifted her hand, and pressed his smiling lips gently against the hollow between her first two knuckles.

The softness of his lips, the heat of his breath against the back of her hand, unleashed a storm of emotion inside her, like a flock of startled birds taking off, a fluttering rush of wings beating all at once.

It shocked tears into her eyes. She had to tell him . . . what? Her mind was blank. She wrenched her gaze away. This was silly. So a sexy guy was ogling her. Big freaking deal. She should ogle him right back. She was a ruthless headhunter who used men and tossed them away.

Except that this man didn't look particularly . . . tossable.

He stroked her palm with his fingertip. She glanced furtively down at his left hand. No ring. "I've intruded on a busy afternoon," she said.

"Not at all," he said. "This has been the best moment in my day. So far, anyway." His fingers tightened around hers.

It felt so natural to drift ever so slightly deeper into the warm, buzzing force field that surrounded him. "But your schedule—"

"There's nothing I'd like better than to show you around the hotel," he said smoothly. "I'm proud of this place. I live for this stuff."

"And your three-thirty meeting?" She glanced at her watch. "What can we do with only twenty minutes?"

He pressed his lips tenderly against her hand. "A lot, if we focus." His voice was a low, seductive rumble, caressing every nerve. "I'm very focused, Jane. May I call you Jane?"

"Ah . . . yes. Of course." This was most overt sexual come-on she'd ever gotten, and she was actually considering—was she?

Yes, she was. Oh, God, she really was. She dragged a stuttering breath into her lungs. This had never happened to her, an impulse so strong, so shocking, but why the hell not? She was single, independent, adult. What was the harm in taking what his eyes were offering? She *chose* her response, she reminded herself. Big girls made choices. They reached out, and took what they wanted. Why not her?

"So? Let's get to it, then." He opened the door, and seized her elbow. The contact sent a shiver up her arm. He had a fresh, herbal smell. She wanted to rub her cheek against his shirt. Gulp him in.

He led her away from the reception area. "We'll use the back staircase," he said, in answer to her questioning glance. "I don't want to engage with Robin. That would be a poor use of our precious"—he checked his watch—"nineteen minutes and thirty-nine seconds."

His big, warm hand settled possessively at the small of her back. Faraway thunder rolled in her mind as he led her up the narrow staircase. Were there rules governing these situations? Conventions? She didn't have a clue, and their silence was so . . . eloquent. With each moment that passed, she might be tacitly agreeing to any wild, erotic thing that he might want from her. Her head swam with sensual images. She stumbled. He steadied her, his arm circling her waist.

"Careful," he said softly. "I've got you."

Oh, didn't he just. He swept her past the second floor landing with a gentle, decisive push of his hand. "The espresso bar, hair salon, tourist office and fitness center can wait, for now. I want to show you the luxury bedroom suites. They're our big selling point." His low voice brushed over her skin like silk. His hand pushed her gently onward.

She was so excited, she could hardly breathe.

He stopped in front of a door. "Each of the luxury suites has a theme," he told her as he unlocked it. "This is the Baron's Suite."

He opened the door. She took a deep breath, and walked in.

* * *

Mac left the door carefully ajar as he followed her into the room. He flipped on the light and circled around so he could catch her reaction. Bringing her up here was a low-down, dirty trick, but all was fair in love and war, and he felt perfectly justified in a preemptive strike. The Baron's Suite was calculated to make a woman weak in the knees, and judging from the startled delight on her face, it was working.

"This room is a reproduction of a bedroom from an eighteenth century baron's palazzo near Naples," he told her. "The bed is a reproduction of a bed that the baron commissioned for his mistress. This suite is the Kingsbridge Crowne's answer to a honeymoon suite."

"I see. It's, um, remarkable." She drifted closer to the immense bed. The massive gilded headboard writhed with cupids, nymphs and satyrs. Upon first glance, it was just a busy swirl of golden baroque eye candy, but upon closer inspection . . . yes, she was catching on, moving closer. Mac sidled around so he could peek at her face as she realized just exactly what that chubby little shepherdess was doing to that goat-footed boy to justify his blissful smile. What all of the cavorting nymphs and satyrs were doing— in every conceivable position and combination.

She drew in a startled breath and clapped her hand over her mouth. For a second, he was afraid he'd shocked her, but the sparkling glance she darted at him reassured him. She wasn't a prude. God, she was pretty when she blushed. "Let me show you the bathroom," he said.

She followed him through the sumptuous room, taking it in with wide, dreamy eyes. Mac felt as if he'd been split in two. One of him was giving a courtesy tour to a fellow professional, and the other watched Jane like a hawk, just in case his wildest dreams should come true. He wasn't making any rash assumptions, no matter how many smoldering glances she cast at him. She had to give him a clear, unmistakable sign.

And he would gracefully take it from there.

He flung open the bathroom door. "We decided to sacrifice historical realism in favor of luxury. The baron and his mistress would have appreciated modern plumbing. But we used marble quarried from a place near Naples, to stay in the spirit of the palazzo."

He watched her look around at the huge, sunken bath, almost big enough to swim in. The Italian marble was pink tinted and fleshy and sensual. Gold-toned fixtures gleamed. The fantasy rose up; the tub full of steaming scented water. Jane stepping in, her bare bottom rosy from the heat. Smiling over her shoulder at him in sultry invitation.

"Wow. It's bigger than my living room," Jane said.

He stared at her flushed, delicate profile. Her hairdo hinted at thick red waves, rolled up tight and pinned into stern submission. Calculated to tease a guy who loved a challenge. Her body was perfect: trim, but lush, like a juicy peach. Something inside him had stood right up and said *gimme that*. He wanted to peel those clothes off her and then let those satyrs and nymphs look down and learn a thing or two.

She turned back to him. "It's beautiful."

He jerked his gaze away from her tits just in time to smile innocently into her wide, indigo eyes. "This place really lends itself to a lavish pictorial color spread," he said. "What photographer do you use?"

Her eyes flicked away from his. "Oh, I, um . . . I work with a few different people, actually. I haven't decided yet."

"I could make some recommendations for you," he offered.

"Thanks, but I'm covered," she murmured. She brushed past him out of the bathroom, and he sensed her tension in the faint, glancing touch. She was vibrating at a very high frequency, he could feel it humming in the air, but he still wasn't sure what she wanted him to do.

He didn't dare guess. This was way too important.

He followed her into the bedroom and found her transfixed by the painting of Leda and the Swan. In this rendering, Leda was a plump naked maiden with long dark curls. She reclined on a canopied bed heaped with crimson and gold pillows, and her bare skin glowed like a pearl against the shadowy draperies. The swan was poised between her parted thighs, wings spread wide. From the naughty twinkle in the swan's black eye and the voluptuous flush of surrender upon Leda's face, it was clear that a very good time was about to be had by all.

Jane put her hand over her mouth. Her eyes gleamed with

suppressed laughter. "There's no safe place to rest your eyes in here."

"This was painted by Manfredi Cozzoli," he said. "An unknown Sicilian painter, early ninteenth century. I picked up his Zeus and Europa at the same auction. Cozzoli was heavy into mythical subjects."

"Europa?" She frowned, puzzled. "Which one was she?"

"Zeus changed himself into a bull to seduce her," he explained.

She choked on a giggle and looked away swiftly. "Good heavens."

"Yeah, it was a little much," he admitted. "We decided that Leda was our best bet."

"It's, ah, certainly not your standard hotel art," she ventured.

"There's nothing standard about our hotels," Mac said. "Each one is unique. We want every guest to feel"—he kissed her hand, felt her delicate bones, her soft skin against his lips—"caressed by luxury."

Oh, Lord, did that cheesy line really come out of his mouth? He must be getting desperate. He forced himself to let go of her hand. He hoped he wasn't blushing, but his face felt suspiciously hot.

Jane looked at Leda and the swan. She looked at the nymphs and satyrs. She looked back at him. His heart began to race.

She walked to the door, shoved it closed, and turned the key in the lock.

Chapter Two

It wasn't wishful thinking; this was really, truly happening. She felt delirious, lost in a feverish dream. Her heart thudded against her rib cage as if it wanted to get out. And now that the door was shut, she had to turn around and face him. She had to . . . to *do* something with him. She caught a glimpse of herself in a lavish, gilt-edged mirror. Pale, heart-shaped splotch of a face, eyes wide with terrified excitement.

His warm hand came to rest on her shoulder. She turned and looked up. His clear gray eyes asked a question that her entire body longed to answer. That was when she realized why her throat felt closed. She didn't want to lie to him. Even a passive lie felt wrong. She couldn't care less about Brighton Group. This was more important. She'd never felt so alive, poised on the brink of something miraculous.

But if she told him the truth now, the miracle bubble would burst and the moment would be lost. It would be all business: explanations, apologies, a hasty and embarrassed retreat with her tail between her legs. A sharp lecture from her boss to look forward to.

She couldn't risk it. If it came down to a choice between fantasy or nothing, she'd go with the fantasy. For as long as she could.

She reached out and rested her palm against his chest. He jerked as if she'd burned him. The smooth white field of fabric looked as cool and pure as snow, but beneath it, he was all hard, resilient muscle and vital male heat. His rib cage rose and fell. His heart thudded rapidly against her hand. He was so tall, she was going to fall over backward.

He must have read her mind, because he cupped the nape of her neck with a low murmur, slid his other arm around her waist and pressed her against his hard body.

It had been so long since she'd embraced anyone, other than brief social hugs. The intimate contact was a soothing, stimulating rush of pleasure. She drank it in with a tiny moan. "Mac, what are we doing?"

"Isn't it obvious?" His hot breath fanned her cheek, her ear.

His mouth covered hers. His lips were as velvety soft as she had imagined. She knew the pros and cons of teeth and tongue, open versus closed, and all the gradations in between. She had her preferences, like everyone else, but this feeling was entirely outside her experience.

The warm, seeking pressure of his mouth called to every buried yearning in her heart. His faint beard stubble rasped across her jaw. Flames raced through her body like beacon fires over a dark landscape, stirring desires she'd never felt. Warmth unfurled in her chest, her belly, between her legs. Colors exploded, swirling behind her eyes.

His kiss grew bolder, coaxing her wider open. He tasted hot and deep and wonderful, with a hint of coffee in the background. His breath was sweet against her face. She flung her head back, gasping for air.

"Your lips are so soft." She blurted the words out before she had time to wonder if it was a stupid thing to say.

He laughed softly against her mouth and kissed her again. His fingers tightened on her hair, and his mouth demanded more.

She flung her head into his hands and opened to the bold thrust of his tongue. Her mouth danced with his, exploring him with eager abandon. She was suspended in space, a chaos of seething heat.

A thread of panic uncoiled inside her. This shaky, falling apart feeling was not what she'd expected. She'd certainly never felt this way with Dylan, or anyone else. "Mac? I feel—I feel like I'm—"

"I know," he murmured. "All yours, angel. Don't worry."

She pulled away from him, flustered, and stumbled back with her hand clamped over her swollen mouth. Her heel caught in the carpet. Mac dove to catch her, and they toppled together onto a soft, brocade-covered sofa.

Mac lifted his weight swiftly off her body. "Damn. Sorry about that. Are you OK? Did you hurt yourself?"

She started to shake with silent, hysterical laughter. "I'm fine, thanks," she said. "Just . . . falling to pieces, that's all."

He dropped to his knees in front of her, resting his big, warm hands on her knees as he gazed searchingly into her face. She would never have dreamed that knees could feel so much, drinking in his heat, tingling with pleasure.

"You sure you're OK?" he asked hesitantly. "You look like you're about to cry."

She shook her head. "I never cry," she told him.

They stared at each other. He reached up and gently pushed back a lock of hair that was trailing over her cheek. She leaned closer, until she could feel his warm breath. His magnetism tugged something deep inside her—a slow, inevitable pull, an aching hunger for his scent, his heat, his vital essence. Her arms slid around his neck as his lips caressed the side of her face. He smoothed her tight, straight skirt up so that he could move between her parted thighs and slide his arms around her waist. The closer he got, the closer she wanted him.

His weight shifted, and he hoisted her up so she was lying on the couch. He bent over her, his lips moving over her face with sweet, seeking gentleness. She was floating, clinging desperately, barely noticing the buttons on her shirt giving way, one after the other, tiny little silent pops, the pressure of her blouse releasing over her breasts.

And oh, God, he was all over her now, so big and hard and heavy. This was happening so fast. Her body was going nuts. She vibrated beneath him. Her skirt was shoved up to her waist and Mac lay between her splayed legs, giving her all his strength and heat to push against. She wanted all of it. Needed it.

Need? She couldn't afford to need this man. She knew nothing about him. She tried to stop her hips from pressing eagerly up against the hard bulge at his crotch. She couldn't stop. She could barely move beneath his weight, and every breathless, heaving wiggle deepened the pleasure, sharpened the throbbing tension.

Mac's mouth moved over hers, caressing and exploring, drawing out sweetness and giving it back in equal measure. She turned her face away to gather her wits, but he caught her face in his hands and jerked it back, covering her mouth again with a low growl of command. He stroked the sheer fabric of her thigh-high stockings, all the way up until he reached bare skin. "Your stockings drive me crazy," he said roughly.

She clutched his shirt, crumpling the fabric in her fists as her hips tightened, squeezing him. She arched, taut as a bow about to release—oh, God, no. *No.* This was insane. All alone in a hotel room with a total stranger. She would fall apart. Never find her way back.

She wrenched her face away again. "Mac? Please—"

"I know," he soothed. "I feel it, too. I'll take care of you. Relax."

Her panic swelled to a frenzy. What had she done? She'd had no idea the stakes would be this high. She was gambling with coin she could not afford to lose. She'd met this man twenty minutes ago, and these emotions were stronger than anything she'd ever felt. If he took what she'd offered him and then buttoned up his pants, *thanks, that was fun, have a nice life . . . what was your name, again?* It would be no more than she deserved, but she would be destroyed. She didn't do casual sex. She'd wanted it, yes. Ached for it. She'd thought she could handle it, and it had taken this inside-out feeling to realize how thin the veneer of her self-control really was. How vulnerable she was beneath it.

Suddenly she could move. Cool air moved over her damp face and her bosom. It rushed into her shuddering lungs. Mac was up on his knees, unbuckling his belt, yanking his shirt out of his pants. His face was flushed, his eyes fierce and hot and focused upon hers.

She struggled up onto her elbows. "Mac, please stop."

He went still, hands frozen on his shirt buttons. His shirt gaped over his broad, muscular chest. An arrow of dark hair disappeared into low-slung briefs, and she wrenched her gaze away—too late. She'd already seen what was poking out of those briefs, long and thick and hard against his flat belly. Whew. Formidable.

"What?" he said, incredulous.

She was shaking so hard, she collapsed onto her back again. Her breath rasped audibly between parted lips. "I can't just, ah . . . do it."

He stared down at her. "I thought this was what you wanted."

She pressed her hands against his chest, but instead of cotton, her hands found hot, naked skin. She tried to snatch her hands back, but Mac trapped them against his chest. His muscles shifted beneath his skin with each breath. His heart throbbed, quick and hard against her palm. "I know it looks that way," she faltered.

"Looks?" His chest jerked beneath her hands in a soundless laugh.

She bit her lip. "I'm sorry. I know I came on to you, and when you kissed me, I lost my head. But it's too much. I just met you, what, twenty minutes ago? I can't just . . . have sex with you, out of nowhere."

"Jane." His voice was flat. "This didn't feel like nowhere to me."

She squeezed her eyes shut. "Sorry. Really. I'm so sorry, Mac."

The silence was so long, she finally opened her eyes and peeked. He was staring at her body. Taut nipples poking through the lace of her bra, skirt crumpled around her waist, legs sprawled wide. Face hot.

He released her hands, and sighed raggedly. "I can hardly be blamed for getting the wrong idea."

Her face flamed hotter. "I know. I'm sorry." She attempted to button her blouse. A lost cause if ever there was one, lying flat on her back. She couldn't make a single button connect over her breasts.

He lifted himself off and stood, closing his fly. He ran his hand over his reddened face. "I'm the one who should be sorry. I read your signals wrong. I don't force myself on women. It's not what gets me off."

"Of course not!" She struggled to sit up. "It's not your fault! I was very misleading, and I'm the one who should be sorry. Not you. Really."

"Then, kiss me again," he demanded.

Her eyes dropped. She buttoned her blouse with shaking fingers. "I don't think that would be a very good idea," she whispered.

He lifted her chin, forcing her to look at him. "I won't open my pants. I won't force you in any way. Just kiss me again, like you kissed me before." He sank down next to her on the chaise. "Please."

She shrank back. "Mac—"

"Please. Just a kiss. I'll fall to pieces if you don't."

His stark tone silenced her. His face was taut, his hands

clenched into huge fists. She wasn't the only one shaking apart. She was moved. Her emotions felt so clear and bright. The impulse to soothe and reassure him was irresistible. She knew how it felt to fall to pieces.

She leaned closer, and brushed her lips against his grim mouth.

The erotic promise implicit in that tentative kiss made Mac shudder. Every sensation was magnified, amplified. The press of her soft lips, the rush of her breath. The shapes and contours of her mouth, the pouting swell of the lower lip, the sculpted curves of the upper, the borderline where the matte velvet of her lips gave way to the moist, satiny secrets of her inner mouth. The flirtatious flick of her tongue.

She pulled back, gazed at him as she pulled her full bottom lip between her white teeth. She'd chewed the lipstick away, and the natural, hot blush pink showed through.

He clenched his hands into fists and stared into her wondering eyes, willing her to sway forward and do it again before he keeled over and died. He'd never seen eyes like that: storm-at-sea blue. With her pupils dilated, the color faded to indigo, then black. Bottomless lake eyes, against cloud-pale skin, framed by autumn-leaves-on-fire hair.

Yeah, a boner of these proportions could turn the most pragmatic man into a fucking poet. "Please." His voice rasped. "Again."

Her lips moved over his, brushing like a warm breeze, then pressing their yielding sweetness more fully, opening to him.

He'd never read a woman so wrong before. He should have figured it out as soon as he touched her. He'd expected the bold enthusiasm of a woman who knew exactly what she wanted, but she hadn't been like that at all. She'd been like a fourteen-year-old getting her first kiss. Shaking like a leaf. *Vulnerable.* Yeah, that was the word he was groping for. She kissed him again, more boldly. The tip of her tongue ventured shyly inside, brushing his. He inhaled her sweet breath, electrified.

This felt so fragile and tenuous, like she might dissolve into a puff of smoke if he made a wrong move. *Vulnerable.* The word hovered around the edges of his mind as she stretched him out on the rack of this agonizing kiss. Vulnerable implied risk. Responsibility. Unknown quantities that had no place in a bout of anonymous sex. Her tongue flicked against his, and he opened for her with a sigh. She gasped against his mouth when his fingers clamped around her arms.

She rose up onto her knees and steadied herself by clutching his shoulders. Her fingernails dug into the fabric of his shirt like small claws. A flush of arousal painted her face, her lush bosom. She was primed. He could push her right over the edge with a puff of breath. He could take her right now and make her love it.

Some deep, wordless instinct held him back.

She explored his mouth, nibbling and licking, her breath a warm cloud against his face. "I love your smell," she whispered shyly.

"It's just my shower gel," he told her. "I don't do cologne."

"Mmm. Nice." She sniffed. "Tangy. Pine needles in the summer."

He grinned like a fool. So he wasn't the only one waxing poetic. "Want to take a shower with me?" he offered. "I'll share."

He was emboldened by her soft giggle. He slid his hands around the back of her legs, stroking her sleek thighs. He hesitated when he got to the lace border at the top of the stocking, lingering in a sweet agony of anticipation as she tortured him with those moist, smooching kisses. She tasted so sweet and fresh. Lemon drops and mint and springtime.

He let out his breath in a harsh sigh as his fingers strayed into forbidden territory—a humid bower of silk and flower-petal softness. A tiny bit higher, and his fingertips were touching lace. Damp stretch lace, over soft, springy ringlets. Very damp. She was more than ready.

He dug his fingers into the wavy hair that was tumbling down at the nape of her neck and seized full control of the kiss. He wanted to strip that lace away, spread her wide open and explore all those secret female folds with his hungry mouth.

She wrenched her face away. "Mac, you said just a kiss!"

"I'm sorry," was all he could manage. He bore her down beneath him onto the sofa and traced the crevice of her labia with his fingertip. She was shivering and taut in his unrelenting grasp, but she was so close. It was killing him. He had to finish it. He had to make her come.

She clamped his hand tight between her quivering thighs so that only the tips of his fingers reached her mound. Fine. Fingertips would do the job. He flicked his tongue against hers as he moved his fingers in small, teasing circles, found the tight protuberance of her clit, caressed it. That wild squirming was going to feel incredible when he was embedded in her hot depths. Plunging and sliding.

Fucking her was going to be so good. She was small, but strong, with those big soft breasts barely contained by the lacy bra. Lithe, vibrant, well built. She wouldn't break beneath his big body when he wanted to be on top, but just to be on the safe side, he'd put her astride for the first few times. Just to let her get used to his size.

He thrust his tongue into her mouth as he imagined her riding him, the swell of her hips gripped in his hands, rosy tits bouncing and swaying. She would take him in, whimpering with pleasure as he pulled her down and filled her up with his stiff, aching cock. Then the moist cling, the quivering tug as he lifted her up again, sleek and skintight as a leather glove. The fantasy almost made him come in his pants.

She writhed beneath him, as if she were afraid of the climax he was driving her towards, but he couldn't relent. He wanted this edge—every possible advantage, all the points he could garner. He wanted to back her into a corner, claim her for his own.

He caressed, insisted, until she stiffened in his arms and let out a sobbing wail. Her orgasm throbbed against his fingertips, jolted through her body and echoed through his own. He hadn't even gotten her panties off yet. This was going to be the hottest sex he'd ever had.

He nuzzled the side of her face, and waited for the verdict. She panted, eyes squeezed shut. She was afraid to look at him, he realized. He pulled her face gently around. Her bones felt so sharp and delicate beneath the velvet soft skin of her face.

"Hey," he prompted. "Hey. Jane? Everything OK?"

Her eyes fluttered open, and she struggled up onto the edge of the sofa. He followed, pressing his thigh to hers. He didn't want her to shiver outside the influence of his body's warmth as the sweat dried and the doubts started.

Her skirt was riding up, stockings rolling down. Her garter had come loose. A stipple of reddish freckles was strewn across the tops of her thighs. He stroked his hand over them, lingering over the downy softness of her skin. She snatched his hand, blocked it.

"You told me just the kiss," she accused him.

His fingers splayed over her warm flesh, digging boldly into her thigh. "You liked the orgasm, too," he said.

"That's not the point," she said softly.

They stared at each other for a long moment, wordless.

The heavy knock on the door made them jump as if they'd both been struck. Mac swore under his breath. "Who is it?"

"Mac? What the hell is going on in there?"

Mac buried his face in his hands and groaned. His brother, Danny. Chief financial officer of Crowne Royale Group Hotels. A good brother, if a difficult one. A good guy, too, when he wasn't being an uptight son of a bitch, which admittedly wasn't often. Mac was convinced that Danny just needed to get well and truly laid. This was not going to be pleasant.

Jane leaped up. He reached for her, but she evaded his hand. "I'll be out in a minute," he called out.

"What do you mean, a minute?" Danny demanded.

Tension radiating from Jane's small, curvy body. She tried to attach the garter to the stocking, but her frantic fingers couldn't manage it. She squeaked and batted at his head when he sank to his knees in front of her. "Relax. Let me fix this for you," he soothed.

"Christ, Mac! Carlisle and Young have been waiting in my office for over fifteen minutes, and Robin says you've waltzed off to give a tour to a cute magazine writer? Are you out of your goddamn mind?"

"Shut up and give us a minute," he snapped. The shadowy mysteries beneath Jane's skirt deserved his undivided attention. He snagged the fluttering garter and inhaled deep, hungry breaths of her heady female sexual smell as he hooked the garter to the stocking.

Then she got down onto her knees to look under the sofa for her shoes, and he almost forgot his predicament just admiring her ass.

The force of Danny's disapproval radiated right through the door, but Mac ignored it with the stoic fortitude forged from years of practice. Danny was unbearable when he was in one of his controlling, self-righteous snits. Ignoring him had always been the best policy.

Jane had finally struggled into her shoes. He helped her to her feet and cast around for a new excuse to touch her. "Your blouse is misbuttoned," he said. "Let me fix it."

She quivered as he reached for her, but she didn't pull away. He was rewarded for his boldness by a delicious last peek at her lace-covered tits before fastening her up again. He let the backs of his knuckles brush up against the underside of her breast, flicking delicately over her taut nipples. "Have dinner with me," he said.

Her indigo eyes flicked away from his. Damn. He'd come on too strong. He'd overwhelmed her, and now she was bolting. She could disappear from his life as quickly as she had appeared.

"Mac," she said stiffly. "I, uh, have to tell you something—"

"I never gave you a tour," he broke in. "I'll take you to the Copley Crowne for dinner, and give you a tour afterward. Please."

Her nose wrinkled in a cute grin. "You mean, like this tour?"

He straightened her collar. "A real one," he promised rashly. "Any kind you want. You call the shots. No tricks, no traps. I'll be so good."

"Um . . . but, Mac? I, ah . . ." She looked like she was gearing up to tell him something he didn't want to hear.

He headed her off instinctively. "I have to see you again, Jane."

"But I have to tell you something," she insisted. "I'm not really—"

"Say you'll have dinner with me," he persisted. "Just say yes."

"Stop interrupting!" she said tartly. "You never let me finish!"

He stepped back, and let his hands drop to his sides. "Sorry. It's a bad habit of mine. Say whatever you need to say." He braced himself.

She took a deep breath, and tried again. "I'm not really—"

"Mac!" Danny thumped the door. "It's been six minutes. Shall I tell Carlisle and Young you're too busy indulging your animal instincts to discuss their possible investment in our hotels? Just say the word."

"Take a pill, Danny," Mac snarled back.

"Just wondering"—Danny banged until the door rattled—"if you're planning on coming out of that room some time in this century."

The moment was irretrievably lost. Jane was buttoning the blazer beneath the awe-inspiring shelf of her bosom, her face hidden by waves of fiery hair. "I'll just, ah, get out of your way." Her voice was unsteady.

"Please." He seized her arm. "Don't run away. Whatever you need to tell me, you can tell me at dinner. OK?"

She hesitated for so long, he was horribly certain that she was going to blow him off. Then she nodded, and he could breathe again.

He grabbed his phone and punched up the address function. "I'll pick you up at eight. Where do you live?"

She backed away and scooped up her purse from where it had fallen during their tempest of kissing and groping. "Oh, don't worry. I'll just meet you at the restaurant."

She was side-stepping him, leaving her options open. He hated it. "At least your number?" he pleaded. "Your E-mail? Jesus, anything?"

Danny pounded on the door again. "Damn it, Mac!"

Mac stalked to the door, unlocked it and flung it wide. "You're going to pay for this, Danny."

His brother's dark eyes were narrow slits of fury. "I already have. Crowne Royale Group has paid for it, too. I don't think Carlisle and Young have much of a sense of humor about this kind of thing."

Mac glanced back at Jane. Her face was snowy pale, but for the splotches of embarrassment on her high, delicate cheekbones. "Excuse me," she murmured. She pushed past him, out into the corridor.

Danny's glacial gaze swept over her. "This is the writer?"

"This is Jane King," Mac supplied, when Jane seemed incapable of replying. "Jane, this is my brother, Danny MacNamara."

Danny's eyes took in the tousled hair, the crumpled skirt, the lipstick kissed away from her mouth. "I'm going to be very curious to read whatever article you end up writing, miss."

The biting sarcasm in his brother's voice made her flinch. Mac's hands clenched. "Do not be rude to her, Danny. Or I will flatten you."

Danny's dark eyes locked onto his. Not many could go nose to nose with Mac, but his brother was six three, just like him. Danny was thinner, though. Whipcord lean. His dark, intense face was a sharper, narrower version of his brother's, and he wore his black hair long, smoothed back into a perfect, gleaming ponytail which still somehow managed to look classy and perfect with his Armani suits. Go figure.

"I'm not as easy to flatten as I used to be," Danny said evenly. "But whatever, man. Go for it."

Jane tugged on Mac's arm. "It's OK, Mac. Just go about your business. I'm gone." She scurried towards the main staircase.

"Meet me at the fountain in the Copley Crowne rose garden!" he called after her. "Eight-thirty! You know how to find it?"

"I'll figure it out." She cast a wan smile back over her shoulder and disappeared around the corner. Her heels clattered unsteadily down the stairs. He hoped she was holding on tight to the banister.

He turned back to Danny. "Thanks, bro. You scared her away. But of course, that's your specialty."

"Do I need to send somebody up to change the sheets?" Danny bit the words out.

Mac smiled thinly. "That won't be necessary, thanks to you."

Danny snorted as they strode towards the back staircase. "I would consider it a real professional courtesy if you would seduce your women on your own time, and in your own condo."

"Jealous? Been a while, hasn't it, Friar Danny?"

"Grow up. I've been stalling those guys while you—" Danny's gaze flicked down Mac's body. He let out a grunt of disgust. "Go to the john and think about the Wicked Witch of the West. You are not presentable."

Mac surveyed the bulge in his trousers with a casual shrug. "It's on the decline. You should've sent Robin in to distract them. She could've juggled paperweights. Pulled quarters out of their ears."

"Yeah, with her belly button hanging out. That would do wonders for our business credibility," Danny muttered. "You think this is all just a game for your personal entertainment, don't you?"

"What if I do?" Mac had never been able to resist a chance to bait his brother. "If it's a game, I always win. It's the results that count. You're the one who takes it all too goddamn seriously. Relax, already."

"What was my crime?" Danny asked the ceiling. "Why do I always get to be the humorless prick in our surreal family dramas?"

"Lighten up," Mac advised. "I'm not as much of a slut as you think I am. Just because I don't keep my dick in the freezer like you—"

"Ahem. Excuse me?"

They jerked to a halt. A chubby man in a gray suit was poking his head out of the conference room. His eyes bulged with anger. "What a volatile place this is," he said. "Have we come at an unfortunate time?"

"Not at all, Mr. Carlisle," Danny's voice was as smooth as ice cream. "I was just retrieving Mac from his, ah, meeting. It ran late."

"I can well imagine." Carlisle's eyes flicked over Mac with unfriendly sharpness before his head popped back in the door.

Mac punched up his friend Henry's number as he dove for the men's room. "Yo, Mac. What's up?" Henry greeted him.

"Hey, Henry. You still seeing that woman Charlotte?"

"Yeah. Why?"

"She still on the staff of *Europa Air Inflight Magazine?*"

"She sells ad space for them, yeah. Want to advertise?"

"I think we already do, actually," Mac said. "I met a woman who writes for them. I was wondering if you would ask Charlotte to, ah . . ."

"Tell you all the dirty details of this woman's life behind her back? Sneaky, underhanded bastard. You ought to be ashamed of yourself."

"Will you or won't you?" Mac demanded.

"What's this chick's name?"

"Jane King."

"King. Got it. I'm in the middle of something now, but I'm seeing Charlotte for dinner. I'll ask her then, and call you back. How's that?"

"Sooner is better than later," Mac told him.

Henry snorted. "You never change, buddy. Talk to you tonight."

"Later." He hung up, his mind circling uneasily around whatever Jane had been trying to tell him. *I'm not really* . . . Not really what? Maybe something unpalatable, like "I'm not really interested in having dinner," or "I'm not really looking to get involved right now."

Or something really bad, like "I'm not really available." But there had been no ring on that tiny, slender hand. He'd checked, first thing. Oval nails, buffed to a high sheen, pink and shell-like and kissable.

And her response had been real. Raw, honest. No faking that.

So, unfortunately, was his own, just from thinking about that orgasm fluttering against his fingertips, and he'd only just gotten his dick back down to socially acceptable proportions. Damn.

He tried to think about the Wicked Witch, but she kept morphing into Jane. Green skin, black pointy hat, hooked nose, striped stockings, they just weren't as compelling as damp stretch lace strained to its utmost over lush feminine curves, an errant garter dangling over her soft white thigh. Rippling red hair. Storm-at-sea eyes.

He was fried. He wanted Henry to call back right now to assure him that she was single, eligible and relatively sane. He had to be careful. She was skittish and shy. He would court her slowly, seduce her gently, but he was still going to book a suite at the Copley tonight.

A guy could hope.

Chapter Three

She had the situation under control. She'd come here in her own car, to a crowded public place. She had no intention of getting into trouble. She wasn't even going to peek over that cliff at the churning, heaving water, let alone fling herself over the brink. No way. Not her.

She'd been saying that to herself all afternoon. She hadn't even gone back to work. She'd been too rattled, and the only solution for that, of course, was emergency mall therapy—which had resulted in the purchase of an evening dress and matching shoes, neither of which she could afford. To say nothing of the outrageously sexy lingerie.

And once she had the perfect outfit, well, damn. It seemed a terrible shame to stand him up. A tragic waste of time and money.

But she had no intention, absolutely none, of jumping him.

So why the condoms in your purse?

No good comeback for that one. There was nothing wrong with keeping her bases, ah, covered. So to speak.

She pulled up, killed the engine and rested her hot forehead against the steering column. She had to cool down, get a grip. She didn't dare sweat in this dress. She'd spent way too much money for it.

Think Gwyneth Paltrow, she told herself. Cool, calm, collected. She was a strong, capable person. She'd proved Dylan wrong, and she had the professional accomplishments to show for it. It took rock-steady self-control to channel the MeanStreets kids' volcanic energy into art. That meltdown in the Baron's Suite was just a temporary aberration.

And oh, what an aberration it was. Lips locked, writhing, panties soaked, thighs clenched around his hand. She was sweating again.

Compose yourself, Jane. Nobody likes an embarrassing scene.

Jane laughed silently. *Thank you, Mother, for sharing.* Her mother had always been repelled by strong emotions. How shocked Mother would be to see her now, tarted up in a sexy dress. Firmly in the grip of unruly, embarrassing emotions. Terror, embarrassment, lust. Hope.

The hope scared her most of all. It left her wide open.

The Copley Crowne was a turn-of-the-century mansion, frilly with turrets and towers and various other architectural ribbons and lace, but the total effect was one of cheerful exuberance rather than fussiness. She'd looked the place up on the Internet, and found that the Copley Crowne had a famous chef, a five star rating and gushing reviews from famous food critics. Too bad she was too nervous to eat.

She smoothed down her skirt. The bias cut silk clung to her damp hands. She owed her entire next paycheck to Mastercard, but it was worth it. The dark blue dress skimmed her hips and flared out in a luscious frill over her ankles. Spaghetti straps had forced her to buy a black bustier, which shoved up her boobs and created a provocative valley of cleavage. She couldn't actually breathe in the thing, but what the hell. With Mac, she never breathed anyway. Oxygen was overrated.

She'd shaved and plucked and painted herself like a harem slave about to be led to the sultan's couch. She wondered if Mac would look at her with that intense, focused heat in his eyes when he saw her.

Come now, he probably looks at all women that way. Don't read so much into it. Don't be silly and needy and credulous.

Back off, she told the snotty voice in her head. She was on shaky ground as it was. She should never have agreed to a date without telling Mac what she was up to. It wasn't like it was such a dreadful secret, after all. She wasn't hurting anyone, or doing anything illegal. Still, it put her at a terrible disadvantage. She couldn't take the stress.

She would tell him the truth straight off. Then he could decide if he still wanted to invest the time and energy in having dinner with her.

He might be angry, and conclude that she was more trouble than she was worth. Maybe he would be right. Dylan had put her off men for years. Four years, to be precise. No wonder she was climbing the walls.

She kicked that thought back into the dusty corner where it belonged. Thinking about Dylan was a big no-no. She wouldn't sacrifice one more crumb of her attention to that freaking vampire. She'd regained control over her life from him at great cost. She was hanging on to it with a death grip. She marched towards the graceful, welcoming beauty of the Copley Crowne as if going to face a firing squad.

The hostess directed her towards French doors that opened out onto a magnificent garden. A rose-scented breeze lifted her hair, ruffling the dark foliage around her. It misted her face with cool spray from the fountain. Her skirt fluttered around her legs, a caress of moving silk. Trellises draped with climbing roses shaded shadowy nooks. Paths wound through the bushes, all of them making their way towards the central fountain. The marble fountain glowed a pale pink in the deepening twilight.

The noise and bustle of the restaurant was sealed away behind a wall of glass on the opposite side of the garden, creating an oasis of fragrant calm. A few people strolled along the aisles. There were roses of all kinds and colors: white, pink, peach, yellow, crimson—from tight-furled buds to lush, full-blown extravagance. They seemed to float against the dark green leaves. Petals carpeted the walkway like confetti.

Sensual music throbbed in the air. A classical guitarist was sitting in one of the rose arbors, playing Spanish gypsy music.

Mac stepped out of the shadows. He liked the dress. His eyes devoured her. She was out of her element, out of her league, out of her mind. She really, *really* needed to breathe, but it just wasn't an option. He walked towards her. Her legs were rooted to the ground.

He was so graceful and perfectly proportioned, despite his height and solid, heavy musculature. Loose-limbed, sinuous like a big hunting cat. A white linen shirt set off his dark skin, draping elegantly from those wide, powerful shoulders. He oozed potent masculine charisma.

He stopped a couple feet away, no doubt to savor the buzz of anticipation before gobbling her up in a single bite. His eyes dragged over her from head to toe. "Storm-at-sea blue," he said.

She was bewildered. "What?"

"Your dress. It's the color of your eyes. The color of a stormy sea."

Oh, he was smooth. She was so flattered, her toes curled up. "Thank you, but they're, um, just dark bluish-gray."

He reached out, his finger tracing the line of her jaw. "You will learn to accept compliments from me before the night is over."

The soft words sounded like a promise—or perhaps a veiled threat. She couldn't quite tell which. "Ah, we'll see," she said dubiously.

"I'm glad to see you," he said. "I wasn't sure you'd show."

"Why wouldn't I?" Like she hadn't been asking herself that same question all afternoon.

"You wouldn't give me your address. You were keeping your options open."

"Oh. I didn't mean to make you feel like I was—*mmph!*"

The swift, possessive kiss took her by surprise. He was so vibrant and strong, bending her over backward, pressing her against his body. His faint beard shadow rasped her cheek.

She blinked up at him, dazed, when he lifted his head. "You take a lot for granted," she blurted.

He shook his head. "The dress is a statement. I'm just responding to it. You make a move, I make a countermove. Cause and effect. It's a natural law, like gravity. Simple, elementary physics."

She swallowed back her giggles before she could start to sound hysterical. "I must've been absent that day in science class."

He dragged her higher against his long body until she practically dangled in midair, her tiptoes barely touching the ground. "Did you see the way the men looked at you when you walked out here?"

"I didn't see any other men," she admitted. "I was looking for you."

She glanced down. Yikes. From this vantage point, he could see her areolas, peeking right over the edge of the bustier.

"Well, I saw the way they looked at you," he said. "A man has to stake his claim when his woman is dressed like that."

His woman? Whoa. "Mac, I—"

This time the kiss was slower, sweeter. Pure seduction, drawing her into a timeless haze of longing. She softened against him like melting caramel, eyelids heavy, knees quivering. The kiss lightened to a teasing suction at her lower lip, a tender flick of his tongue against hers, a rain of hot, soft kisses against her throat. Shivers raced over her skin as he nibbled her earlobe. "Our table's ready," he murmured.

She realized, with a start, that her arms were wrapped around his neck. "Oh. Ah, yes," she stammered. "Of course."

He wound her arm through his, and she drifted along in his wake, giddy and dazzled. The sweet talk, the soft guitar, the sensual, over-the-top luxury was all just a thin veil over the primal truth between them. She felt it in every cell of her body. He was luring her into position, and when he had her there . . . God. Explicit images assailed her. Herself, naked and helpless, spread out beneath his powerful body. Writhing with pleasure. She wanted him so badly, and it scared her.

Why, oh why was she like this? Why such endless conflict, such tiresome drama about sex? Always a life-or-death production. Always such a big deal. Why couldn't she just relax and indulge herself? What was wrong with her? She was a goddamn freak of nature.

An opened bottle of wine had been left on the table to breathe. Mac poured the wine and lifted his glass. She lifted her own. The stem of her glass wobbled after the crystalline *ting* of contact. She gathered her nerve. It was ridiculous to continue this pointless charade just because she dreaded looking silly for letting it go on so long in the first place. She took a deep breath. Opened her mouth. "Mac, I have to—"

"Good evening!" said a familiar alto voice. "Well, well, well! What have we here? Isn't it lucky that Gary was gone this afternoon?"

Jane looked up into Robin's smiling eyes. She looked very different in the sleek black pants and crisp white blouse of the restaurant waitstaff. Her hair was slicked back into a tight bun.

"Christ." Mac closed his eyes. "No. Tell me this isn't happening."

Dimples very similar to Mac's deepened at the corners of Robin's expressive mouth. "One of the waiters had a family emergency, and Gary asked me if I would cover for him," she explained. "Remember Lecture Number Six Eighty-seven, about being willing to pitch in? Well, I'm pitching in." She laid a basket of fresh bread on the table and cut them a deep, theatrical bow. "You should be proud of me. So eager to lend a hand."

"How did you know I was coming here?" Mac demanded. "Did Danny tell you? That's it. I'm flattening him. He's history."

"Mac!" Robin looked wounded. "Danny and I would never intrude on your private life!" She winked at Jane. "I wouldn't dare. I'm so cowed. If Mac gets into heaven, which I have begun to seriously doubt, St. Peter will take one look at him and put him to work as a bouncer."

Wine sloshed in the glasses as Mac's hand hit the table. "Robin—"

"He'll be the mean-looking, musclebound guy with the mirror sunglasses and the walkie-talkie, checking ID's at the Pearly Gates."

The words that popped out of Jane's mouth surprised her. "You don't strike me as cowed, Robin. On the contrary."

There was a startled silence, but Robin recovered quickly. "Well, that's only because I'm as tough as nails. Lucky for me, because—"

"Get lost, Robin." Mac's voice was calm. "Switch tables with one of the other waiters. Do not bug us. Or else."

"Certainly not. Wouldn't dream of it. I'll send Maurice to take your order. Be good, Mac." Robin flashed her braces at Jane. "Watch out for him. He's nothing but trouble. Enjoy your meal." She spun around and weaved gracefully away between the tables.

Mac was eyeing her thoughtfully when she turned back to him. "Thanks for sticking up for me," he said. "Sorry about the interruption. I thought we'd be safe here, but I was wrong."

Jane thought of the strained politeness that had characterized her interactions with her own family. "She teases you because she trusts you. She's not afraid of you. Be grateful. It's a compliment."

He snorted. "If that's a compliment, I'd hate to see an insult. My brother's no joke, either. We fight like cats and dogs. You got siblings?"

"No. I'm an only child," she told him. "An unfortunate accident late in my mother's life."

"Hardly unfortunate. You look like you turned out fine."

She shrugged. "My mother was unamused," she said dryly. "You're lucky to have brothers and sisters."

He lifted a dubious eyebrow. "Sometimes I wonder. Robin scares me to death. Danny and I raised her on our own, so we've got the worry and responsibility of parents, but none of the respect or the clout."

She was intrigued. "What happened to your—"

"Out of the picture when Robin was a baby," he said curtly.

"Oh," she murmured. "How old were you when—"

"Thirteen. Danny was eleven, Robin was one."

She itched for more, but the brusque way he was cutting off her questions discouraged further probing. "It looks like you did a fine job."

"We'll see." He rolled his eyes. "Now she wants to be a clown."

Jane smiled. "She certainly is high-spirited."

"Oh, no. I'm not speaking figuratively. I mean that literally. As in Bozo the Clown." He sounded aggrieved. "She wants to go to clown college. Wear a red plastic nose. Make kids laugh for a living."

She was taken aback by the stony disapproval in his voice. "What's wrong with that?" she asked hesitantly.

He looked incredulous. "It's ridiculous, that's what's wrong with it. Danny and I busted our asses to give her career opportunities in the hotel industry, and what does she want? A red plastic nose. She'll be juggling eighty dollar bottles of wine before her shift is over."

She couldn't stifle her laughter, despite his glowering face. "Face it," she told him. "She's a dreamer."

"She's young and rebellious, and she doesn't know what's good for her. She'll come around. Everybody has to accept reality sometime."

Ouch. Time to get going on her own reality check, before she lost her nerve. "Heaven help your own kids when you have them," she said.

An odd silence fell. "Well," he said slowly. "At least no kid of mine is ever going to have to wonder whether or not I give a damn."

Jane's eyes dropped. "There's, ah, something to be said for that." She took as deep a breath as the bustier would allow, which wasn't saying much, and pressed on. "Mac, there's something I have to—"

"So she showed up, after all. You get points for nerve, Ms. King."

They looked up. Danny loomed over them, white teeth flashing in his lean, dark face. His hair fell loose and gleaming over the shoulders of his elegant jacket. A discreet diamond stud winked in his ear. It was unreal. The whole family was drop-dead gorgeous. All three of them.

Mac stared up at his brother. "So what's your excuse?"

Danny shrugged. "I wanted to check on Robin. You know, just to make sure she didn't decide to do her shift wearing her bra outside her shirt. With Robin, it pays to be vigilant." He glanced at Jane, and a charming grin lit up his chiseled features. "I also wanted to apologize, for being rude to you this afternoon. Forgive me."

Jane blinked at him, bewildered. "Oh. Ah, thanks for the thought, but I didn't notice any rudeness."

"I did," Mac said wryly. "Rule number one, Jane. Watch out for Danny when he's smiling. That's when he's at his most dangerous. Danny, what do you want from us?"

"Nothing." Devilish amusement gleamed in Danny's eyes. "You're doing your ogre act, bro. Try to be suave, like me, while you're having dinner with a beautiful redhead. May I call you Jane?"

"You may not," Mac said. "Stop sucking up to my date. I don't appreciate being tortured by my family while I'm trying to enjoy a private, quiet evening with my lady friend."

Danny's mouth twitched. "You'd have more luck with your quiet, private evening if you stayed the hell away from your own restaurants."

"Tell me about it. I would have, but I promised her a tour."

"Oh!" Danny laughed. "Like this afternoon's tour? Yowza!"

Mac's eyes narrowed. "Stop ogling her cleavage and go find your own date, Danny. Good-bye."

Danny seized Jane's hand and kissed it, his eyes fixed on his brother's face. A delighted grin spread slowly over his face.

"You're certainly territorial tonight," he observed. "Enjoy your evening."

Jane looked at her hand as he strode away, flustered. She looked at Mac's face, and stuck the just-kissed hand swiftly under the table.

"I suppose I should be grateful that my brother busts my balls, too?" Mac asked. "Just another compliment, huh?"

She knew he was being ironic, but the words popped out anyway. "Yes, actually. It is. He's not trying to hurt you. He's just curious. You guys play rough, all three of you, but there are rules."

"Rules, my ass. He thinks he's so slick."

"Complain all you want," Jane said. "I envy you. I can't imagine what it would be like to have someone in my family interested enough in my private life to pester me in a restaurant."

Mac rolled his eyes. "Robin says we form an unholy trinity. Like Kirk, Spock and McCoy from the really old *Star Trek*."

Jane laughed out loud. "And I bet you're Kirk, right?"

"I don't look like Kirk, so how do you figure? Is it the masterful way that I use my phaser?"

"I haven't seen any phaser action yet," she said demurely. "I figured you for Kirk because he always grabs the girls and kisses them."

Mac reached across the table and took her hand. "Why waste time?"

She stared at his long fingers. "Do you do that in every episode?" she asked timidly. "Grab the girl, I mean?"

"I've grabbed my share," he admitted. "But I've gotten more discriminating with time. Lots of episodes go by these days with no girl-grabbing. But I'm hoping to make up for lost time. Real soon."

A cell phone rang. Mac pulled it out of his pocket and checked the display. "Would you excuse me while I answer this?" he asked. "I've been expecting this call all day. I promise I'll be quick."

"Feel free." She stared at the perfect rose that adorned the table, trying not to listen to his low conversation and failing utterly.

"Hey, Henry. Did you talk to . . . yeah? And? . . . Yeah, that's the name . . . Oh. Wow. That's really weird. No, can't talk right now. Uh-huh . . . yeah, I will. Thanks, anyway. Thank Charlotte for me, too. Later."

He clipped the phone shut and stared at her for a long moment. "Bad news?" she asked timidly.

"You could say that," he said. "But I'm handling it."

The silence lengthened. The frequency between them had changed somehow. The teasing warmth in his eyes had disappeared. He looked tense and cautious.

He reached for her hand, turned it over, and splayed her fingers wide, as if to read her palm. "So tell me about yourself," he said quietly. "What's it like to work at *Europa Inflight?* Tell me your deep, dark secrets, Jane."

That was an opening to confess if she'd ever heard one, but she had wanted to broach the subject herself, of her own free will. She most certainly did not want to be put on the defensive and have her embarrassing confession interrogated out of her. "It's, ah, a little early for deep, dark secrets, isn't it?" she hedged.

He tilted an eyebrow. "Let's start with simple biographical data," he suggested. "I'll make it easy for you. Ever see those info sheets about centerfold models that you find in men's magazines?"

She shook her head.

His thumb stroked her palm with hypnotic slowness. "Of course you haven't. Along with the naked pictures, we get the vital stats. Like, for instance, Kaia Marie, twenty-three years old, Libra, 38-24-36, born in Anyplace, U.S.A., graduated from U. of Wherever. Loves: kittens and open-minded people. Hates: broccoli and bigots. Want me to go first?"

He waited for her short, nervous nod. "OK," he said. "Michael MacNamara, thirty-six years old, Sagittarius. Born in Las Vegas. Six foot three, two hundred ten pounds, graduated from U. of Washington. Loves: winning. Hates: . . . liars." He lifted her hand, and kissed it. "There's nothing I hate more. Your turn, angel."

Her stomach fluttered anxiously. "You're making me a little nervous," she said. "Can't we, ah, savor the mystery a little longer?"

He studied her face for a long moment. "OK. Fine. If that's the way you want it, there's no need to waste time playing games."

She felt like an actress who'd been handed the wrong script. "What on earth are you talking about?"

"Never mind." He shoved his chair back. "Come with me."

"But . . . dinner?"

He grabbed her arm and pulled her to her feet. "We'll have it sent up to the room."

Jane barely managed to snag her purse before he slid his arm around her waist and swept her out of the dining room. She scurried to keep up with his long strides as they hastened across the rose garden.

She'd been aroused all day at the thought of having sex with Mac, but his quiet, purposeful urgency made her nervous, and she'd been plenty nervous to begin with. Another dim back staircase, another dark corridor, another portentous silence broken only by the scrambling click of her heels, her panting breath. "Mac," she protested. "Slow down."

He swung around, lifting her off her feet so that she straddled his muscular thighs. He pinned her against the wall, and his mouth claimed hers in a kiss of pure sensual possession. She opened to the bold thrust of his tongue, too busy kissing him back to be intimidated.

Oh, yes. Here it was again, that feeling that she'd glimpsed in the Baron's Suite. It was real. She hadn't been dreaming. It wasn't wishful thinking. Every muscle in her body was wildly alive, every inch of her skin screaming for his touch. She wrapped her arms around his neck with a low, throaty moan.

"Why slow down?" He nuzzled her neck until her insides went soft, liquid and quivering. "Let's get on with what we started this afternoon. We can do it right here, in the corridor if you want, or we can take to the room. Ladies' choice, sweetheart."

"In the *corridor*?" Her heavy-lidded eyes popped open. "Are you crazy?"

"Nah. Just out-of-my-mind horny." He hauled her skirt up and stared down at her gartered hose, her skimpy black lace panties. "Oh, man. Look at you. To hell with the room. I vote for right here."

He trapped her breathless protest against another delicious, marauding kiss. She forgot what she had been trying to say. It lost all its importance when he slid his finger beneath the damp lace of her panties. She gasped against his mouth as he teased it along the plump, slick folds of her labia. He flicked it over her clitoris, swirling with slow, wicked skill, and thrust his finger slowly inside her with a ragged sigh. "Oh, God. Jane. You're so hot," he muttered. "You're incredible."

Her mouth was full of his thrusting tongue, his finger was shoved inside her body. Pinned against the wall of a corridor lined with doors that could open at any second, and she actually didn't care. She couldn't stop clenching around his caressing hand, couldn't stop making rough mewling sounds. He caressed a marvelous spot inside her that made her squirm and whimper out loud.

"Here?" His voice was utterly confident. "Now?"

It took a second to remember what he was talking about. "No!"

"The room, then." He let her slide down his leg. When her tiptoes hit the carpet runner, he seized her arm, and they practically sprinted together to the end of the corridor. It was something she would never have dreamed of doing in four-inch heels, but she practically floated on his strong, steely arm. Her feet barely touched the floor.

Mac groped in his pocket for a key, unlocked the door and swept her into the room. The door swung shut with a slam that rattled her overstimulated nerves. She backed away into the dark, panting. She was about to explode with excitement.

Just enough fading twilight sifted in the sheer curtains to make out a sofa, wingback chairs, the sitting room of a bedroom suite. That was all she saw before he shoved her against the wall. His hands were all over her, sliding over her silk-covered curves, under her hair, over her back looking for a zipper, but there wasn't one. This was a dress she had to shimmy out of, but things were hurtling forward far too fast for any seductive shimmying. She reached down for the hem of her skirt and jerked it up over her thighs, to give him a hint.

He laughed and shoved it higher, fumbling for her panties. He ripped out the gusset, and she was bare to his tender, probing fingers. His breath was hot against her throat. He smelled so good. She was so sensitive to his caressing hand, she jerked and shuddered in his grasp. She grabbed his shoulders to steady herself, and a framed picture bumped her shoulder and slid to the floor. Glass crashed and tinkled.

"Damn." He lifted her higher, letting her feet dangle. "Hold tight to my neck. Lift your feet up off the floor and watch out for that glass."

He set her down in the middle of the room and started to unbutton his shirt. She backed away into the dark unknown on rubbery ankles. She was trembling on the brink of a blinding revelation that could transform her completely. Turn her world on its head.

He advanced on her, unbuttoning his cuffs. He shrugged the shirt off and let it drop. The powerful muscles of his shoulders and arms and chest gleamed in the faint light. He was lean, hard, perfect. An arrow of dark hair disappeared into his waistband, where his hands were busy unbuckling his belt. He herded her through a door. He picked her up with shocking ease and tossed her backward into a dark nowhere.

She landed, bouncing on a big four-poster bed and struggled up onto her elbows. "Whoa! Hold on, Mac! Take a deep breath, and chill. This is very intense. I hardly know you."

"I tried to get to know you," he said. "You said you wanted to savor the mystery. So here's your chance, Jane. Savor it." He bent over and pried off his shoes. They thudded off into the darkness.

His cool tone stung her, and she scrambled up until she sat on the edge of the bed, just as he stepped out of his pants and briefs. He stood before her, his magnificent body stark naked.

She forced her mouth to close. Forced herself to inhale. Tried to remember what she'd planned to say to him. It was gone, beyond recall.

She tried not to stare, but it was impossible. His penis jutted out before him, thick and long and heavy.

"Scared, Jane?" he asked softly. "Want to run away again, like you did this afternoon? Please, don't. I could please you. If you let me."

She tried to swallow. Her throat was too dry. "Can't we just . . . ah, lighten up? Take this a little slower?"

He shook his head. "No. I can't." His voice was stark. "Sorry. It's just not going to be like that. Not tonight."

They stared at each other's faces through the shadows. Mac reached out for her hand, and drew it slowly towards himself, his eyes fixed on hers as if silently daring her to pull away.

She didn't. He wrapped her fingers around his penis. Her hand jerked like a drop of water sputtering on a griddle, the sensation was so startling. So hot and hard and solid. So velvety smooth.

He stroked her hand slowly over his hard flesh, more roughly than she would have dared to touch him on her own. "This is how it is," he said. "This is how I am tonight. Take me or leave me, Jane."

"But I—"

"Touch me." His low voice was ragged with intensity. "Squeeze, with your hands. Please."

She was electrified, intensely aroused by the thick, blunt head of his penis, the broad stalk, the suede-soft skin, the raised, throbbing tracery of veins. His heart pumped against her hand. She wondered how he would react if she sank down and pressed her tongue against him. So much of him, thick and taut and swollen to bursting.

Wow. She wasn't sure he would even fit into her mouth.

His fist tightened, swirling her fist, spreading the fluid until his penis was slick with it. He pumped her hand slowly up and down his length. "Do you want me?" His voice was a hypnotic whisper.

She leaned her forehead against the damp skin of his chest. That liquid that lubricated him was magic stuff, more slippery than any oil. The force of his desire made her tremble and sweat. It was so raw, so visceral—the urgent pressure of his big hands wrapped around hers, the hard, stabbing thrust of his thick shaft into the slick recesses of her clenched hand. "Yes, I definitely do want you, but this is too—"

"Shhh." He bent down and slid his tongue seductively along her swollen, trembling lower lip. "Yes, or no. There is no middle ground."

"But I—"

"If you want it, I'll give it to you. My way. I can't make nice and be a good boy tonight. You have to just trust me."

She pressed her face against his chest, tasted the salt tang of his skin against her open mouth, felt the pulsing heat of his penis clutched in her hand. She sank her teeth into the muscle of his shoulder, hard enough to make him gasp. He was so beautiful and compelling, and the only way she could have him was to give herself over to him completely. It wasn't fair of him to drive her into a corner, but she had to have him.

"Yes," she whispered.

"Say please." His triumphant tone made her grateful for the darkness to hide her blush. He waited. "Say it, Jane. Set me free."

She hesitated for one last second, pressed her face against his neck, and whispered it into his ear like a guilty secret. *"Please."*

Chapter Four

Things moved swiftly after that. He rolled on the condom and knocked her back onto the bed. So this was how it would be. Straight-up Neanderthal. Fine with her. She was in no mood to be teased.

He climbed on top of her, surrounding her with his heat. He made her feel small, but not fragile. She felt lithe and strong, like a wild animal. She reached around his big body, stroking the thick muscles of his back, his shoulders. His smell was woodsy, herbal—the sweetness of soap, the sharpness of salt. She buried her nose in his sweat-dampened hair and tried to wind her fingers through it. It slipped right through them, too slick and glossy and short to get any grip.

He tossed her skirt up and shoved her legs wide. He wasn't even going to undress her. Fine. Their tryst in the Baron's Suite was foreplay and then some. She'd been clenching her legs around a damp throb of arousal all day, now. Enough agony, already.

His body vibrated with a low rumble of approval when he brushed his fingertip over her mound and slid it between the slick folds of her labia. "Oh, wow. You do want me."

She ran her hands over his big shoulders. "All day, I've been like this," she admitted. "I had to change my panties twice."

"Tell me about it. I've had this hard-on all afternoon," he told her. "And my problem is bigger than yours."

"Oh, much," she murmured.

He laughed as he thrust his tongue into her mouth, and slid his fingers tenderly around her clitoris, spreading the slick moisture. He thrust his tongue into her mouth with the same seductive, pulsing rhythm as his hand. She was too aroused to be embarrassed at the soft, liquid sounds his fingers made as he caressed her. He pushed the thick head of his penis against her, moistening himself.

The blunt pressure made her stiffen up with alarm.

He was big. Bigger than anyone she'd ever been with, and it had been a very long time. And she'd never quite gotten the knack of just relaxing and letting this happen. She always tensed up, tried too hard.

He went still, and kissed her face gently. "Relax. I won't hurt you."

She tried not to brace herself, but it was an involuntary reflex.

She waited, but nothing happened. He lodged the tip of himself inside her, barely clasped in her moist folds, and there he stayed, motionless.

Finally she opened her eyes. He held her gaze intently as he slid his penis along her labia, a gentle, caressing slide. He lowered his head to her mouth and echoed the same light stroke with his tongue along the sensitive inner part of her lip. Slow, seductive and delicious.

He was waiting for her to tell him to go on. She hadn't expected patience, or sensitivity. Particularly since he hadn't promised it.

Something softened and relaxed inside her. She lifted her face to him and arched herself open. He had demanded her blind trust, and in some quiet, instinctive way, he had earned it.

A rough sigh shuddered out of him. He rocked against her, tiny, teasing thrusts until the head of his penis was firmly wedged inside her, and then he slowly pushed himself inside. The pressure tightened into a wonderful, burning ache. She was distended around his thick shaft, the nerves in that sensitive place shocked to full awareness at the heavy intrusion of his body. Her sheath clung to him, quivering and stretched.

"My God, you're tight," he muttered. "You feel amazing."

She couldn't reply. Her throat was vibrating too hard.

He shoved himself all the way inside, and withdrew himself, with maddening deliberation. It was getting easier to accommodate him. She was slicker with each stroke. She was starting to sense his rhythm and cautiously enjoy his thick, hot, sliding presence inside her when he flexed his hips and thrust himself deeper.

The intensity of the sensation made her gasp.

He froze. "Damn. I'm sorry." Mac trapped her face between his hands and kissed her gently. "I'm really sorry," he repeated. "I'm just so turned on. I didn't mean to do that so hard. It got away from me."

Her heart thudded so hard it seemed to fill her chest and leave no room for her lungs. She could not acknowledge his apology, or tell him it was all right, or that it wasn't. She was overwhelmed.

"Hey. Jane?"

His pleading tone pulled her into focus, and she dragged in a shallow breath and kissed him back. "It's OK," she said. "I'm fine."

"You sure?"

"Fine. It just, um, surprised me. You're touching a place that I don't think has ever been touched. In there, I mean." She patted his face.

Mac's big chest vibrated with silent laughter. He rested his hot, damp forehead against hers for a moment, panting. Then curved himself over her body, and began. Slowly and carefully at first, but his movements became deeper and harder as her body softened to accept him—and then demand him.

Jane had always imagined that if she ever got it right, that good sex would feel sweet. Pleasant. Nice. *Hah.* The gliding intrusion of his penis, his sleek, hot, beautiful body pinning her down, melding with hers, it was marvelous, terrifying tension that ratcheted higher and higher. Anything but nice. Each time he thrust inside her, she wanted more, she wanted *now,* she didn't even know what she wanted, but if he didn't give it to her she was going to scream and claw and bite him for it. It was thunder, lightning, lashing rain. Her body tingled—fingers, toes, face. Her hair practically stood on end. Her chest ached like she wanted to weep. Her hips bucked up to meet him, hands sliding over sweat-slicked skin, nails digging into his muscles. He angled himself so that every stroke of his thick shaft caressed the hot glow inside her sheath, sliding heavily over and over it. Churning her into a frenzy.

The bed squeaked in the dark room. There was no sound but the slapping of flesh on flesh, panting gasps she was helpless to control. His thrusts were rough and deep, driving her exactly where she needed to go, just not fast enough, damn it. She wanted everything he had. *Now.*

She clenched her arms and legs around him at every ramming stroke. It was wild, earthy, crazy, perfect. She yelled at him, shoved and slapped furiously at his chest because she knew he would trap her hands over her head, bear down harder, thrust deeper. Give her all the ballast she needed to push off and launch herself into glittering space.

She almost dragged him along with her when she exploded. He used every trick he knew to hold it back. He sucked in his breath, clenched the muscles around his cock, balanced on the head of a pin inside his head as he chanted the silent mantra: *not yet not yet not yet.*

He wasn't going to be winning any prizes for finesse tonight, but Jane seemed to like it raw and uncomplicated. She was white-hot, stunning. Perfect, but for the small detail that she was a scheming liar and a con artist. But for the fact he was hurt and disappointed. He'd been fighting his anger, ever since Henry's call. And being more turned on than he'd ever been in his life didn't help matters any.

Aftershocks fluttered through her lush, delicate body. He waited until she relaxed and lay still beneath him, limp and soft and panting.

She made a low, startled sound as he folded her legs wide and started right back in on her. She probably needed a break. Too bad. He didn't mean to come for a while yet. He had one shot at this before he confronted her with the truth, and he would make it last.

"I'm not done," he told her.

She stared up into his face, and gave him a nod, wiggling beneath him for more freedom of movement. He adjusted his stroke so that it didn't rub her oversensitized clit. She might be trying to scam him, but she was still small and delicate. He didn't want to hurt her. On the contrary. He wanted her to remember this night for the rest of her life.

He reached out to flip on the bedside lamp. Jane blinked, startled. He needed light to brand every detail of her onto his memory—even if they gave him sweat-soaked fevered dreams for the rest of his life. Her stockings were shredded, which must be his doing although he didn't remember it. He liked the effect, the slutty contrast to her fine-textured white skin. The scent of her tight, slick little cunt made his head swim.

She still had those spiky blue sandals on. The panties he'd ripped open were sheer black lace. Her dress was crumpled around her waist. Her breath was shallow, her fathomless eyes blue-black, wide with wonder. The moist folds of her cunt peeked out of the nest of reddish ringlets. He pulled out and surged back in, savoring the snug kiss of her inner lips, distended around his cock. "I knew it," he muttered.

"Knew what?"

"That red hair of yours is for real." *If nothing else.*

He unbuckled her fragile sandals and flung them behind him. He gripped her ankles and opened her wider. She sighed and undulated beneath him as she took in his slow, lazy thrusts. She loved it like this, with him looming over her. She got off on being dominated, which suited him fine. They were perfect for each other.

The fleeting thought made his stomach tighten. He tried to block it. This was a one-shot deal. Stupid to blow it by getting emotional. He dragged his mind back to the sexy details of her body. "I love your underwear," he told her.

Her laugher was so open and shaky and sweet, it rattled him. "It sure doesn't look that way. You tore them to shreds. I bought them just for you, Mac, and they weren't cheap."

"Oh, yeah?" He pressed her thighs wider. "I'm honored. It was a good investment. I'll make sure it was worth your while."

"You're hard on underwear, Mac. You ruined my stockings this afternoon, too," she told him.

"Sorry about that." He braced her feet against his shoulders, folding her completely in on herself. The angle allowed him to penetrate her even more deeply. Her mouth opened in a soundless gasp as he shoved himself inside her, to the limit. She squeezed her eyes shut. Tears squeezed out between her sooty lashes and flashed down her face.

The tears alarmed him. "You OK?" he demanded.

A short, jerky nod was his only answer, and it didn't satisfy him. "You like it?" he persisted. What a bonehead, bleating for reassurance from a professional liar. "You want more?"

Yes. Her trembling lips made the shape of the word, but no sound came out. Her eyes opened, glittering and overflowing. She nodded.

Vulnerable. Just like this afternoon. It made him frantic and confused. Everything about this was perfect. The way she took him in, like they were one mind, one body. Like he knew her by heart.

Turning on the light had been a big mistake.

He wrenched her low-cut bodice down. Her plump breasts had overflowed the confines of the black lace corset. Her nipples were tight, flushed raspberry red. His breath rushed out of his lungs. Those tits deserved hours of foreplay on their own sweet merits, but he couldn't stop now. Not if someone put a gun to his head. He had to cram a lifetime of sex into one, single, explosive lay.

He pressed his hand to her heaving bosom, between her breasts, over her heart, felt the rapid, wild throb of her pulse against his palm.

She reached up, pressed her own hand against his heart. Her dark blue eyes accepted him, made room for him. All of him, even his anger, even his darkness. Oh, man. Oh, no. The look in her eyes was more than he could take. He had to finish this. *Now.*

He shut his eyes, opened the gates and hurled himself into the orgasm which had been gathering momentum all day. Pounding black waves of agonized pleasure rolled over him and blotted him out.

Oblivion was short-lived. His gut ached as soon as he drifted back to full awareness. He pulled himself out of her clinging body. She reached to touch his face. He jerked away. He climbed off the bed and took off the condom, avoiding her gaze. He was drenched and shivering.

"Mac?"

He turned his back and headed for the bathroom without a reply.

He cleaned up, and stared into the mirror with bleak eyes. The orgasm had actually made him feel worse, amazingly. He'd planned to make this last all night, but he hadn't expected to feel this bad.

He didn't have the heart to string it out for a second go at her, no matter how sexy she was. Best to wrap it up, put on his clothes and get out of here. Maybe get drunk someplace that was walking distance from his condo. It wasn't his thing, but tonight was a special case.

What irony. He of all people should be proof against a con artist's smooth, lying charm. Those liar's tricks were mother's milk to him.

She'd suckered him, with those stormy blue eyes. Vulnerable, his ass. He'd been eating out of her hand, dreaming about matching his-'n-hers terry cloth bathrobes, all the way up to Henry's phone call. He'd never met anyone better than his own daddy until today.

Time to find out what she was mixed up in. He cursed into the mirror. He hated the look in his own eyes. Hadn't seen it for decades.

Get the fuck on with it, he told himself. He shoved open the door.

Jane was curled up on the edge of the bed, arms wrapped around her knees. "What's wrong?" she demanded.

He could tell by the look on her face that his feelings were showing. He'd never been able to hide them worth a damn. That was Danny's gift, not his. "How about you tell me?" he challenged her.

She was the picture of innocent bewilderment. "You're angry. Why? What happened? What did I do?"

He crossed his arms over his chest and reminded himself to play it cool. "Do you have something to tell me, Jane?"

Her hand crept up to cover her mouth. "Oh, dear."

He let out a long, measured breath, stared at her, and let several seconds tick by. "You don't work for *Europa Inflight,*" he said flatly.

Jane squeezed her eyes shut and shook her head. "Ah, no. Actually . . . I'm an executive recruiter."

He was completely lost. "Come again?"

"A headhunter." She hid her face with her hands. "I was looking for a candidate for a general manager. I was scheduled to meet Gary Finley. Posing as a writer was just a ploy to get past the receptionist." She peeked out between her fingers. "I certainly never meant to meet the CEO. Robin stuck me in your office, and . . ." Her voice trailed off.

He was dumbfounded. Headhunter? *That* was her horrible secret? Holy shit. His mood shot towards the stratosphere, but he didn't dare relax just yet. "Prove it," he demanded.

She slid off the bed and padded into the other room.

"Watch out for that broken glass," he called after her.

"Yes, thank you." She came back rummaging through her purse. She found her wallet, fished out a card and held it out to him. Gingerly. The way one might hold out a chunk of meat to a starving predator.

He took it from her shaking hand, and stared at it. *Jane Duvall, Executive Recruiter Grayson & Clint.* "I'm calling your boss," he told her.

"Please do," she said. "I'll give you her home number. You might get me fired, but that's fine. At this point, I think I would be grateful."

He kept staring at the card, as if he could squeeze reassurance out of it. He was starting to feel like an idiot, but that was no big deal. It wasn't the first time he'd lost his cool and done something stupid.

"Who needs a general manager?" he asked.

She hesitated for a moment. "Brighton Group," she admitted.

"No shit. So Rick Geddes finally told that constipated old man where to get off. I'm glad he finally found his balls."

"So you know the Brighton people, then?" she asked hesitantly.

"I don't give a rat's ass about the Brighton people," he said. "All I want to know is why you lied to me."

She sank down onto the edge of the bed again and twisted handfuls of her skirt into her hands. "At first, I just didn't want to blow my cover, but then . . ." She looked miserable. "I meant to tell you as soon as we got to the Baron's Suite this afternoon, but then . . ."

Her hesitation was driving him nuts. "But then what? Why didn't you? Do you enjoy playing games?"

She slapped her hands down against the mattress. "No! I do not! I didn't tell you because you were coming on to me, and I liked it!"

He turned that over in his mind a few times, but he couldn't make it fit. "Uh, Jane? Hello? I would've wanted to go to bed with you no matter what you do for a living. You have to do better than that."

She crossed her arms over her middle. She wouldn't meet his eyes. "I didn't want to break the spell," she whispered.

"Spell?" He squinted at her. "What spell? This is way too deep for me, babe. Help me thrash through it."

She threw up her hands. "It was like magic, this afternoon," she said desperately. "I'd never felt anything like it. I got swept away."

He gestured impatiently for her to go on. "Yeah? So? Magic, swept away, that's cool, that all works for me. And your point is?"

She made a sharp growling sound that Robin sometimes made when she was frustrated at him for not comprehending some insanely complicated girl thing. "If I'd told you I was a headhunter, everything would've changed. I would've spent that time apologizing and explaining and being uncomfortable, instead of . . . you know. Kissing you madly."

"Ah. I see," he said cautiously. "Uh . . . that sounds really weird and convoluted to me, but whatever. I guess I'll buy it."

"I tried to tell you this afternoon, and your brother interrupted," she said heatedly. "I tried again, tonight, and your sister popped up. Then whoops, your brother again. I swear, it was like a bad joke. Then you got that phone call, and—oh. It was the phone call, wasn't it? You changed, right then. You turned into a . . . a conquering barbarian!"

"Barbarian?" He tried not to grin. "Yeah, it was the phone call. I know a woman who works at Europa. She knows everybody on staff. She'd never heard of a Jane King contributing anything to them."

"I see," she whispered.

"I figured you must be a con artist, running some sort of scam. I meant to play you along, find out what your game was."

Her eyes widened, horrified. "Running a scam? You thought I was a *criminal*? Good God! Then why did you bring me up here?"

He shrugged. "I wanted to fuck you anyway."

She flinched back. "Ouch!"

"Yeah, that's how I felt when I found out Jane King didn't exist," he said. "But I figured the ugly scene could wait until I'd nailed you."

Her face went white. "How could you do that? You are ice-cold."

"Actually, I feel like I'm running a fever," he told her.

She slid off the bed and backed away. "Oh, no. Don't you look at me like that. Don't even think about touching me again. I can't believe you thought I was a thief and you still wanted to . . . to . . ."

"To fuck your brains out? Welcome to reality, babe. The little head doesn't always agree with the big head. Compromises have to be made."

A hot buzz of sexual tension still shimmered between them. Sex hadn't dissipated it at all. Jane lifted her chin. "I don't use language like that, under any circumstances," she said. "And I don't compromise."

"You will," he said slowly. "If you want something, you will, Jane. And maybe I'm rude and nasty, but you still want me."

"No." She shook her head warily. "No, Mac, I don't. I've changed my mind. This has gotten too weird for me."

"It's not my fault it got weird," he said. "I'm not the one who told the lies." He lunged for her before she could back away farther, and hooked his fingers through the thin straps of her dress. "Can you believe I still haven't seen you naked? And after all this drama, too."

She pulled back, batting at his hands. "No way. You're not going to see me naked. This is my cue to go."

He caught her around the waist, and she kicked and flailed in his grasp as he dropped down onto the bed, pulling her onto his lap. "I think you got your cues mixed up," he told her.

She struggled furiously. "Hold it right there, buddy—"

"Jane," he said. "I like that name. I'm glad it wasn't fake. Short and sweet. A no-bullshit name. Where do you think you're going, Jane?"

"Home," she snapped. "You can't keep me here."

"Sure I can," he said calmly. "Watch me."

* * *

Being trapped against Mac's hot, naked body, his thick arms clamped hard around her waist, was not soothing. To say the least of it.

His arms were like steel. She twisted around to glare into his face, and the hot, purposeful glow in his eyes made her stomach flutter. Predator eyes. He pressed his lips against her shoulder. His hot breath caressed her skin, and she felt it everywhere.

"You're scaring me," she said. "Don't do this, Mac."

"Don't be scared," he soothed. "I won't hurt you. Or force you."

"Then let . . . me . . . go!"

Her struggles didn't budge him. "Don't wimp out on me, Jane. We're going to get through this. All the way to the other side."

"I am not wimping out!"

"Then stop flopping like a fish on a hook and talk to me! I won't let you go, so don't waste your strength. You're going to need it."

She stiffened. "It's comments like that, that really make me nervous."

He let out an impatient grunt. "Cut the ravished maiden routine. I know you liked what I did to you. I felt it. Every detail."

"That's not the point," she snapped. "Besides, why even bother to make me come if you thought I was out to screw you over?"

He grinned, and nibbled delicately on her shoulder. "I wanted it to be memorable for you. I wanted to make you scream with pleasure."

"Don't hold your breath," she said stiffly. "I'm not the screaming type. Even if I were staying the night with you. Which I am *not.*"

"You don't even know what type you are," he said. "You're figuring it out right now, as you go along. Right?"

Her sharp reply faltered. How the hell did he do that? He made her feel as if all of her secret needs and guilty fantasies were wide open to him, written on her forehead. He could maneuver her so effortlessly.

His lips curved in a triumphant smile. "Stay with me tonight," he urged. "You'll find out exactly what you like, sweet Jane. Don't be afraid. Or ashamed. I'll help you. I was born for this."

"You are arrogant," she informed him.

"I'll show you arrogant, sweetheart. I've only had you once, but I bet I know more about what makes you hot than you do yourself."

"Oh, please," she sputtered. "That's just ridiculous."

"Oh, yeah? Look me straight in the eye and tell me you didn't love it. Just the way I gave it to you.'"

His boasting infuriated her, but she was tuned to his frequency, now. She saw beneath his words to the steely tension of his body. The rough timbre of his voice betrayed his vulnerability. He wasn't quite as confident as he pretended to be, and that observation calmed her down.

"I loved what you did to me in bed," she admitted. "But I hated it afterward, when you pulled away and wouldn't look at me. It was like being slapped in the face. I'm still jittery from that."

He looked puzzled. "I'm not angry anymore," he pointed out.

She shoved at his arms. "Maybe you're not, but now I am!"

He scooped her legs around until she sat sideways on his lap. "One thing I might as well get straight with you, being as how you're a headhunter and all," he said. "Leroy Crowne, the owner of these hotels? He's my uncle. These hotels are successful because Danny and I worked our asses off to make them that way. Having been my uncle's employee since I was sixteen, I know how to treat employees, and how not to. I know what keeps them loyal. Put your arm around my neck."

She draped her arm tentatively across his hot, muscular shoulders. His arm tightened around her waist, cuddling her closer. "I pay Gary Finley very well," he continued. "I doubt he could be tempted to screw me over, particularly not for a humorless old fart like Brighton. But I invite you to try it. Call him. I'll give you his cell phone number."

She licked her lips. "No, thank you," she said carefully. "I haven't the slightest interest in calling Gary Finley right now."

"Good. I'm glad to hear that."

They stared at each other silently for a long moment.

"So here we are, then," he said. "No con artists, no scams, no business agenda, no fake names. No bullshit of any kind. Just a man and a woman naked in bed."

"I'm not naked." She meant the words to sound defiant, but her husky murmur sounded almost inviting.

"Yeah, and I'm going to fix that problem right now."

He grabbed the straps of her gown and pulled her down to kiss her again. Jane put her hand over his mouth and chin and shoved.

"Hold it right there," she said. "Don't you strong-arm me. Just because you're not mad anymore does not mean anything goes!"

He kissed the palm of her hand until she snatched it away. "I just want to feast my eyes on your beauty," he coaxed. "Take it off, Jane."

She felt silly, but she couldn't bear to take off the dress. She already felt so vulnerable. It was ridiculous, after having had such intense sex with him, but the thin silk of her dress felt like the last fragile barrier she had left over her dignity and self-control.

"Come on, Jane," he wheedled. "You'll like being naked with me."

"Sorry. No. Right now, I need my space," she whispered.

"You need more than that." He cupped her breast, and her nipple tightened. "You've got plenty of space in your life already. Too much."

His comment was so dead on the mark that angry humiliation reddened her face. Her loneliness and longing was her own private business. "You do not know me," she hissed. "And I do not *need* this."

"I do," he said baldly. "I'm dying for it. I would do anything to get some more. I'm not ashamed to admit it, so why should you be?"

"I'm not ashamed!"

"Then why do you run away, and lose your nerve, and tell lies, and put on fake names?" His voice was soft and relentless.

"I did it for my job!" She jerked her face away. "Leave me alone!"

"No." He tossed her onto the bed. "I don't want to leave you alone. And you don't want me to, either." He slid down the length of her body, tossing her skirt up over her waist. "You don't need to pretend with me, Jane. I don't know why you ever thought you needed to."

She caught his face in both her hands. "What makes you think I'm so unsatisfied?" she demanded. "How do you know I don't have a whole stable full of lovers? One for every damn day of the week!"

He pressed a lingering kiss against her inner thigh, and tenderly licked her groin. "I know it from the way you act when I fuck you."

She shoved at his face. "My God, you are crude!"

He trapped her hands and held them still. "Sorry. Can't help it. I can't explain how I know, but you don't open up easily. And you haven't done this in a long time. It's true, right?"

She couldn't look into those bright, piercing eyes and lie at the same time. She nodded reluctantly.

A triumphant grin split his face. "Of course not. You're too shy and uptight to go after what you want. You need a rude, crude barbarian like me to storm the gates. Am I right?"

"Don't get any ideas, MacNamara."

"Too late. I've got more than ideas. At this point, they've already solidified into plans. Shy Jane." He shoved her thighs wide and stared down between them. "Oh, man, look at you. Juicy and hot. I'm going to have to take you lingerie shopping, but the stuff turns me on even more when it's ripped to shreds. Is that kinky?"

Her body vibrated at the sight of his face poised over her mound, his hot breath fanning her most secret flesh. "Very kinky. Mac, don't."

"Yum. Why not?" He rubbed his face against her inner thigh.

She said the first thing that popped into her mind. "Because I must taste like latex."

"Not when I'm through with you, you won't."

Chapter Five

She flinched at the first touch of his mouth. The sensation was unbearably sweet, so electric that she arched right off the bed, but his big hands held her wide open no matter how she writhed. His mouth fastened onto her, suckling and lapping like he could never be satiated.

He shoved her legs high, fluttering his tongue delicately across her clitoris, then sliding with voluptuous deliberation along her inner folds. He plunged his tongue deep inside her, licking her greedily.

The sensation was unspeakably, deliciously intimate. He trapped her splayed thighs flat against the bed as she bucked and writhed. She absorbed his rumbling laughter into her body, her shivering tension rising higher and higher to an agonizing crest.

It broke, and washed over her, sweetly, endlessly.

When she finally managed to open her eyes, he was staring at her, fascinated, his head pillowed on her thigh. "You taste so good, Jane," he said. "I could eat you forever and never get tired."

She tried to laugh, but her muscles didn't remember how. She wanted to tug him up so she could embrace him, but her limp fingers found no purchase against his hard, thick shoulders.

Mac slid up her body and pressed his face to her breasts while he thrust two of his fingers deep inside her sheath.

She stiffened with shock. "Enough," she pleaded. "Let me rest."

"You don't have to do a thing. Just lie there and gasp and come."

"Damn it, Mac—"

"Shhh." His fingers slid deeper, pressing in tender circles inside her. "When I'm going down on you, I concentrate on your clit. But I don't want to neglect this place right here . . . right? Isn't this the spot?"

She answered with a whimper of shocked delight. It almost

hurt, but a deep, diffuse pleasure was building inside her, spreading out in concentric rings, getting deeper, wider, sweeter. She closed her thighs around his hand, clenching and pumping.

"That's good." He crooned his approval. "That's beautiful, Jane. Move against my hand. Show me how much you like it." He tugged the cups of her bustier down. He tugged at her nipple with light, teasing suction, then swirled his hot, wet tongue lavishly over her breasts while his thumb circled the taut nub of her clitoris. She arched, thrust herself against his hand. He drove it deeper, muttering rough encouragement until she was carried away on yet another long, shuddering wave.

She was dimly aware of him climbing off the bed, moving around the room. She let her head fall to the side. Her eyes fluttered open. He stood by the bed, his enormous erection bobbing inches from her face.

He smoothed a condom over himself. Her embarrassment was gone. It was the most natural thing in the world to wrap her fingers around his thick shaft, and stroke him. He hissed with pleasure and turned her so she faced him, her legs dangling over the bed.

She struggled up onto her elbows, moving in slow motion. She lifted her legs, pulled her skirt up, and mutely offered herself to him.

He dragged her hips down to the edge of the bed and piled pillows behind her, propping her up. He dragged her hand down, wrapping it around his penis. "Put me inside you, Jane. Show me you want me."

She was so startled, she almost laughed. "It's a little late to try to be politically correct now, isn't it?"

"I don't give a damn about politically correct. I just want to be sure we're on exactly the same page."

"Don't worry. We are," she assured him. "I want you."

"Put my cock inside you." His voice had the edge of command.

She gripped him with a trembling hand, pressing the thick head of his shaft against her drenched folds until it nudged her open.

He seized her hands, and placed them on his hips. "Pull me in."

She shook her head. "Don't play games with—"

"Just *do* it."

Her eyes widened at his harsh tone. She gripped his hips, pulled. Both of them groaned as he slid slowly, heavily inside her.

Their eyes locked. "All of me," he said softly. "You can take me."

She embraced him even more deeply, and gasped at the aching intensity of his hard flesh pressed deep against her womb. She wrapped her legs around his waist. "Satisfied?"

"Almost," he said. "Now ask me to fuck you."

She almost screamed in frustration. "Damn it, Mac! Why are you doing this? I'm ready! Go for it! What more do you want from me?"

"Everything you've got. Ask me, Jane." His voice grated, his fingers dug into her waist. His eyes were glittering, relentless.

"OK, fine," she yelled. "Please, Mac. I'm asking. Are you happy now? Have I abased myself enough to suit you?"

"Use the words I used. The exact words."

This strange drama had the feeling of a ceremonial ritual. She opened her mouth, and closed it again in consternation. "I can't," she said helplessly. "I just can't do that. It's not in me."

"You have to," he said. "I want to hear you let go and say that nasty, naughty, dirty *f* word. That would really rock my world, Jane."

"It would be completely artificial," she said. "I would feel stupid."

"We'll never know until you try it, will we?" He teased her clitoris with his fingertip, and slid the head of his penis ever so slightly deeper, teasing. Rocking. Making her frantic.

"You evil, controlling bastard. This isn't fair!"

"I'm sorry you feel that way," he said. "Ask me to fuck you, Jane."

His voice was implacable. She was so furious, she pounded her fists against his chest and tried to squirm away from him. He trapped her hands, pinning them down. "Do it!" he snarled.

She stared into his blazing eyes. "Please fuck me," she forced out.

He drove inside her. An intense orgasm tore through her almost instantly, she was so primed. Mac waited and watched the pleasure shudder through her before he began to thrust. She lifted herself for more, crying out with savage joy at every hard, driving stroke.

"You see, Jane? Now I can give you what you need, and you can't say I muscled you into it. You don't want polite." His eyes were bright with triumph. "Polite would bore you. You're such a wild woman."

She swatted him on the shoulder for his smug arrogance and braced her feet against his hard, sweaty chest. "You talk too much, MacNamara. Shut up and do your duty."

He let out a harsh shout of laughter and obliged her with a deep, sensual grind, a maddening friction that drove them up and over the top together, into a long, soaring fall through nowhere.

She lay on top of him, drifting in a timeless haze. Even half awake, she was conscious of Mac's vibrant, thrumming energy beneath her. She floated into a sensual dream where he was her boat, and she was adrift upon him in a rippling blue ocean of endless pleasure.

"Hey. Jane. You awake?" he asked softly.

She pressed a kiss to his hot, salty chest in reply.

His arms tightened around her. "You still mad at me?"

She nuzzled him. "For what? Manipulating me with sex? Not at the moment. For taking me for an unscrupulous con artist? Hmm. If I think about it for a minute, I will be."

"Better keep you from thinking, then." His fingers slid down and tangled into her damp pubic hair.

She wrenched his hand back up to her belly. "No way! I am wiped out! If you touch me there again, I'll go right through the roof."

"How am I going to make you forgive me?" he asked plaintively.

She giggled and struggled as he tried to fondle her. "I forgive you, I forgive you! No orgasm required. I'm too tired to be mad, anyhow."

He rolled her over and kissed her deeply. "Actually, it's lucky things went this way," he said. "We cut through a lot of red tape."

"Oh, please," she scoffed. "Exchanging polite conversation

over dinner is your idea of red tape? What a typical guy thing to say."

He looked aggrieved. "Don't be sarcastic. I'm serious."

"So am I." She pulled herself out of his arms and sat up. "What would you have done differently if you hadn't taken me for a criminal?"

He rolled onto his back and folded his muscular arms behind his head. "Well, I would have taken things slower. I would have been witty and charming. I would have tried to make you laugh. Tried to impress you with how hip and cultured I am."

She thought about it. "That sounds like fun."

"I would have tried to get to know you better before I took you to bed, so you wouldn't think I was a superficial, oversexed animal."

She giggled. "God forbid."

"But I don't have to pretend anymore. My cover's blown. You already know I'm a superficial oversexed animal. I can't fall any lower. What freedom. It thrills me." His hand slid under her skirt.

She slapped his hand away. "Watch it, MacNamara! I am resting!"

He gave her a lazy grin and stretched, making his big, lovely body ripple and flex. "I would have been gentle and careful when I took you to bed," he went on. "I would've tried to get you to relax and trust me."

"That sounds nice, too," she said primly. "Nothing wrong with that scenario at all, Mac."

He reached for her hand and massaged it between his thumb and forefinger. "No, there's not. But I would never have known that you like it wild and rough. Because you would never have told me. Right?"

She stiffened. This turn in the conversation startled her.

"I bet you didn't even know it yourself. It's a first for you, right?" His words vibrated through her body like a plucked string.

"I would never have known that you go for it really raw, just like me," he went on. "Think of all that precious time I would have wasted, trying to be a good boy so as not to offend you."

She felt like the fingers of a powerful, invisible hand were closing around her. "There's nothing wrong with gentleness," she whispered.

"Nope," he said lightly. "Gentleness is great. So is nice, polite sex. It's a lot better than no sex at all. But sex like this . . ." He shook his head. "Unbelievable. You clawed me when you came, you know that?"

Her eyes widened in shock. "I did *what?*"

"Oh, yeah." He looked triumphant. "Big time."

"Let me see!" she demanded.

He rolled over obligingly. She clapped her hand over her mouth. Angry red weals raked his back, and she didn't even remember doing it.

"I'm so sorry," she said faintly. "I've never—"

"Good. I'm glad you never. I'm proud of them, Jane. I bet you've never slapped a man and yelled at him to fuck you harder, have you?"

She slipped off the bed and stood, unnerved and aroused by his provocative questions. "I'm not comfortable with this conversation, or your choice of language," she said. "Please don't talk to me that way."

"I'm not interested in making you comfortable. I'm a lot more interested in making you come. I'm on the right track." He inhaled deeply, and his feral grin stood her hairs on end. "I can smell it."

"You're being rude again." She took a step back. "Don't."

Mac's hand shot out, his fingers clamping over her wrist. His posture on the bed was the picture of lazy relaxation, but his hand around her wrist was like a steel manacle. "You think that's rude? I'll show you rude. Lift up your skirt, Jane."

"Mac, please. For God's sake," she protested.

He jerked her towards him, dragging handfuls of her skirt up, and pulled her until his face was pressed against her pubic hair, his warm breath tickling her. "Hold still, Jane. I was rude and bad, and you're a prissy ice goddess. Let me beg your forgiveness—with my tongue."

His long, strong tongue delved into her cleft. The hot, luscious swirl of bliss made her knees shake beneath her. He suckled her clitoris until she was clutching his head, knees shaking violently.

"Can you come on your feet, or will you fall?" he asked.

"I don't know." Her voice was breathless. "I've never—"

"Good. Another first. I like that. Come here. Climb up on the bed."

The fingers of that invisible hand tightened around her again, despite the wild pleasure of his touch. She wrenched out of his grip with a burst of desperate strength and stumbled backward. "No!"

"I just want to please you." His muscles rippled like a big, sinuous cat as he sat up. "Come here, Jane. You know I won't hurt you."

She stood up as straight as she could. "You're cutting through too much red tape, Mac. It's too much, too soon. It isn't right."

His eyes narrowed. "It would upset you so much to sit on my face?"

She jerked back. "God! That is so—"

"Rude. Yeah, that's me." He slid off the bed and stood. His naked body towered over hers. Fiercely erect. The man was insatiable.

"I'm serious." She struggled to make her voice steadier. "If you'd gone through all the dull bureaucratic channels of getting to know me, there would be ground beneath our feet. This way, it's . . . too intense."

He crossed his arms over his chest. "Let me get this straight, Jane," he said slowly. "The bottom line is, if I want to give you another screaming orgasm, I've got to get to know you first? *Now?*"

She steadied herself on the dresser as she tried to stare him down. "Oh, you poor baby," she snapped. "What a terrible chore."

He shrugged. "You're trying to lock the barn door after the horse is gone. What's the point, Jane? Just let go."

"No, I would say this is more along the lines of going out to look for the horse so you can put it back in the barn where it belongs."

He pondered this with calculating eyes. "Excuse me if I get gritty and practical, but how quickly does this process have to take place? Is there an exchange rate? A point system? Like, for oral sex, we exchange childhood reminiscences, but for full-penetration sex, we have to get down and dirty and tell the first time we ever did it in the—"

"You're being deliberately crass and rude!" she snapped.

He threw up his hands in mock helplessness. "Babe. This is me, uncut and uncensored. You'll get to know me quicker if I don't pretend."

He had a point, but she still felt outmaneuvered. "You're overdoing it, though," she said tightly. "As always."

"Ah," he murmured. "I see how this works. You don't want to hear anything that makes you uncomfortable. This is another game for you to hide behind, like your fake names and your lies, right? You run away from the truth whenever it scares you."

She shook her head. "No. That's not what this is about."

"If you want to know me, you've got to deal with the real me," he said. "And I want the real you. Not just what you feel comfortable with. Otherwise, there's no sense to it. Are you ready for that, Jane?"

He'd turned the tables, put her right back on the defensive, but she was the one who had started this, and she had to see it through.

She stuck out her chin. "I'm ready."

They stared at each other. Mac gestured towards the bed. "Come on back to bed, then," he said. "I won't jump on you."

She walked past him, and slowly reclined on the bed. Mac stretched out his long, gorgeous naked body next to hers. "So? Let's get started," he said. "Go for it."

She stared into his bright eyes, intimidated. "Where am I supposed to start?"

He slanted her an ironic glance. "This was your idea, angel. Tell me everything about yourself."

"Everything is pretty broad. Let's establish a jumping off point."

He skimmed his hand over the curve of her thigh. "Start with the naked centerfold model vital stats."

It was as good a starting point as any. She thought for a moment to recall the format. "Let's see. Jane Duvall, twenty-eight years old. Pisces. Five three, a hundred and thirty pounds. Born in San Diego, graduated from UCLA. Likes: . . . that's tough. There's a lot that I like."

"Pick a random one," he suggested, when she hesitated too long.

"Violets," she began. "Shakespeare. Fine dark Italian chocolate."

"You were suppose to pick one," he reminded her. "Two, max."

"Oh, I'm just warming up," she told him. "Raw honey in the comb. Flowering cactus. Silk. Rainbows. Antique perfume bottles."

"You can't get a one-word answer out of a woman," he grumbled.

"You expect me to decide between silk, rainbows and chocolate?"

"Let's just move on," he said in a long-suffering voice. "Hates?"

She felt his warm hand against her skin. In the course of petting her thigh, Mac had pulled her skirt up over her legs. She yanked it down. "Stop that. Let's see, hates . . ." Her euphoria evaporated as she thought about it. "Meanness," she said. "Spite. Back-stabbing."

He propped himself up onto his elbow, frowning. "I didn't mean for this to be a downer," he said. "Don't take it so seriously, Jane."

She snorted. "That's the story of my life. Your turn, Mac."

"We need a system," he said thoughtfully. "This is like a get-to-know-you party game. Truth or Dare, or Psychiatrist. Or strip poker."

"No strip anything, please," she said hastily. "How about childhood dreams? Tell me what you wanted to be when you grew up." It was as neutral and nonsexual a topic as she could think of.

"Astronaut," Mac said without hesitation. "I wanted to walk on the moon, be the first man on Mars, and wear a bubble on my head."

Jane laughed out loud. "So what stopped you?"

"Physics." He grimaced. "My brain wasn't wired that way. I saw the Indiana Jones movies and figured being an archaeologist would be better. Less math, more adventure. Then my snotty little brother told me I would spend the rest of my life dusting off pottery shards with a toothbrush. Trust Danny to take the bloom off of a dream. In the meantime, when I wasn't keeping Robin from running off cliffs, I was working like a bastard for my uncle. I was good at it. I studied business and hotel management, one thing led to another, and here I am."

"Very nice," she said. "Well done, Mac. This is exactly the kind of conversation we should have had over dinner."

"You liked it?" He surged up onto his elbow. "What's it worth? How many points did I earn towards another bout of hot, grinding—"

She shoved at his chest, knocking him onto his back. "Hold it right there, buddy!"

He blinked up at her in exaggerated innocence. "Huh? What?"

"This is not a game!" she protested. "You do not win points!"

He looked genuinely puzzled. "But everything's a game, Jane. It all comes down to winning in the end."

"You're wrong. This is about trust and communication!"

"Yeah. The direct advantage of which is that they lead straight towards another bout of hot, grinding, pounding—"

"Stop!" she snapped. "You are deliberately driving me nuts! Trust and communication are their own reward, you . . . you animal!"

He shrugged. "It all depends on your priorities, babe."

The sparkle in his eyes made her suspicious. "You're just teasing me, right?"

He gave her an evil grin. "Which answer earns me more points?"

She seized the pillow and swatted him with it. "You are hopeless!"

Mac yanked the pillow away and pulled her into the crook of his shoulder. "Relax. This hug is an affectionate gesture meant to facilitate trust and communication. OK, let's have it. Your childhood dreams."

Her heart galloped madly at the contact with his hot, smooth skin. It was hard to think. "I wanted to be an actress," she confessed.

"No kidding," he said. "Like, Hollywood?"

"No, a stage actress. I liked the classic stuff. Shakespeare, Ibsen, Molière. It started in high school. My folks . . . well, they're older. They never wanted children. I had a very quiet childhood. It was important to never bother them. No scenes allowed."

He nodded for her to go on, his eyes intent upon her face.

"So my sophomore year in high school, I was stage manager for the school musical. We were doing *Li'l Abner,* and the girl who was playing the femme fatale broke her arm the day before dress rehearsal. I was the only one without a part who fit into the costume."

"Femme fatale?" He grinned. "I can see it. Yum."

"It was just a bit part, but all the sudden, I found myself in a tight slinky dress, walking out on the stage as Appassionata Von Climax."

He shook with startled laughter. "You're kidding!"

"Nope. Cross my heart. Anyway, it was a revelation. Some switch flipped on inside me. I projected this sexy energy. It was magic. The guy who played the lead asked me to the prom, of all things."

"You don't say."

"Don't laugh," she said. "He was one of the popular boys, I was a nobody, and his girlfriend was playing Daisy Mae to his Li'l Abner. It was a huge scandal. I almost got lynched in the girl's locker room."

"I'm sorry for your trauma," he said meekly.

"I just bet you are. The problem was, once I took off the outfit and wiped off the makeup, the magic disappeared. I went to the prom, but I was so shy, I couldn't think of anything to say to the guy, so it fizzled out fast. But that's how it started. I was bitten by the theater bug. What a relief, to let it all explode out of me in a big, loud voice."

He waited for more. "You studied theater in college?" he prodded.

She nodded. "It was great. I got cast as Juliet once, and it was like *Li'l Abner* all over again. Romeo fell for me—during the run of the show, that is. Then I was Kate in *The Taming of the Shrew,* and Petruchio got a mad crush on me—for the duration of the show."

"And after the show closed?"

She laughed uncomfortably, and wondered what had possessed her to volunteer such embarrassing details to him. "They lost that loving feeling. On stage, I sparkle, but offstage I'm pretty stiff and shy."

"Not with me, you're not," Mac said, with clear satisfaction.

"I never even got a chance to be stiff and shy with you!"
He stuck his finger into her neckline and tugged it. "You see the advantages of cutting through that pesky red tape?"

She slapped his hand away. "Down, boy! You haven't earned anywhere near enough points yet to take those kind of liberties."

"Arf, arf," he said. "So why didn't you become an actress?"

She hesitated for a little too long. "It didn't work out," she said lightly. "It's a tough business. I had to pay the rent somehow."

"You're holding something back," he murmured. "I can feel it."

She pulled herself out of his arms. No way was she telling him about Dylan. Talk about downers. "That's the story. Take it or leave it."

"Let's see. What can I make of this?" His voice was low, musing. "You blocked your emotions and only let them out on stage. Interesting. You like playing roles. You love control, almost as much as you love losing it. Complicated, challenging. I like mysterious women. You play at intimacy, but you're afraid of the real thing. Right?"

She forced herself to laugh, although his analysis made her want to squirm. "Are you psychoanalyzing me, Mac?"

"Hell, no," he said readily. "Real men don't do that." He stared at her, narrow-eyed. "You're not on stage now, Jane. And feel this." He took her hand and slid it down to his hot, rigid penis. "I haven't lost interest for a nanosecond. I'm the one who's stiff. Not you."

She giggled. "You must've broken the spell I was under."

He looked pleased with himself. "Prince Charming, huh?"

"Hah!" She wrenched her hand away. "Prince Un-Charming is more like it. Once you get me alone, the charm goes right out the window. You could try a little harder. This is a first date, after all."

He yanked her back down so that she lay half across his broad chest. "This isn't a first date conversation. I don't know if I've ever had a conversation with such a high reality quotient, let alone on a first date. It's not first date sex, either. It's more like thank-God-we-were-saved-from-the-river-of-boiling-lava sex."

"I might have known we'd get right back to sex," she grumbled. "You're obsessed, Mac."

"No, just focused. And really tired of this goddamn dress." He seized her skirt. "We've had sex twice. I've gone down on you twice. We've even had a deep, meaningful conversation. I'm being as charming as I know how to be, and I still haven't seen you naked."

She tugged her skirt back out of his grasp. "Mac—"

"Don't fight me, Jane. If you don't take the dress off right now, I'm going to rip it off you."

Their eyes locked. "I . . . I paid way too much for this damn dress," she sputtered. "So don't even think about—"

"So strip, if you like the dress," he cut in. "Otherwise it's going to be sacrificed upon the altar of my immoderate lust."

She scrambled off the bed. "Do not order me. I don't like that tone in your voice."

His eyes flashed. "Maybe not, but it works for you. I've got you figured out, Jane. If we'd had nice, polite sex, you might have been able to keep me at arm's length, like you're trying to do right now. But we didn't, babe. You know you can't control me. That's why I turn you on."

She wanted to scream with frustration. "I'm not trying to control you, damn it! I'm trying to communicate with you!"

He shook his head. "Wrong again. You hide behind words. I have to look deeper than just words if I want to unlock my shy, complicated Jane. For you, words are the wall, babe. Not the key."

"You're pretty damn sneaky with words yourself."

A slow, merciless smile spread across his hard face. "I try."

Jane covered her trembling mouth with her hands. "I'm not in the mood to spar with you, Mac. I told you intimate details about myself, and now you're turning them on me. It's not fair."

He stood up and stroked her upper arms. His hands left a tingling shiver in their wake. "Life is never fair," he said. "That's how the game is played, Jane. Find your opponent's weak point— and exploit it."

She gave him a sharp, angry push which barely budged him. "So I'm your opponent, then? All you want is to vanquish me?"

He lifted her hair off her shoulders and bent to kiss her throat. "Sure, if being vanquished turns you on. That's what I want. Whatever makes you hot. I'll hunt it down . . . and I'll pin it right to the wall."

The savage intensity of his voice made her tremble. She turned her hot face away from his demanding kiss. Mac jerked it right back around. "That turns you on, doesn't it, Jane?" he crooned. "Admit it."

It did. His dominating power turned her inside out. He'd broken the spell that bound her, not with a chaste fairy-tale kiss, but with his wild desire, with his unflinching honesty. Her Prince Un-Charming.

He'd wakened not just her passion, but everything that had been crushing it down—stones of petrified anger and sadness. But a paradox was at the heart of his sexy power games—something treacherous and painful. She didn't dare give in to him. He would run right over her.

She took a slow, calming breath, and gathered her power as if she were about to step on stage. "Back off, Mac." She said it in a clear, strong voice, designed to carry to the very back row.

His eyes widened. He let go, took a step back and lifted his hands in mock surrender. "Yes, ma'am."

She studied him. So far, so good. "Even if your macho posturing did turn me on—and I'm not saying that it does—I won't just lie there whimpering and conquered," she said. "You need a sharp lesson."

"Oh, yeah? Going to spank me, Jane?" he taunted. "Handcuffs?"

"I don't need props," she said coolly. "I'm learning from an expert. I just have to find your weak point . . . and exploit it."

He frowned. "What's the use of that?"

"Ah, I see," she mocked. "It's OK for me to be vulnerable, but not for you, hmm? Heaven forbid that the big, bad hunter—"

"You like to lose control, and I like to make you lose it," he said impatiently. "Why mess with that? I just want to give you pleasure."

"And you want to run the whole show," she said.

"Sure, I do. Why not? I'm good at it," he said. "Trust me, Jane."

"So you can exploit my weak point?"

"No!" he snarled. "So I can please you, goddamn it!"

She tried to look down her nose at him. A neat trick, since he was a foot taller than she. "Maybe it would please me to vanquish you, Mac."

The tension humming between them got thicker every second.

Mac folded his arms, and shrugged. "OK, Jane. Let's see how long you can keep this up. Vanquish me if you can. Do it quick, though, because I'm going to rip that dress right off if you don't make a move."

His challenge rang in the air. Her mind raced. He didn't look like he had any weak points. How on earth was she going to dominate him?

"Scared, huh?" he taunted. "What would Appassionata do?"

Ah. Of course. She had the answer to her dilemma, and Mac had handed it right to her. A smile curved her lips. "Appassionata would eat you alive, Mac," she said softly. "It's dangerous to invoke her."

"Anything to get things going," he grumbled.

She shoved his chest, driving him across the room towards the chair. "Sit." She knocked him back, a sharp, imperious gesture.

He was so startled, he actually obeyed her and fell back heavily into the chair. An excellent beginning. Beyond her wildest hopes.

"Don't move until I say so," she said. "Or else. Understand?"

He nodded, his eyes quietly watchful.

"Now watch, Mac." She began to strip.

Chapter Six

The change that came over her was unnerving. He couldn't pin it down exactly; maybe it was the wild glow in her eyes. The shape of her lips changed, her posture, the tilt of her eyebrows. She was someone else, confident and armored, completely closed to him. Then she began to shimmy the dress down over her tits, and all coherent thought fled.

The dress dragged the lace cups of her bustier down along with it. He almost whimpered when the fabric snagged on her taut nipples. It stretched, strained . . . and finally popped over. Her breasts were bare, propped up on the shelf of the provocative black lace corset.

There was another moment of delicious suspense when he wasn't sure she was going to get it all the way over the rich swell of her hips. Her tits jiggled, her hips swayed as she worked it steadily down. It slid to the floor, and she kicked it aside and struck a pose for him. Leg lifted, foot arched, arms over her head. She tossed her hair, swiveled her hips. She turned her back to him and bent over, back arched.

His breath stuck in his lungs as if it had turned solid. He gaped at the rounded globes of her ass, the shadowy glimpse of her cunt.

She reached down, unhooked the garters from the lace-trimmed stockings. He could barely make out her face beneath the swirling red curtain of her hair as she reached behind herself to unhook the corset.

He reached for her. "Hey, let me help you with that."

"Get down." Her voice stung him like a slap in the face. "If I want something from you, I'll ask for it."

He fell back into the chair, shocked into total stillness. Whoa. She was dead serious about this, but he didn't have time to feel weird about it, because right then the corset fell to the floor, and the world stopped.

The graceful totality of her naked torso stole his breath. Her skin was so luminously pale, marked with the scratchy lace. He stared at the swells and hollows and delicate curves. Her breasts were abundant, the taut nipples high, the rich undercurve perfect to lick and nuzzle.

He reached for her. She shoved him back into the chair, hard enough to make him grunt. "Bad boy," she said. "Slow learner, hmm?"

He panted up at her, his cock as hard as a railroad spike. "What the hell's the matter with you, Jane? What are you doing?"

"Looking for your weak points," she told him. "Suffer . . . baby."

"What do you care about my weak points?" he demanded. "What good are they to you? It's my strong points that can serve you."

She scooped her hair up over her head and let it tumble back down in a witchy tangle to veil her mysterious eyes. "Hush, Mac. You think too much." She lifted one graceful, arched foot, and placed it on the arm of his chair, giving him a ringside view of the folds of her cunt pouting out of the curly red thatch. "Pull my stockings down," she commanded. "With your teeth."

He leaned forward, irresistibly drawn to the hot, damp nest of woman-scented hair. She kicked him back into the chair, her foot pressing hard against his chest. "The stocking, Mac," she repeated.

He tried not to pant as he seized her stocking in his teeth. This was strange, not his usual vibe, but any opportunity to rub his cheek against her skin was fine with him. He pulled the stocking free. Tiny pink toes, toenails painted frosty silver. He wanted to suckle each one.

She patted his face. "Good boy. Now the other one."

She turned and lifted the other leg for him to service. If he leaned forward, he could just bury his face in her juicy, delicious—

"No." She slid her fingers through his hair and jerked his head back, hard. "Focus, Mac."

He dragged the other stocking down. He realized, to his dismay, that he was trembling. She lifted her foot so he could pull the stocking free, and ruffled his hair, as if praising a dog that had retrieved a stick.

"Very good." She widened her stance. "Now my panties."

He took the elastic between his teeth and pressed his face against the silky, yielding warmth of her belly. Incoherent anger gripped him. She knew damn well this servile love-slave routine came hard to him. She wanted to see how far she could push him before he snapped.

Problem was, he wasn't sure himself. The one thing he was sure of was that he wanted to know Jane Duvall. He wanted to learn her by heart. He wanted the keys, the codes, the goddamn operating manual.

That was the only reason he was playing along. If she needed so badly to be in control, he would grit his teeth and see how much he could take—to a point. He buried his face in her pubic hair, thrust his tongue deep into that hot, slick furrow. She made a startled sound and seized his face in both hands as if to push him away. She didn't.

She let him worship her for several silent, trembling minutes, until her knees started to buckle. She stumbled back, dazed. Staring down into his face. He wiped his mouth. He was unable to hide his triumph. Her eyes focused, and her chin lifted. "The panties, Mac," she said. "And don't take liberties." Her body shook, but her voice held firm.

What the hell. He was secure in his sexuality. He could indulge a woman if she wanted to play the dominatrix bitch, as long as they both knew damn good and well who was boss. It cost him nothing.

But something very weird was happening—this burning in his chest, the ache in his gut. He couldn't stop shaking. He hated the mysterious, impenetrable look on her face. It made him feel lonely and desolate. It messed with his head. She could take him apart. She didn't need whips or chains. She did it with her eyes.

He dragged the panties down. She was finally naked, thank God. Never in his life had he struggled so hard to get a woman's clothes off.

"Now, sit." She sank to her knees beside him and seized his cock. Her bold grip made him gasp and jerk. "Don't be afraid," she purred. "You've been very good, Mac, and now you're going to be rewarded."

She grasped his cock firmly, licked the tight, swollen head, and sucked him deep into her mouth. Oh, God, she was good. Passionate, voracious, skillful. She sucked him deep, sliding her tongue along his length, flicking it across the most sensitive spots with teasing, fluttering strokes. Her strong, slender hands followed the slippery path of her mouth, gripping and stroking him. It was shivering agony, the tight, dragging suction as she drew him out of her mouth, the luscious glide as she took him back in again. Deep and yielding and wonderful.

She took her time, and she didn't get tired. She drew his cock into her mouth deeper than he'd imagined possible, and then peeked up at him through her lashes. A wicked smile gleamed in her eyes as she watched his reaction to the clutch of her moist pink lips, the lash of her tongue. He shuddered and groaned, all his attention narrowed down to her swirling, suckling mouth. Just when he thought it couldn't possibly get better, she cupped his balls, caressing them with her fingertips, and pressed that sensitive spot beneath them.

He fought back the orgasm that was about to flatten him, and Jane lifted her head, sensing it. "Don't even think about coming yet," she said. "I have other plans for you. Understood?"

He nodded, and then shook his head, confused. Yes, he understood. No, he wouldn't come. Yes, no, whatever. Anything she said, anything she wanted. Anything at all. Just more. Just *now*.

"Where are your condoms?" she demanded.

"Box in the bathroom," he managed to say.

Off she went, to the bathroom. Mac hoped whatever she had in mind involved fucking him, hard and soon. Otherwise he was going to be in urgent need of medical help. She posed in the bathroom door like a Venus, all voluptuous curves and creamy paleness and rippling hair.

She advanced on him, smiling, and knelt down, smoothing the condom over his cock. She stood up, backlit by the bathroom light. Her hair was a fiery halo. Her face was wreathed in mysterious shadows.

"Scoot down in the chair, so I can straddle you," she commanded.

He trembled in pathetic eagerness to do her bidding. Her hand cupped his chin, jerking his face up. "Look at me, Mac."

He looked. She stood astride him, eyes in shadow, hair lit from behind like a corona of flames. Terrifying and gorgeous and pitiless.

He loved it and hated it. She'd stripped him of all the power and self-control he'd worked so hard to gain. He was an ignorant, vulnerable boy again, and she was a cruel, unfathomable goddess with the power to bestow life or death. He burned with need. He was prostrated with fear, terrified of disappointing her, failing her in some way.

"Ask me to fuck you," she said. "And say please."

He opened his mouth, but the words stuck in his throat. He swallowed, and tried again. "Please fuck me," he said.

She smiled, caressing his cheek, and guided his cock, nudging it between her legs. She lodged it in the tender opening of her body, and sank down with a moan, shoving him deep inside herself. The muscles in her cunt fluttered around him. It was too good. It was killing him.

He was terrified to move, he was so close to orgasm, and he would die of shame if he lost control of himself now. Jane sensed his dilemma. She waited, motionless, until he opened his eyes and gave her a nod.

Then she started to ride him. It was perfect, it was heaven, it was hell. He was miserable. Her body rose and fell against his in an urgent rocking slide. Her skin had a pearly sheen of moisture. She was so goddamn beautiful. This erotic bitch goddess was wildly sexy, but he hated the look on her face. He missed that sweet, open look, the soft vulnerability. He wanted it back. He wanted his sweet Jane.

She pried one of his hands off her hips and pressed it against her mound. "Touch me," she said shakily. "Make me come, Mac."

Hell, yes. That was his ticket out of this bizarre sexual torture. He bucked beneath her and caressed her clit. His hard, stabbing strokes from below were just what she needed to detonate the explosion. She arched back, cried out and came violently, clenching him inside her.

He fought his own orgasm back. He couldn't climax with her

now. It would make her victory too complete. He had his limits, and he'd reached them. She'd had her fun. He was done.

"Come back to me now," he said. "I've had enough."

She lifted her head. Her hair clung to his sweat-dampened skin. Her eyes gleamed with laughter. "Who asked you if you'd had enough?"

His fingers dug into her waist. "Do not fuck with my head, Jane."

Her eyes widened, and she fluttered her lashes. "Such intensity. You think one spectacular orgasm gives you the right to run my world?"

"Come off it," he demanded. "The dominatrix routine is a flaming turn-on, but I've had enough of it. I can't take it anymore."

A mocking smile played about her lips. "Oh, no? Well, then. Here we have it. This must be the weak point I'm supposed to exploit."

He shook her. "Cut out the man-eating bitch act and talk to me!"

"Talk?" Her light laughter grated on him. "I thought it was only girls who ruined sex with talk. And just when I'm moving in for the kill."

"Don't push me, goddamn it." His voice shook. "I'm warning you."

"And give up my advantage?" She touched his face, and he jerked away from the caress. "No, Mac. That's not the way the world works. You told me so yourself."

That was it. Something exploded inside him. He slid off the chair to his knees, carrying her down to the floor beneath him.

She must have seen something in his face that scared her, because her eyes went big, and she pulled away, scrambling out of his grip with the swiftness of panic. She rolled over and tried to crawl away.

He seized her ankles. She flailed and struggled, but he flung himself on top of her, pinning her down on her stomach.

Even better. This position suited him just fine.

She twisted around to look at him. "Mac, I—"

"Be quiet," he snarled. "Everything you say makes me angrier, so just *shut up*."

He slid his arm beneath her hips, dragging her up onto her knees. He knocked her legs apart and drove his cock inside her. She cried out, and pitched forward onto her forearms. He was possessed, shaking with strain as he held her down and pounded his body into hers. Sharp gasps jerked out of her at each heavy stroke. His cock gleamed with her slick, hot moisture. He knew it was too rough, but he couldn't ease off. Not many of his lovers had been able take his whole length. Neither had Jane, at first. He was used to holding back, but he wasn't now. She was made for him. He could plunge to the hilt.

She was *his*. He let out a guttural shout as triumph and dark fury prodded him over the edge and into a blinding, explosive release.

He lifted himself off when he drifted back, so weak he could barely move. He collapsed onto his back and covered his face with his hand.

His gut ached. The formula to this man-woman thing was beyond his understanding. Love could be given and taken away. No warning, no explanation, no apologies. He accepted that fact, even profited from it. He'd given and taken it as it pleased him, when it was convenient, when he was in the mood. He'd left it behind without a second thought.

He'd never wanted to keep a woman under lock and key. To force her to love him. Ironic. If there was one thing he'd known since he was a kid, it was that love couldn't be forced. There was no commanding it, no controlling it. It did what it goddamn well pleased.

He should ask if she was OK. He should be solicitous and apologetic. Fuck it. It was beyond him.

"Mac?" she asked cautiously.

At least she could talk. He was the destroyed, humiliated one.

"Mac, please say something," she urged.

He turned his face away. "What do you want me to say? You were looking for my weak point. Looks like you found it. I hope you liked it. I hope you had a great time. Because that'll make one of us."

He measured the silence by his own pounding heartbeat.

"Do you want me to go?" Her voice was soft and timid.

"No!" His hand flashed out, clamping around her wrist.

Jane slid the condom off his cock, and tugged gently at her wrist until he released it. She got up and went quietly to the bathroom.

He was limp, motionless, exactly as she left him, when she came back. She knelt down and started to pet his damp chest. "I'm sorry, Mac. I shouldn't have done that. I didn't mean to hurt you."

The irony of it made him laugh. "Uh . . . I think that's my line."

She shook her head. "No. The minute you weren't having fun anymore, I should have given in. I don't know why I didn't. I had something to prove, I guess. You, ah, sort of challenged me to a duel."

"Don't remind me." He shivered. "You were just getting back at me for being a controlling dickhead. I guess I deserved it."

"No. You didn't," she said. "You pushed me hard, but you never went too far. I went too far."

He made a sharp, angry gesture of negation. "Forget it. Please."

"No," she persisted. "It was cruel, and I'm sorry."

Her apology shamed him, made him feel even more vulnerable. "Let it go, for Christ's sake," he growled. "I don't want to think about it."

Her hair coiled in silken loops on his face and chest as she bent to kiss him. "All right," she said softly.

"You're OK, right?" he asked. "I didn't hurt you, did I?"

She hesitated. "No biggie. My knees are stinging from the carpet, and I might have a bruise or two. But I'm fine."

He reached up and ran his hands over her body. "Damn. Where?"

"Don't worry." She put her mouth to his ear. "Actually, it really excited me," she whispered. "But that's a deep, dark secret, so don't you dare throw it back in my face."

"Hell, no," he said fervently. "I've learned my lesson."

The real Jane was back. He could finally breathe. He closed his eyes. Her soft kisses were soothing, like warm raindrops. They eased the burning in his chest, made the clenched knot in his belly relax.

His stomach rumbled. "I'm hungry," he said. It sounded so prosaic, after the thunder and lightning and crazy sex, but there it was.

"So am I," Jane said. "You made me skip dinner. You were in such a tearing hurry to plunder the fortress."

He peered into her face, and cautiously concluded that she was teasing him. "Plundering fortresses is hungry work. I'll order up some dinner. How about you go run a bath?"

"Dinner?" She glanced at the bedside clock, and back at him, amazed. "You can get dinner sent up at this hour?"

His chest jerked in a derisive laugh. "I run this place."

"Ah." Her eyes widened. "The lord of the manor is back, I see."

"He was never gone," he said shortly.

"Oops! Excuse me, Your Exalted Masterfulness. I'll just trip obediently off to the bathroom to do your bidding now—"

"No more," he barked. "I have had *enough.*"

He instantly regretted his tone, but she just covered her mouth with her hand, eyes sparkling. "Sorry. I'm so bad. Didn't mean to push."

She left the door wide open as she set the bath running. That was a good sign. So was the fact that she . . . wow. She was humming.

He'd been so sure he'd fucked up beyond redemption, but she was still here. Humming, for God's sake. Go figure.

He grabbed the phone and dialed the kitchen. "This is Michael MacNamara," he said to the guy who picked up. "Send a bottle of Dom Perignon up to room twenty-eight. Put together a cold dinner for two, whatever's good tonight. Lots of it. Knock loudly and leave the cart outside the door. But I want the champagne right now, so grab it, and run. Got it?"

"Yes, sir. Right away, sir," the kid assured him.

He hung up the phone and stared at the open door. Steam wafted out the door in curling streamers. The tub was big enough for two. She was singing now. She had a pretty voice, husky and rich and soft.

Damn, he was confused. He would never understand how this stuff worked, but he wasn't stupid enough to waste time worrying about it while a beautiful naked woman waited for him in the bathtub.

Jane hummed the refrain to the sappy old show tune as she sank into the steaming water. It stung as it covered her sore spots, the deep ache between her legs. The world was shimmering with possibilities. She felt so alive. Poised on the edge of disaster. Like a dream where she was flying and knew she might fall, but flying was worth the risk.

Mac appeared in the doorway, a bottle of champagne in his hand. She gave him an encouraging smile, and admired his spectacular naked body as he walked in and held out a champagne flute. She caressed his muscular flanks, and the weight of his dangling penis and testicles, heavy against their thick nest of springy dark hair.

She accepted the champagne. "You're beautiful, Mac."

He grunted, lifting a heavy brow. "Thanks," he said doubtfully.

She sipped the icy cold, frothing champagne. It stung against her throat. A bold impulse struck her. "Would you do something for me?"

"Uh, what, exactly?"

His narrow-eyed caution made her giggle. "Turn around," she said. "I want to look at you from behind."

He frowned. "No funny stuff."

She laughed out loud. "No! I just want to admire your, um . . ."

"My ass," he supplied. He shrugged, and turned around, widening his stance. "There it is. In all its glory."

Oh, dear. It wasn't fair, it wasn't right. His body was superb. Powerful shoulders, his muscles lean and graceful, not at all like the swollen bulk of steroid-popping body builders. His back narrowed to a lean waist, a tight butt, thickly muscled thighs, ropy calves. Even his ankles and feet were beautiful. Masculine perfection personified. She wanted to grab him, assure herself that he was real.

The throbbing ache between her legs reminded her that he was very real indeed. She put the champagne down and rose up onto her knees. He jerked as she put her hands on his hips. "Don't worry," she soothed. "Your body is so perfect, Mac. I just want to touch it."

"That's what I'm supposed to say to you," he complained.

"Move closer to the tub, please." He hesitated, and she tugged at his resistant body. "What's wrong?" she teased. "Am I so scary?"

He allowed himself to be pulled closer. "Yeah," he admitted. "You are pretty damn scary, Jane. It feels strange, to have my back to you."

"No funny stuff, I promise," she assured him.

She stroked the curve of his spine, the smooth, resilient dips and curves of his flanks. She pressed her lips against the dimples over his buttocks, the tuft of hair at the small of his back. He smelled of sex. He tasted hot and salty. She slid her hand into the heat between his thighs. Her fingertips brushed the warm, velvety skin of his scrotum.

He stiffened, shuddered. "Oh, Jesus. Don't get me going."

She deepened the caress, nuzzling his back. "Do you like that?"

"Yeah." He turned around, his erection bobbing in her face. "See?"

She fell back into the tub, startled. "Good God! You're insatiable!"

"I know. This isn't normal. I feel like we're just getting started."

She ran her fingertip over his erection. "How long are you?"

Mac laughed. "You mean, my cock? I've never measured it."

She flicked water at him. "That is a big fat lie! No way have you never measured that thing!"

"It's true. Running for a ruler is the last thing I think about when I'm hard. I'm more interested in measuring, say, these." He knelt, slid his hands into the water and cupped her breasts. He stroked his hands tenderly around her ribs, her waist. "Thirty-four-D," he said. "Dress size, ten."

She stretched and purred at his touch. "Bingo. You're good."

"I know. Measure me if you want, Jane." He pulled her hand out of the water and wrapped it around his penis. "I thought we were taking a time-out, but if you want to get right back to it, that's fine."

"I'm not ready to have sex again," she admitted. "I didn't know you'd be so quick to, um . . . that is, I didn't mean to lead you on."

He looked like he was trying not to grin. "Yeah, you said that this afternoon. After kissing me senseless and coming all over my hand."

"It's your own fault, for having such a tempting body," she said primly. "The bath is very nice. Want to join me?"

"Hell, yes." He refilled their champagne glasses and climbed in.

She curled up to make space. She felt wild and free, almost drunk. Their dynamic had changed. Mac seemed less arrogant, almost wary of her, and she felt more confident and relaxed with him. Maybe it was perverse, but if it worked, it worked. She was being more honest with him than she'd ever been. Saying what popped into her head, not thinking it to death for fear it would get her into trouble. It felt fabulous.

His big body displaced a huge amount of water. It sloshed perilously near the rim. He arranged her legs so they floated on either side of his knees. His indefatigable erection lay high against his belly. He slanted her a crooked smile. "I knew it was too soon to seduce you again, but I had to try," he said. "Nothing ventured, nothing gained."

She laughed. "That's what I tell my kids all the time."

"Kids? You have kids?"

She giggled at his startled expression. "Not my biological children, silly. The kids in my theater troupe. The MeanStreets Players."

"MeanStreets?" His face turned thoughtful. "Robin mentioned them a while back. There was a buzz about a Shakespeare production using a bunch of local gang delinquents. It got good reviews."

"That was us," she said proudly. "Except they're not delinquents. They're the MeanStreets Players, and they rule. A few years ago, I got asked to direct a skit with some at-risk teenagers at the youth center where I volunteered. It went so well, we decided to keep on with it. We're doing *A Midsummer Night's Dream* this fall. In fact, my boss promised to help fund our fall show if I bagged your GM."

His eyebrows twitched. "Oh. So by thwarting you, I'm destroying the dreams of underprivileged urban kids? As usual, I'm the bad guy."

"Hardly," she scoffed. "I don't need your stupid old GM. There's more than one fish in the sea. We'll fund that show somehow."

"I'm sure you will," he said. "You're a force to be reckoned with, Jane Duvall. Those kids are lucky."

"Theater saved me when I was young," she said simply. "It gave me a place to dream. Every kid should have a place to dream, whether it's sports, music, whatever. I just want to give that back to those kids."

"That's great. I salute you for it." He lifted his glass to her.

The warmth of his smile was like a physical caress. She took a gulp of champagne and beamed back. She felt giddy and fearless. "Your turn, Mac," she announced.

"For what?" he said suspiciously.

She nudged his hard belly with her foot. He pulled it to his mouth, and she giggled and squirmed as he suckled her toes. "Stop that! Our party game, Mac. You know things about me that I've never told anyone. Your turn. Tell me one of your deep, dark secrets."

He shrugged. "I don't have any deep, dark secrets. I suck at secrets. Can't keep one to save my life. Danny is the secrets man."

She rolled her eyes. "Don't be difficult, Mac."

"It's true," he protested. "I swear. I'm a what-you-see-is-what-you-get kind of guy. A real simple creature, when you get right down to it."

"Yeah, right," she scoffed. "We can pick a tame, easy topic if you're feeling nervous. How about hobbies? I just told you mine."

"Hobbies?" He laughed derisively. "I've never had time for hobbies. I was always either working or dealing with Robin."

"Forget hobbies, then. Tell me how is it that you got left with a baby sister to raise," she suggested. "I've been itching to know."

His eyes slid away from hers. "I don't want to talk about that."

She drew designs on his chest with her foot and waited.

Mac sighed, drained his glass and set it down on the shelf. "I'll give you the short version," he said grimly. "If you insist."

The silence was marked by the hollow plop of water from the faucet. Mac's eyes were far away. "Any version is fine," she prompted.

"My daddy was a con man," he said, in a halting voice. "He drifted around the country, swindling people. He was in Olympia running a real-estate scam when he met my mom. When he had to run from the law, he persuaded her to run with him."

"Oh." She blinked, and forced her gaping mouth to close. "That must have been, uh, hard," she ventured timidly. "On your mother."

"Don't waste any sympathy on her. She worked with him when

he needed a partner. So did I, sometimes, but mostly he used Danny. Danny was sneakier than I was. A better actor. My daddy used to say that Danny had the makings of a good grifter, but not me. I was hopeless. I wear my heart on my sleeve. Like I said, I suck at secrets."

"I, ah, see."

"So the short version of this saga is, when I was thirteen, somebody from my daddy's past caught up with him—with a baseball bat. The guy was still very pissed for having been ripped off, even years later. Daddy died ten days later in the hospital. Internal bleeding."

"I'm sorry," she whispered.

He didn't acknowledge her words. "My mother fell apart," he said. "We went to stay with my uncle Leroy. But when she got out of the hospital, she never came to get us. She just couldn't deal, I guess."

Her heart twisted in sympathy. "You never saw her again?"

He shook his head.

"And your uncle Leroy? Did he, um . . . was he—"

"No." He dismissed his uncle with a gesture. "He was an older man. He gave us a roof over our heads. School. Work, when we were old enough. That was as much as he could do. I did the rest myself."

She studied his tight face for a long, careful moment before she risked the next question. "Do you even know where she is?"

"Leroy kept tabs on her. She ended up in Texas. Married again, had a couple more kids. I don't know the details. Don't want to know."

"So that would explain why you assumed I was a—"

"Yeah," he said curtly.

"And why you were so upset about it," she finished softly.

"That's right. Liars and swindlers make me violently angry. Anyhow, I made excuses for her for as long as I could. I waited for her like a faithful dog. Finally I realized that I was on my own with Danny and Robin. For good. That was the worst day of my childhood."

The silence that followed his words had real, physical weight.

Jane fished around the water for his foot, and propped it up onto her knee. She lathered her hands with the lavender scented soap, and massaged his feet. "You never forgave her, did you?"

He looked incredulous. "Why the hell should I?"

"Not for her sake," she said. "For yours. To drain the poison."

"I don't feel any need to forgive her, for my sake or anybody else's. She ran away from her baby girl. I crossed her off my list."

The stony anger in his voice made her hands falter for a moment.

"She screwed me over but good." He pulled his foot away, let it slop into the tub. The water sloshed and heaved around their chins.

Jane stared at his brooding face. There was nothing simple about Michael MacNamara, no matter what he said to the contrary. He was a tangle of contradictions. Calculating and spontaneous. Tender and rock hard. Angry, competitive, sensual, with a fierce sense of honor and responsibility. Raunchy and shocking in bed. Complicated. Passionate.

She would never be done figuring him out.

His eyes met hers, shadowed with old pain. "So, Jane? Satisfied? Any other dirty secrets I need to reveal before I can fuck you again?"

She decided to push her luck. "Yes, actually," she said. "Why do you call yourself Mac? Michael's a perfectly good name."

He dropped his head back against the bathtub with a sharp sigh. "Michael was my daddy's name. It's bad enough that I'm a dead ringer for him physically. Robin and Danny take after my mom, but I'm pure MacNamara. A surname is as much as I can stand to share with him."

She decided that it would be prudent to lighten the mood, by brute force, if necessary. Mac was quite a handful when he was badly upset. "You could get your name legally changed," she suggested.

"Jesus," he muttered. "How about we get the subject of this conversation legally changed?"

"It's just a suggestion," she protested. "Let's pick out a brand new name for you. Alfred? Bartholemew? Or how about Cedric?"

She was encouraged by the reluctant smile that tugged at his mouth. "Try it out," she urged. "Oh, Cedric, touch me like that again. Please, Cedric. Oh God, Cedric, *yes*. Has a nice ring to it, doesn't it?"

He lunged for her. Water sloshed over the edge as he dragged her up over his body. "You just don't know when to shut up, babe."

"Actually, I've always suffered from the opposite problem," she admitted. "You do something strange to me. It's only with you that I can't shut up. I just feel compelled to torture you, for some reason."

"Wow. Lucky me," he said sourly. "I feel so unique."

She kissed the tip of his nose. "How about Raymond? Or Murray? Or Hubert? Oh, Hubert. Please, Hubert—do it again, Hubert—"

"Shhh." He slid his fingers into her hair and covered her mouth as he maneuvered her into the position he wanted, astride him. He slid her sensitive labia slowly, sensually, up and down the length of his penis.

A loud knock sounded on the door. She jerked, startled. "What?"

"It's the food," he grumbled. "The kid's timing sucks."

She scrambled to her feet, conscious of his eyes on her body. His eyes dragged over her. "Turn," he said. "I want to look at your ass."

Well, it was only fair. He'd been a good sport, and so should she. She undid the knot on top of her head, letting her hair tumble down. She slowly turned around. "No funny stuff," she warned him.

It felt strange, to have her back to him. The water heaved around her legs as his hot, wet hands seized her hips, stroked the curve of her waist. He pressed kisses down her spine while he stroked her backside. The sensitive skin of her bottom went wild in tingling, ticklish delight.

"You have the most gorgeous ass," he said. "I love this view." His teeth grazed tenderly along the curve of her buttock.

She trembled at the bold caress. "Ah . . . biting my butt definitely falls under the heading of funny stuff, Mac. Stop that."

"I can't help it. You're perfect," he protested. "I want to open you up, like a peach. Find all the sweet, delicious juice hidden—right here."

He slid his finger inside her sheath, and she almost fell.

He steadied her, and rose to his feet, curving his body over hers. "Bend over. Brace your arms against the wall. I'll hold you."

She was so tempted, but she was so giddy, from hunger and hot water and champagne. She couldn't let him sweep her away. Not yet.

"No, Mac. Time out. Feed me, and we'll see." She waited, breathless, to see if he would do as she asked.

It was like holding a wild beast at bay, with her willpower alone.

Chapter Seven

Mac lifted his hands from her body. Breath rushed into her lungs.

She stepped out of the bathtub onto quivering legs without looking at him. He placed a terry cloth robe over her shoulders.

"Dry off," he said. "I'll go out and get the dinner cart."

When she emerged from the bathroom, Mac was laying platters of food onto a tablecloth that he had spread out on the carpet.

"I figured we'd do this picnic style," he said. "All right with you?"

"Sure." She stared down at the sumptuous feast, openmouthed.

There was a platter of roasted glazed ham, one of rare roast beef, one of smoked salmon. Caesar salad, frilly greens with grilled swordfish strips strewn across them. There was fresh bread, herbed butter, a platter of grilled vegetables. Puff pastries filled with artichoke hearts and cheese, pasta salad dressed with goat cheese, sausage, sun-dried tomatoes and Greek olives. A bowl of black-red cherries. A glass bowl filled with trifle: sponge cake layered with berries and Bavarian cream. She almost fainted. Her abandoned lunch was still sitting on her desk at work. She hadn't eaten since her breakfast bran flakes.

"Did they know there's only two of us?" she asked faintly.

"They knew that I was one of us," he said. "More champagne?"

They dove in, and Jane quickly concluded that the food critics were right. Every bite was savory perfection. When they finally began to slow down, Mac loaded his plate up with sliced ham and stretched out on his side. "Let's get on with the party game," he said. "Your turn."

She dug into a plateful of savory, tender swordfish and greens. "The database is vast," she said. "I need a key word to begin my search."

He tossed up a cherry, caught it in his mouth, and gave her a crafty grin. "Tell me about the very worst day of your childhood."

She winced. "Oh, God, Mac."

"Don't even try." His face was implacable. "You made me do it."

She covered her face with her hand. "But it'll make me feel like I'm trying to make you feel sorry for me. I hate that."

"Did you feel sorry for me when I told you my worst day?"

"Not exactly. I felt compassion, but you weren't looking for pity."

"Well, neither are you. Just tell me. No matter how gut-wrenching it is, I won't pity you. I'll just say, jeez, is that all? I can top that with one hand tied behind my back. Then we can do a fucked-up childhood one-upmanship competition. That's always fun."

She giggled so hard she started to cough. "OK." She popped an artichoke pastry in her mouth and washed it down with a fortifying gulp of champagne. "But my childhood didn't have any traumas that they make made-for-TV movies about. It's hard to pick out a particular—"

"Stop waffling." He forked some more roast beef onto his plate. "There's got to be a worst day. Just pick one."

She dragged her eyes away from his stunning nudity with some effort. "Here goes. When I was eleven, my uncle came to visit us. He—"

"Oh, Christ, no." He jerked up onto his elbow, so suddenly that he almost knocked over his champagne. "Don't tell me."

She was startled. "What? You're the one who wanted this!"

He covered his face with his hand. "Uncle-come-to-visit stories. They can get really weird."

Comprehension dawned. "Oh! No, no, no! It's not that kind of story." She petted his arm. "Relax. My uncle is a very decent man. The nicest, kindest person in my whole family."

"Thank God." His hand dropped. He gave her a sheepish smile. "I'm sorry. I shouldn't have reacted like that. But the thought of anybody hurting a little girl like that . . . it's like an electric shock."

She stroked his bare, muscular leg. "You can relax," she soothed him. "I don't have any stories like that to tell."

"Lucky for your uncle. If you had, I would have to hunt him down and take him apart. Chunk by bloody chunk."

His vehemence startled her. "Do you want to hear this, Mac?" she asked gently. "We can change the subject if it's too upsetting for you."

"Just get it over with." He sat up and wrapped his arms around his knees, scowling. He looked like he was bracing himself for a blow.

"Uh, OK," she began cautiously. "So this sweet, innocent uncle of mine gets the bright idea to give me a chocolate Labrador puppy for my birthday. I had him for a week, the whole time my uncle was visiting. He was the cutest puppy that ever existed. His name was Brownie."

"Aw, shit," he muttered. He clapped his hand over his eyes again. "I see where this is going."

"I warned you," she said. "You promised, Mac. No pity."

"Of course not." He crossed his arms over his chest and squeezed his eyes shut. "So? What happened to the damn puppy? Did he die in a heroic leap off the roof after saving you from a burning building? Go ahead. Tear my heart out of my chest and stomp on it."

"My uncle left," she said simply. "My mother took the puppy to the pound. He made too much of a mess, she said. But the truth was, I think he was just too happy for her. All that jumping and wagging and licking. She was horrified by emotional excess."

She waited. Mac was glaring into the remains of the pasta salad as if they had offended him deeply. He would not meet her eyes.

"So?" she prompted gently. "There it is. I was so heartbroken, I thought I was going to die. But I lived to tell the tale."

He rubbed his jaw, and swallowed hard. "Icy-hearted *bitch*."

The raw fury in his voice jolted her. "You said no pity."

"I don't pity you," he snarled. "I'm pissed. Which is different."

He looked like he wanted to hit something. "Mac? I'm OK now," she reminded him. "It was a really long time ago. Seventeen years."

"It's one thing to say no from the get-go," he fumed. "Some-times you have to. But to let a little kid get all attached, to let a whole goddamn week go by, and then take the dog away? Jesus, that's cold!"

Tenderness for him bloomed in her chest. "You know what, Mac?" Her voice was soft with wonder. "You're a great big softie."

His jaw dropped. "Me? Hah!"

"Yeah, you. You can't fool me. You try to come off like a bossy, arrogant hard-ass, but you're all soft and squishy inside."

He looked alarmed. "Not me. Check me out, Jane." He let his thigh drop to the ground and revealed the thick jut of his erection. "Hard as a rock. And just as pitiless."

"Of course," she said. "A classic macho defense mechanism. You're so predictable, Mac. Put you on the spot, and you steer us right back towards sex. Safe and familiar ground."

He shook his head. "No. Sex with you is not safe and familiar. It's way out there. Places I've never, ever been."

She started to smile. He was sensitive and tenderhearted, no matter how he tried to deny it. She wanted to give him all the sweetness and gentleness he craved. To feed his hunger, and her own.

She took the bowl of trifle and two dessert spoons, and scooted over until their knees touched. She shrugged her robe off and scooped up a spoonful of sponge cake layered with custard and cream and syrupy berries. It quivered on the end of the spoon.

"You try so hard to be Mr. Macho, but you're just like this dessert, Mac." She closed her lips around the spoon and moaned with agonized pleasure. "Sweet. Tender. Full of cream." She scooped up another spoonful and held it out. "Here. Try some."

This damn party game of hers was dangerous. The more he knew about her, the more he wanted to know. The more possessive and raw he felt. And now she was hand-feeding him manna of the gods, a voluptuous, naked nymph of paradise. He was a goner.

He took the spoonful she offered and scooped up another one for her so they could have simultaneous sugar orgasms. That touched off a dance—feeding spoonfuls of dessert to each other with lazy, sticky, nibbling kisses flavored with berries and cream between each bite. A glob of custard fell onto his chest. Jane hastened to lick it off.

"Jane?" He couldn't control his shaking, pleading tone.

She kissed the burning heat of his cheekbone. Her damp hair was cool against his fever-hot face. "Hmm?"

"Go down on me again," he begged. "But no weird games this time. I'm not in the mood for kinky stuff. I just want my sweet Jane."

She leaned her forehead against his. "You have to be sweet, too," she said. "Sweet like cream custard. No scoring points, or nailing me to the wall, or storming the fortress. No chest pounding of any kind."

"Deal. I'll be an éclair, a cream puff, a tiramisu. Anything."

He shoved platters aside to make room, and she curled up in front of him and pillowed her head on his thigh. She began to play with his cock with her soft, cool hands, stroking him with tender eagerness.

When she took him in her mouth, it was so sweet it brought a hot lump to his throat. He dug his fingers into her hair and tried not to whimper. He'd always loved blow jobs, not just because they felt so damn good, but because of the way they made him feel about himself. Pumped up. Powerful, like a prince, or a god receiving his due of worship.

But this was completely different. He felt helpless, vulnerable. No ego inflation, no prince, no god. Just a man, shaking with emotion, desperate for her tenderness. *Her love.* He shoved the thought back down to the depths from which it had arisen, but the damage was done.

He curled around her, moving his trembling hands over her body, mapping every inch he could touch: the freckles, the milky paleness, the faint blue tracery of veins beneath delicate, flower-petal softness. Lush curves, delicate bones, strong, lithe muscles. A miracle of nature, holding him with all her strength, pleasuring him with all her skill. She pulled his cock into her mouth with long, lazy, caressing strokes.

He put his hand between her thighs. She was hot and drenched, quivering around his thrusting fingers. Going down on him turned her on, just like burying his face between her thighs did it for him.

He rearranged their bodies so he could stretch out alongside her and spread her legs. She shuddered and moaned as he thrust his tongue hungrily into her slit, lapping up the warm, sweet flavor of her lube. He'd never much cared much for the sixty-nine position before. He preferred either to relax and receive his pleasure, or to exert himself to give it with single-minded precision. He'd never seen the point in doing both at once, clumsy and distracted and half-assed.

But there was nothing clumsy or half-assed about surging with her on wave after wave of pleasure. With every luxurious stroke of their tongues, he blended more wholly with her. His pleasure and hers were a single moving, sighing, melting swirl. Over and over he came to the shuddering brink. Every time he dragged himself back, unwilling to let it end, until her pleasure finally burst and throbbed against his mouth.

He drank it in, then turned around and mounted her damp, spread-eagled body. He forced himself inside her just in time to feel the end of her long orgasm pulse through her. He was already plunging and sliding in a liquid agony of bliss before he realized that there was a reason why his cock felt so amazingly, deliciously, *unusually* good.

He'd forgotten the condom.

She remembered at the same moment. Her eyes popped open. They froze, clenched around each other. Both unwilling to stop.

"Uh, Mac?" she whispered, wide-eyed.

"I'm sorry," he pleaded. "I should be safe. I never do this without a condom. I've never just lost it, and forgotten. I swear to you."

She cradled his face. "I believe you. Me neither. I haven't done this in years, and I was always safe. But I'm not on the pill. So, ah . . ."

He rested his damp forehead against hers. He should pull out and suit up with latex like a responsible male of the third millennium, but his body wouldn't obey him. It kept surging, in waves that just got higher, stronger, rocking him farther and farther from the shores of sanity or good sense. "I won't come inside you," he promised, but he was in no condition to promise anything of the kind. The normal Mac could have, but not this madman. "I can't stop. It's too perfect."

Her stormy eyes were endlessly deep and gentle. "Yes," she said. "It's too wonderful to stop."

He was speechless at her trust. She deserved compliments, love words, poetry, but he was helpless to provide them. She put her arms around his neck and moved herself against him with sinuous grace.

She was so soft, so strong, giving herself to him with a generosity that humbled him. They surged and danced, heaving against each other, giving and taking, following the shining path together towards the bright perfection that beckoned them. He barely managed to pull out before he exploded and spurted his hot seed across her trembling body.

Some time later, Jane extricated herself from the damp knot of their bodies, and stumbled to the bathroom. She shut herself inside. The sink ran. The water stopped. Silence. He sat up. Waited some more.

More silence. Too damn much silence.

He got up, knees still shaking, and knocked on the door. "Jane?"

"I'm OK." Her muffled voice through the door sounded strange.

He waited some more. "What does OK mean?" he demanded.

She didn't answer. Fear yawned in his belly. She was slipping away from him, and he didn't know why, and there wasn't a goddamn thing he could do to stop her. There fucking never was.

His knocking turned into banging. "Jane! Open the door!"

"Just give me a minute." Her voice sounded even stranger.

"I'm coming in," he warned her. "Stand back."

"I'm fine, Mac. Please don't—oh, God!"

His blow to the door ripped the brass hook-and-eye lock out of the door frame. Jane stood in front of the mirror, hands clamped over her mouth. Her eyes were wide and startled, her face shiny with tears.

He was horrified. "What did I do? Jesus! What's wrong?"

"It's not you," she quavered.

"Then what?" His voice cracked like a whip. "Tell me!"

She flinched. "Don't worry."

"Don't worry? How the fuck am I not supposed to worry? Jane, just tell me what's wrong! Let me fix it!"

"You can't fix it!" She shoved past him into the bedroom. "I'm sorry! I never cry. I don't know why I'm crying now. There's no reason for it. I swear to God, if I could stop, I would!" She scooped up her dress from the floor, and turned it right side out.

That was a bad sign, very bad. He wrenched the dress out of her hands and flung it away. "Forget it, Jane," he said. "No way."

She hugged herself and backed away, still sniffling. "I can't handle the barbarian routine now," she warned him. "Don't, Mac!"

"I'm not letting you run out on me." He tossed her onto the bed, and climbed on top of her. "I'm going to hold you till you sleep."

"You can't do this!" She struggled wildly beneath his weight. "I can't sleep! How the hell do you expect me to sleep like this?"

"So I'll hold you while you don't sleep. If you want to cry, cry. Tears don't scare me. You running out on me, that's what scares me."

He tucked Jane between himself and the wall and wound his leg between hers, braiding them together. She was going nowhere unless he said so. He waited patiently, hoping she would initiate the conversation. Even spitting insults were preferable to this tense silence.

He decided to take the initiative. "You asleep?" he whispered.

She jerked her head. "Hah," she muttered. "Dream on."

"You're not crying anymore," he said. "Maybe you should."

"I can't do it on command." Her voice was sharp.

"Oh." He nuzzled her fragrant hair. "You want to talk about it?"

"Now I'm the one who wants to get the conversation legally changed," she grumbled. "You're like a pit bull, MacNamara."

"I just don't want to screw up again." He kept his voice neutral.

Her body shook, with laughter or silent tears. "It's not your fault."

"How so? How not? Tell me, for Christ's sake."

She sighed. "For various reasons too tedious to recount, I get freaked out when I lose control," she said. "Something about you makes me lose it, and it seems to be getting worse. Like an earthquake."

"Oh." He pondered her words. "Yikes."

"It's not . . . your . . . *fault*," she repeated, emphasizing every word.

"Yeah. I'll comfort myself with that the next time you're cowering inside a locked bathroom."

"I was not cowering!" she shot back. "And it didn't help to have you rip the lock out of the door and muscle me around like a caveman!"

"So shoot me," he said. "I was scared."

The silence began to feel ominous again. Mac gathered his nerve. "If you can't sleep, let's do a round of our party game," he suggested.

"Oh, get real," she snapped.

"I think we should." He kissed her neck soothingly. "You still haven't told me why you didn't become an actress."

Her body went rigid. "It's your turn. I went last with the heart-rending puppy story, remember?"

"I will never forget the puppy story, unfortunately," he said wryly. "But I already told you about my blighted dreams to be an astronaut and an archaeologist. So I skip my turn. Back to you, Jane."

The heavy quality of her hesitation rang his alarm bells. They'd been circling around this moment all night, spiraling closer and closer.

"This won't calm me down," she said. "It's not a nice story."

"You have to tell me now, or I'll die of curiosity," he told her.

She stared up at the ceiling for so long, he started to twitch. "My senior year in college, there was a guy on the faculty of the theater department," she said finally. "Dylan. Charismatic, talented, conceited."

His muscles contracted. "I hate the dickhead's guts already."

"Good. Be my guest," she said. "So I got involved with Dylan. I was so flattered that he wanted shy little me. How lucky, to be molded by someone so experienced, I thought. And at the very beginning of my career, too. Oh, thrillsville."

A sound came out of him that could only be described as a growl.

"Mac? Can you deal?" she asked. "Do you want me to stop?"

"I'm not that fragile, goddamn it," he snapped.

She sighed. "Dylan was an egomaniac. He had to be at the center of attention at all times. And he didn't want me to find theater work. That would have diverted my attention from its proper place—squarely focused on him. When I figured this out, I tried to leave him. He freaked out . . . and then he cut me off."

"Come again?"

"He had me blackballed," she explained. "He was very connected. He knew all the directors and producers in the business. He spread it around that I was mentally unstable, that I used drugs, you name it. Suddenly, I was uncastable. No more summer stock, no more student films, no more nothing. I got rejected from the grad schools I applied to, even the ones that had been courting me. Nobody wanted to take a chance on me after he was done. My reputation was trashed."

Mac's world turned bloodred. "What's this guy's last name?"

She looked over at him with a wary frown. "Why do you ask?"

"Just curious."

"Curious is how you'll stay, buddy," she said. "Dylan loves attention. Even negative attention. What he truly hates is to be ignored. So please. Ignore him, for God's sake."

"He wouldn't love my attention," Mac said. "I guarantee it."

There was a short, nervous pause from her. "Be that as it may, I would prefer it if you let it go," she said tightly. "It's old news."

"It wouldn't be that hard to find out who he is," he mused. "Some time on the Internet, a few cross-referenced facts—"

She jerked up onto her elbow. "Don't, Mac!"

"OK, OK. Calm down," he soothed. He tugged her back against the warmth of his body. "So how did you get loose of this prick?"

She buried her face against his chest. "When I figured out what had happened, I ran." Her voice was muffled. "I didn't have anyplace to go, so I ran home. The ultimate mistake in a long series of mistakes."

He petted her hair. "And why was that a mistake?"

She shook her head. "Dylan had been calling my mother for weeks, working on her. Telling her how messed up and hysterical I was. She didn't believe my story. She took his part."

He went rigid with outrage. "Shit! No way! Your *mom?*"

"To be fair, I must have seemed unbalanced, with all my wild stories about being sabotaged. My mother thought studying theater was a sign of insanity already. This was just one more confirmation for her."

"So she sold you out." His voice was harsh. "Like with the puppy."

"She lectured me for giving him so much trouble," she said wearily. "Advised me to be grateful to have such a patient man. Then she called him. He came to pick me up. They had a prior agreement."

She fell silent. The suspense made him want to scream and pound his feet on the bed. "And?" he prompted. "So? What happened?"

"At that point, I was almost convinced they were right," she whispered. "I was a mess. Dylan and my mom had a good time analyzing me. Two rational adults clucking their tongues and shaking their heads, and one freaked-out girl who couldn't stop crying. Dylan took me back with him to L.A." She paused for a moment. "It took me a week to work up the nerve to run again."

He could tell from her voice that she wasn't going to talk about that week, now or ever. Just as well. Imagining it was bad enough.

He cuddled her to his chest, sick with anger. "Where did you go?"

"I came here, to Seattle," she said. "I camped out on a friend's couch. I waited tables, temped. I discovered headhunting. It was a pretty tough time, but I suppose I should be grateful to him."

That comment threw him. "How so?"

"If it hadn't been for him, I would never have founded the MeanStreets Players. I was a pretty good actress, if I do say so myself, but I think I'm a better director. And I love the artistic control."

He stroked her back. "Now that's what I call a good attitude."

"I had to think of it that way, or I'd have gone nuts." She was silent for a moment. "I haven't seen my mother for four years now."

Mac snorted. "Hah. That's nothing. I haven't seen my mom for, let's see, almost twenty-four years. I've got you so beat."

He was relieved to hear her giggle. "OK," she said. "You win, Mac."

"No pity," he said.

She shook her head. "None."

"Your mother's a heinous bitch, though."

"That's enough," Jane snapped. "She's not a cruel person. Just misguided. She truly thought she was trying to help me."

"Whatever." He snapped off the light, organized their limbs in a braided tangle, and wound a lock of her hair around his fingers, to be on the safe side. No way was he letting go of her now.

You're so intense, Jane. Pull yourself together. No one wants to deal with an emotional black hole. It's embarrassing for everyone.

A square of moonlight crept slowly down the wall. Jane watched it with eyes that burned and stung. She'd spent five years trying to prove Dylan wrong. Mac had swept that work away in one wild night.

It had been a huge mistake to tell Mac about Dylan. It woke up all the frustration, the anger, the confusion, the shame. Dylan had used her own emotions against her, and he'd been diabolically clever about it. He'd provoke her into a frenzy, then manipulate her into discrediting herself. The more she fought him, the crazier she'd looked, and the more he'd played up his martyr act. Her only solution had been to develop an artificial calm, as deep and thick and cold as a glacier.

And Mac had shattered that calm to smithereens.

She couldn't face what was underneath. She was a mess. A black hole, like Dylan used to say. Look at her, sobbing uncontrollably after sex, spilling her guts about all her past traumas. A total basket case.

She wondered why Mac was hanging on to her so tightly. Maybe he felt sorry for her. Maybe he felt responsible. His body felt so good. She loved the weight of his muscular leg thrust between hers, his thick arm wrapped around her waist. She wished she could just relax into his solid warmth, but she kept seeing tomorrow morning's scene.

Stark reality, revealed by the pitiless light of day. The discomfort in Mac's eyes as he searched for a polite way to tell her he didn't want to deal with her emotional baggage, her intensity, her "issues."

It would be unbearable. She felt like she had no skin as it was.

She started, very slowly, to shimmy out of the tightly wound cocoon he'd made around her with his body. Her hair was caught fast. She reached up to free it, and found his hand snarled in it.

She squeaked as he grabbed her wrist. "I knew it," he said.

His quiet voice made her freeze. "Knew what?"

"That you were going to try the vanishing act. I fucking *knew* it."

Her heart thudded as if she'd been caught doing something bad. "That's why you grabbed my hair? That's creepy, Mac."

"You're not running away." The bed shifted, and Mac climbed on top of her, pressing her facedown into the tangled sheets. He shoved her legs apart. She pressed her face against the sheets and gasped silently as he penetrated her in one deep, relentless shove. She was wet and soft, but very sore, and his invasion was so complete.

"Close your legs," he commanded.

She was confused. "What?"

He straddled her thighs with his own and pushed her legs together, settling his weight against her bottom. He rocked against her, wedging himself still deeper between her tightly clamped thighs.

She felt breathless, trapped. She could barely move. She struggled, and he responded by clamping her wrists together and trapping them against the pillow in front of her face. "Mac? I—"

"Shh." He slid his hand beneath her, in front of her hips, and slid two fingers into her slick folds, catching her clitoris between them. The deliberate friction against that swollen bud and the deep penetration of his body from behind kindled a glow of delicious excitement inside her.

She strained against the calculated weight of his body, his ruthless grip on her wrists, but with every stroke she became hotter, softer, more liquid around him. Tears of frustration burned in her eyes. His penis pressed against the mouth of her womb. "Squeeze your thighs around my fingers. Around my cock." His voice was soft, but there was a cold, sharp bite of anger to it that she felt throughout her body. "You'll like what happens. Harder. Good, like that. You like that?"

"Let me up, Mac." She tugged at her wrists. "This is not OK."

"Yeah, that would explain why your clit is practically vibrating between my fingers. You hug my cock. All of it. You like me inside you." He swiveled his hips with slow, sure skill. "You want me." He seized her earlobe between his teeth, bit it, and suckled it to soothe the sting. "Or else I wouldn't be doing this to you. I'm not stupid."

"I never said that you were," she protested. She tightened, clenching around him instinctively. "You don't have to hold me down."

"Oh, no?" He thrust into her, hard enough to make her gasp. "You plot to steal from me. You start out the evening by lying to me. You finish it up by trying to run from me. Yeah, you really inspire confidence, sweetheart. I'm not letting go of you for a goddamn second."

"I wasn't running," she lied. "You were pulling my hair. I was just trying to get comfortable—oh, God, Mac. Please."

"Please, what? Please, harder? Deeper? Why run, Jane? Because you're embarrassed? Because you cry when you come? Big fucking deal. Cry all you want. I love to see you come apart when I get you off."

She shook her head. His furious, insatiable sexuality was melting her down, making her crazy, desperate. "I don't want to come apart."

"Too bad. I don't care," he said. "I love it when you sob and writhe and clench yourself around my cock. I know that you need me."

"Mac—"

"I need you to need me, Jane." He ground his hips against her, stoking the pleasure to a searing blaze. "Don't run away."

She moaned, writhed beneath him. "I wasn't!"

"Don't lie. The more you hide, the more I see. Don't lie, Jane."

She shook her head frantically. "I won't."

"And don't you dare disappear on me, goddamn it."

"No," she sobbed. "No, I won't."

"Promise me!" His hips heaved and pounded, driving her relentlessly towards wild, seething chaos. "Promise it!"

"I promise," she gasped. "Don't make me fall to pieces, Mac."

"I have to." His rough voice shook. "Let me make you come, Jane. Let me have that much. Come for me. Give it to me."

She pleaded, but neither one of them could stop. They were both long past the point of no return. The harder she struggled, the bigger the feeling that swelled inside her—a crescendo of emotion.

She loved him. That was the realization she'd been fighting against all day. She'd known him for twelve hours, and she was madly in love with him. He had the power to break her heart to pieces, and she'd never felt more vulnerable and fragile in her life.

The world exploded. She lost herself in chaos. Throbbing darkness swelled up and sucked her under.

Dawn lightened the window to deep grayish blue. Mac held Jane's soft body tightly against his. His cock was still stone-hard and aching, clamoring for its own reward, but he'd wrestled the orgasm down.

Unfortunately, his hard-on wasn't so readily commanded. It throbbed hopefully against Jane's round, sexy ass. Clueless, as always.

He was miles from sleep. Wired, wound up, horrified at himself. Pinning her down and fucking her after she tried to run, whoa. Thousands of years of human evolution, wiped out in the blink of an eye. He'd never forced a woman, even in play. Never wanted to. Something about Jane drove him nuts, made him desperate. Sure, she'd been hot for him, but that meant nothing. The body didn't always agree with the mind. He, of all people, should know that.

If she didn't want him, he couldn't hold her. The harder he tried to pin her down, the more it would tear him up when she left.

And knowing that didn't help worth a damn.

He pulled away from her, and sensed the subtle tension that

came over her body. She was awake. The air felt chilly after her heat.

She stirred behind him, sat up. He swung his legs over the bed and waited, hunched over, for the axe to fall.

It wasn't in his nature to wait. He wasn't a patient man, never had been. He was restless and edgy, wound up tight as a coiled spring, and he'd never been able to bear the weight and chill of silence.

He turned around. She was so pale, her eyes huge and shadowed with smudged mascara. She looked fragile, and very nervous. Probably wondering if he was going to leap on her like a slavering wolf.

Either she wanted him or she didn't, he told himself. Either she could handle him, or she couldn't. He'd fucked up. He shouldn't have tried to hang on to her last night, but what was done was done. Period.

She reached out her hand, but changed her mind at the last minute. Her hand fell short and landed on the sheet. "Are you all right?"

"You keep stealing my lines," he said grimly.

"It's not a line." Her eyes flicked down to his unflagging erection.

"Sorry about that," he said. "Pay it no mind."

"Nothing to be sorry about." Her voice was wary.

His body's blunt, humiliating betrayal made him furious. His hope and hunger, naked to her. "I wouldn't want to embarrass you," he said. "I'm trying to play it cool. Too much jumping and wagging and licking will get me taken to the pound for sure."

Her face contracted. "Oh. Ouch, Mac. That was unnecessary."

Smooth move, asshole. Being gentler wouldn't hurt his cause.

A lock of tangled hair had fallen over her eyes. He reached towards her to smooth it back. She flinched away.

He snatched back his hand as if he'd burned it. He was screwed. She was afraid of him, and he had no one to blame for it but himself.

The silence between them got heavier. The fear lying on his belly got colder, sharper, until it transformed itself into hard anger.

"Mac, I, um . . . do you want me to . . ." her voice trailed off to a frightened thread of sound. He couldn't stand it. "Do you, ah, want—"

"Whatever," he burst out. "Do whatever the hell you want. I'm not going to tie you to the fucking bed, Jane. I'm taking a shower."

He stalked to the bathroom and slammed the door shut before she could see his face crumple.

He had to let go. He couldn't force her to love him. To wake up with him every morning and go to bed with him every night until they were old and toothless and doddering. Love did as it goddamn well pleased, every time. He knew that. He'd always known it. This was no surprise to him. He got under the shower. Turned the dial to ice-cold.

But tears still came out hot, even with icy water pelting down.

The bathroom door was so blank and mute, and yet so terribly eloquent. It whispered things she didn't want to hear. Wasn't this what she got for falling wildly in love with a man after one sweaty night? Besides, how could she have been so stupid as to hope he would still want her in spite of everything? He knew too goddamn much.

He couldn't even bear to look at her. This was worse than the discomfort and embarrassment she'd been afraid of. The suppressed violence in his voice sounded as if he almost . . . hated her.

Do whatever the hell you want. I'm not going to tie you to the fucking bed. She slipped off the bed and went to the bathroom door. She leaned her hot forehead against the wood, listened to the water hiss.

There was no lock on the door. He'd torn it off last night. So? What was the plan? Climb into the shower, beg him to love her? Maybe she could drop to her knees, all desperate and submissive, and give him a supplicating blow job. That would be right in character.

She'd summoned that image to punish herself for being so stupid, but it backfired on her, sparking a flush of feverish lust. Miserable as she was, it weakened her knees, it curled her toes to think of it: the hot water pounding down on them, his muscular legs planted in that wide, aggressive stance, his big hands holding her head, his fingers tangled in her wet hair as she pulled as much of his thick, hot penis into her mouth as she could take without choking on him.

She was stupid, crazed, undone. Her legs shook, from violent emotion, lack of sleep, too much sex. He could tie her to the bed if he wanted. Her body went nuts for him, no matter what he did. Gentle and sweet, rough and wild, it didn't matter, as long as it was Mac. Everything her mother and Dylan had said about her was true. The grain of the dark wood swam before her eyes. He wielded such power over her. She'd given it to him freely, and she had no idea how to get it back. She felt as fragile and transparent as blown glass.

He didn't want her. The only thing to do was run. Quick. Salvage what was left of her dignity before she started to snivel and beg.

She looked around for her dress. There it was, a crumpled tangle under the bed. She was lucky it was in one piece. The bustier with all its hooks and eyes would take too long, the panties and stockings were completely trashed. Her fingers trembled so hard, she could barely tug the dress over her body. She snatched her purse, tiptoed out the door.

She was blocks away from the Copley Crowne, running like a stumbling lunatic through the misty dawn before she noticed that she was barefoot, and only because she stubbed her toe on a sidewalk crack and pitched forward, scraping the skin off her hands and her knees.

She was sobbing like a child by the time she reached her car.

Chapter Eight

"One thousand forty-eight dollars and eighty-one cents is the grand total of the damage to the room." Danny flung the manila folder on Mac's desk and gave his brother his patented dark, brooding look.

"I'll write out a check," Mac growled.

"And there are the complaints. Robin and I are used to your tantrums, but the guests and the cleaning staff aren't. I don't think Rosaria even wants her job back after seeing you naked on the rampage in the hotel corridor. Jesus, Mac. The poor woman has high blood pressure to begin with. She can't stop crossing herself, they tell me."

"Leave me alone, Danny."

"Word is out that the colorful, eccentric CEO of Crowne Royale Group needs his thorazine dosage adjusted," Danny informed him. "You've always been high-strung, but smashing a roomful of antique furniture is over the top, Mac. Even for you."

"I'll write the fucking check," Mac repeated grimly. "Then go."

Danny had that look on his face, as if he were puzzled and alarmed to find himself related to such a strange, exotic beast. Mac was familiar with that look. What he wasn't used to was the shadow of anxiety in his brother's eyes. The hard, worried line of Danny's mouth.

Not that Danny would ever admit to such feelings, thank God. Mac wouldn't know what the hell to do with him if he did.

"You've run through more women than I can count, but I've never seen you like this," Danny said fretfully. "You're not eating, you're even more rude than usual, you look like shit. Get a grip. There are thousands of women out there, throwing their goddamn phone numbers at you by the truckload. This writer chick is not worth it!"

"She's a headhunter, not a writer. She was going after Gary."

"Yeah, you told me." Danny's voice was suspiciously gentle. "We're lucky she never got her claws into him. If this is what she did to you, she would've made hamburger out of poor Gary."

Mac surged to his feet, and Danny skittered back warily, his reflexes honed by a lifetime of brotherly wrangling. "Take the check, apologize to the staff and leave me the hell alone," Mac snarled.

Danny stalked out and slammed the door. Mac was one of the few people on earth who could goad him into doing that. Usually he enjoyed the challenge, and savored his little victories. Today, he couldn't care less.

The door opened just as he sank back down into his chair. Only one other person would dare come into his office without knocking.

Mac didn't look up when he felt her cool hand on the back of his neck.

"Hey, you," Robin said gently.

"Don't be hurt, but I need to be alone," he said. "Get lost, shrimp."

As usual, his little sister ignored his command. "This is awful," she said. "I feel really bad, because it's partly my fault."

He grunted suspiciously. "How do you figure that?"

She dropped a kiss on top of his head. "I knew I should have rescheduled her to meet with Gary, but I decided I wanted you to meet her. I know you go for the sweet, luscious type with big, pillowy ta-tas."

He buried his face in his hands. "Oh, Christ, Robin. Why?"

"It seemed like a good idea at the time," she protested. "She was cute, and she looked smart, too. You need a challenge. You bore easily."

"A challenge she was," he mumbled. "No question about that."

"So why are you moping?" Robin demanded. "It's not like you. When you go after something, you always get it. You're like a pit bull."

He flinched to hear the exact words that Jane had used. "News flash, shrimp. She ran out on me. Which is a pretty big fucking clue that I'm not perfect for her, get it? I'm too much. Over the top."

Robin perched on his desk. "I see. Well, you do take some getting used to. But you're worth the effort. When you bother to exert yourself."

"Gee, thanks. What a sweet, loyal baby sister."

"Sweeter than you deserve," Robin said crisply. "So did you?"

"Did I what?" he snarled.

"Exert yourself, silly."

"Hell, yes!"

Robin looked superior. "I don't mean sexually, you big pig."

"Don't talk about sex, damn it. You're too young."

Robin rolled her eyes. "What I meant is, did you exert yourself to be charming? You know, compliments? Sweet talk? Making her feel cherished and special? Standard, romantic stuff like that?" She stared searchingly into his face and her dark eyes widened in dismay. "Oh, Mac. You've got that look on your face. You didn't. You big idiot."

That final, ugly scene with Jane flashed through his mind, in all its painful detail. "It wasn't like that," he hedged. "It's complicated."

"Then the ball's in your court," Robin snapped. "And you don't need my sympathy. You need a swift kick in the butt. Stand up and turn around, Mac. Good thing I wore my pointy shoes today."

He sprang to his feet. Robin stumbled back. "She's the one who ran out on me!" he bellowed.

Robin stuck out her lower lip like a belligerent toddler. "Only because you were rude and horrendous, I bet."

"Get lost, Robin. For the last time. Or else."

"Or else what, big brother? So she ran out on you. Big deal. You're notorious for never staying the night with your conquests. You're practically an urban myth. Michael MacNamara, sexual superhero. He uses up a whole box of condoms, and poof, he's gone by dawn."

"Stop talking about sex!" he roared. "You're pissing me off!"

Robin was undaunted. "You know what your problem is? You're used to winning, and you sulk like a big baby when you lose. But love isn't a game. Seduction, maybe, yes. But love, no. It's not like closing a deal, or winning a tennis match, or getting the last word, Mac."

"What the hell do you know about love or seduction?" he demanded. "You're just a kid. Go play clown. Stop lecturing me."

Robin started to reply. She stopped herself, and pressed her lips together. "I'm not a kid anymore," she said tightly. "But you'll never accept that, so why do I waste my breath?"

She stalked out. His door was slammed, for the second time in five minutes. He was on a roll. The whole world was pissed at him.

Robin was right about his sexual track record. He never invited women to his condo, or slept a whole night with his lovers. It was a big waste of time, he'd always thought. Sleep he could get in the privacy of his own bed at home. If he was in bed with a naked woman, why sleep? There were better things to do. Hours of them.

But he'd slept with Jane. Tried to, at least. He wanted to sleep with her on his own big bed, snuggled under his comforter. He wanted to pull the covers up over her sweet body to keep her warm. Cuddle her all night. Make breakfast for her in the morning.

Why was he torturing himself? It never stopped. This feeling sucked. He hated it. He'd tried everything, and he couldn't shake it.

He collapsed forward onto the desk, rested his head on folded arms and tried to think it through, but reason had never been his default setting. He'd always had more luck with action, impulse, instinct. Reason came hard to him, especially with that feeling roiling in his gut. A sickening, sinking feeling, horribly similar to fear.

He'd distanced himself from the world by making everything into a game, but Jane had unmasked him. He was hunched over an ugly, unhealed wound. He'd distracted himself from it all his life by pumping up his ego, trying to be smarter, faster, better.

Now look at him, flat on his face, stomped to a pulp beneath Jane's ridiculous sandals. Which were currently locked in his desk like Cinderella's glass slipper.

How pathetic. Reduced to fondling a woman's shoes in secret.

Prince Un-Charming. The details of that night were etched on his mind. Every rude, mean thing he'd said and done to her. His courtship strategy had been the emotional equivalent of running her over with a tank. Hardly a way to convince a woman that he was husband material.

Whoa. He lifted his head. His heart sped up and started to thud anxiously against his ribs. Yeah, that crazy thought had originated in his own thick, hard head. No point in playing dumb. One night, and he was convinced. Life would be flat and stale without her. He wanted that zing, the vibrant push and pull. He wanted to shock her, make her laugh, drive her wild with pleasure. Make her open up like a flower.

Something in him stopped struggling, relaxed into its proper place with a sigh of dumb relief. The odds were against him, but he had to try. She'd already ripped his heart right out of his chest. He might as well do something useful and flashy with it, like fling it at her feet.

The idea exploded in his head like fireworks. Oh, man. Of course. He was so brilliant, he blew his own mind. He knew what she longed for, what she valued. He could start racking up points right away. He would put his most aggressive pit bull tendencies right to work on it.

Project Prince Charming was under way.

He grabbed the phone, dialed the Crowne Royal Group program director. "Hi, Louise? It's Mac. . . good, thanks, and you? . . . great, great . . . I have a question about our corporate contributions to the arts this year. I've decided to take a more active interest in our . . . yeah, I know . . . well, there's this local youth theater group that's doing great things, and I was just wondering what we could do for them . . . "

"Mr. Mysterious strikes again! Here's another one!" Mona called out to the office at large. The receptionist bustled into Jane's office and laid the box on her desk. "God, this is fun. Hurry, Jane. Open it."

Four more of her female colleagues instantly crowded into the room. "Get a move on!" Maria demanded. "Need some scissors?"

Jane stared at the box and put her hands over her hot cheeks. The diabolical, seductive bastard. She ripped open the box and peeled away layers of tissue paper. A collective gasp of delight went up.

It was an antique perfume bottle. Iridescent rainbow tints shimmered on its surface. No card, no note. Just a silent message, like a kiss on the back of the neck. The confident caress of a man who didn't have to ask. He knew what she liked. No need for words.

"Oh, Lord." Erica sighed. She took it reverently out of Jane's hands and held it up to the light. "A Kessler. Original. Beautiful. Circa 1870. Would fetch, oh, say, nine hundred bucks on eBay, minimum."

Jane winced. "It's a gift," she muttered. "Don't be crass."

"Crass, my ass," Erica said. "For God's sake. Say yes, or at least give us this guy's phone number so we can have a crack at him."

Jane hid her face in her hands. "I can't take much more of this."

"Good." Her boss's crisp voice rang out from the doorway. "I can't, either. The suspense is cutting into our corporate productivity. Give in, or the man won't have enough money left to buy you a decent ring."

Jane's spine straightened. She plucked the bottle out of Erica's hand, swaddled it in tissue paper and stuck it in her purse. "I'm cutting out early today," she said. "Bye-bye, ladies. Have a good one."

Charlene glanced pointedly at the wall clock. "At three-twelve?"

"Fire me if you like, Charlene," Jane said. "I need some time to myself. I'm feeling a bit crowded."

Shocked silence followed her words. Her colleagues tiptoed out, eyes frozen wide. The door clicked shut. Jane and Charlene stared at each other across the desk.

"You've developed quite a little attitude, Jane," her boss said.

"It's about time, wouldn't you say?" Jane kicked off her pumps, and slipped into her walking shoes. "Haven't you always told me I should find out where I put my spine?"

"Well, yes," Charlene admitted reluctantly. "But did you have to find your spine during office hours?"

"You'll live." Jane shrugged on her suit jacket. "Or not."

"I don't want to fire you," Charlene fretted. "You're good at this."

"In that case, I would like to draw your attention to the fact that we still haven't renegotiated my contract. Twenty-five percent of each commission I bring in would be more than fair, at this point."

"Don't push me." Charlene fluttered her hand. "Off with you. I'll talk with Pierce about your contract. He'll be reluctant, but—"

"I'm worth it. Pierce knows it, too. And if he doesn't, he'll learn."

"Out! Enough! You're unbearable when you're like this. Go call that poor man and put him out of his misery. Heartless hussy-pants."

"I'm holding you to your promise," Jane said. "Talk to Pierce."

"Out! Shameless opportunist. You try my patience! Out!"

Jane pretended not to notice the covert glances as she walked out of the office. Over a week had passed since that wild night, and her skin was still thinner. Her glacial shield was utterly gone.

She was dancing a whole different dance with the world. Sounds were louder, smells stronger, colors brighter, lines sharper. And the tears were ridiculous. Even dog food commercials made her cry.

She got angry faster, too. She spoke her mind without thinking. She didn't even care if Charlene fired her. She didn't love this job. She wouldn't starve. She could always temp, or wait tables. She felt fearless, reckless. Strange. Her priorities were so clear, they shone.

She'd lost her cool—and she didn't miss it. Not one tiny bit.

And Mac's silent, devastating courtship was weaving a thread of bright suspense through her days, a teasing tug that kept her constantly off balance. It had started with the bunch of violets, breathing out whiffs of elusive sweetness. The next day, a gold foil box of flowers molded in exquisite detail out of the finest dark Italian chocolate. The next day, a silk scarf, the exact color of the dress she'd worn to meet him. Storm-at-sea blue.

A chunk of glowing honeycomb in a wax-paper lined white box, dripping and golden like trapped liquid sunshine. A miniature cactus with one luminous pink blossom floating out to the side, a gossamer dream of a flower. It faded away in two hours, leaving only a dry violet thread. The messenger who had delivered it had been sweating for fear of damaging it. He'd had to calm down in the conference room with an iced coffee, patting his shiny brow with a tissue.

Each day a lovely surprise. A leather-bound volume of *Romeo and Juliet*, dated 1714, in near-perfect condition. Erica had gotten onto the Internet and priced that item, too. The sum had made Jane sink into a chair and put her head between her knees. Better not to know.

Then it had been a faceted crystal window ornament. Mac was working his way steadily through her centerfold model's list of likes—and he'd dreamed up a way to give her rainbows.

Rainbows, for crying out loud. It was pure psychological warfare.

Every gift was a message designed to bypass her head and zing straight on to her heart. She would never have dreamed that such a volatile man could be possessed of such seductive delicacy. It brought back all the marvels of their night together. The shocking intimacy, the almost unbearable pleasure. The honesty, the tenderness, the passion.

But she was so vulnerable to his overwhelming personality. His brutal last words were still ringing in her head. She was wide open to him. She couldn't shield herself to Mac as she had with Dylan. Mac was too intelligent, too powerful, too crafty at slipping past her barriers. He knew her too well, after only one night. He could hurt her so easily.

He wanted her, but she didn't dare speculate why he'd changed his mind. She was confused. So tempted and allured, as if by the haunting whistle of enchanted pipes, luring her to sensual doom in the hall of the mountain king. So seductive. Almost worth the risk. Almost.

She swallowed over an aching lump in her throat as she watched the city go by. Her loneliness had sharpened, taking on a poignant edge. The silence of solitude was more profound. Harder to bear than before.

The message light was blinking when she got home, but she headed to the bedroom to change first. She placed the perfume bottle carefully on her vanity next to the chocolates and the cactus. She opened the gold foil box and yielded to her new after-work ritual, which involved struggling not to take out a chocolate flower.

The struggle lasted about three seconds today.

She broke off the outer petals of a chocolate rose, placing them on her tongue. She would *not* chew, she told herself. She would savor the chocolate bliss turning liquid on her tongue for her whole shower.

Afterward, she dried off and tugged on sweatpants and a skimpy white tank top—one of the reinforced kind that were theoretically designed to hold your bosom in place even without the benefit of a bra. In her case, the tank top made a valiant and commendable effort, and if it fell short of its goal, who was ever going to know? She lived alone.

That fleeting thought depressed her even more. She stared at herself in the mirror and bounced up and down on the balls of her feet. She caught herself wondering if Mac would appreciate the Jell-O jiggle.

The ache of longing that brought on made her stuff the rest of the chocolate rose into her mouth for instant comfort. She sucked on it as she trotted barefoot down the stairs to listen to her messages.

She punched the message button. "Jane, this is Patti," said the stage manager of the MeanStreets Players. "The most incredible thing just happened! I tried you at work, but they said you'd gone home. I hope you're not sick, but if you are, this news will cure you! Call me!"

She dialed Patti's number. "Hey, Patti, it's me. What's up?"

"We got a corporate contribution!" Patti crowed. "A big, whopping mother of a donation! We're set for the fall show! We're in fat city!"

Jane's backside connected hard with the kitchen chair. "We what?" she squeaked. "How? From who?"

"Crowne Royale Group Hotels, whoever the hell they are! I never even knew they existed!"

"Mac," Jane whispered. "Oh, my God. Mac funded our show."

"Who? No, honey, you're not making sense. The program director is a woman named Louise Reardon, and she says . . ." Patti's words flowed out in a high-pitched, unbroken stream, but Jane could no longer follow them. She clutched the phone to her ear, bent over a keen ache in her belly. Mac had funded her show. No one had ever stirred themselves to help her. No one had ever given her a gift so valuable.

". . . Jane? Hey! Jane, you still there?"

She dragged her attention back to Patti. "Sorry. I'm in a daze. This is incredible news. Patti. I've got to go. I'll call you back, OK?"

"OK, fine! Till later, then."

Jane placed the phone in the cradle and stared out the kitchen window. Beams of golden afternoon summer sunshine slanted in, split into lazily spinning rainbows by the crystal that hung in the window.

Rainbows, everywhere. Mac's gift to her. Flashes of extravagant, sensual beauty. She was surrounded by them, on all sides.

She pressed her hands against her wet eyes and started to laugh. It was so Mac, this careless, flagrant generosity. He was nothing like Dylan. He was passionate, complicated, difficult, but he was also kind and gentle and immensely tenderhearted. He was pulling strings behind her back, like Dylan, but while Dylan had done it to punish and control her, Mac pulled his strings to make her dreams come true.

He was a magnificent sweetheart. Her heart had known the truth from the start, but she hadn't dared to listen to it. She'd been too busy trying to keep her heart safe from him. A pointless exercise if ever there was one. Her heart would never be safe from Michael MacNamara.

She grabbed the phone and dialed. "Crowne Royale Group Hotels," said an older woman. Not Robin.

"May I speak with Michael MacNamara, please?"

"I'm sorry, he's out of the office. May I take a message?"

The doorbell rang at that moment. "I'll, uh, call back, thanks," she said. She hung up, went to the front door and peeked out the spy-hole.

No one appeared to be standing on the porch. Her heart thumped heavily as she unfastened the deadbolt and opened the door.

A high-pitched whimper pulled her attention down. A loose-woven covered basket sat on the porch. She crouched and flipped open the lid.

A puppy poked its fuzzy head out. It whined and licked her hand with a tiny pink tongue. A chocolate lab puppy. Its small body vibrated with emotion, its dark eyes woeful with fear and tremulous hope.

She lifted the squirming animal out of the basket and settled it into the crook of her arm. She rubbed its plump, naked pink belly. A male puppy, she noticed. He wiggled, practically bursting with love.

Her heart swelled till it felt like it would explode. She rubbed her face against him and breathed in that odd, sharp smell that only puppy fur had. Woo hah, crying again. Big deal. She had Kleenex in her pocket, she had industrial strength waterproof mascara. She was set.

She walked down the porch steps and out onto the sidewalk. The pavement was hot against her bare feet. She cuddled the puppy and looked around, realizing that she didn't even know what car he drove. Their party game had never gotten around to such mundane details.

She walked out into the middle of the quiet residential street, and turned like the dancing ballerina in a jewel box, eternally spinning to a tinkling, romantic tune. The pop of a car door jerked her gaze around.

Oh, please. She might have guessed that he would drive a black Jag. Bold, sexy, eye-catching, extravagant. So very Mac.

He got out of his car. His physical reality was like a blow to the center of her chest. God, he was beautiful. Even taller and broader than she remembered. He was wearing jeans and a snug white T-shirt that did nothing to conceal the muscular perfection of his body. His face looked hard and wary. Leaner. A quarter inch beard shadowed his face.

He walked towards her, and stopped a few feet away, his eyes wary. "I'm not stalking you," he said, in a low, careful voice.

She cuddled and soothed the trembling puppy as she feasted her eyes on him. "Of course not. I would never have thought that you were."

"I'm only here at your house because I thought it might be awkward to have a puppy delivered to your workplace."

"Very thoughtful. I loved your presents, by the way. Thank you."

"You're welcome." He shrugged. "You, uh, never called me. So I did kind of wonder. If you liked them, I mean."

She hid her smile against the puppy's fuzzy head. "You never left a note," she pointed out.

"I was trying to be restrained," he said wryly. "For a little change of pace, you know?"

"You act more like a fairy godmother than a stalker," she said.

"Oh, great," he said sourly. "What a turn-on. Bippity boppity boo."

She started to laugh. "You know that movie?"

"I raised a little girl." His voice was long-suffering. "Believe me, I know my Disney. Better than I ever wanted to."

The puppy tried to crawl up onto her shoulder, and she gently rearranged his wriggling body. "Fairy godfather, then?" she teased.

"That's problematic, too," he said gruffly. "Makes me sound like some bad-ass Mafioso, about to make you an offer you can't refuse."

"Are you?" she asked.

His mouth hardened. "You can always refuse, Jane," he said. "Always. And I'll respect that. I promise. You get what I'm saying?"

Her eyes filled up. She blinked the tears away and nodded. "Thank you for getting us the donation," she whispered.

"You don't have to thank me." His voice was tense. "I'm not trying to buy you, or anything sick like that. I just wanted you to have it."

"Try not to be so twitchy and defensive, Mac," she suggested. "Just take a deep breath . . . and try. It's going to be OK."

"Oh yeah? Easy for you to say. I'm the one who's out on a limb. I'm the one who scared you away. I don't want to fuck this up, but I—"

"You won't," she said simply.

He closed his mouth. His throat bobbed. "I won't?"

She took a careful step closer. "I only left because I thought you didn't want me," she confessed.

He shut his eyes. "I felt bad," he said tightly. "For losing control, and pushing you around like I did. I thought you wouldn't want me. That's why I, uh, took that shower. To give you an out. So you could cut and run, if you didn't want to deal with me."

She bit her lip. "Oh, Mac," she whispered.

"You ran," he said. "I wasn't surprised. I didn't blame you, but I can't stop thinking about you, Jane. I'm sorry about what happened. I want another chance. Please."

She couldn't get any words over the lump in her throat, so she went up on her tiptoes, and kissed him gently on the mouth.

He accepted her kiss, but did not return it. His body was rigid. "I'm not like that asshole who trashed your life," he said.

"I know," she said. "I'm so convinced." She swayed forward, caught a whiff of the sweet-smelling detergent his clothes had been washed in. She strained for the warmer scent of his skin and hair and breath. She had so much to say, she didn't know where to start.

"Don't torture me." His voice sounded strangled. "Say something."

She touched his chest. "Do you want to come into my—"

"Yes. Please."

He followed her into her house and looked around, fascinated. "Weird, that I know so much about you but I've never seen your place."

"I know. I felt that way when I was looking for your car," she told him. "We crammed a six-month affair into one night."

"Yeah." He peered at the photos on her wall. "Emotional overload. No wonder we had a meltdown."

She put the puppy down, and he rolled onto his back, presenting his quivering belly hopefully. She crouched down to pet him. "He's the cutest puppy that I've ever seen," she crooned. "Absolutely adorable."

Mac turned, a frown tugging his brows together. "I know it's a risk, a gift like that, which is another reason I wanted to give him to you in person. I can take him back, if you don't have time for a—"

"No power on earth could take this puppy from me." Her voice rang with authority. "This puppy is *mine*. Body and soul."

Mac's big shoulders visibly relaxed. "So he's an OK gift, then?"

"He's a spectacular gift," she said firmly. "Inspired."

A cautious grin woke his mischievous dimples. "I picked out the most jumpy, wiggly, waggy, emotional puppy in the whole litter for you."

She let out a watery giggle. "You know me so well."

"So have I succeeded in my campaign of tricking you into thinking I'm a deep, sensitive guy?" he demanded.

She folded her arms beneath her bosom as she pondered her reply. She noticed his eyes drift down to her chest. She deliberately hiked her boobs up a couple of inches. "Face it, Mac," she said.

"You *are* a deep, sensitive guy. A total sweetheart. A complete honey."

"Yeah, right," he said. "And that is the most provocative article of clothing that I have ever seen in my life."

The air crackled with the heat that arced between them. "Here you go again," she said. "Turning the conversation to sex when I tell you you're sensitive and sweet. You're so predictable."

"I didn't say a word about sex. I was talking about your tank top."

She waved an impatient hand at him. "Don't even try. I am so on to you, Mac. Whenever things get sticky—"

"You think this is sticky?" he cut in. "I'll show you sticky, angel."

The silence grew even heavier, more sexually charged. Mac blew out a sharp breath. "Damn. I didn't mean to do that."

"Do what?"

"Come on to you, before I even get things straightened out. Keep looking at me like that, and I'm going to nail you right here in your foyer, up against the wall."

She pulled in a quick, startled breath, and steadied herself against the wall. "Let's straighten things out quickly, then, shall we? Go on, Mac. The clock's ticking. The foyer wall is waiting."

He started to grin. "Oh, man. I am so in for it."

"And speaking of sticky, I've got some chocolate flowers we could put to creative use. This deep, sweet, sensitive guy I know sent them to me. And when we run out of those, I've got some raw honey we could lick off each other's, ah, tender spots. It's got a flavor that just explodes in your mouth—like some other things that I could think of."

"Whoa. Slow down, sweetheart." He held up his hands, his eyes feverishly bright. "Let's get this straightened out first. I've been thinking up some new questions for our party game, and I want to try them out." He seized her upper arms and tugged her towards him. "Like, for instance, where do you want to spend your honeymoon?"

Her eyes widened. "Oh, Mac."

He tilted her chin up and kissed her with exquisite gentleness. "Do you want a big wedding, or a small one? Do you want kids?

How many? Do you want to start trying now, or would you rather wait? Do you squeeze your toothpaste from the top, or the bottom?"

Her body was turning rosy pink, a deep glow starting in the center of her being and radiating out like the sunrise. "I've never thought about the honeymoon, so I'll pass on that one for now," she said. "Small wedding. Two to three kids. I'd love to start now, but I would wait if you wanted to. And I squeeze from the bottom. I hate waste."

The silence had the breathless suspense of a diver about to leap off the board. Mac leaned his forehead gently against hers. "Uh-oh," he said. "Trouble ahead. I'm a spendthrift, wasteful top squeezer. A sucker for instant gratification, as you know."

She swayed against him, giggling helplessly. "Oh, dear. What a dilemma. What are we going to do?"

"Separate toothpaste tubes," he said promptly. "Problem solved."

"Thank goodness," she murmured.

His smile faded, and he gazed at her with searching, shadowed eyes. "You know what I'm like," he said. "In bed, and out. I'm a very aggressive person. Always will be. I take up a lot of space."

"I love the kind of person you are," she said.

"I tend to act before I think," he went on, as if rushing to get the worst out. "I like to be the center of attention, but I'm not pathological about it. I get angry easily. I've been known to say stupid things that get me into trouble, but it never lasts. I know how to apologize. And I'll treat you like a goddess, Jane. You don't ever have to be afraid of me."

She shook her head. "Oh, I'm not. I can handle you, MacNamara. And I will. Very skillfully. Using some of my sandalwood bath oil, so my hands can slip and slide all over that big, thick—"

"Hold it right there, babe. Let me do this right. Here I am, trying to do the right thing, and you . . . is this all just about sex for you?"

She laughed at his outraged tone. "Are you accusing me of being superficial and oversexed?"

"Actually, I'm just trying to figure out if I'm dreaming," he said.

She reached down to his crotch, cupped him, and squeezed. "You're awake, Mac," she said throatily.

"Uh . . . yeah." He shuddered, groaned. "You've convinced me. OK, Jane. I've sounded you out, and it looks promising. I'd better get this over with while I can still talk. So, ah . . . here goes nothing." Mac swallowed hard, and sank down onto one knee. "Jane Duvall, I love you. Please don't laugh at me. I know this is trite, but I wanted to stick with the classic Prince Charming schtick—"

"It works," she whispered. "Don't stop. It's fine. Really."

His face lit up with pure joy. "Marry me, Jane." He seized her hand and kissed it. "Be my bride. I'll love you till I die."

His beautiful face wavered and swam. She brushed the tears away. "I'm a great big crybaby," she warned. "In case that bugs you."

"I don't care. I think I even like it. Is that kinky? Marry me, Jane."

"And I've got a pretty hot temper myself," she said. "I almost got myself fired today. And even if your conquering barbarian routine turns me on in bed, get this, Mac. I will not take any crap from you. Ever."

His eyes widened. "Whoa! Strict Jane! Marry me quick, babe. I can't wait to be put in my place by a gorgeous redhead every night." He embraced her hips, nuzzled her belly and looked up through fluttering lashes. "Just don't be too cruel to me," he pleaded. "You know how sensitive I am. Be gentle with my tender feelings."

She cradled his face, laughing through her tears. "We've only spent a total of maybe twelve hours together. It's, uh, kind of quick."

"I knew in the first ten seconds," he said simply. He pulled a little velvet box out of his pocket, snapped it open and held it out to her. Her jaw dropped, her voice snagged in her throat.

It was a stunning, square-cut sapphire, flanked with diamonds.

"It's that storm-at-sea color," he said hesitantly. "I love that color on you. If it's too old-fashioned for you, we could reset the stones—"

"It's perfect. I've never seen anything more perfect." She sank to her knees and wound her arms around his neck. "I love you, Mac. I would love to marry you. I would love to spend my life with you."

Mac unwrapped her arms so that he could slip the ring on her finger. His arms circled her, pulled her tight against him. He dropped light, sweet kisses against her face, and his hands moved over her with anxious care, as if he were afraid she might break. His caution made her want to cry with tenderness for him, but she was starved for raw passion. Time enough for gentleness later.

"Hey." She pulled away, and shoved him down onto the floor on his back. "It's been over a week, buddy, and I'm not made out of glass!"

"What's that supposed to mean?" he said belligerently.

"It means you don't have to be so damn careful. You've proved that you're capable. It's gone onto your record. You've racked up more than enough sensitivity points for a bout of hot, grinding, unbridled sex." She straddled him, whipped off the tank top and shook her bare boobs in his delighted face. "So get to it, Mac. Satisfy my carnal lust."

The puppy chose that moment to join the romp. He jumped onto Mac's chest and licked everything his tongue came in contact with, which in short order became Mac's face. Mac lifted the squirming animal into the air with a sigh. "This isn't going to work."

"What about the wall in my foyer?" she asked.

He laid the puppy to the side, shaking with silent laughter. "I, um, thought that might be a bit too raw for your delicate sensibilities."

The puppy yipped excitedly and scampered away into her kitchen, tiny toenails clicking and skittering against the linoleum.

"Wrong." She clambered off him, rose to her feet, and shoved her sweatpants down. "There's nothing delicate about my sensibilities."

They came together in a tender fumbling haste. She clawed off his T-shirt, unbuckled his belt. They shoved his jeans down so that his magnificent erection sprang out, swaying heavily in front of him.

He fished a condom out of his jeans and sheathed himself in

latex, too quickly for her liking. She'd wanted to run her hands over that hot, velvety club of male power and pleasure, but Mac was running the show with his usual high-handed style. No biggie. She knew she would get her chance to whip him into line. The struggle would be endless fun. Enough push and pull and laughter to last a lifetime.

He shoved her against the wall. The wild look in his eye made her chest tighten with excitement. He scooped his arm beneath her knee and jerked her leg up high, stroking his finger down her tender cleft.

"You're so wet and soft. You drive me crazy. I love you, Jane."

"I love you, too," she said shakily. "Please, Mac. Now."

He pushed himself inside her, shoving deep until his hips pressed against hers, until she was utterly filled. He scooped up her other leg and began the deep, plunging invasion that she craved. He rode her deep and hard, pinning her against the wall with the strength of his powerful body. She sobbed with pleasure at each heavy thrust.

"The wild beast is unleashed, baby. And you've got nobody to blame but yourself," he panted.

"Give me everything you've got, MacNamara," she said.

And with a groan of pure bliss, he did.

Exposed

Donna Kauffman

Chapter One

Austin Morgan got paid to shoot beautiful women. And he was very good at his job.

Had been, in fact, since he'd caught Cindy Harper in only her bikini bottoms, sunning herself on a raft out in old man Ramsay's pond when they were both seventeen. He'd never forget that hot August day. He'd staked out his spot in the woods for hours, hoping to get a shot of the great blue heron who'd made a habit of coming in every afternoon, usually just as the sun started its descent.

Instead he'd zoomed in on Cindy Harper. Her soft breasts, plumping out along the side of her body as she floated, facedown, on her bright orange raft. He remembered as if it were yesterday, how he'd skimmed his lens along the tight curve of her very sweet ass, feeling it as deeply as if he were stroking her for real. He remembered admiring the way her hamstrings flexed those perfect cheeks of hers when she flip-kicked her way back from the center of the lake. Girls Volleyball State Champ two years running. And the payoff was a body boys drooled over. And made his fingers twitch on the trigger.

He remembered thinking he couldn't figure out which had excited him more . . . the idea of wading out in that water and flipping her off the raft . . . and wrapping those strong legs of hers around his waist. Or capturing for posterity the exact element of her that had him rock hard in his shorts. Considering Cindy was dating his older brother Tag at the time, he'd opted for posterity.

Austin closed his eyes, shut out the sounds of people shuffling up and down the narrow aisle outside his private rail car, ignoring the stream of anxious chatter that filled the air that was growing more still and stifled the longer the train sat motionless on the snow-covered tracks. Instead, his thoughts continued to drift back through the years, as they had since he'd boarded the damn train in Florida, twelve interminable hours ago. This time to that day on Ramsay's pond. To that one snap in time that had changed his whole life.

The endless hours spent dreaming of a future spent traveling to exotic locales, photographing wildlife, capturing them in their native element, examining their power, how they fit in on the playing field of life . . . all forgotten the instant that shutter had clicked. The hunger to capture the primal glory of an entirely different kind of wildlife sprang to life inside him that hot afternoon, making him feel alive in a way he never had before. A hunger that, with a great deal of perseverance, and support from everyone back home in Rogues Hollow—except his father, of course—had led to a very lucrative career, traveling to all those exotic locales he'd dreamed of and many more he hadn't. Still focusing on the primal beauty of nature . . . only now it came wrapped in a string bikini.

The corners of his mouth kicked up just a little. And he owed it all to Cindy Harper's sweet ass. Now, a dozen years and a hundred magazine covers later, he was heading back home to Rogues Hollow. And any urge he had to smile vanished.

Home. He could be in Milan right now, shooting that bathing suit layout for *Elle*. Instead, he was stuck on a train, plunging headlong into a howling winter storm. Heading to a house, to a past, that—Cindy Harper's ass notwithstanding—held memories he'd traveled the world to forget. But what the hell, it was that time of year, right? Peace on earth, goodwill toward men?

Yeah, he thought as he stared out at the heavy white swirl beyond the fogged passenger window. *Merry fucking Christmas.*

Delilah Hudson loved Christmas.

But not for all the traditional reasons most people cherished and lovingly tended to every year. In fact, she loved it for all the reasons that had nothing to do with tradition or sentiment. Christmas was a season when everyone packed up, bundled up, and trundled home to friends and family, leaving work, the hassle of day to day living behind, to embrace the warmth of that impossible-to-duplicate familial cocoon.

Del hadn't come from a cocoon, familial or otherwise. She liked to think she'd emerged from the chrysalis fully formed and totally independent. She allowed herself a little smile, her first in hours, and a dry one at that, thinking the nuns who ran the orphanage she'd been raised in would agree on that last part. Her knuckles, however, still bore the scars of their opinions on the former.

Unlike the people presently milling past her, up and down the aisleway, she had no desire to revisit any of the places or people who had been a part of that time. She'd rather embrace a city empty of expectations and demands. For two glorious weeks, from the days just before Christmas, through the New Year, everyone hustled and bustled around town, thoughts focused on gift giving and partygoing . . . not on work, not on deadlines. And not on Del.

For two glorious weeks she felt like she had the whole place to herself, a place out of time, where she could wander as she pleased. Just her, and her camera. Only the pictures she took during that time weren't for the print ads that dominated her working hours. They were for herself. A reflection of who she was, what she saw in the city that had given her a life she loved. Museums were empty, the park cold and windswept, the harbor barren of sails. For those two weeks, New York City was hers.

Or it would be, if I could get the hell back to it, she thought grimly. Instead she was snowed in on a goddamn train . . . and snowed out of getting home anytime soon.

She drew her attention away from the grumbling of her fellow passengers and back to the fogged window. When she'd boarded the train in Atlanta early this morning, she'd seen expectant faces and chubby-cheeked smiles. People happily leaving work and home behind, heading off to spend the holiday with family or friends. Now those same faces were weary, frustrated, the littlest ones tear-stained. She could hardly blame them. It was Christmas Eve and they'd just been informed their train was temporarily stalled on the tracks.

Another train coming the other direction had partly derailed due to icing. The conductor had informed them that there had been thankfully few injuries, but that with the storm still ongoing, and the wind picking up, causing heavy drifting and near white-out conditions, rescue and repair efforts were being severely hampered. They'd been forced to stop a dozen miles away from the next station. Which was still hours short of Penn Station in New York City, so what difference did it make?

At least she didn't have anyone waiting for her: no relatives tipsy from too much eggnog, no family worrying about her safety, no significant other hoping he'd found just the right gift to surprise her with. "No me, wondering breathlessly if this is going to be the night he finally proposes," she said, lips twisting into a wry smirk.

Only, somehow, the acerbic internal monologue didn't quite give her the perspective she'd been hoping for. She'd always prided herself for not falling into that trap. The trap of expectations that others inevitably placed on those they loved. She took pride, and a significant amount of pleasure, in the fact that the only expectations she had to live up to were her own.

How often had she watched her friends and coworkers succumb to the lure of letting someone else define their happiness? Infatuation was great, lust even better; she was a firm believer in enjoying both. But only up to the point where you forgot it was just for fun. Once you started to rely on it, depend on it . . . Big mistake letting it progress beyond that point.

So, it was ridiculous to feel even the tiniest twinge of . . . what, loneliness? After all, she'd set the boundaries, right? What to others might appear a too solitary life, was, to her, a life filled with the sweet intoxication of complete freedom. She'd spent the first eighteen years of her life totally dependent on others to define her existence. The day she'd been emancipated from the orphanage, the day she'd first faced the actual reality of being completely in charge of her own fate, awash with the twin sensations of terror and exhilaration at the very prospect, had been every bit the defining moment in her life she'd always assumed it would be.

She clung to that freedom with a fierceness that only someone who had walked in her shoes could hope to understand. Almost ten years later, she still wasn't willing to give up an inch of it to someone else's demands, expectations, needs. Selfish perhaps, but she figured she'd earned the right. Maybe someday she'd cross paths with someone who'd make her reconsider those boundaries.

And, okay, maybe, that little twinge she'd felt just now was the first inkling that she was ready to even consider it. But that was up to fate, wasn't it? Hardly something she could control, so why worry about it?

Del shifted in her seat, tired of watching the blizzard of white on the other side of the fogged windowpanes. Tired of the tension that filled the air. And supremely tired of the muck and mire of her own thoughts. Trapped. She felt trapped. "Well, hell, I am trapped," she muttered, not wanting to admit the sensation had nothing to do with being stuck in this metal matchbox. So she did what she always did when the world closed in on her, made her think too much, question herself. She grabbed her camera. Always easier to focus outwardly, rather than inwardly.

Pushing out of her seat, Del forged a path through the passengers clogging the aisle. She wasn't even sure where the hell she was going, or where there was to go. She only knew she had to move, had to find some space to breathe. She wove her way to the end of the car, wanting, needing fresh air. It would be frigid, and she hadn't grabbed her coat, but no way was she going back. Freedom, temporary though it may be, was too close.

She ducked into the hatchway that spanned the distance between the cars, disappointed to discover it was fully enclosed. She'd envisioned those little rear balconies. "Gotta stop watching *Fugitive*," she murmured, even though she knew she wouldn't. She and Harrison had a long-standing Friday night date. Pathetic but true, Harrison Ford was the most constant man in her life.

She stood in the hatchway, camera in hand, shivering, debating on what to do next. She looked back, then ahead. One car was the same as the next. Full of grouchy people thwarted by the Snow Grinch who'd stolen Christmas.

But the car in front of her had one thing going for it. It was one car closer to the end of the line. Surely if she made it to the very back, the caboose, if there was still such a thing, would have an open-air platform or something. Resolved, she plunged forward.

Eight cars, two stubbed toes, one banged elbow and a dozen swallowed invectives later—okay, so there was that one that didn't quite get stifled, but the guy who'd pinched her ass deserved it—she made it to the last car. God help them all if that door was barred. Any goodwill toward men she might have scrounged up had disappeared with that pinch. Men could be such assholes.

Probably even Harrison. She sighed. And shoved through the door. No alarms went off, no bells clanged. At least none that she heard. Even if someone came after her, she had at least a few minutes of total solitude.

She stepped through the narrow door and into an artic wall of white. The cold air hit the back of her throat, making her gasp. Snow immediately clung to her hair and eyelashes, blew into her mouth, and eyes. Ducking her head, she moved back against the wall under the narrow overhang, pressing her back next to the door. Squinting, she tried to make out her surroundings.

White pretty much summed it up. It was dusk, although she was going more by her watch than anything else. The sky had been a deep gray all day. But the heavy blanket of snow illuminated the landscape as far as she could see, which wasn't very far as the wind was driving the snow sideways and upways, downways and swirlways. She could, however, see that the tracks behind them were already deeply drifted over. She had visions of being trapped in this chain of tin boxes for days on end. Apparently there was a fate worse than death.

Teeth chattering, the tip of her nose already growing numb, she fumbled with the camera she'd tucked under her arm to protect it from the snow. She'd come this far, she was going to take a few shots. "What I Did on My Christmas Vacation," she muttered, already mentally framing a shot of the buried tracks. She set the f-stop on her Nikon, shifted the ISO speed, absently wishing she'd brought her wide-angle lens and a few filters with her as she lifted the viewfinder to her eye. She exposed frame after frame of film as she maneuvered around the narrow confines of the rear landing, the cold and damp forgotten as her entire world narrowed to the view captured by her lens. Escape, pure and complete. Thank you, God.

She shifted so she could lean her weight back over the railing, wanting a direct shot up at the sky, capturing the flakes as they drove directly into her lens, when the door shoved open. She jerked in surprise, sending her feet slipping out from beneath her.

One arm flailed out, grappling at the slick railing as strong hands braced her hips.

"Sorry," came the deep male voice that accompanied those hands.

She was blinking snow from her eyes, so all she could make out was a big, dark blur. "It's okay," she said, assuming he'd let go when she regained her balance.

He didn't.

Chapter Two

As surprised to discover another person on the landing as the woman apparently was, Austin said, "And here I thought I was the only lunatic driven to risk frostbite rather than—"

"Risk death by claustrophobia?" she shot back dryly.

Austin's lips quirked. "Something like that."

It was only when she tugged her hips from his grasp that he realized he was still holding her. Even with snowflakes frosting his eyelashes and obscuring his vision, he was completely drawn in by her face. Her angular chin was offset by a small but very lush mouth. Her overly defined cheekbones stood out in stronger relief when combined with her choppy dark hair. But the capper that pulled it all together for him was the exotic slant to her almond shaped eyes—dark eyes that gazed directly, almost starkly, into his. Demanding . . . what? he found himself wondering.

He was already framing the way he'd shoot her as she took another step away. He ducked back under the slight overhang as a gust of wind eddied the snow into a swirl around them. It was only after he scrubbed the dampness from his face that he noticed the camera in her hand. And it was no little point and shoot. His interest increased. "Nice gear," he said with a nod, moving to make room for her against the wall. "Pro? Or serious enthusiast?"

She didn't glance at him. Instead she spoke as she cleaned her lens and examined her camera, dabbing off the damp spots with the hem of her thick pullover. "Both." She jerked her chin out, motioning to the snow. "This current bout of insanity would be driven by the latter." A wry smile kicked at the corners of those little bowed lips.

Sweet Lord, what a mouth. The lens would eat it up, drink it in. Such a contrast. Stark, almost harsh planes of her face, coupled with a courtesan's mouth and a concubine's eyes.

"It's the former that allows me to indulge in such insanity," she went on, still cleaning her lens. "In fact, some days I think that's the only reason I go to work."

"Doing what?" he asked, more intent on studying the contrasts of her face, imagining what lighting he'd use. Black-and-white film, definitely.

"Advertising."

It wasn't until the mouth he was mentally framing and shooting pulled down at the corners that he realized he was staring. He glanced up to find her staring back. Those eyes sucked him right in. Damn but she was a treasure trove of surprises.

The complete lack of artifice, not a speck of makeup on that skin, those lashes, that mouth. The total disregard to her hair, her appearance in general, he thought, as he noted the too long sleeves of her faded green pullover, the baggy khakis with the beaten tips of leather boots peeking out beneath the battered hem. Was she unaware of the impact the total package presented? Probably. But that was something he understood. Photographers were like that. So intent on capturing the world around them, they sort of forgot about their own impact on it.

She tucked her camera under her arm, out of the direct path of the driving snow the slight overhang was doing little to thwart. "What?" she finally said.

He should have looked away then, perhaps a bit guiltily. Only he didn't feel guilty. "Professional hazard. I'm usually not so obvious about it, though. You just took me by surprise."

She lifted a brow in silent question.

He grinned, already reaching for his own camera, thumbing off the lens cap and pressing the power button even before it cleared his pocket. Then he did something he'd ordinarily never do. Not without permission, tacit or otherwise. And given her expression when he swung the camera up and clicked, he knew he had neither.

"Well," she stated, unblinking. "That was rude."

"Yeah, I know." He didn't apologize as he snapped one more, then pressed the button that called the image up on the LCD screen. The framing, the lighting, it was all shit. And yet . . . "Sometimes, the alienation risk is worth it," he murmured.

She looked away, didn't ask to see it. "Pro?" she queried, her tone dry as dust. "Or annoying enthusiast?"

"Both." He clicked to the first image he'd taken, noting her glancing out of the corner of her eye. Not at the image. But at the camera itself. "Just so you know," he said, "that shot was for the latter."

She said nothing to that, but looked back out to the snow. She had to be freezing. He sure as hell was. But neither of them seemed in any hurry to go back inside.

"Why?" she finally asked.

He smiled, amused at the grudging tone. "Impulse. I don't give in to too many. But when I do, the gut instinct is rarely wrong."

She sighed, shook her head. "I didn't mean that." She flicked a glance his way, nodded at his camera. "I meant why digital photography? Professional choice? Or curiosity of the impulsive annoying enthusiast?"

His mouth curved. "I can see I'm going to have to work at rectifying my first impression."

"Why? You don't seem the type to be overly concerned what your targets—I'm sorry, your subjects—think."

His grin spread wider. "And yet you make such a fascinating . . . subject."

She frowned at that, but not before the corner of her mouth quirked a little.

"See for yourself," he said, clicking the picture back on the LCD screen and turning the back of the camera toward her. "Not my best shot, but the promise is all I was after."

"Promise?" she asked, sounding supremely disinterested, but pointedly not taking so much as a glance at the image of herself.

"That there is something worth studying, capturing. And since I know you won't ask, I'll just go ahead and tell you. A gold mine of promises."

She shook her head, her laugh short and dry. "You're a smooth one. How many women fall for that line, anyway?"

His look of surprise was sincere. "Believe it or not, I meant that professionally."

She shifted then, pulling her gaze away from the snow, turning her body slightly toward his, toward the shelter of the wall. Her hair and lashes were crusted with snow. Her shoulders were damp from it. They should go inside. But he wasn't quite ready. And her next question proved she wasn't, either.

"And your profession would be?"

"Shooting women." At her arched brow, he added, "And, on occasion, men."

"Ah. And you showcase your trophies where?"

"Magazine covers," he said, with complete immodesty. Those stark eyes of hers demanded nothing less.

She didn't ask for credits, didn't ask his name. Instead she shrugged. "Then we're in the same business. More or less. Layouts are layouts, after all."

"I suppose you're right."

There was a pause, then she said, "Although I imagine I get less attitude from my subjects than you do yours."

He laughed. "I don't know. Inanimate objects can be inordinately stubborn. Hard to get them to understand they have to shift slightly to the left to catch exactly that hint of backlight you're looking for."

"True. But you can kick them when you're through and they don't walk off in a huff threatening to sue."

"I'm beginning to see the advantages of advertising photography." Austin shifted so he faced her, using his shoulder to block as much of the snow as possible. "Are you based in the South?"

She shook her head, gaze still focused beyond him, out at the snowswept landscape. "New York. I was on assignment in Atlanta."

"Tough time of year to take assignments away from home."

Another shoulder shrug. "I don't mind. I offered to go."

He smiled. "What, you stopped believing in Santa Claus?"

Now she looked at him, and although her lips were curved in a deeply bowed smile, her eyes were more . . . inquisitive.

Good, he thought. He was curious, too.

"Something like that," she said. "What about you?"

"Work."

"So, you're heading home to New York, too, then."

He paused, unsure how to answer that question.

She must have sensed the little arc of tension, because she immediately pulled back from him. Not physically, but the open curiosity on her face a moment ago, returned to the more shuttered expression she'd had since he'd stepped out here. "Sorry. None of my business."

"No, it's not that. I just wasn't entirely sure how to answer."

The dry smile reemerged. "You don't know where home is?"

He grinned. "I travel a lot. It's a quandary." He sobered a little when she turned away from him again, wanting to keep her there, in the moment, rather than off to the side as a casual observer. It was easy, entirely natural, even, for people in their line of work to slip into that role. He found he didn't want her doing what was easy. For that matter, neither did he. "Your lips are starting to turn blue. Allow me to buy you a cup of whatever warms you best. Consider it my apology for being, what was it you called me? An impulsive annoying enthusiast?"

Her lips twitched. "First impressions can be hell, but in my experience they're often accurate. Or accurate enough, anyway."

"I hate to admit it, but you're probably right. Can I ask . . . which part is keeping you from saying yes?"

She laughed then, shook her head. "I'm thinking we can add *direct* to the list." She shot him a sideways glance. "The growing list."

He grinned. "Well, as long as it's growing, that means I can still add one or two things in the positive column."

Her expression told him she wasn't placing any bets. But that little kick at the corner of her mouth told him he still had a shot at changing her mind. And he found he wanted to.

"So?" he nudged. "Consider it a public duty."

"What, to the next poor woman whose privacy you intrude on?" She snorted.

Austin couldn't remember the last time he'd had such an odd . . . and stimulating conversation. "Well, if I understand my shortcomings, I might work harder to overcome them."

She just shot him a look that said *nice try.*

Maybe it was the snow clinging to her lashes, or the way the lighting cast shadows in the hollows of her cheeks, playing up the plump fullness of her lips, but it was in that exact moment that Austin's interest went from professional . . . to personal. He didn't just want to capture those lips on film . . . he wanted to taste them.

Which, in and of itself, wasn't that amazing. It certainly wasn't the first time he'd been aroused by the look of someone. But this was different. This was no simple stirring of interest. It was more like a punch to the gut. And he couldn't recall the last time he'd felt it. Or if he ever had. Maybe it was that for all she couldn't be more than twenty-five or -six, she was no naïve ingénue. Unlike most of the women he met these days. Models got younger and younger every year. He didn't. But this was more, even, than that. There was a life lived here, he thought, looking into those dark eyes of hers, experiences had.

And he realized he was hoping for the chance to hear about them.

"I'm guessing coffee isn't enough to redeem me. How about dinner?" It was odd, but he actually found himself sort of holding his breath, anticipating her answer.

"I have a feeling you're too used to getting your way."

"So, I'm being turned down because I know what I want and I'm not afraid to pursue it?"

She turned to him then, facing him fully, and gazed directly up into his eyes. She didn't say anything for several, eternally long moments.

Austin knew he was being judged, summed up, and it was a little disconcerting to realize just how much he wanted to add up to something worth investigating further. *Chalk it up to being stranded, needing to kill time,* he told himself. And how better to spend it than with a prickly woman who, in less than fifteen minutes, had managed to intrigue him in ways he'd forgotten he could be intrigued.

Then she slipped her camera out, raised it deliberately to her eye. Austin was surprised, but, after all, fair was fair. Still, he had to work not to shift his weight, or tense up as she took her time focusing in on him, getting the shot she was looking for. He was never on this side of the lens, and the intrusion was more of an invasion than he'd thought it would be.

Those eyes of hers saw too much. And, at this specific point in his life, there would be a lot to find in his. She would capture that. And despite the fact that he'd likely never see the proof of it, he didn't want it in existence in the first place.

He was just about to lift his hand, and—fair or not—cover the end of her lens with his palm, when she rolled off a series of shots.

He frowned. She grinned.

And he couldn't look away. It was like the sun peeking out beneath two dark storm clouds.

She reached past his waist and tugged on the door handle. "I'm freezing."

He stepped away so she could open the door, still deciding how he felt about . . . well, everything that had transpired out here.

She paused on her way through the door, looked back at him. He still hadn't moved. "About that coffee? I take mine black." Then she ducked inside.

And just like that, it didn't matter how he felt. He ducked in the door after her. He wasn't going to lose her. Not yet.

Chapter Three

What in the hell am I doing? Del pushed her way through the throng of passengers clogging her path. Flirting. That's what she was doing. Well, in her own fashion, anyway. She was not a flirter by nature, not the type of moth that had to flutter in a man's glow, batting away at his resistance until he caved to her greater charms.

Charms. There was a laugh.

And yet . . .

No, she shook that thought clean from her head. He was charming, despite her indication to him that she thought he was anything but. She, on the other hand, was usually described as being a bit bristly, somewhat unapproachable. It was a defense that had served her well, that she derived a sense of security from, creating that little foyer of space between her and those around her. Choosing who to let in, who to keep at bay.

And yet, he'd seemingly had no problems approaching her. She thought about the pictures he'd taken, thought about the promises he claimed to have seen. She wasn't unaware of herself as a woman, quite the opposite. But she understood beauty and knew she wasn't the embodiment of it. She was scrawny, her hair was a perpetual fashion faux pas, and her face was an asymmetrical construction of angles and curves. Perhaps it was her very oddity he'd found interesting. After all, she thought with a self-deprecating smile, he hadn't said exactly what promises her face had made.

But that they were professional in nature she had no doubt. There were certain men who went for the funky-artsy types. Based on her experience, he wasn't likely to be one of them. Of course, the same could be said in reverse. She wasn't typically drawn to what she called the God's-gifted. This man had certainly been showered with them. Thick dark hair, blue eyes that danced, a killer grin. The body wasn't bad, either. When he'd asked about her equipment, she couldn't deny she'd already been checking out his. This being before she knew he was carrying a camera.

Her smile lingered as she thought about the payback she'd exacted from him. He hadn't liked having his picture taken, but he'd endured it. An honorable man, perhaps? Did they still make such a thing? Of course, she'd pushed it, intentionally taking her time framing her shot, dragging out the torture. Though, truth be told, the lens loved him. He was disgustingly good-looking. Likely he knew it, though she hadn't picked up on that particular vibe. He seemed far more intent on studying her, than projecting himself. But she'd known even before lifting her camera that there would be no bad shots of this man.

Promises indeed.

She felt him behind her, keeping pace with her as she plunged forward, through one car, then the next. The club car was a number of cars in front of hers, and they weren't even close to that yet. They were forging their way through the third sleeper car, when he touched her briefly on the shoulder, then leaned close to her ear. "Wait."

Del paused, tried to shift out the flow, but was inadvertently shoved up against him. It occurred to her that she didn't even know his name . . . and a second later she forgot she'd even had the thought. Or any other thought. Except how his hands felt on her.

His hands—big hands—came up to steady her elbows, but as the steady stream of passengers maneuvered through the narrow passageway, they were pushed to the side, their bodies pressed together. He turned slightly, sheltering her from the flow with his body. She'd never been one for big men, not buying the bullshit theory of needing a big man to make her feel small and feminine. She was quite feminine enough, thank you.

Which did nothing to explain the hot little thrill she got at the feel of his big, muscled frame pressed against her admittedly narrower, softer one. She didn't know that it made her feel all that feminine . . . but it did elicit certain animalistic tendencies that were a bit shocking.

Hmm. Who knew?

His body completely blocked hers, and when she looked up into the shadow of his eyes, well, she might have gone a little crazy then, because the hard length of him, pressed so intimately against her, the intense focus of his gaze, made her think of every train fantasy she'd ever had.

Okay, so she'd never once had a train fantasy. But the longer she let herself stay snagged in the serious depths of his blue eyes . . . well, one or two sprang to mind. In quite indecent detail.

"Sorry," he murmured, as they were continually jostled up against each other.

I'm not, she thought, but didn't quite muster up the nerve to say it.

In fact, this was nerve racking . . . or nerve sensitizing. Whatever. Maybe it was all this body heat coming so swiftly on the heels of all that numbing cold, but her skin was buzzing as if some kind of electrical current was sizzling along its surface.

"What—" She cleared her throat. "What did you want?" she asked, vaguely recalling he'd asked her to wait.

His eyes flared, and there was no doubt the response he'd have given her if they'd known each other better. Or at all, for that matter.

She found herself wishing he'd put voice to the thought. What would her answer have been? Two strangers, on a train, headed nowhere.

He tried to speak, but any real conversation was made almost impossible by the steady stream of conversation eddying around them. Instead he fished in his pocket and came out with a card. Before she realized his intent, he'd slid his hand past her waist, into the lock of the private car they were pressed against. The door came open behind her back and he gripped her elbows as he back-walked her into the private car. He heeled the door shut behind him, and the sudden vacuum of silence made her ears ring.

Finally out of the insanity, she thought . . . except they were still tangled up with each other, and neither was making an effort to move apart. Her gaze was still hooked into his.

And the silence changed, became charged. He started to dip

his mouth toward hers, then stopped as if realizing only after the fact what he'd been instinctively driven to do. But they continued to stare into each other's eyes. Until the air in the cramped space fairly crackled around them.

Then, with an excruciating slowness that only served to jack up her anticipation, he began lowering his mouth to hers once again. His intent clear, he was giving her every opportunity to stop him. It was in that instant she decided not to, that she realized she'd only now stepped into the real insanity.

A breath before his lips brushed hers, she shivered in acute awareness. Of what she was about to do. Of what she was about to let him do. But when he slid those big hands of his from her elbows, up along the backs of her arms, he didn't have to tug her closer, urge her to move in. It was as if they flowed together.

Sweet, she thought, when his lips finally—*thank you, God*—took hers. Warm and sweet. Soft. None of the things she'd have expected from a man with such hard hands, such a hard body.

She let him into her mouth with an ease that should have shocked her, moved into his arms as if she'd looked for safe haven there often. Safe. Haven. She should have laughed. He was certainly neither. A man she'd only just met, one who thought nothing of taking indecent liberties with a stranger.

A stranger who had no desire to stop him from doing just that.

Two strangers on train, heading nowhere.

The phrase echoed in her mind, the fantasy resonating within her. Was this merely a knee jerk response to that twinge of loneliness she'd felt earlier? A quick fix? A way to treat the symptom so she didn't have to face whatever the larger concern might be?

And, so what if it was? she rationalized.

She kissed him back, as a test of sorts. Not in the hands-fisted-in-his-hair kind of way that she wanted to, the way those primal forces he'd somehow unleashed in her prodded her to. No, she had to retain some semblance of sanity here.

Didn't she?

Those long fingers of his slid up along the column of her neck, cupped her face, her chin, angling her mouth so he could plunder deeper. She moaned. Or maybe it was him. It didn't really matter. Damn, but he tasted sweet, and hot.

Her fingers twitched to touch him, to run her hands all over him. But the overload of sensations created by his mouth on hers, his tongue sliding along hers, was the center of her universe at the moment, all she could focus on. His kiss was deep, yet slow, almost lazy. As if they had all the time in the world, just to explore each other's mouths. Which was directly at odds with the almost ravenous hunger now clawing at her, to have him, all of him, immediately. But she welcomed the steadier, saner pace he was establishing, thinking it would give her time to gain some control, over herself, over him.

Instead, the exquisite torture of muscles clenching, nipples tightening, as he slowly continued to claim her mouth, drove her to a fever pitch. How was it he knew how to play her, so beautifully, so perfectly, right from the start? No awkward motions, no aborted moves. How was it he knew her mouth so well?

His body was rigid, taut against hers, the mere feel of it rocked her. And yet his fingers, his lips, his tongue, were gentle, smooth, deliberate. He slid free of her mouth, then took her bottom lip and suckled it, a groan building deep in his throat as his fingertips flexed, ever so slightly, against the side of her neck, then slid into her hair. Again she shuddered. Her breasts ached painfully now for those fingertips to brush across their tightly budded tips, for that mouth of his to suckle them, make love to them in the same exquisite way he'd made love to her mouth.

It occurred to her, in some deep recess of what was left of her mind, that she had to stop this, him, before they went much further. Regroup, pause, think things through. She'd thought herself a fairly cosmopolitan woman when it came to sex, but even she wasn't the type to go for something quite this daring, fantasy or no.

But then he was shuffling her backward, moving them until her spine came up against the narrow, smooth strip that ran between the two windows. The wall was ice-cold. His hands as they moved down over her collarbone were blistering hot. She didn't know which sensation made her shudder the hardest.

He trailed his tongue along her jaw as his hands shaped the outward swell of her breasts. And the need for him to do something to assuage the reckless need he'd aroused in her obliterated whatever lingering idea she might have had to call a halt to this.

When he began to slide his hands down her body, moving his body down along hers at the same time, she gasped and arched against him. Her knees wobbled dangerously and she flung her hands out, grappling at the edges of the sleeper bunks that jutted out, shoulder height, on either side of her. She shoved her camera still gripped in one hand onto the padded surface, then curled all ten fingers deep into the cushions as he moved lower, and lower still.

What in the hell was she doing? What in the *hell* was she letting him do to her? He was a goddamn stranger she'd only just met and—*Dear sweet God,* she thought, moaning as his hands cupped the slight weight of her breasts, but stopped shy of brushing over their now agonizingly sensitized tips. *Just touch me. Don't stop touching me.*

She heard the ragged edge to his breathing as he lowered himself to his knees. She wanted to beg him, might have, but he was nudging the hem of her shirt up with his nose, tracing his tongue around her naval. And just as he dipped his tongue into the soft recess, he flicked his fingertips over her tightly budded nipples, wrenching a guttural growl from her, a noise she'd never made once in her entire life.

He made her want to tear the clothes from her body, bare herself to him and his clever tongue, magic fingers, perfect mouth. Made her want to rip at his shirt, his jeans, until he was as naked in fact as he'd already made her feel in spirit.

He slid his hands down, gripped her pumping hips, hips she hadn't been aware she'd been moving until he pinned them back against the wall. He pulled the buttoned tab of her khakis open with his teeth, his thumbs pressing against her hipbones as he tugged the zipper down. He peeled the sides back. She tensed, paused, waiting, waiting . . .

"Don't move," he said, the words a hoarse command.

It was all she could do to breathe and remain upright at the same time. When his hands left her, her eyes opened of their own volition. *No, don't stop now, dammit.*

She froze. Bastard, he had his camera aimed right at her. "What kind of shit do you think you're pulling—"

"Don't," he repeated, still on his knees before her. He ripped off a shot before she could do more than glare at him.

"Talk about a mood killer," she ground out, heart still pounding, only now in growing fury.

Which only mounted further when he dared to grin—grin!— at her as he tossed the camera back on the bench seat before moving toward her once again.

"Oh, you don't seriously think I'm going to allow you to—"

"I'm not thinking, I'm reacting," he said, his tone one of utter sincerity. "And I would apologize for that gross invasion of your privacy," he said, negligently flicking another button loose on her khakis, "except I plan on doing a whole lot worse than that."

She would have smacked his hands away, surely she would have, if she'd only managed to pry hers loose from their death grip on the berth cushions before he'd gotten those hands of his on her again.

"You have no idea the absolute primitive way in which you're affecting me," he said against the tender sliver of exposed skin just below her naval. "I had to try to capture it, define it. Make sense of it," he said, as if that made it all better. "But it's only for me," he vowed as he pressed those sweet, deliciously hot lips of his against her tender, still-sensitized skin. "I swear it."

And, God help her, she didn't rip his head away, or knee him back on his ass. Both of which he deserved, manipulating bastard.

Manipulating bastard with a mouth that was this close to showing her nirvana, her little voice so helpfully added. And damn, damn, damn if she were going to stop him before she got hers.

"Next time, though," he murmured, as he pushed his questing fingers beneath the hem of her shirt, began to smooth them upward as he continued pressing soft kisses against her belly, "no glaring."

"Next time," she gasped, stunned at his arrogance. But the are-you-out-of-your-fucking-mind? tone lost any punch it had when he finally discovered her breasts, unfettered by a bra, and brushed the pads of his fingertips across her bare nipples.

Damn if his timing was as exquisite as his touch.

But dammit, she wasn't going to let it be that easy. "Do you," she began, then stopped to squirm as he fingered her nipples, while tugging the fly of her pants open wider with his teeth. He dipped his tongue along the edge of her panties and she shuddered as the pleasure of it rippled over her. "Do you," she tried again, determined to have at least a shred of say in this, "always . . ." That was as far as she could get before the groan that started somewhere deep in her belly, crawled up and out, long, and low. She might have whimpered, too, when his hands left her breasts, and moved to begin to tug her pants down.

Stop him, she told herself. *Make it clear you have some control here. Don't let him just have you like this, dictating what will happen and how.*

But his mouth was already brushing against her soft, springy curls, and her inner muscles clenched so tightly in anticipation of what he was about to do it caused her physical pain. Pain he could—and would, by damn—assuage with one dipping thrust of that clever tongue of his. Just one dip, and she'd fly apart. Just one little dip. Then she'd stop him cold. After all, it was the least he owed her for that damn picture.

"Do I always what?" he murmured, just the feel of his breath caressing her there enough to make her jerk and twitch. His fingers digging into her hips was the only indication of what this little pause was costing him.

It took her a moment to realize what he meant, her thought scattered by the edge she was tottering on. "Take pictures," she ground out, knowing he wasn't going to do anything else until she answered him, and wishing like hell she'd never asked the damn question. So close. So. Close. She fought the urge to keep from grabbing his head, shoving him where she needed him most. "During sex."

"Never."

He said it instantly, sincerely. She barked out a laugh, because it was ridiculous how much she wanted to believe him. And, honestly, what did it matter? For all she knew he could have his entire bedroom papier mâché'd with pictures of his conquests. Who the hell cared? All that mattered was that he finish conquering her. And if it was as good as she suspected it was going to be . . . well, then he could keep the damn picture. Frame it.

Her lips curved in supreme satisfaction as his fingers curled around the elastic edges of her panties . . . tugged them down.

But first he was going to have to earn it.

Chapter Four

She was not what he'd expected. With those long, nail bitten fingers and the almost hard line to her jaw and cheekbones, he'd expected to find more of the same beneath her baggy clothes. Jutting hip bones and taut skin, hard muscle wrapped about slender bone. So it was with deep and abiding pleasure that he reveled in the discovery of the plump swell of her small breasts, the plumper swell of her belly. And it was to his everlasting gratitude that, as he slid her pants down her legs, that he uncovered hips, and thighs that were lush, soft. Despite her small stature, she was made to cushion the weight of a man.

And damn if that man wasn't going to be him.

He'd stared through lenses at rail thin women for so many years, he'd all but forgotten what it was to unwrap such abundant treasure, to sink himself into it. Fingers, tongue, body. She was steam heat and sweet musk and soft moans and how in the hell had he denied himself this for so long? So long, apparently, he'd lost track of the existence of it altogether.

Tag's words floated through the last shred of his brain that wasn't fogged with lust. *When your work is your play, you've found nirvana, haven't you?*

He'd always thought his older brother had it exactly right. Had smugly, in fact, basked in his own luck and good fortune. Grown men would weep to experience, even once, the opportunities he was offered monthly, weekly. And got paid handsomely for.

Yet, when he slid his hands around the back of her legs, and softly kissed the insides of her thighs, he wondered if maybe he'd missed something vital somewhere along the line.

His heart was pounding, his fingers trembling, and he couldn't clearly say when was the last time they had done so. And despite the absolute certainty of what he was about to do, and precisely how he planned to go about doing it, there was some level of . . .

what? Not fear. Not even concern, really. He wanted her, and that he would get what he wanted was fairly assured.

So why, when he nuzzled her thighs apart, gripped her hips harder when her legs threatened to go loose on him, urged her to hold on tighter to the berths while he dipped his tongue right where it so badly wanted to go, did he feel a thrill in the pit of his belly that he couldn't quite explain?

Dangerous lust? Sex with a total stranger? Neither had ever called to him. Until now.

He lapped at her, groaned himself when she proved to be sweeter than expected. His cock surged to rock-hard proportions as her hips began to move, as she let herself go, alternately moaning and swearing. It was the swearing that made him almost come in his pants.

He pressed her back hard against the wall, drove his tongue inside her, exulted in the way she intentionally rapped her head against the wall several times and cursed like a sailor as she came. She shocked him, delighted him, jacked him up, and . . . and . . . he had no words for the rest. He slid his hands beneath her shirt, took her nipples between his fingers and prodded them, tugged at them, slid his tongue over her again, even when she was squirming to get away from it.

"Can't," she panted.

"Can," he assured her, continued to stroke her, even as she gasped, twitched hard, told him she couldn't possibly—that he couldn't possibly think she could ever—then grinned like a fool against her slick wetness, taunting her with his tongue as she came again, this time quivering and laughing like a damn loon.

He spread wet kisses over her thighs, held her as she shuddered, trembled, her gasps somewhere between laughter and stunned disbelief.

"I've changed my mind about Santa Claus," she finally managed.

He laughed, and at the time, was so hard he was in physical pain. But he didn't rip his pants down, yank those lovely lush legs of hers around his hips and bury himself in all that incredible hot wetness he knew only too well was waiting for him.

He wanted to, but he'd looked up. Her almond eyes were a bit glazed, making them look more exotic than ever. Her bowed courtesan lips were slack, inviting him to do lascivious things to them, between them. If she only knew the things he could envision the two of them doing. He spent a moment wondering how many of them they could do in the narrow confines of this cabin.

"And here I thought I was the lucky one," he told her. "Best present I've opened in a very long time."

Her fingers were still fisted in the thin cushions that lined the beds. His fingers twitched with the need to pick up his camera. Just to shoot her hands. Her mouth. Her eyes.

He must have given himself away, because her gaze briefly shifted to the bench seat, where he'd tossed the digital earlier. Her gaze flicked back to him, and he expected to see accusation, heated anger. Not uncertainty . . . tainted with just a bit of . . . curiosity? Arousal?

He was picking it up before she could make up her mind.

"Just don't—not—"

He shook his head. "I won't." He worked the buttons without looking at them. As if he could take his eyes off her. She seemed to understand she wasn't to move. He lifted the viewfinder, aimed it at her, and she trembled. She pulled her bottom lip between her teeth, and he twitched hard as he zoomed in on her mouth, caught the white of her teeth sinking into that plump bottom lip, twitched again when he snapped the shot.

He immediately lifted the lens, caught the stunned look in her eyes, the glaze of shocked excitement. He moved to his right, her gaze stayed forward. He snapped. Jerked.

He shifted, zoomed in on the white-knuckled grip she had on the cushion, moved so the gray light from the windows caught the tension perfectly. Snap.

Jesus. He'd always found his work stimulating . . . but not quite like this. In fact, despite the focus of his work, never like this. He'd always thought it was his ability to let his mind go there, but keep his body separate, letting his mind float free of that restriction, that made him the photographer he was. Totally in tune . . . and yet completely out of touch.

He questioned that now.

Still kneeling, he shoved her trousers and panties down to her ankles, pulled them off, over her boots. He glanced up, caught her frown. She tugged the hem of her shirt down, holding it between her thighs, covering herself. Just barely.

"There. Don't move." He rolled to his heels, moved back, still crouching. Her hair stuck up in wayward spikes. Twin spots of color had bloomed on her cheeks. Her bottom lip was puffier still from the pressure of her teeth. And yet the ferocity in those eyes of hers, still aroused, still damn hungry . . . she was woodland nymph and Amazon goddess all in one. Vulnerable, dominant. Defiant, needy. He framed the shot, took his time. Her hands twisting the hem of her shirt topped the frame, thighs rubbing one in front of the other, booted feet turned in at the toes. Snap. It was his. A part of her was his. Forever.

He moved back farther. "One more." He needed this one. The other shots were the artistic side of his brain, the elements of passion. Broken down, zoomed in on. But this . . . the need for this shot came from some other part of him. Made it harder to frame, made him want to be analytical, categorize it neatly that way, only to find he was incapable of it.

He framed her face as she stared steadily at him. Now his hands trembled. And it had nothing to do with art. She would haunt him. He understood that, even as he rejected it. Hundreds of faces filled his portfolio. None of them were imprinted on the back of his brain when he closed his eyes at night.

Hers would be.

His throat tightened, his finger twitched on the button. And, as if she could see through him, into him, understand the power she wielded, the corner of her mouth kicked up in the subtlest of smiles.

He took the shot without thinking. His, he thought. Forever.

He threw the camera on the bench even as he surged to a stand. *Haunt me,* he thought as he moved to her, even as he forced it from his mind. This was pure fantasy. Two strangers on a train. Heading nowhere. Except into each other.

He slid his hard fingers over her tough face, drove them into her spiky hair, gripped her head, held her. Swallowed her gasp when he crushed his mouth to hers.

Her hands immediately came up between them, fisted on his

chest. But she only shoved him once. Then she was tearing at his hair, and shoving her tongue into his mouth. His lip caught on her teeth, she took him so hard. Animal. Primal. Alpha. The urgent need to mate.

And goddamn if he didn't need to mate. The hunger was almost a vicious clawing inside him now. The way she dragged his shirt over his head, then raked her fingers down his back, clutched into him, dragging him to her, told him he wasn't alone.

She ripped at his pants. He held her head pinned to the wall, plundering her mouth the way he wanted to plunder her body. And then she was climbing onto him, wrapping herself around him. And when he shoved himself inside her, she swore long and loud, bit his lip, then swore again as she pummeled his back with her fists, urging him deeper. Faster.

Growling, he complied. Dear sweet Jesus, she was tight. So damn wet. Her back slapped against the wall as he drove into her. His grunts and groans alternating with her steady stream of "shit, fucking goddamn shit." Her fists pounded harder; she found his mouth again, took him, driving her tongue inside his mouth, showing him what she wanted. Pistoning, deep, hard, fast.

The wave came rushing at him so fast, the force of it draining the blood from his head so fast he thought he might black out. Sanity, some small shred of it, prevailed at the very last possible moment. He pulled out, let her legs drop from his hips, then shoved himself down between her thighs, held her hard up against the wall, and shuddered so hard as he came he was sure he'd buckle and take them both crashing to the floor.

"Goddammit, no," she wailed. "I'm on—the pill. Fuck."

He couldn't help it, he started to laugh. He held her tight when she started to squirm, pressed his face against the damp skin of her neck. "Does Santa know you talk like a trucker?"

She sighed, then made a noise somewhere between a sigh and a laugh. "It's only when I'm—I'm usually able to censor myself, keep it in my head. But with you—" She turned away from him, cheeks stained the most becoming pink. He just followed, continued to nuzzle her neck, tickling her ear, making her smack at him, even as her legs trembled.

"*Uninhibited* is the word I think you're looking for. And before you apologize for it, don't." He lifted his head then, found her staring at him curiously. "What can I say? It worked for me. Who knew?"

Her lips twitched, once, twice, then she lost the struggle and grinned. "No apology, then. But don't tell Santa. I was finally enjoying Christmas Eve for a change."

And just like that his heart came into play. It made no sense. None. Hot sex was an incredible physical release, but he never put his emotions into play. Not ever. Observer, that was his role. Occasional enjoyer, but never full participant. Not that way. It muddled things up. Screwed with his objectivity.

Haunt me. The thought he'd had, as he'd moved to take her, rolled through his mind again, echoed over and over. He wanted to look away from her, from those eyes, that face, her entire being, pull back into the protective mode where they were two consenting adults, enjoying a moment out of time. An incredible, intensely erotic moment. But a moment all the same.

But he didn't look away. And when her smile faded, when her gaze grew serious, when neither of them looked away, yet stood there, half naked, sweaty, and sticky . . . the moment to save himself passed.

And he couldn't seem to care all that much.

Instead, he lowered his mouth to hers, and kissed her. With the mating urge sated, this wasn't about hunger. Not physical hunger, anyway. *So what was this yearning then?* he asked himself, as he gently took her mouth, kissed her slowly, tenderly. Soothing the lips still puffy from their voracious feeding frenzy. Soothed some part of himself as well, in the doing of it, the caring for her.

What was this yearning, this need? he asked himself again. But then she was kissing him back. With the same care. The same tenderness. And the question was lost, the answer no longer so urgent.

Chapter Five

Where was this coming from? Del wondered, even as she kept kissing him. This urge to be sweet, to be tender, when this was supposed to be all about hot, about sizzling.

She shifted, let their lips part, slowly disengaged herself from him. He didn't stop her, but when she edged away from the wall, he reached out, let his fingertips brush hers, then dropped them when she paused.

"I've—I know we need to, you know, clean up. I have some—" He stopped stammering and moved instead to a leather duffel that sat on the bunk he wasn't using. He opened it up, pulled out a small pack of Kleenex and handed it to her. "I'm sorry, it's all I have." He pulled a bottle of springwater from another satchel and handed it to her. "Will this help?"

It was awkward, she thought, hating that. Mostly because the sex hadn't been. How could that have been so easily magnificent, and now they could barely string two sentences together? They were apparently fine with screwing the daylights out of each other. It was only when they'd slowed down enough to—to—get involved in whatever that last kiss had been about. That was what had messed it all up.

She struggled to come up with something blasé, dry, amusing, to put them back on track. But when she took the Kleenex and water from him, she made the mistake of catching his gaze. Where did that curiosity she found in them stem from? He had carnal knowledge of her. What more did he need to know? Shouldn't he be wanting her to clean up and get on back to her seat right about now? Shouldn't she?

She thought about that kiss. And didn't know what to do about that part. "Thanks," was all she managed.

He nodded, then turned his back, pulled on his clothes. "I'm going to step out," he told her. "Use the rest room."

She nodded, then realized he wasn't looking at her, was carefully giving her some privacy. Considering what they'd just been doing, it should have made her laugh. It didn't.

"Can I bring you back anything?"

"I'm fine," she said, finding herself curious, too. What kind of guy seduced a woman one moment, took her like an animal the next . . . then turned into a decent, gentlemanly sort?

The kind you want to get to know better, she thought. Then had to swallow the sudden urge to snicker. She knew him carnally, too, right? What else was there to know? "I'll be right behind you as soon as I—you know." Try as she might, the amusement came through anyway.

He paused at the door, his lips kicking up a bit, too, as he glanced briefly back. And just like that, it was comfortable again. "We never got around to that coffee."

"No," she said, no longer caring that her eyes were likely dancing. The hell with being blasé. Blasé hadn't gotten her the best sex of her life, now had it? She grinned. "No, we never did."

"Still interested?"

Oh, yeah, she thought instantly. "Here?"

"Would you rather go to the club—"

She shook her head.

His eyes darkened. Very sexy, she thought. Damn sexy. She wondered what his recovery time was like. Then mentally slapped her wrist. Greedy girl.

"Black, no sugar?" he said, and at her nod, added, "You want anything else?"

She let her smile be her answer.

Rather than respond in kind, he simply held her gaze for the longest moment. "Don't disappear on me."

She shivered a little, liking that intensity. A lot. "What, do I look like a mirage to you?"

A grin split his face, but it just made the intensity ratchet up another notch. "No, but I damn sure couldn't have hallucinated a better moment than this one." He flipped his cabin card on the bunk. "Take this with you. In case you get back first. It might take me a while to get the coffee." And then he was gone.

As it happened, she did get back first. The buzz among the passengers as she'd made her way to and from the bathroom was that the storm was surpassing forecasters' predictions, further hampering rescue and clean-up operations. The conductor had announced they'd likely be there until past daybreak at least.

"Merry Christmas to me," Del had sung beneath her breath, smiling unashamedly when other passengers gave her curious looks. She refused to feel guilty. The buzz still warming her insides was too good. Besides, though she understood there were many unhappy people on this train, they were at least safe, warm, and dry. She wasn't going to pretend she was upset by the current set of circumstances.

It was only when she'd gotten into the bathroom that she'd noted the high color in her cheeks, the razor burn at the base of her throat. Ah. That might explain some of those curious looks.

And she still hadn't felt guilty. In fact, her grin had been rather wanton as she splashed water on her face and neck. Like it was going to magically fade away. Like she cared. She'd all but danced her way back to his cabin. Let the rest of the passengers get their own fantasy train lover.

Only now that she was back in his cabin, alone, with nothing to do but think about what she'd done, what she'd allowed him to do . . . right there against that wall, did the second-guessing begin to creep in. She sat by the window. The sun had gone down now, and with the sky still heavy with clouds and snow, there was nothing to see but endless darkness, and the reflection of her own face in the glass. Why had she so blatantly disregarded any reasonable standards for her safety, possible health concerns, all of it? All for a quickie with a man whose name she didn't even know.

And yet when she closed her eyes, pictured in her mind every detail of what she'd done with her stranger, what he'd done to her . . . well, she shifted in her seat, her body still vividly aware of recent pleasures, and found she couldn't quite quash the grin that accompanied the mental replay. "Del, you naughty, naughty, girl," she murmured, shaking her head with a little laugh. So she'd been irresponsible. She figured she was due. And hell if she hadn't picked the best possible time, place . . . or man.

She opened her eyes, and her gaze landed on his camera, still lying on the opposite seat. She remembered then, the pictures he'd taken. A little shudder of fresh arousal skated over her, twitched at muscles that amazed her with their apparent unending need. He'd been so intent, she thought, so specific about what he was after.

She pictured him, kneeling before her, like she was some sort of goddess to be worshipped. She was hardly that . . . and yet, when he'd aimed that lens at her, something had shifted in her. She was neither exhibitionist nor repressed maiden. Far from either. She was comfortable enough with her body . . . but in the way a person was comfortable in the house they lived in. She never thought about herself, not in the way he'd made it clear he was thinking of her. When he'd aimed that lens at her, she'd felt more than naked . . . and terribly aroused at the thought of what he might discover. What it was he might see in her, that she'd never revealed before . . . maybe even to herself.

She shifted on the seat, needs and desires stirring in her all over again. It was silly, really. They were just stupid pictures. She'd probably cringe if she saw them. But her gaze lingered on the camera. Did she want to know? Want to know what it was he'd seen in her? What he'd felt so compelled to capture? What would it say about him? About her? It was that last part that kept her in her seat.

She looked up at the satchel, and the leather duffel on the bunk. What would its contents tell her about the man who had just taken her, like some kind of half wild warrior, starved for the feel, the taste, of a woman.

Any woman?

She shrugged that off. So what if she'd merely been convenient? He surely came under that heading, didn't he? She smiled. So she'd gotten the better end of that deal. *Shut up and thank Santa for early presents.*

She looked back out the window. So, if their almost unnatural ability to perform mind-blowing sexual acts with each other, first time out of the gate, was their only purpose in spending time together, why was she sticking around? What did they have to say to each other? After what had just happened, what else would they choose to reveal?

Don't disappear on me.

He didn't want her to go. Not yet. Did he want to take more pictures? Did he just want another shot at nirvana while he had the chance? Did she?

It was what fell under the "or what" column that had her standing, pacing the few steps in the narrow space between the bench seats.

He was smart. Had a swift sense of humor. A devout interest in pleasing a woman. All good things to know. Did she really need more? Right now the fantasy was pretty damn near perfect. Coffee, conversation . . . might ruin it all. Did she want to risk it?

She snagged her camera off the other bunk, fiddled with the settings, thought about the picture she'd taken of him. What would she think about when she looked at it? A week from now. A year from now. What memories did she want it to elicit?

She looked at the door. Leave now, and know? Or stay and risk ruining it?

She was reaching for the door when it slid open. She snatched her hand back, rubbed it along her pants leg and smiled as he stepped in, carrying a cardboard tray with two cups and a paper bag.

"Hey," he said, "sorry it took so long. Club car is now chaos car."

"I can imagine," she said, moving to the window, taking her seat.

He sat across from her, handed her a cup. "It's really hot."

If you only knew, she thought, thinking how the temperature had spiked the moment he'd stepped in the cabin. Or maybe it was just her temperature. "Thanks." She took the cup, wrapped her hands around it as she watched him set the tray to the side, and dig into the paper bag.

"I went ahead and got some sandwiches, some chips. I had no idea what you like."

That's where you'd be wrong. She had to duck her chin and pray that hadn't shown on her face. But the little snort gave her away. Damn her impulses. She glanced through her lashes over at him.

He'd paused in his bag search, was looking at her, one eyebrow raised. "You're really something."

"Yeah, but what?" she said on a laugh, immediately raising her hand. "Don't answer that."

He tossed a bag of chips on her lap. "Why? You so sure it's something you don't want to hear?" He held up two sandwiches. "Turkey or ham?"

She put her coffee in the side cup holder and reached over to snag the turkey. He was fast, caught her wrist before she could shift back to her seat. "What?" she asked, her pulse bumping up a bit at the unexpected move. But not in fear. This man meant her no harm. In fact, if the look in his eyes was any gauge, his intention was quite the opposite. A promise she was well aware he could deliver on. If she wanted him, to.

"Fascinating," was all he said, then he tugged on her wrist, pulling her from her seat. The bag of chips fell to the floor.

"Huh?" she asked, all lost in his darkening gaze.

"The 'something' you are. Is fascinating. Come here."

She should have resisted, just to see what he'd do, what he'd say. But she didn't want to. Besides, doing things his way had worked out pretty damn well for her so far.

He shoved the tray with his coffee down the bench and she moved to sit next to him. He just shook his head, took her by the hips and pulled onto his lap so she straddled his thighs.

She gave him a questioning look; he gave her a totally endearing, lopsided smile, and said, "You were too far away."

"Define too far," she said, not quite settling her weight on him yet.

"Not in constant contact with some part of my body."

Now it was her turn for a quirky grin. "Ah. I'm guessing there's a specific part you're most interested in having . . . constantly contacted?"

He laughed, but didn't tug her down tight against him. "Naturally, but I'm not that picky at the moment." He nudged her back, so she was perched closer to his knees than his lap. "Mostly you just felt too far away. Now you don't."

Maybe she should have moved, taken some control. But she liked where she was sitting, liked him wanting her there. She realized she was still clutching her sandwich, and decided what the hell, she was starving. So she unwrapped it as she talked. "And do you always shift things to suit your needs?" she asked, biting off a corner. "Never mind, don't answer that," she said, or tried to, while chewing. "After all, it's your job to shift your surroundings to suit your needs. No surprise you take that approach in every sense, I suppose."

He picked up his sandwich from where he'd tossed it, unwrapped it and took a bite as he thought over what she'd said, finally nodding. "I guess you're right."

"I guess the real question is, do people always allow you to get away with it? Do they ever get to call the shots, move things to suit their needs, even if they're not in line with yours?"

He grinned, sunk his bare teeth into the sandwich, and bit off a chunk, still smiling as he chewed.

"I take it that's a no," she said, unable not to smile in return. He was being completely alpha, and he knew it. Somehow, that didn't bother her too much. After all, she was only going to have to handle it temporarily.

"I didn't say that," he said. "Actually, I was thinking that you of all people should know exactly how much I don't mind putting others' needs above my own."

Her eyebrows climbed a little, as did the tiny blush of heat into her cheeks. Ridiculous, considering they weren't exactly trying to pretend what had just happened . . . hadn't.

She polished off the rest of her sandwich rather than respond. Her flush had answered for her anyway. He finished his sandwich in silence, too, never taking his gaze from hers. It was both reassuring and quite disconcerting, being the total and complete focus of this man's attention.

"You realize," she said finally, "that under normal circumstances, I'd have never allowed you to do what you did."

"Define normal."

"Meeting under almost any other circumstances." She balled up the wax paper and shot it at the paper bag, pumping her fists when it went in clean.

"Nothin' but paper," he agreed, nodding.

"What can I say," she boasted, buffing her nails on her shirt. "Some of us have it."

He surprised a squeal out of her by snagging her hips and yanking her snug up against him. She flung out her hands to brace herself on the wall behind his head, just before her breasts hit his chest.

"And some of us want it. Badly." Then he took her face between those big, wide hands of his, and crushed her mouth to his.

Chapter Six

He felt like he'd been drugged. Intoxicated by the taste of her. Her smart, hot little mouth. The scent of her. He couldn't get close enough. His fingers had twitched from the moment he'd stepped back in the cabin.

She hadn't fooled him. He'd seen the quick flicker of guilt. She'd been one step away from leaving. So he'd shamelessly done whatever he had to, to get her to stay. And that meant capitalizing on the one thing, the only thing, they shared—heat. Basic animal attraction.

And yet, it wasn't the soft curves, the delightful scent, or even the taste of her, that had driven him to this, to this need to have her. It was her laugh, her absolute insouciance. The fact that he was pretty damn certain—despite every evidence to the contrary—that she was no more likely to jump a stranger on a train than he was. And yes, that she'd allowed herself the freedom to take and be taken by him, made his blood pound.

He wove his fingers through that spiky hair and took her mouth, plundered it, the way he already burned to plunder her body again. This time staying buried deep and long, all the way to an incredibly explosive end. He began to stir when she kissed him back, slid her lips over his, took over. With her weight on his lap, hands braced on the wall behind him, she pressed him back into the seat, sunk herself into his mouth, took him. Took him in deep, needy thrusts, in the exact way he wanted to take. To be taken?

That thought shocked another surge through him. Was that it? he wondered, as his mind spun out and his hand slid down her sides, then up her back, meshing her body even more tightly against his. Was it her conviction in this interlude they'd embarked upon, her matched determination, openly seeking what he sought, wanting what he wanted? All this heat, but nothing more. Not even his name.

The perfect train fantasy.

Then their kisses began to slow, move to a deeper, more languid pace, and questions became answers and daring new feelings pulsed to life. Curiosity, the desire for more. And, perhaps a little temper, too, that she could be part of something so explosive, so intense, so fast, and not want more than the fantasy. Not demand to know what more there might be. Like he wanted to.

His fingers tensed on her back, causing her to pause briefly in her thorough seduction of his mouth.

So he wanted more. Which was asking—no, begging—for disaster. If he made a push, opted to try to explore this further . . . and she opted to walk, then what had been the stuff of dreams would become the stuff of disappointment and regret.

Except . . . now that he'd acknowledged he wanted to know her further, forge a type of intimacy that went beyond merely discovering they could pleasure each other physically, well, he'd already altered that dream anyway, hadn't he? Now there would be regret, and a lifetime of "what ifs" if he didn't try.

With both anxiety and anticipation, he slowly nudged her mouth from his, then captured her face once again between his palms.

Her eyes were huge, dark, and bottomless as she stared into his. He was insane to screw with this, to not just sit back and literally enjoy it. But he was already speaking, his pulse spiking as he took the first step. Risk, it appeared, came in many forms.

"I—I, we—" He broke off, sighed. Jesus. Perhaps he might have thought this out a tad better first. But what the hell, they'd pretty much been winging it this far.

Instead of frowning in confusion or concern, she chose to smile, all soft and smugly content. "I—I—we, what?"

His heart thundered, but no longer in anxiety or indecision. No way was she stopping now. Did she know what she was doing to him? How could she when he was still trying to figure it out? It was like being hit with a semi. "You know, you absolutely stun me."

"You had to stop kissing me to tell me that?"

"I absolutely did. And you absolutely do."

"So. Define stun," she said, taking one hand off the wall, tracing his bottom lip with her fingertips.

He ached—ached—to take those fingers into his mouth, suck on them, pull both of them right back under the wave of sensuality that flowed so easily around and through them, forget all about forging new paths and just do what came oh so naturally. He fought the urge, that ache, because this other path, this new exploration, was even more tempting to him now. "Amaze. Defy logic. And certainly all expectations."

She touched the end of his nose, then shifted her weight back a little more on his legs so she could sit up. "You had expectations? Before or after meeting me?" Her eyes were still lit with this amused gleam. "Was there some previous plan? A scheme? A dream? A fantasy, perhaps?"

"Funny you should use that word."

"Which one?"

"Fantasy. Up to just a few seconds ago, I've been very willing to file this rather mind-blowing experience away as just that."

"Only now . . . what?" She toyed with the collar of his shirt, no longer meeting his eyes.

He ducked his chin, looked up into her face. "Only now I don't know if maybe I'm shortchanging myself. And you. By accepting that this—phenomenal as it is—is all there could be. Or should be."

She didn't say anything, but she hadn't tensed, hadn't pulled away. She continued to toy with the button at his collar, her expression thoughtful. Which meant she'd wondered about it, too.

"So what are you asking, exactly?"

He rubbed his thumb across the hard angle of her jaw, up along the indentation of her cheek. "I haven't the faintest clue."

Her lips quirked at that, and she darted a glance at him, through thick, stubby lashes.

"I could be a fool for chancing ruining this," he said, "for not just going with the flow. And if that's all you want, then please, with all due haste, let's go back to where we were just a minute ago and forget I said anything." And yet his heart pounded, heavy and deep in his chest, as he waited what seemed like an eternity for her response.

"What else can there be?"

He smiled now, heart lifting, just a little, anticipation growing, excitement spiking all over again. "That's what I'd like to know."

She straightened now, raked her fingers through her hair, making it stand out even spikier than before, but seemingly unconcerned with her appearance. Perhaps one of her biggest draws to him, he thought. Her total lack of concern about beauty, allure. Even more, her lack of arrogance or assumption about those very things. Instead, she seemed simply willing to accept that his actions spoke for his attraction to her and therefore no other proof was required, verbal or otherwise.

For a man who spent his life immersed in the arrogance of allure, of beauty, her easy acceptance of their physical combustion, with no explanation necessary, was downright intoxicating.

She folded her arms loosely between them as her gaze locked on his once again. "Okay. So let's play twenty questions. And see what we see."

Amused, even as his pulse thundered at her agreement to pursue this new course, his lips curved. "Twenty questions?"

She lifted a shoulder, smiled back at him. "We've already discovered how well our bodies react to one another. You want to know how we'll do with a melding of the minds. Seems the most direct way to me."

He rested his hands on her thighs. "Oh, my mind has been engaged for some time now."

"Yeah, screaming sex does tend to get one's attention."

He laughed. "With you, that's definitely true. But I wasn't referring only to that." He traced patterns on her legs with his fingertips. "You have a way about you that fascinates me. Very direct, no bullshit."

Her smile was dry. "You get a lot of bullshitting women in your life, do you?"

"As a matter of fact, yes. Professionally, anyway. I work with models. It's a tough, vicious industry, with a great deal of pressure placed on a group of men and women who, while seemingly worldly and perfect, are in fact very young in more than just years. And yeah, a lot of them have to bullshit their way through it, just to survive."

"So that's professionally. What about personally?"

"Does this count as question number one . . . or two?"

Her smile deepened. "One. The bullshitting women was more of an observation."

"Ah. Okay, then. Personally . . . I've been pursuing my line of work, dedicated my life to it, in fact, for over a decade, now. In the beginning, I definitely enjoyed the fringe benefits, as it were, of moving and shaking in a world filled with more beautiful, exotic women than I'd ever suspected existed in my rustic, rural youth."

Her eyebrow lifted at that last part, but all she said was, "Go on."

"Patience," he said approvingly, glad she wasn't peppering him with questions all at once. "Another trait I don't see often enough. But back to the question . . . as time passed and my career took off, the women circulating around me stayed quite young—"

"But you did not," she finished for him.

"Thirty-two might not be ancient to the rest of the world, but where models are concerned, it's downright prehistoric."

She snorted. "When it comes to seeing other models, maybe, or pursuing guys not involved in their world. But you're the man behind the camera, the man seducing them with his lens, peeling back the layers, exposing them. You can't seriously expect me to believe they don't feel seduced, read that intent their own way, and hit on you no matter the age difference."

"I think I've just been complimented. Sort of."

"I'm just stating fact, probable fact anyway."

"Is that how you felt? When I aimed the lens at you? That your layers were being peeled away?"

Her gaze sharpened, and her thighs tightened, just a fraction against his. But he wasn't sorry he'd asked. Quite the opposite.

"I'm counting this as question number one for you," she finally said. "And yes, I suppose that's exactly how I felt. It was both disconcerting and, given the specific situation, arousing. The latter was the part that surprised me."

Direct. Honest. Where had she been all his life? "So then you think photo sessions are foreplay for me? Or, for the model, perhaps?"

"Of course not. Not always, anyway. But for some of the models, some of the time . . . I'm sure it feels like it. And some of them probably act on it." She lifted a shoulder. "It just stands to reason. Nothing wrong with that."

"Except I don't mess around with my models."

"Not ever?"

He shook his head. "Lines get blurred that way. I want to be the observer, maintain perspective. It gives me the edge I have to have. Hell, even in the beginning, anyone that strolled behind my camera never strolled in front of it. Life is complicated enough. And, the simple fact was, there was plenty to go around without complicating things."

She grinned. "Well, that's a relief. Now I don't have to worry about those shots you took of me showing up in some magazine."

"They could," he said in all seriousness. "The quality would be very raw, but all the more powerful for it. But, no, you're right, they won't. The subject was personal. And I was very serious when I said those were just for me."

She stared at him for a long moment, their gazes steady on one another. Then she nodded, accepting his word. Just like that. Which, with someone—anyone—else maybe, would seem an enormously foolish thing to do, given their relative newness to one another. But she'd taken his measure, and decided him worthy of trust. Temporarily anyway. And she was no fool. Of that he was certain.

"You said 'was.' That there *was* plenty to go around," she clarified. "But now that you're so ancient and they're all so young, you're not comfortable strolling, as you put it, for companionship with the women you meet during the course of doing your job?"

"Not that young, no. I still find my subject matter endlessly fascinating, as it pertains to the work itself. But no, that world as a whole no longer calls to me when it comes to finding companionship. As you call it," he added, amused when she merely lifted a cocky brow in response.

"What would you call it?" she asked. "One-night stands? Random caboose pickups?"

"Well, that last one is admittedly a new one for me, but seeing as it's proven pretty damn successful, I might just stick with it."

"Might you?" she asked wryly. "So, you're calling it a pickup, I call it companionship. Pretty much the same thing, don't you think?"

"Wait, whose turn are we on now?"

"Mine. Question three. And I get to rephrase it."

"My, my, we're all for making up the rules as we go along."

"Absolutely, as long as they favor me."

He laughed. "Good to know that going in. Rephrase away."

"Referring to the opposite sex only, for clarification purposes, I call reaching out, looking to make some kind of connection, a search for companionship. Sometimes the need driving it is physical, sometimes it's just friendship. If you're lucky, it can be both."

"What about love?" He raised a hand. "Clarification. Doesn't count as a question."

She just batted his hand down. "Yeah, yeah. Okay. You can look for companionship. You can't look for love. Well, you could, but it would just be a deeply frustrating and ultimately fruitless exercise, I think, since it's not something found, but something that happens as a result of something else."

"No belief in love at first sight?"

"Lust, yes." Despite her frank assessment, the most becoming color bloomed in her cheeks. "But for love you need friendship, an attraction that goes beyond sex. Respect, trust. That can't happen in an instant."

Had someone made that statement at any time in his life, up until about two hours ago, he would have heartily agreed. It was a definite, a black-and-white issue. Now? Now there were all these shades of gray.

His gaze dropped to follow the patterns he was tracing on her thighs with his fingertips. "And yet," he said thoughtfully, "within a very short time, we've proved we have attraction. We've trusted each other, enough to allow a degree of intimacy beyond heat-lightning sex. And the attraction grows, expands. Which is somehow scarier than the physical part." He glanced up, caught her intently gazing at him. "But here we are, pursuing it anyway."

She didn't look away, but covered his fingers with her own. "Pursuing isn't the same as having, or being. It's still not love."

He turned his hand over, laced his fingers through hers, then drew her hand to his mouth, turned it so he could press a kiss to her palm. He curled her fingers inward, tucking them inside his hand. "You're right. But it's a start. And a start is all anyone can ask for."

Chapter Seven

Del trembled as he curled her fingers inward, closing his kiss—his promise, request?—into her fist. She tried for a light laugh, but the fact of the matter was, she kind of wanted the same thing. "I think *scary* is an understatement."

He tugged her hand, pulled her closer. "Absolutely," he murmured, his eyes going all smoky with desire again.

She pushed against his chest at the last second, just before their lips touched. "Uh-uh. This is territory we've already covered."

He closed the gap, smiled against her lips. "Any burgeoning relationship should be built from a position of power, right? I'd say this part is pretty damn rock solid."

She couldn't help but smile. "You're incorrigible."

He kissed her, hard and fast, then set her back, grin still in place. "See, you've already learned something new."

She laughed now. "Oh no, I pretty much had that pegged back on the caboose."

"That transparent, am I?"

"Have you forgotten the list?"

"No, but I was sort of hoping you had. I was kind of hoping I'd burned it right out of your brain earlier."

She felt her cheeks heat again, a startling discovery each and every time. Mostly because she wasn't exactly the blushing type. She seemed to be going off type a lot today. "Yes, well, maybe you did. Temporarily."

"Now I've learned something new about you." He pulled her close. "If I'm in the doghouse, I'll know how to get out of it."

She arched a brow. "Big words."

He turned her face to his. "You weren't complaining earlier."

This close to him, seeing the teasing glint in his eyes, she began to seriously reconsider her lust vs. love at first sight. Ridiculous, sure. But how hard would it be to love a man who could make her laugh, make her sigh . . . and, well, make her come, all with such ease? *Danger, danger, Del.*

"No, I most certainly wasn't," she answered him.

His expression shifted then, turned surprisingly gentle. Given how they'd exploded earlier, she wouldn't have taken him for the type who appreciated tenderness. But then she remembered that final kiss, when the little lights were still twinkling in the air before her eyes . . . when things got a little awkward, a little too intimate. Which should have been laughable, considering . . . but hadn't.

She wondered if it would get awkward again now. Nothing had really changed. She didn't know much more about him now than she did an hour ago. Except that she wanted to know more. And so did he.

Which was potent enough.

He lowered his mouth, brushed warm lips across hers. Soft and sweet, he kissed her. Short kisses, dropped across her lips, on her chin, along her jaw, until she sighed and let her head fall back, allowing him to trail that soft mouth along her neck. She sunk her fingers into his hair, let the low buzz in her belly begin to build, swell, move outward, fill her with warmth, with anticipation.

When he lifted his head, she slowly brought her gaze back to his. And got her answer when she looked at the intensity, the desire, the curiosity so baldly apparent in his eyes. Not awkward. Still scary. Extremely potent.

She traced her hand over his face. "How is this kind of power possible?" she murmured with a bit of awe. "I thought I had things pretty well figured out. Then this. You make me ache. For all kinds of things."

"I was just asking myself the same question," he said, smoothing his fingertips along her hairline, cupping the back of her head.

But when he would have drawn her back, kissed her again, she pulled away. He let her go, let her shift back, straighten, saying nothing, but his gaze held the silent questions all the same.

"I said before I don't do this. Could have never even imagined—" She broke off, shook her head. "And yet, it's almost too easy between us. That scares me more than anything."

"Maybe it's easy for a reason. Maybe we should take that as a sign. I don't know about you, but this . . . this feeling, like I've been struck by lightning or hit by a truck, it just doesn't happen. To other people, maybe. Is that a little terrifying? Yes. But you're feeling it, too. So maybe that's how it is when it's right. I'd be crazy to walk away just because it scares the shit out of me."

Her lips twitched. "You sound so rational. And yet there's nothing rational about it. The truth is, we don't know each other. I don't know you."

"You know I can please you. Make you laugh. Make you think. At least I hope I do. You've already proved you can do those things for me."

She leaned forward until her nose and forehead touched his, almost going cross-eyed in an effort to stare him down. "And yet I don't even know your name," she said distinctly, plainly. She shook her head, moved back again. "If you were to get up and walk out of here, I'd have no way of ever finding you. Nor you me. I'd say that makes us strangers."

He shifted her off his lap, surprising her. Gripping her hips to keep her balanced, he pushed to a stand right along with her. He set her apart a few feet, then stuck his hand out. "Hi, I'm Austin Morgan. I'm thirty-two and live out of a suitcase—although I have an apartment in Chicago I'm rarely in, and a hotel suite in Milan that feels like home. I make a good living shooting pictures of beautiful people who are usually at least ten years younger than me, but make me feel at least twenty years older than them on a regular basis. I don't smoke, I occasionally enjoy a couple of drinks, I always enjoy sex, but never more than I've already enjoyed it with you. I've never been married, but have nothing against the institution.

"I'm the second of four boys—no sisters—all of whom were raised in a tiny place in the Blue Ridge foothills called Rogues Hollow. A bucolic, rural setting founded by three Scots highwaymen several hundred years ago, one of whom happens to be an ancestor of mine. I haven't seen any of my brothers in years, although we all get along. We're all presently heading back to Virginia to see each other and settle some family business. And while I'm excited about that, I'm dreading going back.

"Both my parents have passed away. I don't remember my mother. My father was a son of a bitch who just recently died, hence the reunion. I'm okay with being orphaned, which probably makes me at least a little bit of a son of a bitch myself and I'm not sure how I feel about that. Or about stepping foot in a house I swore I'd never go back to. But I'm dealing with that. Much better now that I've met you." He grinned. "Pleasure to make your acquaintance."

She took his hand, laughing a little, dazzled a lot. "Fine, okay. Um, well, I'm Delilah Hudson." She narrowed her gaze before he could comment or even react. "Everyone who knows me, and wants to live to tell the tale, calls me Del. I'm twenty-eight, I live in New York City, where I make a decent living by New York standards, shooting advertising layouts that never involve people of any age, but do involve working with clients who make me grow old before my time on a regular basis. I've never been married, but have several bridesmaid dresses in my closet suitable only for very bad Halloween costumes.

"I used to smoke, but that was mostly to make the nuns who raised me shake their heads and worry for my immortal soul. I also enjoy a few drinks on occasion, which has nothing to do with the nuns, but my enjoyment of sex—especially, it seems, with you, given the language you elicit with very little effort—would likely shock them speechless, and therefore makes it all the more gratifying. Which only proves they were right to worry about my immortal soul all along, I suppose.

"I've been to Chicago, but never Milan. Or, for that matter, anywhere out of this country, though I have gauzy dreams about what it would be like to traipse the globe and live out of a suitcase, probably all very over-romanticized, which would definitely shock my friends as they wouldn't believe I have a romantic bone in my body.

"I'm an orphan, too, only I've been one since I was six weeks old. I don't know anything about either of my parents, except at least one of them thought I'd have a better shot at life if I started it out in an abandoned grocery cart in an alley behind a Greek deli on Third. The nuns did their best, and despite their probable opinion, I don't think I turned out too badly. I occasionally won-

der about the kind of people I came from, if I ever had any siblings, that kind of thing, but not so much anymore. The fantasy
stories I made up as a child, of where I really came from, were always far more interesting and probably have a lot to do with
those gauzy dreams I mentioned earlier, and why my closest
friends will never know about any of them." She paused for a moment, her dry tone softening a bit. "I can draw, but it's very raw
talent, I have no formal training. My secret dream was to write
these amazing epic adventures for children, all illustrated by me of
course, so kids like me would have an alternate universe to escape
to.'"

She shook her head now, laughed, more than a little embarrassed by the revelation. "And I've never told that to anyone. I got
into photography as a teenager, as a way of trying to define myself. I spent hours strolling the streets of Manhattan and the bor-
oughs, making my own sense of the world, my sliver of it anyway,
through the lens of my camera. Still do, when I have the time. I
never thought of actually making a career taking pictures, am still
kind of surprised I do. The ad job sort of happened by accident, a
friend of a friend found me a job, and so on." She shrugged. "I
was good at it, it supports me well, and life went from there." She
smiled. "Occasionally even taking me to exotic foreign ports of
call, like Atlanta. And here I am, on a train back to the city, where
I have a glorious week to myself to wander those streets and once
again make sense of my world."

Her smile faded a little as she looked into his eyes, so intent, so
focused on her. "I think it might be a little more difficult this time
around. Seeing as my world has recently been turned upside down
and shaken up a bit."

"Lightning," he murmured, then closed his hand around hers
when she shook his, and yanked her up against his chest. In one
smooth motion, he spun so it was his back against the wall and
she was flush up against his body. "You have no idea what a pleasure it is to meet you, Del Hudson. And the more I meet, the more
it pleases me." He wrapped his arms around her. "So, now that
introductions are out of the way, where were we?" He took her
mouth without waiting.

And truth be told, she was glad he had. Her mind was spinning, her heart pounding. She loved the way he kissed her, the way he just knew her mouth, how he somehow managed to take and give at the same time. The way he knew exactly how to kiss her. Strangers indeed. She'd meant her little recitation to be acerbic, a little dose of reality into their fantasy world, a raw glimpse into her real world. Maybe make him realize just how close to being strangers they were. And yet, the result had somehow done the opposite. It had drawn him to her . . . and when he'd pulled her into his arms, she realized that's exactly what she'd secretly hoped he would do.

"What happened to the rest of the twenty questions?" she asked breathlessly, when he moved from her mouth to the side of her neck.

"I think we just gave each other at least that many answers. Besides, we've got the rest of our li—trip to ask and answer anything we want to know. I'm an open book. You can ask me anything you want to know. Right after I get done with this very important study I'm conducting."

Her snort turned into a surprisingly delighted giggle when he nuzzled her neck all the while sliding her arms out of her sleeves, stopping only long enough to tug the garment over her head. Surprising because she wasn't a giggler either. She supposed the new things she was learning weren't necessarily all about him.

"And this study would be?"

"To see if you look as fabulous naked as you felt."

"Ah," she said. Not exactly a stinging retort. Much less a roadblock to his continued exploration. "And?" she asked baldly. "How do I stack up? Although," she added, gasping a little when his warm palms spanned her waist, "stacked is probably not the right word here." She'd said it dryly, well aware of the fact he'd had no problem finding her arousing before. When his wide palms closed over her breasts, barely filling his hands, she let her head drop back. "Don't answer the question. But—Jesus, that feels good," she said, when he softly rubbed her nipples across the ridges and valleys of his fingers.

"Swearing already. Point to me."

"Two points, I believe," she said, as her nipples hardened painfully.

He chuckled, then banded one arm around her back, snuggling her up tight against the hard length of him, the rigidly hard length. Thereby removing any shred of doubt about his final judgment regarding her naked breasts. He leaned her back over his arm so he could trail his tongue down the center line of her chest, then moved torturously slowly to the tip of one breast. The deep groan of appreciation as he finally took her plumped nipple between his lips was matched by her own.

Her hips were twitching up against his, the muscles between her thighs clenching almost viciously. She finally ripped his head up and, catching him off guard, shoved him up straight against the wall and yanked at his shirt. "Fair's fair," she reminded him, and off it came.

He was beautiful everywhere. Hard, leanly muscled, with a spray of fine dark hair across perfectly molded pecs. Perfect pecs with their own tight little buds. Well, she thought, turnabout was just. She pinned his shoulders back. "Uh-uh, no hands."

He held his hands up in mock surrender.

She merely nodded approvingly. "Keep them there, you're entirely too sneaky with them."

"Anything you say, ma'am. What, uh, are you planning to do with me?" He tipped his head back, closed his eyes, and with an air of mock drama, said, "Just be gentle."

Which was the only reason she used her teeth—just a little—when she closed her lips around his nipple.

His whole body jerked. Most impressive was the part that had jerked between her thighs. "Ah," she said, trying to sound detached, scientific. "Knee-jerk reaction, or . . ." Keeping him pinned to the wall with her hands on his forearms, she ducked down and swirled her tongue around the other one.

A little moan escaped. She thought he might have breathed something that sounded like, "Shit. Jesus Christ," when she pinched the hard nub between her lips.

She licked her way up to his chin, bit the edge of his jaw, then the edge of his ear. "You know, it is sort of arousing to make you swear."

He turned his head, so his eyes blazed into hers. She knew he was fully, completely aroused, and, this close, not entirely tame about it. The inherent whisper of danger didn't remotely make her feel like backing down. No, it sent a hot thrill right through her. Made her wonder just how far she could push him, provoke him. And just how incredible it was going to be when he lost control.

Since when had she become a thrill seeker? She, who had worked very hard to create stability, sameness, a solid foundation that only changed when she allowed it to. A life she controlled. And here she was, all but daring him to take control away from her. And just the mere thought of him actually doing it soaked her panties.

He continued to stare into her eyes. She felt his pulse thunder through the veins in his forearms, now flexed beneath her fingers. "Any other little experiments you want to conduct on me, Del?" he said, his voice low, rough.

"Maybe," she taunted. Only hearing him say her name did something wacky to her insides. Simultaneously jacking her up, and stunning her a little. How much she'd enjoyed just hearing him say it. Made no sense. People said her name all the time. But this . . . now . . . it was personalizing things between them in a way that—well, considering just how up close and personal they'd already been . . . and from the looks of things, please, God, were about to be again—was a little ridiculous to think was any different. But it was different. Enough that she wanted to see if it would send that same jolt through him.

She leaned closer, until his mouth was as close as it could be without her actually touching it. "I want to know what I'd have to do to provoke you, to make you lose control."

His lips curved slowly, but the resulting smile was more primal than amused. "And your method would be?"

She drew her hands down his forearms, pushing them before she moved on down, signaling him to keep them there, which he did. Having him pinned, willingly, against the wall, was intensely arousing. Undoing his pants was even more so. She moved her body down, so it slid against every inch of him as she dropped into a crouch . . . taking his pants and his briefs down along with her.

He was gloriously hard and thick. And when she looked up at him as she drew her hands back up bare thighs, now locked in a rock-hard stance, his cocky smile faltered. But the hot gaze turned almost molten. She brushed along his inner thighs, keeping him jutting close to her mouth, but not touching her.

She allowed her breath to caress him as she slowly cupped him. His cock jerked. When she wrapped her hand around him, he swore. She glanced up, found his head back, hands pinned to the wall, eyes clenched shut, jaw tight. The mere sight of all that power, leashed, controlled, allowing her full possession of it, however she wanted to avail herself of it . . . made her almost light-headed with desire.

She stroked him, making him groan, making him growl. She let the tip of him brush her cheek, her closed lips.

"Holy Mother of God," he said through clenched teeth, his chest rising and falling.

She drew her hand to the tip, back to the base, then up again, before stopping to look up at him again. "Austin," she commanded quietly. His whole body twitched.

"Yeah," he grunted.

"Watch me."

"Jesus," he breathed.

"I want you to watch me."

"Del—I don't know what you meant by lose control, but the minute you put your mouth on me—"

"Austin," she said, voice quivering just a little. She liked the taste of his name on her lips. Now she wanted to find out if she liked the taste of something else. "I dare you."

He swore. In both English and Italian.

She grinned.

He pried his eyes open, slowly lowered his gaze. "And you say you don't know me."

"I'm about to." She wet her lips.

He groaned, "Fuck me."

She said, "Most definitely," then took him fully into her mouth.

Chapter Eight

Austin was pretty sure the top of his head was no longer there, blown off by the intense sensation of her lips, tongue, and mouth sliding up and down along his—Christ, it wasn't like no one had ever . . . but when she—he sucked in air, tensed, shocked to feel the surge begin to gather. He'd just come an hour or so ago . . . no way was he going to—but damn, it sure felt like it.

He spent a split second thinking he should tear her away, pull her up, bury himself deep, so he could come inside her sweet, hot body—but just the thought of it was enough to send him flying over the edge.

Del kept him pinned hard to the wall, not letting him take any control. Taking him. And taking him. Until there was nothing left, and he could barely stand upright, his knees were suddenly shaky. He wanted nothing more than to slide down the wall, pull her into his lap . . . and just drift on the intense waves of pleasure still flowing over and through him.

His head was tipped back, his eyes squeezed shut. "Never," he managed. "Twice. Jesus." He shook his head. He was still half hard; in fact, he wasn't sure he'd ever go limp again. His body had been hard-wired for her and it simply wasn't going to quit until they were both either completely spent . . . or unconscious.

"Austin," she urged, her voice all throaty. She kissed one rigidly locked thigh, then the other.

Something in her voice had him opening his eyes, looking down at her, still kneeling there, looking up at him, eyes still dark with desire, mouth curved in a damned dry smile. It was the smile that did him in completely. He laughed even as his throat grew strangely tight. Unsure what to do with all the emotions she so easily elicited, he only knew she shouldn't be kneeling before him. He yanked her up, tugged her so she fell against him. "I want to feel all of you," he said, not aware of what words he had to say until he was saying them. "Against all of me."

Her smile faded, and maybe her throat was a little tight, too, because she swallowed hard.

"I want us out of these clothes and up there," he jerked his chin toward the bunk he'd used as a bed. "I want to feel your legs entwined with mine. I want to lie there and imagine how it would feel to sleep with you all wrapped up with me." He stroked her cheek, ran his thumb along her lip, knowing this was probably way too intense, yet unable to stop. "I want to fall asleep with you in my arms. And I want to wake up next to you in the morning." He brushed a kiss across her lips. "At least once."

She shifted enough to look into his eyes. Held his gaze for the longest time. Then moved out of his embrace . . . and slowly took the rest of her clothes off. He kicked free of his own clothes as she turned, placed her hands on the upper berth, intending to push herself up. He moved in behind her, tugged her hips back against his. Would he ever get enough of her?

Leaning over her, he dropped kisses along the nape of her neck as he wrapped his arms fully around her waist, nestling himself between her legs. Her grip on the berth tightened as she pushed back into him, arched her neck to give him greater access.

His pulse raced again, the blood pounding in his veins. It was almost like a sickness, the depth of need she stirred in him, so effortlessly. The clean line of her neck, the supple curve of her spine, the swell of her hips, the soft roundness of her buttocks. He ached to capture them on film, so he could forever remember this moment, each perfect instant of her body meshing with his. And yet he already knew he wouldn't need a tangible reminder. Not when so many images would be forever indelibly burned into his brain.

She moaned softly as he slid one hand up to cup her breast, and slid the other down between her legs. He groaned as she moved against him, against his questing fingers. Her nipple grew hard and tight as he rolled it between his fingers. Her breathing grew ragged as he moved to the other breast, her moan deep and long as he slid first one finger inside her, then another.

She pushed down, moaning, gasping . . . swearing.

Smiling, he pushed himself between her thighs from behind,

gently bit the ridge of her shoulder, then soothed it with his tongue. She started moving faster, clenching around his fingers. He shifted her so her back arched more fully, then slid his fingers forward, to play with her, so slippery and wet, then slid them back inside her. The moment he pushed them fully inside her, she came hard, spasming around him, crying out.

He continued to stroke her, toy with her nipples. He bit her ear, licked her neck, and drove her up and over again. Dear God, he could lose himself completely in her. In her scent, her sound, her softness.

Intoxication. Addiction. Obsession.

She was trembling, her legs shaky, when he finally withdrew. Rather than turn her in his arms, he lifted her up onto the berth, and followed behind her. Saying nothing, he stretched out and pulled her to him. Legs and arms flowed together far too easily. But nothing about her, about them, surprised him any longer. He was deep in a sensual fog and he had no desire for the mists to clear, for reality to rear its often ugly head. She snuggled against him, her breathing slowing until she dozed on him. He stroked her hair, her back, the length of the arm she'd draped across his belly . . . and tried not to think about what would come next.

Too many things were in turmoil in his life at the moment. Well, one thing, but it was a major one thing. This trip home. Had he so willingly leaped into this . . . whatever it was he was having with Del, as a way to avoid dealing with what lay ahead? Or, at least, forget about it for a while? Possibly. She'd certainly taken his mind off things. But he'd been under all kinds of stresses throughout his life, and he'd never once reacted by having spontaneous, mind-blowing sex with a woman he'd only just met.

He shifted, looked down at the woman sleeping in his arms. She didn't strike him as a woman who trusted easily, or probably often. Her background intrigued him. Hell, everything about her intrigued him. Would he have given her a second look had their paths crossed anywhere else? He had no way of knowing. He only knew that from the moment he'd stepped onto that tiny, snowy balcony, she'd had his complete attention.

He brushed at the spiky ends of her hair. She wasn't his type, if he had such a thing. She was a quixotic mix of hard and soft, both physically and emotionally. The women he spent his quiet time with were usually easier, less complicated. Less likely to snag at his heart? Probably. He moved around a lot. Women, clingy women, complicated that. He'd never consciously made the decision to stay unattached, but subconsciously? Yeah, he could see now where he might have kept things light, easy, simple, on purpose.

So when, he wondered, had he stopped taking risks? His work challenged him. He was good at what he did, demanding of himself. He didn't settle, but neither had he truly pushed himself lately. Professionally . . . or personally. Until today.

His thoughts drifted to the call he'd gotten from Tag, telling him Taggart Sr. had succumbed to a heart attack. He hadn't known what to feel about the news. He'd always thought he'd be indifferent to the bastard's passing. Their lives hadn't intertwined in over a decade, hadn't impacted each other's really in even longer than that. But the fact was, he was his father. The man who, for better and oftentimes worse, had raised him. Austin had always thought he'd become the man he was despite his father's harsh hand and even harsher mouth. But perhaps he was who he was because of those things. It was an unsettling thought.

He shoved it all aside. For now, he was tucked away on a snowbound train, with a naked woman sprawled across his chest. He had no idea how he was going to feel, walking into the house he'd been raised in, how it would be between him and his brothers, all together after so many years apart. So many memories. Most bad, but maybe some good. He stroked his hand down her spine and his lips curved a little as he smoothed his palm over the sweet fullness of her buttocks. Like Cindy Harper on that lake. That had been a good day.

There would be other memories. When four boys grew up under one roof . . . there would be stories, plenty of them. He smiled, wishing he could be more cynical about the little spurt of hope that sprang to life inside him. The hope that he and his brothers could concentrate on those times. It wouldn't be so simple. There was a will to be read. Ancestral property to be dealt with. Who would stay? Who would be responsible?

No. He didn't want to think about it. Much better to dwell on the more immediate concern. What to do about Del? Did he want this to be the perfect interlude? The one golden fantasy that he could resurrect at will, and likely would, repeatedly, in years to come? Or did he want to push it beyond this chance meeting? This chance blending of bodies . . . and souls. It was a little sappy, but that's what he was feeling at the moment. Two souls, buffeted about by life, victorious either despite or because of their pasts . . . tossed into each other's paths. Was it any surprise, then, the tempest their meeting had created?

He shook his head, closed his eyes. Soul mates. He'd never believed in such a thing. But it was hard to deny the connection he felt to Del. A connection that had begun physically, but had already expanded beyond that. The . . . fear? Yes, fear, that he'd wake up and find it had all been a dream. Or worse, that she'd somehow slipped away from him before he could convince her to . . . what? E-mail him? Have intercontinental phone sex?

He swore silently, not wanting to deal with things like logic and reason. Nothing about this was either of those things. And yet, the fact was she was rooted in New York. He wasn't rooted anywhere. He thought about her revelation, that she wanted to travel. Be an artist. A writer. What if he offered to give her an opportunity to do those things, discover what might be? Both within herself . . . and between them? It might amount to nothing. They might be horrible together day-to-day. Or it might open a world for her in which he'd be no more than a stepping-stone. It might lead to pain, heartache.

Or, it could lead to something even more terrifying to contemplate. Something like happiness. Contentment.

Love. Commitment.

He turned his face so that the tips of her hair tickled his cheek. Risk. It all came down to risk, to his willingness to chance it. "Well," he murmured, "what the hell do I have to lose?" The idea of never seeing her again seemed a far worse, very immediate reality. He knew if he didn't try, he would forever ask himself "what if?"

He blew out a surprisingly shaky breath, shifted to his side and pulled her more fully into his arms. Her body was warm, pliant. And his, he couldn't help but think. A man who had never had a possessive bone in his body. He felt a sudden, almost desperate need to wake her, demand to know if she felt that same sense of possession. Was she, even now, dreaming of what a life with him could be like?

He tucked her head on his chest, amplifying the beat of his heart as it thumped against the pressure of her cheek. Would he wake up tomorrow and ask himself what in the hell he'd been thinking? Would she?

There was only one way to find out.

Chapter Nine

She woke to the sound of the train rumbling along the tracks. Judging by the dim gray light seeping through the windows, it was early morning. She'd slept all night. In Austin Morgan's arms.

She'd recognized the name. He wasn't famous on the level of Bruce Webber or Helmut Newton, his name wouldn't be recognized outside the industry. But inside it was a different story. He had quite a reputation as a photographer. As an eligible shark swimming in a pool of the world's most beautiful fishes . . . well, surprisingly there was really no buzz about him in that regard. Which meant, of course, that most industry people probably had him pegged as being gay and still in the closet.

She grinned against his chest. This man was definitely all hetero.

"What's funny?" he murmured, his voice drowsy and deep.

She began to shift away and his arm immediately came up, his fingertips stroked the length of her spine, encouraging her to stay where she was.

It was the proverbial morning after. Their glorious one-night stand over. The train was moving and in a few short hours, they'd go their separate ways. It would be awkward, possibly even painful. There was no reason to linger or draw things out. It would just make the inevitable more difficult.

And yet it took no more than the gentle urging of his fingertips on her back to keep her staying right where she was. "I was just thinking that you've spoiled me for travel by train."

He chuckled, the sound rough and gravelly, then rolled to his side, pushing her to her back. Without so much as opening his eyes, he found her nipple, gently brushed his lips across first one, then the other, making her gasp and arch.

How did he do that? The merest touch and her body came alive. She'd gone from drowsily sated to needy and achy in an instant. She nudged him away, not wanting to lost control again. It was time for good-byes, and her head was already cluttered enough with odd feelings and emotions. She needed to clear it out. Say the right things. Find some way to leave this. Leave him.

Then his hand was sliding down her belly, and she was wet and writhing before his fingers found her, stroked her. So sure, so confident that she was ready for him, that she'd open for him. And damn if that didn't turn her on, too.

"Austin—"

"Shh," he whispered against her neck. "Let me. Please."

His quiet entreaty tugged at her. She closed her eyes, pushed her fingers through his hair, held him as he stroked her, built her up slowly, then took her effortlessly over the edge. She was still shuddering from the climax when he shifted his weight over hers, pushed the rigid length of himself, warm and velvety smooth, deep inside her with one slow thrust. They'd never done it like this. Traditional, man on top. After all they'd done to each other, with each other, this should have seemed generic, standard.

Instead, the feel of him, on her, covering her while he took her, was somehow more primal, visceral. He pushed his fingers through her hair as he stroked her. Slowly, thoroughly. He nuzzled his face into her neck. Nothing frantic about this, or hurried. Just slow, deep thrusts, as he dropped soft kisses down the side of her neck.

"Ah, Delilah," he murmured.

Instead of jerking her from the moment, it pulled her more deeply into it. It sounded right for the moment, right coming from him. Her nails dug into his back as she slid her legs up, circled his waist. They both gasped, then groaned together as he slid deeper. "The way you fit me," he whispered, sounding awed. "So perfect."

She realized there were tears building behind her eyes, and it stymied her. The sound of her name, the way he'd said it, the way he filled her. This was no longer hot sex with a stranger.

This was lovemaking . . . with Austin.

Before she could decide how to feel about that, he began to thrust more deeply, more intently, as his body tensed and tightened. She realized, dimly, that he'd never come inside her. And she wanted that. Almost desperately. Why, she couldn't say. It was like some elemental necessity. The thought of possessing him, some small part of him, had her tightening around him, lifting her hips, raking her nails down his back. He groaned and began to push harder, faster.

Their breaths changed to hoarse, rapid pants as their gentle give and take took a turn for the primal. He held her tightly, his lips pressed against her temple as his body gathered up, tensed, rushed ahead. Then, even as he was growling at the beginning of his release, he turned her head, took her mouth in a fierce, almost branding kiss. And when he came inside her, the combination of his claiming every part of her body, so fully, so completely, drove her over the edge as well.

Shuddering, he collapsed on top of her, his weight both unbearably heavy, and perfectly excessive. He shifted almost immediately, but drew her with him, wrapping himself around her, keeping her wrapped around him. His fingers were tangled in her hair, his chest still rising and falling rapidly. Neither said anything as seconds became minutes.

She didn't want to speak, didn't want to say anything that might ruin what had turned out to be a more powerful union than those they'd shared before. It had been more personal this time. More intimate. He'd made love to her. And it was going to make walking away from him that much more difficult.

Her body vibrated with the feel of the train racing over the tracks. Her head was tucked beneath the crook of his chin. He stroked her hair, her back. She knew she had to get up, start putting distance, both physical and emotional, between them. Her emotions were all over the place and she needed to get out of here, get her head clear and back on straight. They led very different lives. Did she want to tangle herself up further with him? Was she up to seeing him whenever he happened to be in town? Could she be so casual about this, about him, for the long term?

The way her heart leaped at the very idea of seeing him again was exactly why she knew she'd be fool to sign on for that kind of see-you-whenever relationship. She didn't need to ride that emotional roller coaster. And neither did her heart.

And yet . . . she couldn't seem to find the strength to pull away from him quite yet. This felt too . . . right.

She swore silently. At best they had a couple of hours more together. *Time to let go of him and embrace reality, Delilah.* But it was damn hard when the fantasy was so much more tangible and real to her at the moment.

"Merry Christmas," he murmured.

Her heart bumped up, and squeezed painfully. She'd forgotten. Completely. But he hadn't. And somehow, that made it all the more sweet. Poignant.

If only she could look at this—at him—as a really great Christmas present. A present that she'd unwrapped and enjoyed thoroughly. Sure beat the hell out of anything she'd ever received before. And yet, even as the intent formed, to say that very thing, with a droll tone, a little laugh, she stumbled. It would have been the perfect way to put this . . . whatever it was . . . back on track, situated where it belonged, squarely in the it's-been-fun, consenting-adults category.

Would have been.

Instead, she couldn't help but think of every Christmas morning looming in the future. She'd long since relegated that day to something more in the way people thought of Memorial Day, or the Fourth of July. A vacation day. Now? That had all changed. Although, when she thought about it, there *had* been plenty of fireworks.

He slid his fingers beneath her chin, tipped her head up so he could see her face. "I can feel you smiling."

She looked into his eyes, warm, drowsy, sated . . . and knew she was doomed. All those carefully honed defense mechanisms she'd ruthlessly developed were useless. She opened her mouth . . . and the truth came tumbling out. "I've never been a Christmas person."

His embrace tightened for a moment. "Actually, neither have I."

She thought about that, about what little he'd revealed about his background, then took a breath, and finished what she'd started to say, "Well, you changed all that."

His smile was immediate, dazzling. "Funny, I was thinking the exact same thing." When she would have ducked her head, taken a moment to absorb the impact of his easy acceptance of what was happening between them, he nudged her chin so she kept looking at him. "I don't want this to end when the train stops, Del."

"I don't, either." There. She'd said it. God help her.

"But?" he asked. "It's in your eyes," he explained.

"This . . . this is fantasy. Illusion. Two people, stranded on a train "

"It started that way."

"Maybe it's fantastic because this is all it needs to be. We start trying to make it something else—"

"It's a risk I'm willing to take. Tarnish all my Christmas mornings to come on the chance that maybe there'll be more Christmas mornings like this one."

She sighed, even as her pulse spiked. And her heart leaped. "I'm heading to New York, and you're heading off around the world. So . . . what, we see each other when you're in town? I don't know that I'm capable of that." *With you*, she added silently. Any other time, this might have been the perfect solution for her. A man who embraced his independence as tightly as she did hers, willing to hook up when it was convenient, but not intrude on the rest of her life.

But she already knew he would be different. Less than a day, and her heart was already engaged. No, she couldn't do this. It would start out wonderful, and then she'd want more . . . hell, she already did. No, crushing disappointment and heartache she did not need. "Maybe it's better to leave it like this, the perfect interlude."

He didn't say anything, just kept his gaze on hers, his fingers tracing lazy patterns up and down her back. "Tell me about New York. About your work, your life."

She sighed, laid her head back on his chest. So he wasn't going to talk about it. She should resent that, manipulation by avoidance. But what difference did it make? It would all resolve itself in the next couple of hours, one way or the other, anyway. "I live in the Village. I rent a small second floor apartment from an older couple. A coworker of mine actually had the place first, then she got married, and I was tired of living with roommates, so I took it on. It's been a good fit. They travel often, don't intrude much. I water their plants, get their mail, and they leave me pretty much alone."

"I can see where that would be ideal."

He traveled constantly, so it wasn't surprising he understood the pleasures and simplification of a solitary life. But it touched her anyway. Dammit. "Do you travel by train often?"

"First time, actually. In the States anyway."

At least he wasn't trying to gloss over the fact that their lifestyles were literally worlds apart. And yet, she couldn't help but want to know more. "How does it compare?"

He laughed. "Well, considering my closest companion on my last trip by rail was a woven coop filled with chickens, I'm thinking this is the better deal."

"You think?" she said dryly. "Of course, if we'd been stuck much longer, you might wish you had the chickens. At least they could be eaten."

He pulled her closer. "I'll let you know if I start to get hungry."

Her heart sighed, even as she nudged him in the ribs. Their easy camaraderie was something she'd miss almost more than the sex. Almost. "You know, I didn't book a sleeper car because it seemed like an unnecessary extravagance. But now I'm rethinking my opinion on that."

He pressed a kiss to the top of her head. "Me, too."

Why did this have to feel so easy, she couldn't help but think. When it was anything but. Why couldn't he be some guy she bumped into in SoHo, a guy who lived around the corner from a deli, spent time traipsing through the same museums she did. Now *that* would at least have given them a fighting chance. No, there was nothing really easy about any of this. "So, when you're not taking the very exotic Eastern Seaboard train, where else does your work take you?"

"I should be in Milan right now. Paris next week."

She sighed wistfully. "I've always wanted to go there. And Spain. Barcelona." She fiddled with the hair on his chest. "Ever been to Barcelona?"

He nodded. "They're both beautiful." He paused for just a second, toyed with her hair. "You should go."

"Yes, I should," she answered quickly. Too quickly. He hadn't made it an invitation . . . but her heart had skipped a beat at the mere idea of it anyway. "Unfortunately Atlanta is about as exotic a locale as I get on my business expense account."

"Atlanta is an interesting city."

"It's not Barcelona."

He smiled. "That's just another city."

"Yeah, to the people of Barcelona."

"Well, think how exotic Atlanta would seem to them."

She shook her head, laughed. "So, what were you shooting in Atlanta?"

"I was actually in the Keys."

She snorted. "Of course. Shooting women in bikinis and getting paid for it. Tough life."

"I'd apologize, but I'd just be lying if I said it was hell."

"Thanks ever so much for sparing me."

He nodded magnanimously and Del rolled her eyes.

"So, what were you shooting in Atlanta?" he asked.

She sighed again, but in disgust this time. "Myself. In the foot."

"What happened?"

"I went down there to salvage a layout we were doing on bachelor pads. You know, the simplistic affordable look in living furnishings for the single male."

"Couches. Hate working with them. Always reclining on the job."

She pretended to jot something down on an imaginary list. "Makes bad puns."

"Still keeping the list, huh? Which column did that go in?"

She just gave him a look.

He grinned. Incorrigible, indeed. "So, the couches didn't show up? What happened?"

"No. The studio shots my colleague had taken were crap. So I was sent down to salvage the job. But when I went into the studio, nothing I tried was working any better. It was all flat, distant. It was contemporary furniture, very clean lines, Dutch influence, but the setup made them look flat, alien. Unapproachable."

"Not what you want when selling furniture."

She shook her head. "So it was my bright idea to move the shoot outdoors."

"But didn't Atlanta just get hammered with that freak winter stor—" At her glare he broke off. "I'm guessing the skies opened up after you'd unloaded the stuff?"

"Pretty much."

"Ouch."

"Oh, yeah. Sleet, ice. Saggy couches, water-stained ottomans. Not exactly the clean, crisp look we were going for."

"Is that why you're taking the train? Delay the inevitable, sneak in over the holidays and pretend no one will notice?"

"Gee, where were you when I was planning my career?"

He shrugged, guileless to the end. And damn if it didn't work on him. "Hard to say."

"Barcelona probably," she deadpanned. "Shooting women with nothing on at all."

"I hate to say it, but that is a strong possibility."

She smacked at his chest, but was smiling as she did it. "Does it get old? Traveling the globe to exotic locales? Living out of a suitcase?"

He grabbed her hand, tugged it up to his mouth. He kissed her fingers, then the palm of her hand. But before she could tug it away, he pressed it back to his chest, over his heart. "Lonely at times. But I like what I do."

He'd sounded off the cuff, but the look in his eyes was saying something else.

He noticed her staring, shifted his gaze to hers. "What?"

She lifted a shoulder. "I don't know. I got the impression you were thinking about something else. Are you anxious to get back to work? Do you miss it?"

He didn't answer right away. "I love taking pictures. Love what I can capture if I just look at something the right way. But this trip home to see my brothers, well it's bringing back an avalanche of memories."

"About?"

"A lot of things, but I've been reminiscing a little about when I started to get into photography, why it's always been a dream of mine." He lifted a shoulder. "I wonder if somewhere I stopped pushing it, stopped dreaming, settled, in a way. I know my way around a shoot, I always give it my best, but I've done so many . . . Maybe I rely on what I know, instead of seeking out what I don't." He let out a short laugh. "Yes," he said, "short answer is, I miss it. I want to get back. See what else there is to see. But now maybe, hopefully, I'll see some things I never saw before." He tilted her chin up. "Meeting you . . . finding this . . . it makes me think. About possibilities."

Del's throat tightened. She was thinking about them, too. Or, more aptly, impossibilities. She'd crafted a stable career she was good at, that provided well for her. She'd made a home for herself, a secure one, in New York City. Security, stability. Key foundations for her. "Yeah," she managed, not sure she wanted to know where he was heading with this. Then her stomach chose that moment to growl. Loudly.

Mercifully, it broke the tension that had been rapidly filling the air between them.

"Why don't I go round us up something to eat," he said, kissing her forehead, then her lips, before disentangling himself from her.

"I, uh, I could use a trip to the lavatory," she responded, letting out a silent whoosh of relief.

He was already off the bunk and pulling on his pants. He dug around in his duffel for clean clothes. "Do you need to borrow anything?"

She sat up, watched him move about the small space below. Her heart squeezed. "No. Thanks. I'm going to head back to my seat and grab my bag. I've got stuff in there."

He tugged on his shirt, then reached to help her down from the bunk. He turned her into his arms. "You want more than coffee? Eggs or a bagel or something?"

She shook her head, just looked into his face. Memorizing each feature, capturing them with the lens of her mind's eye. "Just coffee." Her stomach was a knot, and she felt the stirrings of a headache coming on. Probably a result of her brain cramping from analysis overload.

His expression grew serious. "Del, I—" He broke off, shook his head just a little, then took her mouth in a kiss so fierce, so sudden, it took her breath away.

And when he broke free and left the room without saying another word, he took a piece of her heart with him.

She pulled her clothes on, thinking how foreign her body felt in them. They'd been so comfortable without them. He'd made her feel . . . worshipped. Tended to.

"Fantasy," she muttered, wishing like hell she still believed that. It would make what she was about to do a hell of a lot easier.

She unearthed her camera, then looked around for something to leave him a note with. She picked up his camera instead. Turning it on, she spied the small speaker on the side, then fiddled with the buttons until she figured out how to toggle the movie mode on.

She took a moment, blew out a deep breath, aimed the screen at the pillows where their heads laid, and hit Record.

Then she began telling Austin good-bye.

Chapter Ten

Austin knew the moment he stepped back into his private car, even before he saw his camera propped on his pillow, that she was gone. As in not coming back.

He was torn between panic and anger. The former made him want to canvass every single car on this train until he found her. But the train had made a stop while he was picking up breakfast. He suspected Del had debarked early. The anger took over then. Although he wasn't sure who he was angrier with. Her for not having the balls to say good-bye. Or himself, for pushing her. Or maybe not pushing her enough. Hell, he didn't know what to feel. Except lost.

He shoved the drink carrier and the paper bag with their food onto the unused berth, then reached for his camera. When he flicked on the screen, he was further disappointed to discover she hadn't left him with an image of herself . . . but of their empty bed.

Then her voice drifted from the tiny speaker . . . and he realized she'd said her good-byes after all.

He sank onto the bench seat and tried to slow his heartbeat down enough to hear her words.

"You're probably pissed off at the moment. I would be. But . . . this . . ." There was a break, and he could hear her draw in a breath. "We shared something . . . indescribable. Such a short time, and yet I feel altered in some way. Permanently. I—I didn't want to leave you. Not in my heart. But, my heart, well, I've been safeguarding it for a very long time, and I guess I'm having a little bit of a hard time dealing with the shock you've delivered it. So effortlessly, too. I don't know what to do with that." There was another pause, then, "We've obviously connected in a way that is hard to explain, or at least I can't. We're both independent, both the captains of our own destinies. That's probably part of it. But those destinies have played out very differently. I need to operate from a secure base. You need to be able to move at will." A little sigh, then, "I don't know how long this thing records, so I hope you hear this. It's so trite, so cliché . . . and yet I've never meant anything more. I'll never forget you, Austin Morgan. You taught me to step a little closer to the edge of that secure base. Reach out a little, take a chance. I—it was a good lesson. One I'm going try to learn from. But I can't—I'm sorry—I can't take any bigger of a leap. I hope—" She broke off, then he heard her swear, rather fluently, which made him smile despite the fact that he felt like his heart had just been ripped out and handed to him on a platter. But it was the unshed tears he heard in her voice when she ended by saying, "Good-bye, Austin," that haunted him.

For the rest of the train ride. All the way back to Rogues Hollow. Through the reunion with his brothers. Through the reading of his father's will. She haunted him.

He supposed he should thank her. He'd been so preoccupied, thinking about what he could have done, what he should have done, how he could have convinced her to stick around and at least give them a chance to figure things out . . . that the homecoming he'd been dreading passed by in sort of a distracted haze.

It didn't help that his younger brother Jace had crossed paths with his childhood sweetheart Suzanna York, that the two of them had just spent a tumultuous, snowbound weekend reuniting. Or that, from the look of things, they might stay united . . . for life. He was thrilled for them both, but seeing them together, so obviously besotted, made his heart squeeze in a way that at any other time in his life would have surprised him. Or terrified him. Instead it made him hunger. Made him ache.

So, by the time his older brother Tag took him aside to ask him what in the hell was up, he was more than ready to pour it all out.

"I don't know what to do," Austin finished, having given Tag the basics, leaving out any specifics. What had happened between him and Del would stay between him and Del. He dropped his head to his hands, raked them through hair that was likely standing on end by now.

They were sitting in what had been his father's study. It was a place that held memories he could go his whole life not thinking about. This was where the lectures were delivered. And the whippings. This was where, when his father discovered that his second son's dream was to become a wildlife photographer, that Austin's endless hours spent cutting grass had been to support the rolls of film he went through every month, he'd been very deliberately told he'd never measure up. That, in his father's eyes, he was a failure. That he was not only letting Taggart Morgan Sr. down, but every Morgan before him. And probably every Ramsay and Sinclair along with them.

Of course, as he got older, he understood that anything shy of actually becoming his father was going to make him a failure as a man, a human being, and a Morgan. Not that their father would list them in quite that order.

Taggart Morgan Sr. had thought his sons were daydreamers, wastrels of the worst sort, because they refused to follow in his footsteps. Taggart Sr., the first reputable Morgan. In his eyes, anyway. First Morgan to go to college. First to become a lawyer. First to become a judge. A respected citizen by all who lived and breathed.

Well, Austin had always thought of himself and his brothers as simply carrying on the Rogue tradition. The original Ramsay, Sinclair and Morgan, Scots highwaymen who had left a life of crime in their homeland, followed their dreams to the colonies, and began anew. Building a life that had eventually become a legacy spanning, so far, hundreds of years.

A legacy he'd run from and happily never looked back on. He'd always thought his great-great however-many-great grandfather Teague Morgan would have been proud of him for chasing his dream.

When Austin heard his father had died, he'd spent some time wondering if he shouldn't have come back sooner, tried to at least begin some kind of dialogue. That maybe as grown men they could have found some way to communicate, to learn who the other really was. Sitting here now, in his father's library, staring at the imposing desk and the rows and rows of leather-bound legal texts that lined the walls . . . he knew he never would have. And he couldn't find it in his heart to regret it.

210 / Donna Kauffman

"So," he said, blowing out a breath. "That's what I did on my Christmas vacation. Fell head over heels for the first time in my life . . . and got dumped for the effort."

Tag was leaning against one of the bookshelves, arms folded. "Sounds like a lot of that going around. Except Jace managed to figure out that last part better than you. Makes me glad I drove in. Alone."

Austin leaned back, braced his hands behind his head. "Yeah, yeah. Easy for you to be smug. You won't be when it happens to you."

Tag snorted. "Never gonna happen."

"Uh-huh. That's what I said."

Tag pushed away from the shelves. "So, what are you going to do about it?"

"What can I do?"

Tag just rolled his eyes. "You've built a career out of nothing more than a roll of film and the cheesy Kodak you and Burke earned cutting the Sinclair's back forty. And yet you can't manage to figure out how to hold on to the only other thing that has captured your full attention since?"

"She said good-bye. Or did you conveniently not hear that part?"

"Oh, I heard it. I also heard that she didn't want to say good-bye. So, because it's not easy and smooth you're going to agree with her that walking away is the best option?"

Austin shrugged. He felt miserable. He rarely felt miserable. Of course, it didn't take a degree in psychology to figure out that was because he'd long since made a practice out of not feeling much of anything. "You know," he said quietly. "I never realized how cut off I've become. I give everything to capturing a moment on film. But I don't exist *in* any of those moments." He stared at his hands. "Then I opened the caboose door, and— bam!—there she was. I even tried to keep her framed in my mind. A shot to be taken, something to observe, study. But she wouldn't let me retreat like that. And the thing was, I didn't want to. And more than that, she's a lot like me in that respect . . . and yet she didn't retreat, either." He didn't have to add "until it was too late."

"So you're both charting new territory. No hard and fast rules in new territory. She wants to cling to what's safe. So do you. But you'll never know if there's a compromise unless you try."

Austin lifted his gaze to his brother's. "And if she turns me down again?"

Tag's crooked smile emerged. "You sell yourself way too short."

Austin sighed, shoved to a stand. "Yeah, well, that's easy for you to say, Mr. I Spend My Life in the Jungle. You just wait, some woman is going to come along and want to play Jane to your Tarzan and then we'll see who's giving advice to whom."

Tag just laughed. "Uh-huh." He reached out and snagged Austin's arm, pulled him into a back-slapping hug. "You and Jace go find your happily ever after and leave my and Burke's enduring male bachelor fantasies alone, okay?"

"I hear you." Then he shot Tag a look and a smile. "But man, you have no idea how much better that fantasy can be."

"Well, since you won't share the actual details of hot train sex, then could you just please get the hell out of here and go find her already?"

"Yeah. Maybe I will." He stood there for a moment, let the decision settle inside him a little, feel it out. It felt . . . right. "I will." He looked at his brother. "Thanks. For listening, for kicking my ass when I need it."

Tag grinned. "Always a pleasure."

"Just keep a bottle or two of something strong on hand in case said ass gets royally kicked all the way out of New York City, okay?" Austin was halfway out the door when he stopped, turned back. "Hey," he said, serious now. "I've been so wrapped up in my own shit I haven't asked you about . . . you know. Any decisions? You want to talk about it?"

For all that Taggart Sr. had been an equal opportunity son of a bitch, he'd reserved a special place in hell for his eldest and namesake. So it had come as a shock to them all, when the will was read, to discover that their father had left the entirety of the Morgan's share of Rogues Hollow to Tag. And nothing to the rest of them.

The last part had been more of a relief than an insult to Austin.

But that didn't negate his concern, or Jace's or Burke's, for their big brother. They'd tried to talk to him about it then, but he'd stormed out of the lawyer's office and hadn't shown up on the property for two days. When he had come back, it had just been sort of understood that they'd let him bring it up. He hadn't.

Tag just shook his head. "No. I'm—I'll handle it."

Austin struggled to find the right words. "We'll all help, you know. In whatever way we can. If there's a tax burden or—"

Tag lifted his hand, but said nothing else.

Austin fell silent, then said, "Since Jace is moving back permanently, maybe you two can work something out. Burke and I were going to talk to him, but we haven't seen much of him."

Tag's lips quirked. "Understandable. Zanna turned out pretty damn fine."

Austin smiled a little. "Damn, if she didn't." He fought to keep the tone light. "I just want you to know we're all here for you. I know we've all spent our lives off doing our own thing, but don't think that just because of Dad that we don't respect family. We—"

Tag lifted his hand again, only this time he closed the distance and pulled Austin into another hug, this one tight, emotional. "I know. Thanks," he finally said, his voice rough. "But this is something between me and Dad. I want—no, I need to work this out on my own."

"Yeah," Austin said, his own voice a bit raspy. "Okay. Just—well, anything you decide is going to be okay with us. Know that, too."

"I do." He shoved Austin out the door, finding a smile. "Now do us all a favor and go get this woman and make her understand she'll never do better than a Morgan." He winked. "And if she needs an endorsement—"

Austin laughed. "Right. No thanks. You stole every girlfriend I ever had. This one is all mine."

Tag leaned in the doorway as Austin took the stairs two at a time, intent on packing and booking the next flight to New York.

"I hope she appreciates it," Tag murmured. "She's got herself one of the best."

Chapter Eleven

"Oh good, you're still here."

Del sat hunched over a specially lit bench table, her eye pressed to the magnifier. She didn't look up. "God help me, Enrique, yes I am." The pictures on the proof sheet were all crap. Row after row of crap. How hard was it to take pictures of sandals, for God's sake? Apparently it was beyond her meager talent. Three weeks. It had been three weeks, dammit, and she still hadn't gotten her head back together. Or her heart.

"Someone left a package for you."

"Great. More shitty proofs I don't need to see."

"I don't know what is it. I was asked to bring it to you. You want me to put it on your desk?"

She sighed, looked up at the night maintenance man. "Yeah, sure. And thanks, Rique. You shouldn't have to play delivery man after hours. I don't know why they can't leave after-hour deliveries at the lobby desk like they're supposed to."

The older Spaniard lifted a shoulder in a simple shrug, but his eyes twinkled. "Some are just more persistent than others in getting their way. And I didn't mind. Got me away from a faulty sink in the men's room on seven."

Del gave him a tired smile, and took the flat, rectangular package from his outstretched hands. It was surprisingly heavy for a relatively small package. Definitely not contact sheets.

"Don't work too late," Enrique admonished her, as he often did.

And as she often did, she nodded absently and waved. But instead of turning back to the proof sheets and the layout design she had to deliver in the morning, she stared at the package in her hands. There was no label. No postmark. "Hand delivered?" She glanced at the clock on the wall. "At nine at night? I bet that cost a fortune." The box was long, flat, and wrapped in brown paper.

And she hadn't the faintest clue what it was. One way to find out, though.

She tore at the paper, only to reveal a flat, white corrugated box. She let the paper fall away, and turned it over. Nothing printed on it, front or back.

"'Curiouser and curiouser, Alice,'" she murmured. She opened the flap and pulled back the tissue paper. A thick white envelope lay on top of a picture frame, but when she lifted it, saw what was in the frame beneath, the envelope fell from her hands. Her mouth fell open on a gasp. And her heart teetered and fell right after it. "Oh. Austin. Oh."

In a thick black frame, matted exquisitely beneath textured white board, were four photographs, positioned vertically, all shot in subtly lit black and white. Below each picture, in carefully scripted black ink, was one sentence.

The first photo was a close-up of a pair of eyes. Nothing else. But she knew they were her own. The desire so naked in them clutched at something deep inside her. Below the picture, it said: *I want to look into these a hundred times a day.* Her throat tightened as she dragged her attention to the next one. It was her hand, tucked flat between her legs, as one thigh rubbed in front of the other. The line below it read: *I want to run my tongue here.* She shuddered, and felt those very same muscles twitch in remembered pleasure. The next shot was of her fist, gripping so tightly there was no color in her knuckles. Below it: *I want to make you hold on to me this tight.* Tears had gathered in her eyes by the time she got to the last picture. It was taken from the caboose. Gray skies and snow-filled tracks. Desolate. Lonely. Beneath it was: *I don't want to let you go.*

She pressed a trembling fist to her mouth as she stared at each picture again. Tears tracked down her cheeks unbidden. She could marvel over his technique, the lighting, especially given the circumstances under which they'd been taken. But her professional eye was not the part of her that was engaged here.

And her heart didn't care about technique. It was too caught up in the man who had taken the pictures.

It was only when she pulled her gaze away long enough to look for a tissue, that she remembered the envelope. Carefully setting the frame aside, she grabbed a tissue first, blew her nose, dabbed at the tear tracks on her cheeks. She picked up the thick envelope. Dying to know what else he'd sent . . . and terrified all at the same time. She fingered the edges, but didn't open it right away.

"Jesus, Del," she said, angry at her own ambivalence. He was putting it all on the line. She admired him greatly for that, given she hadn't been able to summon up the courage to do the same. Heart pounding, she opened it and slid out a folded note and a slim white packet. With her heart in her throat, she opened the note first.

It took me two weeks to finally decide I couldn't let things end as they did. It only took me a day to find you. But another week has passed while I tried to figure out the best way to contact you. You were right. I was angry. You want to cling to the fantasy. It was a pretty damn fantastic one, so I guess I can't blame you for that. And yet, lingering memories, powerful images, crowd my brain, making it difficult to think straight. Much less to work. Or do much more than sit, and think about you. What you're doing. Where you're going. Who you're seeing. And how much I'd like the opportunity to be doing with you, going with you.

Seeing you.

It's been almost a month. Surely long enough to get over something that happened in a day. Only I find I'm not. I can't. Every minute with you felt like a year, and at the same time, passed in a blink. It felt like I'd made love to you for eons . . . and yet I'd only begun to explore you. I know you, and yet I don't.

But I want to.

You spoke of a secure base. Of risk. I think we all cling to what makes us feel safe. For me, it's independence, calling my own shots. I think in that way, we're very much alike. Somehow, though, all this independence I had to have, hasn't seemed so damn important since you walked away from me. So . . . I'm willing to take that leap, off my base. Risk that, in the cold light of day, we remain strangers. Two people who happened to spend a moment out of time in spectacular,

earth-shattering fashion, but have nothing more to say to one another. I'm willing to risk that it was illusion . . . for the chance that it might be reality.
  It's been three weeks. It's been forever.
  A new year has begun. I'd like to begin something else. With you.

Del wasn't sure when she'd begun to cry again. She dabbed at her eyes with her sleeve, then looked away, and blinked back fresh tears. She felt blindsided . . . and yet, there was no denying the absolute relief that had filled her. He didn't want to let her go. And wasn't page after page of crappy shots, weeks of crappy work, proof enough that just maybe she wasn't ready to let him go either?

She blew out a long breath, pressed a fist below her heart to quell the jumpiness in her stomach.

Because it had been three weeks. And it had been forever for her, too.

A tear tracked down her cheek as she unfolded the large piece of paper that had been tucked in with the note. Inside the first fold, he'd written:

  I'm in town for the next five days. I want to know your world, through your eyes. I've spent too long being an observer of life. I want to step into your picture.

She unfolded the rest of the note, gasping when a plane ticket fell into her hands. On it was another note that read:

  Then, if you feel the same way, I want you to step into mine. Whatever happens after that . . . happens.

She turned the ticket over and saw it was to Milan, Italy.

She stared at it, her first instinct was to run to him, wanting what he offered so fiercely it scared her. What about that secure base? All that bullshit about stability? About a home? She had three projects in the works and four meetings lined up in the next three days with prospective new clients. And after that, there would be more meetings. More clients. More projects.

And none of those things offered her the one thing she truly wanted.

Austin.

And suddenly everything she'd based her life on began to tilt and waver. Her solid base felt like it was crumbling away around her. But instead of being terrified by it, she was . . . exhilarated. Excited. Curious.

Stability, security, reliability were great, but what good were they if they kept her from living? She looked at the ticket. The offer of the trip dazzled . . . certainly. It reached down deep inside and tugged at something she'd denied she wanted, or simply hadn't had the courage to do anything about . . . the temptation to wander. To be a little aimless, to drift . . . to take the risk of letting the chips fall where they may. Even if they all fell on her head.

And yet, more surprising was the realization that showing him her New York was just as dazzling to her. He understood it was special to her, precious. And always would be. That she guarded her feelings about it, protected what she'd built here, the safe, secure haven she'd erected for herself when she needed it most. And yet he'd asked for a glimpse of it, to be part of it, even for a little while. That took guts.

Just the thought of sharing her world with him energized her in a way she couldn't remember ever feeling . . . except perhaps for that brief time stranded on a train in the snow. The sights, the sounds, the scents of her city, experienced like a first time, because it would be with him. He was a connoisseur of the senses. It would be a smorgasbord; sensory overload.

She wanted it. Wanted that. With him.

She looked at the ticket. Italy. She knew what it meant to him. The serenity and peace he'd found there. And yet he wanted to share it with her, bring her into his haven, risk the ripples on the pond that she might create in that world, so far away from the chaos that apparently had been his childhood as well.

Risks. So far he'd taken all of them.

Hand trembling, this time with anticipation . . . she set the letter, the tickets, beside the frame. It was her turn, to reach for what she wanted . . . and damn, for once, the consequences. To give up the sure thing, for a chance to see what might turn out to be the very best thing that ever happened to her.

Except . . . Her shoulders drooped. She had no idea where to find him. How to contact him. Was she supposed to do what he'd done? Do whatever it took to track him down?

Okay, then, she could do that. Prove she wanted this. He deserved that. She thought for a second, who she could call who would likely have any clue who he was working for, or where. He said he was in town. Surely she knew someone who knew someone who knew something.

She spied the clock and swore. But none of those someones were likely to be at their desk at this hour. "Dammit, dammit."

Crappy sandal photos and morning meetings completely forgotten, she shoved off her stool and paced to the door, then back to the window. She stared out at the twinkling lights of the city and sighed. "Where are you, Austin Morgan?"

"He's right here."

She jumped, hand plastered to her chest. Then swung around to find Enrique pushing at Austin, who was standing just outside her doorway.

"I tell him it's okay to come up, but he's no wanting to barge in," Enrique said, eyes twinkling, gold caps gleaming. "I tell him he must. He didn't come all this way to wander around down in the lobby." He gave Austin one last shove, sending him fully into the room. "Now, you two talk about things. Make her smile," he instructed Austin. "She no smile anymore." He ducked out before Del could respond.

Not that she would have. She was hardly listening to Enrique. Her eyes and head and heart were too busy soaking up the reality that had just walked through her door. "Hi."

He stopped beside her workbench. "Hi." He glanced down, saw the picture frame, his letters and the ticket on the surface. He looked back to her, and though he said nothing, it was clear he wanted to know, needed to know, her reaction to his offer.

Her chest was so tight, her heart thundering so loud, she didn't know if she could form actual speech. *Don't blow this, don't blow this,* were the words running through her mind. "It's amazing, Austin." *You're amazing.* "I'm . . . I'm stunned by it."

"I was going to give you time. To think about it, decide. But I couldn't seem to make myself leave the building."

Her lips curved just a little when he shifted his weight from one foot to another. Her confident, worldly, courageous lover was nervous. Thank God she wasn't the only one.

"I know you wanted to leave things as they were. I tried to go along with that, but . . ." He trailed off. "Well, if you read my notes, then you know how I feel."

"I read them." Every word was emblazoned across her heart. "You're a lot braver than me." She took a breath. "I owe you an apology. I should have stayed, talked to you, explained why I had to go. But I was afraid."

"What did you think I was going to do?"

She held his gaze. "Convince me to stay."

He took an involuntary step forward, and she could see the heat flare in his eyes. He stopped himself, but the heat didn't fade. "Would that really have been so bad?"

She wrapped her arms around herself. Mostly to keep from running across the room and wrapping them around him. "Yes. And no. I—you said in your note that you spent your time observing life, that I made you want to step into the picture and live it. Well, that's what scares me about you. I guess I figured if I ever got serious about someone, it would be here, in the city. It's terrifying enough to tie your heartstrings to someone else's, to allow yourself to be that vulnerable. I—I've never even been tempted to do that." She took a breath, made herself finish. "Until you." She raised a shaky hand when he stepped closer. "That would have been a big enough leap for me, but the fact is, you lead a very different life than I do. I—" She stopped, lifted her shoulders, let them fall. "I figured it was better to quit while I was ahead."

He held her gaze, had held nothing but since he'd walked in the room. The intensity came off him in waves. "And now?"

"The truth is, I haven't been able to think of anything but you. Of what we began, of what I was too afraid to finish. I kept telling myself I did the right thing, that it was more important not to shake up what I'd spent so long building. That, in time, I'd be able to put those memories in their proper perspective." Her lips quirked just a little. "And maybe by then I could develop the damn roll of film I took with your picture on it."

His lips quirked, too. "You might have been smart not to. I can't tell you how many hours I've spent looking at yours." He didn't move closer, but the room felt somehow smaller when he said, "They made me ache, Del. Remember I told you I'd let you know when I was hungry? I've never stopped hungering for you. It's like this hollow nagging void that just doesn't subside. I finally told myself—actually, it was my older brother Tag who kicked me in the butt—"

"You told your . . . family? About . . . us?" Color crept into her cheeks.

Amusement colored his expression. "Not *all* about us. But it became pretty noticeable that I was, well, preoccupied. Of course, my baby brother Jace came home with his high school sweetheart draped all over him, which didn't help my frame of mind any. I guess you could say I was mooning. Tag finally told me to do something about it or I'd regret it forever. And he was right."

Del stood there, overwhelmed by his simple honesty, and by the strength she knew it had taken to literally lay his heart at her feet. "I'm not as brave as you. But you make me want to be. You make me question everything I thought I had to have to be happy, to be fulfilled. I thought security meant being rooted firmly into one spot, with definite ties that could never be severed, by anyone but me." She began to walk toward him. "I guess I lost sight of that last part. That the security, the stability, is in having the choice at all. What I do with those choices is also up to me. Somewhere, somehow, I started to confuse sameness with stability. I have a job that I'm good at, but isn't what I really dreamed of doing, and yet I settled for it because it meant a steady paycheck, security. I have a home that's not really mine, but that I can keep as long as the rent check is on time. And because I have a roof over my head, and clothes on my back, all provided by me, I'm safe.

"The rest, love, family, happiness . . . I can't make those things happen." She stepped closer. "So I left that to fate, and controlled the things I could." She stopped just in front of him. "And then I met you. And I couldn't control anything. Not how you made me feel, not the things you made me question. Not the hunger you started inside of me for more. More." Her throat closed over. "You make me want more. When I've always been satisfied to take what I know I can get, what I know I can keep. You make me want more. And frankly, that scares the living hell out of me."

He reached for her as the first tear welled up and spilled down her cheek.

"I don't want to cry, dammit. I want—I want to explain, I want you to understand—"

He tugged her into his arms. "I understand," he said, his own voice hardly a rasp. "Just tell me you'll find your more with me. That you'll try. That you'll reach out and take what you want, and trust that we'll do our best to get it. The rest will get figured out the only way life can . . . one day at a time."

She looked up at him, eyes blurred. But it occurred to her that she'd never seen anything so clearly as what was standing right in front of her face. She nodded. "Okay, then. I want you, Austin Morgan." She sniffled even as she laughed and wrapped her arms around his neck. "I sure as hell hope you know what you're getting us into."

A grin split wide across his face as he wrapped her up in his arms. "I haven't a clue. I only know I can't wait to find out."

He then took her in a breath-stealing kiss, which she sunk into willingly, eagerly. His hands moved down her back, cupped her against him, and suddenly Del wasn't worried about her future or his, beyond the right here, the right now. Maybe that was the way to handle this. Live in the moment. Enjoy what she had, and not worry about what she might lose.

"Just how late do you have to stay at work tonight?" he asked, taking her earlobe between his teeth.

"Definitely all done working," she said on a gasp.

"Does this door lock?"

She was already reaching behind him, clearing off her other workbench. "Mmm-hmm."

He back-walked them to the door instead, flipped the lock. "You know, we really have to figure out how to do this more conventionally."

She spun him around and pinned him to the wall. "We do?"

His eyes went dark. "You know, I'm thinking you way under-estimate yourself in the bravery department."

"That's bravado. Totally different thing." She yanked his shirt from his pants.

"Ah. Well, then, whatever this is, I'm liking it."

"This is me, throwing twenty-eight years of caution to the wind." She tugged his zipper down. "This is me, taking what I want and damn the torpedoes." She pushed his pants down over his hips. "May God save my immortal soul, but—" She looked up into his eyes, eyes she wanted to look into a hundred times a day. "This is me, Delilah Hudson, falling in love." And she allowed her heart to open wide, and the grin that split her own face matched it. "So, watch out, things could get messy."

"I should only be so lucky," he said, turning the tables, and her, so it was her back against the wall. "You know, for the first time I have no idea how to frame the shot." He tugged open each button on her shirt. Then slowly, tortuously, pushed her pants down over her hips.

She was already lifting her legs up around his hips even as he was sliding her up the wall, and down onto him. With a deep groan, he eased all the way inside her. "And goddamn but I can't wait to see what develops."

"You know," she said on a gasp, "I think I like making you swear."

He grinned, and thrust deeper. "Well then, we're going to get along just fine."

And much to their mutual delight, they did.

PURE GINGER

E.C. Sheedy

Chapter One

Precariously high heels, hip-rider miniskirt, white satin tube top—more Band-Aid than cover-up—and humongous gold hoops in one set of her three pierces per ear.

Hmm . . .

Lipstick, red enough, bold enough, slick enough, to make the cover of *Hustler* magazine.

Ginger twisted, assessed, then smacked her backside. The skirt fit like sausage casing.

Perfect.

She tossed her long honey-red hair in the manner of a high-blooded mare and roughly pinned up one side, left the other to fall on her bare shoulder. Straightening enough for her top to lift and display the diamond glittering in her navel, she was battle ready.

Almost.

She scanned the mishmash of jars, bottles, and brushes littering her bathroom counter and chose a scent that smelled suspiciously like sex in a bottle. She drenched herself in it.

Done.

She grabbed a sweater, her outsized black tote, and headed for the door full stride.

She knew exactly where to find him.

Hand on the knob, she paused, closed her mocha-shadowed eyelids. Too hot, too hyped, she took a calming breath. If she didn't get control, and keep it, tonight would be no fun at all. She'd ruin everything. Foreplay—lingering, edgy anticipation—that's what this was about.

He'd taught her all about that. Oh, yes . . .

One private and wicked grin, and she flounced out the door.

Tonight it was her turn to play teacher, and she intended to enjoy the class.

She couldn't wait.

* * *

Ginger knew he—along with every other man in the room—had spotted her the second she stepped into the exclusive restaurant. An audience. Just what she wanted. To hold it, she placed a hand on her hip, swept the room with a bold smile. Finally, she settled her gaze on the darkly handsome man seated at the best table in the room.

And his date.

Perfect.

He looked up and their gazes locked. She was too far away to see if he so much as blanched—*the bastard!*—but she was pretty sure his hand shook the tiniest bit when he lifted his wineglass to his mouth.

Red wine. Excellent!

Resisting the urge to paw the ground à la a charging bull, she handed her sweater to the maître d' as if it were ermine, and sashayed across the room.

She heard a whistle from a nearby table, ignored it. Ginger had learned to tune out whistles at the age of thirteen, if she hadn't she'd be deaf as stone.

She stopped at his table.

"Hey, Tony," she said, trying her best to purr like a month-old tiger. "Fancy meeting you here."

"Hey, baby." He tossed his napkin on the table, leaned back in his chair, and gave her a smoldering once over. The man was cool as winter glass—and handsome as midnight sin. *Damn!* Her stomach lurched. Lust or rage, she wasn't sure, but she'd bet on rage.

"Going to introduce us?" She slanted a look toward his blond, beautiful, and obviously bewildered dinner companion.

He gave her the white-hot smile that had attracted her to him in the first place. The man might be a bastard, but he had great teeth. "Ginger, honey, do you really think that would be smart?"

"Probably not." She picked up his wineglass, took a sip. "But then *smart* isn't exactly what I've been these last few months. I was too preoccupied with this—" She lifted the wineglass, smiled, and poured it on his crotch.

"Jes—Ginger!"

She dumped his girlfriend's fettuccini Alfredo over his head.

"But I got smart real fast when I found out about the wife and two kids you've got tucked away across the Canadian border."

He jumped to his feet, sputtered, and wiped impotently at the creamy mess on his face with his napkin. The blonde marbelized where she sat. "You dumb—" he started.

"—bitch?" Ginger finished sweetly. She picked a strand of fettuccini off his chin, while making sure her voice carried throughout the posh restaurant. "Better a bitch, lover boy, than a scum-encrusted bottom-feeding cheat like you."

She strode off, turned back once to give him and the rest of the room a saccharine smile. "Oh, and did I tell you we're through?"

"At Darios! You didn't!" Tracy stared at Ginger, wide-eyed.

"I did. And it felt good, woman—*real* good." Ginger leaned her head back on the sofa, closed her eyes, and hit the replay button. Warm all over, that's how she felt.

She'd wasted six months of her life on Tony Flora—until his wife called and filled her in on his amorous adventures, Ginger being but one in a string. She felt like dirt about the unhappiness she'd caused the soon-to-be ex Mrs. Flora and her kids. Ginger had made her share of mistakes—but until now, being suckered by a married man hadn't been among them.

"Man, would I have loved to have been there." Tracy took a sip of her coffee. "Pure Ginger, live and uncensored."

Ginger's smug smile slipped a bit. "Yeah, pure Ginger," she echoed and tried to quell the uneasy feeling the description was apt, but not complimentary.

Tracy tilted her head. "You're not having second thoughts are you? The guy was a worm."

"That's the problem, Trace. He was a worm, and I fell for him. Doesn't say much for my judgment."

"We all make mistakes."

"True. I just happen to make a few million more than the rest of my sex." She got up from the sofa, tugged down her miniskirt, glumly confused. "What am I, anyway? Some shallow, incomplete woman, doomed to fall for losers and brainless hunks. Some kind of idiot girl?"

Tracy tugged at a strand of hair, ominously silent.

Ginger shot her a look. "You're not disagreeing with me."

"You're no idiot, and you know it, but . . ."

Ginger frowned at her friend and housemate. *"But?"*

"You are a bit impulsive now and again. You know. A fool rushing in where angels fear to tread and all that."

"You think I'm a fool."

"No, that's not what I'm trying to say." She set her mug on the coffee table. "You're just . . . rash sometimes, or maybe too fearless. I don't know. It's like your heart's the hare and your head's the tortoise." She wrinkled her nose as if her bad analogy had caused a blockage. "Oh, you know what I mean."

"Yes, I do, and I hate it, hate it!" Bad analogy or not, Trace was dead on. Ginger paced. Paced some more. "And I'm getting sick and tired of being a cart-before-the-horse type of person. I'm twenty-eight. I should know better."

"A 'cart-before-the-horse type of person'?" Tracy asked, clearly not getting it.

"Falling in love before falling in like."

"Lust is more like it. You see a good-looking guy, a good-looking guy sees you—TNT in spandex—and you're off to the races."

"We use one more cliché in this conversation, and I'll have to turn in my advertising badge." She frowned.

Tracy giggled.

"But you're right. And it's got to stop. No more races. No more guys. What I need to do is . . . virginalize."

"Excuse me?"

"Clean up my act. Change my look. And give up sex." She didn't like the idea of the last bit, but she was desperate.

"Give me a break." Tracy actually snorted.

"You don't think I can do it." Ginger stuck out her jaw.

"I think you'll dry up trying." Tracy's grin was wicked. "You like sex. A lot. And you're telling me you can say 'no thanks' to some blazing hot guy with the appropriate gear, dutifully erect behind tight denim." Tracy wiggled her brows. "I don't think so."

"You make me sound like a sex addict." Now Ginger was seriously perturbed. Maybe she was. No! "I haven't yet worked my way through a baseball team."

"Not even close, but you do fall off the chastity wagon from time to time. And you do date a lot. Hell, the phone never stops ringing around here."

"Date a lot, think too little." Ginger shook her head, and the clip holding up her torrent of hair fell out. "Okay, maybe I purposely overdid the getup for tonight's occasion, but the truth is I've been trying too hard. Wearing stuff like this," she plucked at her form-fitting top. "And these." She kicked at one of her abandoned stilettos. It lodged under the sofa. "I look like one of those bimbos on a service station calndar."

"You're a little, uh, flashy, but that's just you, Ginger. It's who you are."

Flashy? "That's it!" Ginger stared at her friend, enlightenment filling what, until now, had been her dangerously empty skull. "False advertising, that's my problem. The package I've been presenting is designed for nabbing the bad boy—completely misleading."

"Misleading?"

"Add to that my knack for falling for handsome faces with Chiclet-perfect smiles, and I come up a loser every time."

"So you like good-lookin' guys. That's a crime?"

"If I ever hope to find a nice quiet accountant or plumber, it is."

"So now you're after an ugly plumber?"

"Absolutely. Safe, sane, and serious as a preacher." Ginger was fired up. She should have seen this before. She knew exactly what she had to do. "I've got to retool and repackage."

Tracy gave her a pained look. "Don't start, Ginge . . ."

Ginger ignored her, circled the sofa, and tapped on her chin. "First step. Avoid temptation. Second step. Re-virginalize."

Tracy's gaze shot to hers, alarmed. "God, you're not talking surgery here, are you?"

"Of course not." She blinked. "Can they do that?"

"Ginger!"

"Okay, okay. No, I'm not talking surgery, I'm talking attitude. I need a makeover. I need to look like the serious no-nonsense person I intend to be."

"Oh, no, not the clothes thing," Tracy beseeched. "I can't take another of your closet crusades."

"This is not 'another' anything. I'm serious, Trace. I need to change the way I look and how I think. And that takes time, so I'm going to dress down—way down—and get out of the date race." She took a deep, deep breath. "And I'm staying celibate until I smarten up and can see past the six-pack abs, pearly whites, and sleep-with-me smiles to the real thing."

"Which is?"

"A good guy, a true-blue guy: hardworking, honest, stable as a Plains' farmer. A guy with callused hands and a soft heart who wants to mate forever like . . . like a Canada goose."

"A Canada goose?"

"Exactly."

Tracy sighed and rubbed at her temple. "Is there any wine left? I need a drink."

"Help yourself." She stooped, picked up her high heels, dangled them from her fingers, and smiled. "Me? I never touch the stuff."

Cal Beaumann strode up the aisle of Cinema Neo, smacking the newspaper against his thigh. He ignored the workmen installing the seats in his soon-to-be-opened theater and headed for the office behind the ticket booth in the lobby.

Something seriously akin to worry poked at his gut.

He needed hot, no-fail promotion and he needed it ASAP. Locking up the screen rights for *No Friend At All,* the hottest and most talked about comedy to hit the independent film scene in years, wouldn't mean squat if he didn't get the word out. *No Friend At All* was a sure-fire seat filler, and Cinema Neo needed every buck it could drag in. Hell, his bank loan had more terms and conditions than a paranoid billionaire's prenup. They could call the damn thing if Cal sneezed without a hanky. He needed crowds, and he needed them from day one.

He put the piece of paper holding Ginger Ink's number on his desk. Ellie, his assistant, had given him the number this morning. In Waveside Bay, apparently this Ginger person was it for advertising and PR. She better be.

He stabbed at the keys and tilted back in his chair.

"Ginger Ink. Tracy speaking. Can I help you?"

"You can, if you put me through to Ginger Cameron. I'm the owner of Cinema Neo, the new movie theater in town. I'd like to talk to her about doing the promotion for our opening."

"Ginger's out right now—something about a new bird—but I can make an appointment for her."

"Bird?"

The Tracy woman laughed. "Yeah, she's taken up bird watching, but don't worry, it won't last."

He wasn't worried, he was just trying to picture a bird-watcher doing his PR.

"Okay, how about three-thirty?" the woman went on. "There, I've marked you down." She sounded as though she just completed a hand-rendered copy of the Book of Kells. "Cincema Neo on Front Street, right?— Oops, the other line, gotta go."

Click.

Cal lifted the phone from his ear and stared at it. A bird-watcher and a birdbrain. Really gave a man confidence.

At three-twenty Ginger stood outside the theater looking at the almost finished marquee and the art deco touches on the wide front doors. Nice. Whoever this Cal guy was, he was doing a great job. Waveside Bay needed a movie house, and as a project, it would be fun to work on. More fun than her current stuff: a tire franchise and a discount carpet outlet.

Not that she was into fun these days. She was a serious woman with a serious agenda, whipping her bruised psyche into shape and being a good girl. She'd been a retooled woman for three months, now—no dates, no temptation. Only twenty-one months, two days, and fifteen hours to go. But hey, who was counting? She got a grip on her current goal—*get this account*—and pushed open the door. She stepped inside the theater, firmly in character, a no-nonsense businesswoman who would have made Joan Crawford quiver in her platforms.

And a woman determined to make a sale.

* * *

"Cal?" Ellie called through the gloom of the dimly lit theater. "You there?"

"Yeah?" Cal wrestled the faulty chair seat out of position and set it in the aisle for the installer to replace, a whim of a job he hadn't intended on doing, especially without full overhead lights on.

He was going to tell Ellie to bring the lights up when she added, "Ginger Cameron's here."

"Be right there." He made a couple of mental to-do notes, turned, and headed up the aisle to his office.

A woman strode down the aisle to meet him. She stuck out her hand with the force of a politician fresh from solitary. "Ginger Cameron, of Ginger Ink," she said. "A pleasure to meet you."

He took the hand, but he couldn't make out the face, only a halo of hair glowing like hot coals against the light coming from the theater doors still open behind her. "Nice to meet you," he mumbled, still holding her hand. Or was she still holding his? Either way, they were locked together, her pumping his hand with enough gusto to bring up oil and him squinting to get a better look at her face. "My office?" He gestured up the aisle. "At least we'll have light there."

She released his hand. "Lead on."

In the brightly lit lobby, Ginger turned, worked up her corporate smile, and . . . gaped.

Cal Beaumann was sin in the flesh. Tall, dark, and terrifyingly good-looking. Damn!

Temptation. A woman magnet if ever she saw one.

Oh, no . . .

Her stomach tilted and her mind went snowy. Obviously the goddess of all things virginal was giving her a test. Why else would she present Ginger with six feet plus of male poster material who smelled like musk and spearmint?

Oh, no . . .

Her neck got warm, warmer. Boiling. If she had a fan she'd be working it hard enough to cool the next county. He had green eyes . . . She *so* loved green eyes!

Her stomach sank under the weight of the butterflies. What

now? She hadn't been within sniffing distance of him for more than thirty seconds and her knees were noodles—and that only meant trouble. Because, in her case, instant attraction was a *really really* bad thing, followed by a hormone hurricane that tossed her headfirst into deep water and turned what was left of her brain to rock salt. Her glance fell from green eyes to tight blue denim that fit nicely around all the right body parts. The fabric over his zipper was worn, softly whitened by washing—and other pressures? She wondered if he ever . . . *Stop it.*

She lifted her gaze abruptly. It bumped into his.

The man was looking at her as if she were the biggest disappointment in a life cluttered with them. Interest level?

Point zero and falling.

Perfect! She told herself and started to breathe again.

Cal tried to pull his gaze away. Failed. This had to be a joke. A bad one.

Ginger Cameron was the palest woman he'd ever seen, and she was draped in enough beige cloth to decorate the windows of a new subdivision. He wasn't big on women wearing a ton of makeup, but this one could use a jar or two of something. Anything. And her hair! Except for frizzy bits that fought the leash and caught the light from the open door, it was coiled tight enough to cause brain damage. Interesting color, though, like her eyebrows, kind of a reddish gold, and . . .

Great skin. Clear. Smooth as cream. Which made her—what? He tilted his head, looked harder. Twenty-three tops. He cursed inwardly, first at Ellie, then himself for going along with her suggestion and agreeing to this meeting. No way could this prissy thing have the experience he needed. He was opening a theater, for God's sake, not a damn convent. And what in hell was that scent she was wearing. It reminded him of those lavender sachet things his grandmother put in her linen closet.

"Mr. Beaumann?" She was frowning at him.

"In here," he muttered and pointed to his office. Once behind his desk he planned to get rid of her—as quickly as possible.

"Have a seat," he said.

She sat, the yards of cloth in her skirt draping the chair to the floor. She didn't cross her legs, just slanted them and tucked her feet under the chair as if she were the wallflower at a school dance.

Surprisingly trim ankles . . .

She propped a large portfolio against her chair and smiled again, a bright, earnest smile, the kind that came with dreams and high hopes.

Cal sat down, steepled his fingers and tapped his chin. If he was going to dash those high hopes, he'd best get it over with. "Exactly what kind of work have you done, Miss Cameron?"

"A bit of everything," she said, moving forward in her chair. The action giving a brief hint of actual breasts under her starched shirt. *Interesting. Probably damn lush.*

"Like?" he prodded, surprised he was so intent on surveying her camouflaged territory.

"I have samples in my portfolio. But what matters is what you want and if Ginger Ink can help you. Can you tell me a bit about Cinema Neo? Your plans for Waveside Bay? Is this your first theater?"

"No, this is my sixth. The other five are all located in small to midsize towns in Washington and Oregon. But—"

"That's really impressive!" Her blue eyes widened, and those red-gold eyebrows of hers shot up. "And have you used a local ad and PR firm for all those openings?"

"It generally works out that way." He was getting off track.

"That in itself is good PR. Small communities tend to support their own."

"Uh-huh. I tend to think so, but look, Miss Cameron—"

"Ginger, please."

"Sure." Cal scratched his neck, took a deep breath. He wished she'd stop looking at him like a hungry expectant bird. And more than that he wished he wasn't suddenly intrigued by what kind of body might be under that pup tent she was wearing. Too much work. Not enough sex, he decided, had to be if he was thinking of the Miss Prim sitting in front of him as bedroom material. Hell, she was the least fuckable woman he'd ever seen. And considering that, he'd best get this over with. "Look, Ginger, this opening is critical. I've got a lot hanging on it." *Including a brother with a financial noose around my neck.* "I need someone with a lot of experience. I need great stuff, stuff to let people know Cinema Neo is not some second-rate independent movie house showing artsy crap that won't fly on the major screens." He stared her down. "To be honest, you don't look like someone who can do that."

She narrowed her eyes. Her pale face suddenly not so pale, she said, "What do I look like?"

"Like someone who probably does a hell of a job on ad campaigns for doughnut shops and local home service companies."

She looked a little stunned, turned a dark shade of pink.

Fabulous skin . . .

God, she'd better not cry. He was lousy with crying women. So best he hustle her out of here pronto. He stood. "Thanks for coming to see me, Ginger. Sorry things didn't work out." When she didn't say anything, he added, "You okay?"

"I think so." She stood, looked him in the eye. "I'm just trying to figure out whether I've been insulted."

"No insult intended. But the independent theater scene draws on a particular, and very fickle, demographic: people who are intelligent, young—hip, I guess you'd say. People into cutting-edge film. They want something new, something they haven't seen before." He paused. "Both on the screen and in promotion." He smiled, hopefully the smile of a kind uncle. "Somehow I don't think that's your scene."

"And you've decided that by just . . . looking at me." She stared at him, disbelief and astonishment warring in bright blue eyes. "I've *definitely* been insulted." She picked up her portfolio and clutched it to her chest, eyed him as if he were a cockroach and she a boot-clad army vet.

"But thanks for—" he started, intending to see her out.

"—nothing," she finished. "At least not yet. But don't think you can get rid of me quite so easily."

"I don't think—"

"Obviously not. If you did think, you'd be thinking about how ticking off one of the community's own"—she slapped a hand against the portfolio she held to her chest—"in this case *moi,* is not all that good a PR stroke on your part, especially if the person you ticked off is on a first name basis with all those 'doughnut shops and home service companies' you sneered at." She rammed the portfolio up and under her arm and hooked some kind of granny bag over her right wrist. Cal had the fleeting impression of the queen of England. "The people of Waveside Bay won't take kindly to that at all—should a certain someone decide to make it known."

"Are you threat—"

She raised a hand, went on, "To protect you from hometown backlash, I'll do you a favor. I'll be back in two days, presentation in hand. But for now . . . good-bye, Mr. Beaumann." She walked out and closed the door—none too quietly—behind her.

Cal's jaw hung low enough to warm his chest bone. As sales calls went, this one definitely broke new ground. First she'd blackmailed him, then she'd bullied him. Amazing. He should be mad as hell, instead he felt himself smiling. Who'd have figured it? Under all that tight hair and yards of fabric lay the spirit of a street cop. And maybe a real woman's body.

He shook his head. If he had time, he'd—

But he didn't. He went back to his seat behind his desk. What time he did have, he wasn't going to waste on a PR type who looked as if she stepped off the pages of a 1950s edition of *Ladies' Home Journal*. He punched a series of numbers into the phone, massaged his forehead while he waited for the call to go through. Hudson Blaine would cost him big time, but one thing was certain, he'd give Cinema Neo the kind of promotion it needed.

Ginger Cameron, she of the unfortunate suit and even more unfortunate personality, was history.

Chapter Two

"Tracy? You home?" Ginger shouted, slammed the door, and tossed her portfolio and bag on the nearest chair.

Tracy wandered into the hall munching on a sandwich. "As they say in the movies—yo!"

"Do not talk to me about movies." Ginger eyed her house-mate's sandwich, decided she was hungry, and headed for the kitchen. She wanted to chew on something, and if it couldn't be that smart-mouthed, supercilious, arrogant, condescending brute of a Beaumann—who was the sexiest piece of manhood she'd seen in years—she'd settle for cold cuts. And goddess, she was hot! On her way to the kitchen she peeled off her suit jacket and shirt, and got down to her demi bra and silk-camisoled self. In the kitchen she started beating up on the sandwich fixings.

"What gives?" Tracy popped the last of her sandwich in her mouth. "You look as if you've spent the afternoon on the wrong end of a tax audit."

Ginger slathered mayo on her ham and tomato and clamped the two slices of bread together with enough force to bind them for life. "A tax audit would be a cakewalk compared to a meeting with Cal Beaumann."

"Oh, right, the Cinema Neo thingy."

Ginger rolled her eyes. "A sales call is not a 'thingy.' It's a, uh . . . sales call, for heaven's sake. You know, a front runner to paying the bills, car insurance, the mortgage—those kind of in-conveniences." Firmly under the beady eye of her banker since she'd bought her house last year, Ginger had lately developed a new respect for cash flow—and closing a sale. Before she'd slapped on the beige and cinched up her chastity belt, she'd wasted a lot of time chasing guys instead of customers. And that kind of monkey business had a way of showing up on the bottom line in bold, feverish red. Securing the Cinema Neo account would atone for a lot of past sins.

"Sorry. You know I'm not into business stuff."

Major understatement. Tracy was an artist. Although Ginger suspected she knew more about business than she let on, but ignored it because it bored her.

Tracy walked to where Ginger was pummeling the sandwich. "Let me do that." In seconds she had a neat sandwich and two glasses of milk on the table. "Now, tell Mommy all about it."

Ginger munched morosely on the sandwich. "I blew it."

"Ah. And that would be?"

"My meeting with Beaumann. He didn't even look at my work, just gave me the once-over and decided I couldn't do the job."

"I can't imagine why he'd think that." Tracy said dryly. "You've done such a swell imitation of someone's indigent grandmother, and you're so marvelously . . . billowy." She looked at Ginger's pleated skirt, then lower. She sniffed. "And those shoes . . ."

Ginger stuck her leg out, rolled an ankle anchored by a mottled beige pump. "What's wrong with my shoes?"

"You look as if your toes have tumors." Tracy looked at her shoes as if whatever they had was contagious. "They're positively orthopedic."

Ginger tucked the offending footwear back under the chair. "I want to vent and all you can talk about is my fashion statement."

"Vent away, but if that's a fashion statement, Ginge, I'm an investment banker."

"A little conservative maybe—"

"Humph."

Ginger glowered at her friend. "The point is that whether I wear a toga or a tutu, I deserve a chance to show what I can do. Not to be treated as if I were—"

"—someone's maiden aunt attempting to rejoin the workforce after the Second World War?" Tracy smiled, drank some milk.

"Trace!"

"Okay." Tracy waved a hand as if she were swatting an invisible fly. "I'll shut up, but you're the one always talking about dressing for the job."

"And that's exactly what I'm doing." Ginger smoothed a pleat. "I look sensible, sane, and—"

"Sanitized. The restored-virgin look, I know." Tracy snorted in derision. "It's overkill, plain and simple."

"Overkill or not, it's the new me."

Tracy rolled her eyes. "I give up. So, go on, tell me what happened."

"Beaumann says he's looking for hip, cutting edge stuff, and he doesn't think that's my 'scene.' Can you believe that?" Ginger took a swallow of milk, licked away the frothy mustache.

Tracy suddenly looked puzzled. "Where do I know that name from? Beaumann . . . Cal Beaumann . . ." Her eyes widened. "Can't be. Can't be that Cal Beaumann. Not here in Waveside."

Ginger, who'd barely begun her rant, wasn't in the mood for one of Tracy's digressions. "What are you talking about?"

"What does he look like?"

"I didn't notice." Ginger lied.

"Think! It's important."

Ginger picked up the pickle Tracy had put with her sandwich, stared at the wall, and tried to look as if remembering what Cal looked like was a challenge. "Let me see . . ." A primitive female sigh escaped before she could stop it, and damned if she didn't get a little breathless, and more than a little heated under the silk of her camisole. "Like the Marlboro man after handsome surgery." Another sigh, which she kept to herself this time. "Hot. Super hot. One of those chiseled chin types with a small dimple in his left cheek, makes a crevice when he smiles. Tall. Major shoulders."

Ginger warmed to her topic. She might be beige but she wasn't blind. "And I'd say pec central under that green cashmere sweater he was wearing. Thick chestnut hair, straight with sunny streaks in it. Longish, but not girlish. Oh, and he's got a pale scar on his jawline. Right about here." She touched the spot on her own face, to the left, halfway between her chin and earlobe. She let her hand linger there.

Tracy gave her a speculative look. "You sure you didn't get his shoe size?"

Ginger pulled her hand back, took another bite of her pickle.

She wasn't about to add that her stomach did major aerobics at first sight of the man or that he scared the virgin out of her. One look at him and she'd thought rumpled sheets and sex . . . and more sex. She'd keep that to herself. Sensible women didn't think that way. At least she didn't think so, never having passed Common Sense 101.

"And his eyes, what about them?"

Ginger lifted a shoulder, then her dill pickle, studied it. "Kind of like this."

"He had eyes like pickles?" Tracy echoed, caught in a blond moment.

Ginger had to laugh. "They were green, Trace. Or hazel. Something like that." Actually they were the color of cedar boughs with a touch of Christmas glitter. They were beautiful eyes, full of questions and promises. And humor, she guessed. Her chest kind of caved in. Was there anything better than hot sex and laughter? She didn't think so.

"Then it's him! It's got to be him." Tracy's voice rose in excitement.

"Who? What are you talking about? I'm into serious venting here and—"

"Your venting can wait." Tracy jumped from her chair and ran out of the room. She was back in seconds. "Look at this. Is this who you met today?" She shoved a magazine into Ginger's hand, one of those weekly entertainment things. The top of the page was headlined, "COMEBACKS? WE HOPE SO." Under that was a picture of a man in a tuxedo at some red-carpet do in L.A., the requisite beauty hanging on his arm.

Ginger peered harder. It was definitely him, but who was he? "Okay, I give up." She handed the magazine back to Tracy.

"That," Tracy stabbed the page with a blunt fingernail, "is Cal Beaumann, from *Life and Love*. They killed him off four, maybe five years ago. After that he disappeared."

"You watch the soaps?" Ginger was fascinated with soap operas, but with her work schedule, she never had the luxury of connecting with the story line, so rather than frustrate herself, she left them alone.

"Did, when I was in art school." She touched Cal's image. "I ate my lunch watching this guy make love to women for two years." She laughed. "And from what I read about him, he was as busy with the female sex off screen as he was on. The tabloids loved him. He actually won a contest they ran on which soap star had the best and biggest pe—"

"Stop! I don't want to know," Ginger croaked. She would not go from talking business to penis size. She wouldn't. But his jeans definitely held promise.

"*Pectorals,* Ginger. I was going to say *pectorals.*"

"I knew that." Ginger turned red enough that Trace shook her head.

"Although there were rumors . . ."

Ginger glared at her, but her stomach did a traitorous flip-flop. She'd pegged Beaumann as an A+ woman magnet, but she hadn't factored in playboy status. No wonder she'd drowned in her own hormones when she set eyes on him. She was programmed to fall for these kind of guys.

Typical scenario? One look and her brain shorted out, leaving her dumb as an unmanned hammer.

But not this time! Her loins—or whatever was causing the trouble down there—were seriously girded. No way would she traipse the yellow brick road with yet another guy whose only significant credentials had been earned in the bedroom.

"I can't believe he's in Waveside." Tracy's brown eyes widened in delayed shock. "And I actually spoke to him when I set up the appointment." She looked as if she were going to faint, but rallied to shoot Ginger a steely look. "And you say you *blew* it?"

"So the man says." She was mad all over again. "But I say, maybe not." She rose from the table, put her dishes in the sink, and leaned her backside against the counter. "I muscled myself into one more appointment." She set her mouth into a straight line. "I told him I'd be back in two days. And when I walk into his office, I intend blow him out of his Nikes."

Tracy's expression turned hopeful. "You're going shopping?"

"No." Ginger would get the account, but she'd get it her way. She pulled up her mental socks. An Amazon in beige. That's what she was. All business. All the time. Besides, she didn't want to go to bed with Cal Beaumann . . . her thoughts slid off the rails. There were those rumpled sheets again . . . She shook them flat. She wanted the Cinema Neo account—period. She didn't need flash and style for that; all she needed was her brains and her talent.

And maybe one other thing . . .

The hope in Tracy's eyes faded. "But you've got some terrific ideas, right?"

Ginger's bravado withered to pickle size. "Not a one."

When Hudson Blaine walked into Cal's office, the two men did the male hug thing, quick embrace, manly slap on the back. "Good to see you, Hud," Cal said. "It's been too long."

"Over a year." Hudson dropped his case and took the chair he was offered, stretched his legs in front of him.

"I could have come to L.A."

"I figured I should get a firsthand look at what you're trying to do up here. Makes the job easier."

Cal settled into his chair. "So how's the PR business treating you these days?" He surveyed his friend, lifted a brow, and grinned. "Judging from the Armani on your back, I'm guessing pretty well."

"You'd guess right."

"Better than repping a reluctant soap actor, huh?"

Hudson laughed. "Much. And I don't have to use a cattle prod and bullwhip to get the guy to sign a contract most actors would kill for."

"It wasn't for me."

"Yeah, I know. But we had some good times."

"The best."

"The best food, the best wine, the best women."

"Amen." Cal lifted his coffee cup, didn't have the heart to tell his friend he didn't miss any of it. Okay, maybe he did miss the women, but there were plenty of those, and plenty of ready sex, if a man went looking. Which he hadn't. He'd been doing the monk thing too damn long. Obviously a big mistake, given he hadn't stopped thinking about sex since Ginger Cameron walked out of his office two days ago. Hell, the woman looked so damn tight-assed and proper, you'd think she was a virgin. Could she be? He couldn't buy it. Inexperienced? Maybe. His mind shot to a pristine bed, smooth white sheets, Ginger, knees glued together, arms covering her breasts, giving him a sultry I-dare-you smile. Hell, he was getting hard just thinking about spreading those knees, running a hand up to—

"Ian here?" Hud asked.

The question snapped his attention back to business. He shifted in his chair. "No, he's in Chicago tickling his pork bellies." Ian was Cal's brother. It had been his money that originally funded the business. Cal owed him. Big time.

Hudson grinned. "Still the deal maker, huh?"

"Yup. Still at it." *And still dogging my every step.* Owing came with a price.

"You've managed this far without my big-city rates, Cal. Why now? No local talent?"

Cal had a fleeting image of a woman in tent fabric. *Slim ankles. Soft, soft skin.* "Not good enough." He put his coffee aside and brought the tent image back. Ginger wouldn't work, either for business or pleasure. Well, maybe pleasure.

Hudson straightened in his chair. "Then let's do it. Let's talk movies. What're you opening with?"

"*No Friend At All.* Snagged it at Sundance."

"That's the comedy with that new guy . . . Kiff something."

"Quick. Kiff Quick. And yes, it's as funny as the buzz says it is. I couldn't have a better opener."

"All right!" Hudson pulled out a notepad and pen. "So, let's hear it. What are you looking for?"

Cal leaned back in his chair and started talking, while Hudson listened, questioned, and jotted down the occasional note. Cal felt better already, his guilt about canceling his appointment with Ginger dissipated with every question Hudson asked. For the first time in weeks he stopped worrying about his opening night.

He was doing the right thing here. And with luck he'd never see the Cameron woman again.

Ginger stared at the theater doors, paralyzed. To say she was tense would be the mother of all understatements.

High pressure selling was one thing, but what she was about to do ranked up there with force-feeding and entrapment. She tried the doors, unlocked just as they'd been two days ago. She let out a relieved breath.

Inside the lobby, she heard men's voices: deep, rumbling, and too muted to hear properly. Taking another second to compose herself, she marched to Beaumann's office, a warship on a mission, armored in gunmetal gray wool, white shirt buttoned to the throat, and practical leather pumps. She eased her collar away from her neck with her index finger and rapped on the half open door to Cal's office. With a slight shove, it opened wide enough to show two men sitting at the desk.

Cal's feet were propped on one end, the other man's at the other. Both sets of feet hit the floor in tandem. The stranger stood and Cal gaped. She had a moment of satisfaction at the guilt on his face. He looked like an ex-con who'd spotted his parole officer at an illegal arms sale.

"Am I early?" Ginger asked. She directed her question to Cal and shot a friendly, innocent glance at the other man in the room. She hoped she looked ingenuous but doubted it. She was the world's worst poker player.

"I called," Cal said bluntly. "Cancelled the appointment."

"You did?" She widened her eyes, ever so little.

"I did," he repeated with a read-my-lips expression on his face. "Left the message with your assistant. Tracy?"

"That explains it, then," Ginger said, stepping into the office as if she belonged there. "First off, Tracy's not my assistant. She's my housemate. An artist, actually. A good one. She just answers the phone sometimes when I'm out . . . if she feels like it. This time, obviously, she forgot to give me the message." She stopped, both her babbling and her white lying, and cleared her throat. She'd got the message all right, and decided to ignore it. She smoothed down one of her gray wool lapels, but didn't move to go. "Too bad."

"Yeah." Cal's eyes narrowed. "I can see you're really torn up about it."

She focused on him. "I said I'd be back in two days, Mr. Beaumann, and here I am. I generally do what I say I'm going to do. Of course, if you really want me to leave . . ." She held her breath.

They stared at one another, two cats on a narrow fence.

"Anyone care to introduce us?" the other man said, his expression quizzical—and amused.

"No point. The lady won't be staying," Cal said.

Ginger turned to the other man. "Ginger Cameron, Ginger Ink."

He took her hand. "Hudson Blaine, The Blaine Group. My pleasure."

Ginger's spirit withered. "I've heard of your firm, Mr. Blaine." The Blaine Group was one of the most talked about PR firms in L.A. It didn't take a Mensa member to figure out what he was doing in Cal's office. But she wouldn't quit now. Trouble was, she didn't know where to go from here. "You do fabulous work."

"And that's yours?" He nodded at her bulging portfolio.

She nodded back.

"I'd like to see it."

"Hudson." Cal's tone was low and lethal.

Ginger didn't miss a beat, even though she suspected the polished Hudson Blaine expected she'd fall flat on her unbuffed face. "And I'd love to show it to you." She glanced at Cal. He looked thunderous. She propped her case on his desk and started to unzip it. "I've got some great ideas for Cinema Neo And—"

"Miss Cameron?" Cal put a hand over hers, effectively terminating the unzip.

She looked up at him, unaccountably flustered by the slide of his warm hand over her knuckles. "Yes," she croaked, desperate to look assured, but afraid she'd only managed the desperate part.

Cal looked as if he were about to loose a blister of words, but instead he took a noisy breath, and left his hand to linger over hers. "You've got twenty minutes," he said, then gestured at Hudson Blaine with a jut of his chin. "And you owe it to him. Better say your thanks now, because after you leave he's going to have an unfortunate accident."

Hudson chuckled and pulled out a chair. "Ginger, take a seat. Let's make the big guy squirm."

An hour later Cal walked Ginger out of his office and out the main theater door to the street. The sun hit her eyes with a blinding smack, but she'd barely blinked before Cal had the doors locked behind her.

When she got to her aging Omega, she slumped against it with the sluggishness of a centenarian on tranquilizers, her mind alternately buzzing and whiting out. She brushed an errant curl behind her unstudded ear.

She'd blown it.

She'd given it her best shot and had the biggest misfire in her brilliantly short career. She sighed. Ginger Ink was back to promoting doughnut shops and tire sales.

Hudson was nice enough, but Beaumann? He hadn't said a word during the entire presentation. Sat there and glowered like an old bull moose with a rock in its hoof. Not a question, not a nod, not a sign she'd made any impression at all.

She'd exhale if her lungs weren't filled with lead. Still, she couldn't figure out if she was mad or sad.

She chalked the feeling up to disappointment, got in her car, and fired it up. She needed a cream puff drenched in chocolate, and she needed it fast.

To hell with Cal Beaumann and his precious Cinema Neo.

"You have to go with her, Cal. That was great stuff." Hud poured himself a glass of water and went back to his chair.

"I don't know." Cal shook his head, still in doubt.

"Why the hell not?"

"God, Hud, you saw the way the woman was dressed."

"So undress her. You used to be pretty good at that as I remember."

"Funny," he answered dryly, knowing he'd been thinking the same thing all through Ginger's presentation. *Take it off, Ginger. Take it all off.*

"She's into retro." Hud shrugged. "What's the big deal?"

"The deal is she looks like a nineteen-twenties Salvation Army officer." Cal got to his feet. "Her ideas for radio spots, local ads, and press releases? Great, sure, but the meet-the-people part of this project? I can't see it."

"So tell her to pick up her image. Get some new clothes."

"Tell a woman what to wear? I'd rather face a prison riot with a water pistol."

"Your call, but under that tarp she calls a suit there's a helluva creative person." Hud got to his feet. "I'm going back to the hotel. Call when you decide." He paused. "And remind yourself of this . . . she'll be a lot cheaper than The Blaine Group."

Cal watched him go. Money! It always came down to money.

He leveled his shoulders, committed himself to the equivalent of an hour walking a bed of burning coals. He'd do it. He'd take Hud's advice, tell Cameron to take off her clothes . . . change her style.

He'd be straightforward, businesslike, and above all, tactful with a capital T. He'd call her tomorrow, set up a meeting.

How bad could it be?

"Get up, Ginge. It's the phone. And it's him!" Tracy yelled as if she were trying to hurl her words to the third floor instead of the two feet separating her from Ginger's bed.

Ginger blinked, stared at the phone in Tracy's hand, then grabbed for it. "Hello."

"Cameron?"

"Yes."

"Can you stop by this afternoon? Around three?"

Ginger pushed herself to a sitting position and looped the spaghetti strap of her silky night top over her shoulder. "I'll be there," she croaked, her voice heavy with sleep, her brain still unable to accept that Beaumann was on the phone.

"Are you still in bed?" he asked, his tone an octave lower. "Did I wake you?"

"It's okay. I, uh, overindulged a bit last night."

"On something sinful, I hope." There it was again, that edge of hoarseness in his voice.

Ginger's breathing shallowed. *Not sinful enough. Not as sinful as I could be. With you.* "Hot dogs. Chocolate ice cream. And Kool-Aid."

"That's your idea of over indulgence?"

"Not always. Sometimes it's—" she stopped, not sure what she was about to say, but certain it wasn't the new, improved Ginger who was about to say it.

"Don't stop now, Cameron. You've got my full attention."

"Bananas. I mean splits. Banana splits. I can really go to town on those."

"Ah."

Silence. One of those heavily pregnant ones.

"So . . . should I bring my presentation?"

"Pardon?"

"My presentation. Should I bring it with me?"

"No, just bring yourself." She heard him exhale. "Today that's all I can handle. See you at three." He hung up.

Ginger clicked off the phone. When her chest relaxed, and her heart found its normal pattern, she smiled so hard her cheeks hurt.

"Well . . ." Tracy urged, eyes wide. "What did he want?"

Ginger shot to her knees and bounced on the bed. "He wants me, Trace. He wants to see me."

Tracy plunked herself on the edge of the bed. "Hot damn. I'll get to meet this guy, yet."

Ginger stopped bouncing. "I've got to get dressed." She scrambled off the bed.

"You've got hours yet."

"Yeah, well my, uh, look takes some planning."

"Speaking of your 'look,' as you call it—"

"Don't start." Ginger tossed a pillow at her.

"The black suit, at least it fits," Tracy begged, fending off the pillow, then clutching it to her chest.

Ginger rifled her closet. "The tan skirt, I think. The one with the pleats."

"The pregnant hippo look. Sweet." More rolled eyes.

"It's in good taste and it's comfortable." *And it's enough armor to stop a horny man from a mile off.* Now was not the time to drop her guard and let Cal Beaumann slip in, figuratively or literally.

Tracy threw up her hands. "Okay, I know when I'm beat. Wear whatever you want, but don't plan on dandling my grandkids on your knee because you don't have any of your own." She flounced out, leaving Ginger to make the connection between pleated skirts and grandchildren.

In the shower, Ginger was excited—and smug. Maybe Trace didn't like her new image, but it had worked on Cal Beaumann. He'd clearly seen she was the best person for the job, and he didn't give a damn what she looked like.

Chapter Three

Cal, protected behind the fortress of his desk, figured things had gone okay. In retrospect he could have edited out the remark about tweed underwear, because right now she looked like a cornered badger with a toothache.

"Let me make sure I have this right. You want me to buy new clothes?" Ginger said, her voice lethally low.

"That's what I want."

"And getting the job depends on it?"

Cal nodded. He'd said his piece, and at this point the less foot he put in his mouth the better. The honey-haired woman glared at him, looked ready to combust. And while combustible women were sexy as hell, he preferred meltdowns in bed not his office.

Her skirt smacked her mid-calf as she paced in front of his desk. Cal frowned. He figured a woman's skirt should swirl, not smack. He tilted his head to get a better look at her legs. The six inches of them he could see between there and only looked damn good. But an odd color . . .

"What *are* you looking at?" She sounded mad.

"Your legs." He squinted. "You're not wearing those support things, are you?"

If looks could kill, this would be a bloodbath. "You"—she jabbed a finger in the air in his direction—"are a jerk."

"So I've been told."

"I should walk . . . straight out that door."

"Is that your final answer?"

"No! But I darn well have to think about it."

"How long will the thinking part take?" He looked at his watch. "Time is something I'm short on. Hud either catches a plane in an hour, or stays. It's up to you."

"You really are a jerk."

He looked at his watch again. "And you're repeating yourself. Do you want the job or not?"

She looked mad and mulish. He sighed, got to his feet, and went to stand in front of her. He lifted her chin with the tips of his fingers.

"Look, Cameron, you're a pretty woman with a decent body." He hesitated. "I think." He stopped when her weird lavender scent and some kind of lemony smell drifted up from her hair. And while the two scents warred with each other, he breathed them in. Distracted, he went on. "Although it's damn hard to tell from this side of the drapery. And you have great skin, like rich cream." He smoothed a thumb across her cheek. The warmth and heat in it jolted him. Her gaze, hot and bright, collided with his, and his groin tightened. It surprised the hell out of him. He liked smells like vanilla and rose. He liked women in tight jeans or slinky evening dresses. What the hell he was doing soaking up lavender and lemon worn by a woman who probably starched her bras, he couldn't figure. He looked for words and found some. "I'm not asking you to turn yourself inside out. But for the next couple of months you'll be representing my company. Meeting a lot of people. All I'm asking is that you accentuate the positive for the benefit of Cinema Neo and Ginger Ink."

"And if I refuse, I won't get the job?"

"I'm afraid so. This is a sharp, fast-moving, contemporary industry, Cameron. We're not talking *Sound of Music* and *Mary Poppins*. Cinema Neo is edgy, distinctive, and modern. I want that image projected by everyone associated with it. Especially the person in charge of public relations. So what do you say?"

"I say I *should* be judged on my brain not my fashion picks. I *should* be able to wear burlap and safety pins, and you shouldn't have a thing to say about it. But I want the job." She put out her hand. "I'll revisit my closet, that's all I can promise."

Cal took her outstretched hand, wondered how she made a hand, so delicate and butterfly soft, feel like a carpenter's vise. Even so, he wanted to hang on to it. "I'll settle for anything that dispels the idea you've been in cryogenic storage for forty years."

"Ah, not only is he arrogant and heavy-handed, he's a comedian."

"Laugh or cry. Take your pick." He was sure he spotted a brief curve of her full, pale lips.

Then her face went paper blank. "Right now, I don't feel like doing either one. I'd prefer to work. I'll get my presentation folder. It's in the car."

"You brought it?"

"Of course, I brought it. Why wouldn't I?"

Because I told you not to. "Maybe because we hadn't exactly settled things," he said, suddenly remembering she'd also ignored him when he'd canceled their appointment yesterday.

She waved his comment away as if the settling part had been decided before she'd left home. "Do I get it or not?"

"Sure, why not? While you're doing that I'll call Hud. Tell him to catch his plane."

Ginger headed for the door.

"Cameron?" he called.

She swiveled. "Yes?"

"We have an understanding, right? You *are* going to power up your wardrobe?"

"I said I would, didn't I?"

He stroked his jaw. "You did."

"Then you have nothing to worry about."

Cal watched her walk out the door. Worried? Cal never worried. The twist in his belly was just leftover tension. It wasn't every day a man told a woman how to dress for the job.

The twist morphed into a tight knot.

And it wasn't every day a man decided to trust a woman who'd already snookered him—twice. But there was something about Ginger . . .

Ginger passed her hand in front of Cal to reach for a drawing, and he grabbed her wrist, took a closer look at her watch, and cursed mildly under his breath.

"I've got to get out of here, Cameron. Sorry. My brother's coming in tonight. We're slated for an early dinner."

"No problem." Ginger herded the paper and drawings littering Cal's desk into containment. "Other than Web page design ideas, we're pretty much done for now anyway."

It might have been past five and time to quit, but Ginger was so excited she could have worked for hours yet.

After she and Cal had settled the sticky situation of her wardrobe—or so he thought—they'd agreed on just about everything else, the ads, the radio, the TV spots, even the tone and direction of the local interviews. He'd even agreed to Ginger's ideas for opening night: a Hollywood style premiere with limos, searchlights, the town's who's who in attendance, and a gala black tie post-screening dinner.

Cal had loved it.

Too bad his enthusiasm was so sexy. More than once in the past couple of hours she'd stepped away from the heat of him. And when he'd sat on the couch, put his hands behind his head, and spread his legs, she nearly came undone. And while he'd talked about crossover advertising all she could think of was crossing the room and straddling him—give those jeans of his a quality control test.

Goddess, maybe she *was* a sex addict!

Cal stood, flexed and stretched until his chest expanded to fill his cotton shirt. "Good work tonight." He leveled his gaze on her—warm, unwavering and seductive. "You're smart, Cameron. I like smart women." Something in his eyes shifted, turned silky and dark.

Ginger willed her stomach to quit kicking, was glad when Ellie interrupted with a knock on Cal's door. "Mind if I finish this bit of filing?" She held up a few sheets of paper.

"In a minute, Ellie. We're almost done here." When Ellie left, he turned his attention back to Ginger. "About doing the Web page. Who do you recommend?"

"I'll do it myself. Work up some ideas tonight."

His head came up. "You know all that tech stuff?"

"Under these clothes lies a frustrated techie."

He gave her a speculative look. "Anything else under there a guy should know about?"

"No." She crammed her papers in her case and put a lid on her simmering hormones. "I think we're done here. You better move if you're going to meet your brother. Me, I'm going home and—" She stopped herself just in time. Given the way he was studying her, it wasn't the time to say you were going home to take off your clothes and sink into a bath, the place where she always did her best thinking.

"And what?" He ran his index finger along the seam from her shoulder to her elbow. His eyes were sultry, teasing. "Get into something not made with metal threads."

"Very funny." But she wasn't laughing when he ran his hand back up her arm and her skin got hot enough to bake pizza.

"You're the funny one, Cameron." But he wasn't laughing, or smiling, he was looking at her as if she were wearing a *fuck me* T-shirt and he'd overdosed on Viagra.

As if he were staring into the heart of his fantasy—and she was it. And if he looked at her like that, given the hippo tutu she was wearing, he either hadn't had sex this millennium, which she seriously doubted, or he'd committed himself to screwing any woman who breathed. And she was definitely breathing, too hard and too fast for comfort.

Trouble. With a capital T.

"Well, this 'funny' lady is heading home." She made it to the door in double-time. "I'll call you tomorrow. Let you know how I make out with the Web page." With her hand on the door, she got some courage, said flat out, "And you can save all those sexy looks for someone you *might* get into your bed. Which is *not* me. I don't do the hanky-panky with customers, Beaumann. Best you know that right up front."

"'Hanky-panky'?" Now he did laugh, a deep masculine laugh that rolled out of his chest on strong breaths. Ginger sucked up the urge to laugh with him. God, she loved men who laughed like that. Especially in bed.

"Good night," she said, keeping her lips tight and efficiently prissy, and nuking all thoughts of bed and Cal Beaumann from her head. "I'll call you tomorrow, let you know how the Web page is coming." She closed the door so quickly behind her, her skirt caught, and she had to open it again to free it. Cal was still laughing, and she was sure she heard him repeating, "Hanky-panky," but she didn't keep the door open long enough to confirm it.

When Cal stopped laughing, he put his feet up on his desk and let the smile drift from his mouth.

One thing for sure, Cameron hadn't disappointed him. Once they'd got down to it, working with her had been fun—electric. She might look like a turn of the century prison warden, but she was sharp as hell.

Next up? Ian. His brother with the calculator brain who thought an evening spent reviewing financial statements was better than orgasm.

Cal didn't agree. Idly, he watched Ginger walk down the street, intrigued by the way her hips bumped against that goddamn canvas skirt she'd encased herself in.

He tilted his head for a better look, imagined long shapely legs—leading to exactly where a man wanted to be. What the hell was under all that damn yardage anyway?

It might be fun to find out, uncover the real Ginger Cameron. While he considered the possibilities, she dropped her car keys, and when she bent over to pick them up, he glimpsed a perfect backside.

He whistled softly and let out a long easy breath.

If it was true all work and no play made a dull boy, by now he was the equivalent of a petrified couch potato. Finding out what made Cameron tick—under the clothes and between the sheets— was exactly the kind of *play* he needed right now. Hell, he hadn't had sex in so long he'd probably forgotten how to do it.

He smiled. Not a chance. Any man who could forget the lush enticing curves of a woman, the bone-melting heat and welcome home nestled at the apex of her thighs, had to have had a lobotomy. Of course, he wasn't absolutely certain Ginger actually had curves—but it would be entertaining to find out. And he couldn't think of a better time to start than right away.

He'd drop by her place tonight, after his dinner with Ian, and see how she was making out with the Web site.

God, but he was brilliant when he set his mind to it. He

grinned, locked the theater doors, and looked at his watch. A couple of hours with Ian and he'd be at Ginger's door.

As it turned out, Ginger's house was on the beach about ten miles down the road from the hotel where he and Ian had dinner. A dinner that hadn't gone well.

Cal was left with the gut-wrenching feeling his number-crunching brother had his own agenda. One that didn't line up with his. Cinema Neo might be Cal's passion, but to Ian it was just another money machine. No matter how many times Cal told him he wasn't interested in selling, Ian kept harping on it. Trouble was, there was too much of Ian's money in the business and not enough of Cal's. And if Ian really wanted out, there wasn't much Cal could do about it. It bugged the hell out of him.

He pushed the worry aside. He'd deal with Ian if and when he had to. Tonight he wanted to deal with Ginger.

Where her house sat, the road ended in a dark patch of fir and tall hemlock. Moonlight exposed a sprawling old cedar-shaked house. A black carriage lamp dangled precariously on a tilted fence to cast a yellow light on the driveway entrance.

Even though it looked as if every light in the house was on, it was well after nine o'clock. Cal knew there was a good chance she'd probably slam the door in his face, but even that would be fun.

He stepped out of his Cherokee into the chill of a September wind coming in off the ocean. He shuddered; after months in the Pacific Northwest, he still wasn't acclimated to the cold night air.

He looked for a bell or button but didn't find either, so he knocked.

The door opened, abruptly and wide, and Ginger stood in a fall of light, her face pale under a mass of loose, disheveled honey-red hair that rested on bare shoulders. She wore black sweatpants, so big Cal figured she picked them up at a heavyweight boxer's garage sale, and a white cotton muscle shirt so *small* it must have come from a Barbie dress-up kit. The skimpy shirt showed off straight shoulders and long elegant arms leanly muscled.

Whoa! Cameron did have a body. And more.

She had breasts!

Cal's jaw didn't drop but his gaze sure as hell did—well below the line a sexually correct modern male's should.

Beautiful breasts. Firm and peach size. And a waist he could span with his hands. Hell, this was more than he bargained for—as was the stirring behind his zipper.

She looked shell-shocked. "Beaumann?" She immediately reached behind the door, came up with a ratty old navy cardigan from the same garage sale she'd found the mega sweatpants. In seconds the breasts and tiny waist were enveloped in sagging wool. "What are you doing here?" she demanded.

For a second he couldn't remember; his mind was still processing measurements. "I thought I'd come by and see how you were making out."

She attacked the cardigan buttons with shaking hands. "It's late."

"I know."

"You should have called."

"You're right."

"Being agreeable doesn't make it okay," she said and fumbled with another button.

"So do I stand here until it *is* okay, or are you going to invite me in?"

She closed the last button, tugged the sweater down around her hips, and stepped back. "Come in, then—but next time *call*."

He raised his left hand, crossed his fingers. "I promise."

A smile lifted her lips, and he was surprised when she let it stay. Cameron wasn't much into smiles. "You're a real piece of work. Do you know that?" she said.

"And I'd say, speaking as a man who's just had a glimpse of paradise," he toyed with her top sweater button, "you're a pretty special piece yourself."

She slapped his hand away. "Do not lech after me, Beaumann. For your information, I have legs like tree trunks and an ass the size of Wyoming."

"I don't think so. From that much too brief preview, I'd guess everything is in just the right proportions."

"Previews, as you should know—being in the movie business and all—do not tell the whole story."

"True. But they sure as hell pique the curiosity."

She rolled her eyes. "Men! One boob sighting and they're set to ready."

"One?" He cocked a brow. "I could swear I saw two." He moved toward her. "Maybe I should do a recount."

"A Neanderthal to his bones. Lucky me." She backed away from him.

He grinned, watched her guard go up. He decided to switch gears before she booted him out. "Come up with any ideas for the Web site, yet?"

"Let's go to my office," she said, and this time the look she gave Cal bordered on triumphant. "You're in for a surprise, Beaumann." She started down a hall. "Follow me."

Cal figured he'd already had his big surprise for the night, when Ginger opened the door wearing a form-fitting muscle shirt, but he dutifully followed her down the hall, studying Wyoming all the way.

Ginger still reeled from the shock of having Cal show up on her doorstep. And there she was, tank-topped and half naked. And hadn't he had a darn good look? Then, of course, he'd acted like every man on this side of the primordial soup. He'd grinned like an idiot and put promises in his eyes. Naturally she'd gone all shivery and weak. She didn't even have Tracy here as a buffer; she was visiting her parents for a couple of days.

Goddess! But she was predictable. For three months she'd had her sexual thermostat nicely set to zero, and one Cal Beaumann smile sends it through the roof. She was hopeless. What was it with her, anyway? she grumped inwardly. Why couldn't some sincere, safely suspendered CPA work this kind of magic? Make her skin tingle, her heart race, and her tummy go all funny and tight. Why did it have to be a piece of mouthwatering beefcake with a side order of Texas-size ego?

Doomed. She was doomed.

"This is it." She nodded into the room that was once a three car garage until the prior owner had revamped it into his studio. It was this office, fireplace on one wall, windows that overlooked the beach on two others, that made Ginger hock her unborn children to get into the place.

Cal looked around. "Great place." He smiled again, that crazy breathtaking smile that made her heart jump and her stomach sink into molasses.

"I like it."

He strolled to the fireplace. The small fire Ginger had set earlier had died down, so he picked up a small piece of dry cedar, stoked the fire, and laid the fresh wood across the now crackling flames.

She would have protested if she weren't mesmerized by the way the firelight played over the strong angles of his face—how his jeans hugged the muscles in his thighs and buttocks when he bent over to tend the flames.

"Nice place to work." He stood, leaned against the mantel and tucked his hands halfway into his pockets. His glance slid to the daybed in the corner; he arched a brow.

"I spend a lot of time here. I nap," she said.

He grinned. "I can think of better things."

She worked up a glower. "What do you want, Beaumann? *Exactly?*"

He rubbed his jaw, a jaw with an intriguing ten o'clock shadow, then set his eyes on her as if she were a hero sandwich and he hadn't eaten in a month. "You really want to know?"

She suddenly didn't, but she wasn't about to fold under the challenge in his eyes. And she had asked the question. "Yes."

"I want you, Cameron. I think we'd be good in bed. Damn good."

His directness rocked her; she probably looked like a gasping guppy. "You can't just waltz into my house and ask for—"

"Sex?" His voice was calm, his eyes wickedly teasing and filled with enough raw sensuality to stop a heart at a hundred paces. "Why not?" He stepped close to her, looked but didn't touch. She could smell him, the cedar on his hands, the salty ocean wind in his hair.

"Because—" she stopped, too flustered and warm to say anything remotely logical. She had to get him out of here. Now. "Because I don't want to talk about . . . sex."

"Me, either. I'd rather do it. And I think you would, too." His gaze traveled over her, heated and faintly amused, then locked with hers. "You're like one of those trick packages, Ginger. You know the kind. Lots of wrapping. First the big box, then the smaller box, then the smaller"—he caressed her cheek with his knuckles—"until there's just one small box left. The one containing the perfect gift."

Ginger couldn't take her eyes from his.

"We'd be good together, you know." His eyes shuttered as he looked at her mouth. "And I'd be good to you. Very good."

Her stomach dropped. She opened her mouth, closed it. Her heart thundered around in her chest as if it were a tornado looking for an arena to de-roof. This was crazy. "I, uh, think you should—"

He traced a finger along her jaw, gave her a white-hot smile. "Get started?" he finished for her.

She swallowed, hard. "Go," she blurted out. "I think you should go." She took a step back. "Sex . . . between us is a seriously bad idea. As for me—" she took a breath. "I've been working on the Web design for hours, and now I just want to go to bed." She straightened and her mouth firmed to stubborn. "Alone," she added.

Cal twisted his mouth to avoid smiling. Ginger's face was fever pink. He almost had her. Actually, he was pretty sure he did have her—if not tonight, soon. He closed the distance she'd put between them. "That's a hell of waste. You might want to reconsider that."

She looked at his groin, eyed the bulge he knew was thickening at an alarming rate behind his zipper. She licked her lips, then shook her head. "Men," she said under her breath. Definitely more of a curse than an accolade. She leveled her gaze at him as if it were a firearm. "What I can't figure out is why you're coming on to me. There must be a dozen women in this town who'd leap at the chance to sleep with Cal Beaumann, soap star."

"Former soap star," he corrected. "And maybe it's you I want. I've never met a light hiding under a bushel before."

She cocked that firearm stare. "There's no light. There's just a serious woman, pursuing a serious career." She paused. "I want to *do* my job, not the client—if you get my drift."

He ignored her. "Add to that you smell so damn good"—he bent over, put his face close to her throat, under her ear where he could breathe her in—"like some exotic food." He touched his lips to her neck, soaked up the giving sigh of a ready woman. He damn near came out of his jeans.

"Damn it, damn it, damn it!" She pulled back abruptly. "Okay. That's it. Let's do it. Let's get it out of our systems." She lifted her face to his. "Plant one on me, Beaumann," she instructed, then puckered up like a country school teacher.

Cal studied her stubborn chin, and considered the offer—and a temptingly luscious mouth—while trying to ignore the gyrations and leaps of his feverish below-the-waist brain cells. Still . . . she was fighting this *thing* between them and there was a chance kissing her now would be a waste of her time and his.

"Well?" Her eyelids popped open. She looked annoyed.

"Well, what?"

"You didn't kiss me."

"No, I didn't."

"Why not?"

"I didn't come here for a kiss, Ginger."

"Oh, right, I forgot, you came for sex—the recreational kind, with no strings attached." Her tone was droll.

"Is there any other kind?" He managed a grin, but her barb hit home. That was exactly what he wanted. At least, that's what he'd started out wanting. His mistake was assuming she'd want that, too, that her sexual need was as strong and demanding as his own—despite the dress-up routine she used to hide it. Damn it, he still believed that.

He touched her hair, tucked some curls behind her ear, and resisted the urge to sink his hands into it and do the *planting* she'd suggested. If he did, she'd come to him. He was certain of it. Instead, he glanced at her office door and added. "I'll find my own way out. See you tomorrow."

Still as a plank, she watched him go.

Ginger threw herself on her bed and beat on her pillow, then rolled on her back to harangue the ceiling.

Oh, the injustice of it! Six feet of sin, otherwise known as Cal Beaumann, showing up in her life just when she's bent on taking control. Obviously the Director Goddess of Womens' affairs was out having too many martini lunches.

And what in heaven's name was that "plant one on me thing" about? Sure, she was pushing his buttons, but she'd come dangerously close to pushing her own. Puckering up like a spinster looking for lip service had to be among the stupidest ideas of all times. And then the arrogant son of a baker hadn't even had the courtesy to kiss her.

That stung. That really stung.

But what really scared the sap out of her was that she'd actually wanted him to kiss her. Badly. She moaned, rolled over again and played dead, facedown on the bed.

Same old bad habits kicking in. Put her in proximity of a handsome face, a sexy smile—and a mind that doesn't think past the nearest bedpost—and she becomes the village idiot.

She forked her fingers through her irritating hair, shoved it behind her ears. And as suddenly as that, she relived the touch of Cal's finger teasing the skin of her cheek, stroking the line of her jaw.

Standing, room center, she let her arms drop to her sides and trembled. His touch . . .

Her body and senses humming, half in longing, half in exasperation, she had to admit it; she was in major sexual upheaval, here. It was past time for a reality check.

She stomped barefoot across the bedroom carpet and stared herself down in the mirror over her bureau. She pointed a finger at herself. "Three months ago, Cameron, you made a decision to change your style and your attitude." She sneered at herself. "No more reckless relations with the muscle-bound set. Remember that?" She wagged her finger, metronome style. "You made a commitment, babe, and nothing's changed."

So Beaumann was a sexual tsunami. She'd handle it.

She yanked off her T-shirt. The diamond in her navel caught a shard of light, glittered and shadowed out. If she didn't know better she'd swear it winked.

Chapter Four

Ginger got to Cal's theater at eleven-thirty. A determined fashion catastrophe in shapeless black suit, beige nylons, white shoes, and a hair knot on her noggin so tight blinking required advance planning, she'd arrived to find the theater doors open. She filled her mind with resolve, and walked in.

Inside, she stopped, her interest caught by the clever poster for Cinema Neo's opening film, *No Friend At All*. When Cal stepped up from behind, so close she felt his breath on her nape, she spun to face him.

His eyes scanned her, a dangerous half smile playing sexy games with his lips. *His perfect lips.*

Any thoughts of a businesslike conversation flew from her head like a bunch of disturbed sparrows. Her heart bumped hard into her rib cage, and something tightened between her legs.

"Where'd you get the suit, Cameron, army surplus?" He arched a brow. "I thought you were going to revisit your closet."

She cleared her throat to make room for a lie and did up one black plastic button. "I did. This is it."

His grin was pure devil. He gestured with his chin at her suit. "It won't work, you know. If you wore a circus tent I'd still see what I saw last night under that muscle shirt. Your secret's out, sweetheart."

She ignored his words, his perfect lips, his perfect smile, his perfect *everything* and rifled through her briefcase, all business. "Here's the guest list for opening night. If you have any interest at all in promoting your premier." Yes, she was sarcastic, and yes, he deserved it.

He took it and tossed it on his desk as if it were as relevant as last week's shopping list. "Later," he said and grasped her hand. "Come with me."

"What are you—"

"You'll see."

When she dug her heels in, he tugged harder.

In seconds, despite her ongoing protests, he'd dragged her into the belly of the empty theater and seated her center row.

"Wait here." He strode up the aisle, leaving her to fume at being manhandled.

A few minutes later, the lights dimmed and Cal ambled down the aisle carrying a gigantic bag of popcorn. He took the seat next to her, lifted up the armrest that was between them, and looked up at the shining screen, a screen showing a multi-pierced, shaggy-haired young man skateboarding wildly along a busy New York street in the driving rain.

Ginger stared at Cal. "I came here to work in case you've forgotten." She tried for seriously sniffy, but couldn't tear her gaze from the big screen. She adored movies.

"This *is* work." Cal slouched in his seat, spread his knees wide, and set the bag of popcorn between them. He waved at the screen. "Opening night, Cameron, *No Friend At All*. This is what your PR efforts are all about. I thought you'd like a sneak preview."

Ginger shifted her eyes from the tempting hot buttery popcorn. Too bad she couldn't shift her nose. The aroma was heaven in a bag. And the man offering it to her was seduction in sneakers. "You should have asked. For all you know I could have appointments this afternoon."

He swiveled his head, glanced at her from under shadowed lashes. "Do you?"

She smoothed one narrow lapel. "No, but—"

"Relax, then. You're about to see the funniest damn film made in the last ten years."

"But—"

"Cameron, put a sock in it, okay?"

She glared, then looked down at the popcorn between his thighs. "I'd prefer some of that."

He looked at his lap, grinned. "I take it you mean the popcorn?"

"Leave the humor to the experts, Beaumann"—she jutted her chin toward the screen—"and pass the damn popcorn."

* * *

An hour later, Ginger had her knees propped against the seat in front of her, full possession of the popcorn, and was laughing so hard she barely noticed Cal's arm was draped along the back of her seat. When he rested his hand on her shoulder, she smirked.

He squeezed. Once. "Hell! You're wearing enough padding to repel the entire offensive squad of the Seattle Sea Hawks." He sounded amused.

"That's the idea."

"Waste of time, though."

"Oh, yeah. Why's that?" she asked.

"Because, all your efforts are for a lost cause . . ." He leaned closer and used his thumb to idly caress her nape in that shivery spot between her collar and knotted hair. She shouldn't be doing this. No. But his thumb was warm and expertly insistent as it worked its way up into her hair to softly rub the tense muscles at the base of the skull. When he pressed there, she closed her eyes, rolled her head back into his hand. She sighed, lost in the light, confident touch of his hands, until, his mouth to her ear, he whispered, "You and I are going to make love, sweetheart, and all the shoulder pads in Saks can't do a damn thing to stop it." He ran his fingers into her hair and undid her complicated hair clip with the efficiency of an Indy pit mechanic. "And it's going to be great sex, unforgettable sex. I can taste you just thinking about it. But I'd rather taste this." He licked the side of her mouth.

Finally her brain engaged. She leaped to her feet and her hair tumbled over her face. She shoved it back and slammed the popcorn bag into his lap. "What do you think you're doing?"

He shifted in his chair. "Besides getting hard? Not much."

"Beaumann, I don't want this."

"Sit down, Cameron. And quit sputtering like a spinster aunt." He gave her a stare worthy of the wiliest Baltimore detective. "It doesn't fit what's in the package."

She sat. "I am not a package, Beaumann, and you're not U.P.S."

"Okay, I'll bite. What are you?"

"Give me my hair clip." She held her palm out and kept her mouth closed. She certainly didn't owe Cal Beaumann any explanations. He'd be the last man on earth to understand.

He slapped the clip into her hand, and she started to rebuild her image. Before she finished, Cal reached out, tugged gently on some still-loose strands of hair. He twirled them casually between his long fingers, and asked, "Explain, Cameron. Why does a woman with as much potential as you hide it behind bad hair, bad suits, and a bad attitude?"

"I do not have a bad attitude."

"At least you didn't try defending the suit. So give, Cameron," he said. "What have you got against sex? Scared?"

"Is that what you think I am? 'Scared'? *Of You?*"

"I don't know. I'm asking."

"Well, for your information, 'scared' isn't in the equation."

"What is? In the equation, I mean."

"Avoidance." She eased her shoulders higher.

"Avoidance." He looked puzzled.

She took in more air. It was now or never. "If you must know, I'm taking a two year sabbatical from sex." She grit her teeth. "And I intend to avoid men who like a woman for a good time, not a long time."

"And that's me?" He gave her a thoughtful look. "Something you've decided by just looking at me?"

His words echoed. He was reminding her of what she'd said when he'd tried to throw her out of his office during their first meeting. "Can you deny it? Are you in the market for a double ring ceremony?"

He laughed. "Not this week."

"There you go." She shrugged a padded shoulder. "You've proved my point. You came to my house for sex. You're coming on to me now—for sex. And when you get what you want you'll leave."

"I usually stay for coffee."

"Very funny."

He studied her a long moment. "Burned, Cameron? Some guy leave skid marks on the bed?"

More than one. And for a second the pain of it stalled her thoughts. "You could say that," she muttered.

"That's tough." He ran his finger along the shell of her ear, tugged lightly on her lobe, and nodded. "But maybe you had the wrong idea going in. Maybe you should have left some marks of your own." He touched her jaw. "And maybe you should stop leading with your heart and just have some fun."

She didn't want to admit she'd tried that, and it hadn't worked. "I can't. And I won't."

"I see."

"Good. Then you'll back off." She stood, keen to escape those magician fingers of his currently turning her gray matter into gruel.

Cal stood, too, and faced her. "I don't think the two year thing will work."

"Says who?" They were perilously close. So close she plainly saw the one imperfection in his soap-star handsome face, a half circle scar just under his jaw. It was forgotten when he lifted her chin and forced her to meet his gaze.

"Says me."

He kissed her, brushed his lips over hers with the deftness of a consummate artist. "Ever make out in a movie theater, Cameron?" he whispered against her mouth.

Her breath quivered in her throat, her heart raced, then pounded an irregular jungle rhythm against her ribs. She told herself to pull away, but she wasn't listening. She tried to stiffen in his embrace, but her muscles, soft as butter and melting fast, refused to comply. He had the mouth of a kissing god. She was in the arms of a man who knew what he was doing and how to do it. She was toast!

He deepened the kiss, took her mouth completely. His tongue licked her lower lip as if it were candy, then slipped inside to mate with hers in hot plunging strokes. With the first stroke, she was wet and wanting, with the second she nestled closer to the hard ridge between his thighs. When he lifted his head to smile down at her, his eyes dark and heavy, every neuron, cell, and nerve in her body was waving white flags of surrender. If he stopped holding her, she'd have crumpled to the floor, a thoroughly kissed rag doll to whom two years had just become an eternity.

He shifted his mouth to her throat, her ear, took her lobe in his teeth, tugged, while his warmed breath murmured into her ear.

Ginger slid her hands over the taut muscles in his back, paused at the ridge of belt encircling his lean waist—with no memory of how her hands had arrived at this danger zone in the first place. She was burning. Her face was flushed, and her neck where he kissed and suckled was flame hot.

And she was so close. Close enough to glide her hand between them, cup the impressive weight that lay thick and pulsing behind his zipper. Breathless, she looked up at him. He bucked into her hand and cursed. When he opened his eyes, he settled them on her with grim purpose. "This place is okay for an appetizer but—"

A blast of rap music signaled the end of the movie and the beginning of the credits.

Ginger, as if emerging from the shadowy depths of an enchanted forest into noon sun on a desert, stepped out of his arms. Wordless, she stared at him.

His expression was determined; his voice when he spoke was gruff. "Tonight, Cameron. I'm coming over tonight. Try to wear something . . . accommodating."

At nine o'clock, sitting like a stump in her darkened living room, Ginger heard Cal's knock on her door. Her body jerked, and she swallowed until her throat hurt.

Promises, especially ones you make to yourself, don't go down easy.

She been through her closet, and a storm of decision making, too many times to count since she'd left Cal. Would she sleep with Cal or wouldn't she? Red satin tank top or tweed pants? Ten minutes ago, for the third time, she'd armored herself in baggy beige wool slacks—that scratched like rioting fire ants—and a muddy brown turtleneck a size too big that threatened either strangulation or heat exhaustion. She'd chosen them in an I-won't phase.

Cal knocked again and she headed down the hall.

She saw him through the glass in the door. His collar was up against the wind, and his hair, catching her porch light, shone as the gusts from the ocean blew strands of it over his forehead. He combed it roughly with his fingers but kept his gaze fixed to hers. Waiting.

She thought longingly of the red satin, took a breath and opened the door. *God, he was so beautiful.*

He made no move to come in, and his voice was dark and soft when he said, "If you don't stop chewing that lip of yours, you're going to draw blood." He lifted her chin, looked into her eyes. "Ease up, sweetheart."

Now, a lot of men had called her sweetheart, but no one said it like Cal. Somehow he managed to soak the word in honey and promises. Somehow he made the word sound endearing—for the first time.

Somehow he made it sound . . . sincere.

She couldn't respond of course, because whatever faculties were left after her "sweetheart" analysis weren't enough to spell her own name, let alone plot her next move.

Cal bent his head, brushed his lips over hers in a kiss that would take first place for brevity in the *Guinness Book of World Records*. Two seconds, tops. He stepped back and gave her uniform a long look. "I came because I said I would. Have I made a mistake? Do you want me to go?"

Aghast at the idea, she couldn't answer.

Apparently he took her silence for agreement. He nodded. "Fair enough. See you . . . tomorrow."

He turned to leave. "Coffee," she blurted. "You can come in for coffee, can't you?"

"It's not coffee I want, Ginger. I figured you knew that."

"You don't want coffee?" Stupid response number four thousand nine hundred and eighty-six.

"If I come in and we have that 'coffee'"—he smiled, and her heart stopped mid-beat—"I'll be angling for dessert over the first cup."

"Like sweet things, do you?" She started to breathe, and she started to want. Badly.

He leaned down and kissed her on the tip of her nose, her cheek, then that shivery spot just under her ear. "Definitely," he murmured there. "And I know exactly where to find enough sugar for both of us."

Ginger trembled, and her stomach did the most fluid and wonderful cartwheel. Finally the definitive answer she wanted. *Yes!* She grasped the front of his jacket, pulled him inside, and closed the door with her foot. "As it happens I'm right out of coffee. Not a bean in the place."

"Thank God." He pulled her into his arms. She watched his face as it moved nearer to hers, saw his eyes grow serious and dark in the timeless moment before their mouths joined, hot and uncontrolled. Her last semi-rational thought was a jumbled idea about leaping and a net would appear.

Please, she added, fading further into his kiss, the easy seduction of his tongue . . . *make it a very, very big net.*

He kissed her thoroughly, didn't hide either his need or his impatience. Their tongues met and their tastes and breath mingled. The sharp clean smell of his woodsy aftershave enveloped her, weakened her. It drifted up her nose like a sexual incense, transparent and volatile. She slid her hands up the front of his leather jacket to the back of his neck, ran her fingers through his thick silken hair, breezy and clean from a recent shampoo. A woman was a goner when a man smelled as good as he looked.

With Cal's mouth on hers, Ginger's heart pounded up and into her ears. She pressed herself to him, flush and needy.

But close wasn't close enough. She pressed harder into the heated length of him, knew there was open hunger in her eyes when she lifted her misty gaze to his intense one. Every feminine sinew and nerve in her body strained and spiked, fired by anticipation, the seductive promise inherent in Cal's hardened masculinity.

Cal pulled back, his eyes black in the dim light of the entrance lit only by a nightlight near the door. He took her face in his hands. "You do have a bedroom, don't you?"

"Huh?"

"A bedroom, baby." He touched her lips with his tongue, kissed her again, and whispered roughly, "One of those places where a woman takes a man when she wants to have her way with him."

Ginger forced herself to blink, got lost in visions of exactly what way it would be, couldn't speak. He pulled her against him and kissed her again, then moved back. "I'm dying here, Ginger."

She grabbed his hand. "This way." She towed him down the hall and into her bedroom—to the big awkward moment, the unavoidable segue between the heat of kisses and the turning down of cool sheets for the purpose of hot sex.

Cal shrugged out of his jacket, tossed it on a chair. She saw him roll his head, as if to ease tight muscles.

Instead of throwing her on the bed and himself with her, he looked around. She followed his gaze, saw again the riot of green, blue, and gold—the wild mix of prints that made up her bed. Cal was suddenly anything but wild.

"Nice," he said and nodded toward the glowing nightlight on her dresser. "You sleep with a light on?"

"Only when I have sex," she said, determined to ruffle Mr. Cool's male feathers.

His face held sin and mischief, and his smile was slow. "Which hasn't been too often of late, I understand." He closed the distance between them. Ginger kept her hands behind her and gripped the doorknob as if it were all that stood between her and an eighty-foot wave. The smell of him clawed her, his clean scent mingling with the lavender potpourri she kept on her dresser.

He gripped her shoulders. "Have you ever made love in that bed?"

Ginger was caught off guard by the question. "No," she said, and frowned, for the first time wondering why she'd never brought anyone home. She could have, but she never did.

He lifted her chin with his knuckles. "Ever fucked in that bed?"

A breathy gasp escaped her mouth, and it was a second or two before she got the word out. "No."

"Good." His gaze went from her face to her hair, and he ran his index finger along her hairline, down and across her cheek, then kissed her. "That makes this a first," he murmured, and kissed her again. A kiss with butterfly wings and dark wishes.

"First what?" she asked. "Lovemaking or fuck?"

He gave her a direct gaze. "If we're lucky . . . both." His eyes, rich with desire, settled on her face. He tilted his head to watch when he asked, "You have a preference?"

Ginger's breath grew quiet in her throat. She released her vise-like grip on the doorknob, brought her hands around and rested her palms on his chest. His white shirt was cotton soft, under it his muscles were warm, straight, and firm. "No." She slid a hand to his heart, felt its deep thud under her palm. "I just want"—the words *honest potential* came to mind. She replaced them with, "Sex . . . good sex. No. Make that great sex." *Defined as a series of flame-out, body-numbing orgasms that will make me shift in my chair when I'm ninety!* Add to that she'd be okay with the outside chance of something other than hello-that-was-great-sex-good-bye. Her life so far. In the same instant she reminded herself, Cal was just another handsome face, a fabled womanizer. She would not allow herself expectations. Other than fun.

He tilted his head, and the lazy confident look he gave her made her elbows sweat. "It's been a while for me, Ginger. Truth is, I've been living like a goddamn monk for months now."

"And this is what? An apology in advance for bad sex?"

He laughed. "Nope. Just preparing you for my first rush of enthusiasm."

Ginger ran her hands over his chest. "I've got more than a little of that myself."

He picked her up with the ease of an Olympic weightlifting medalist and carried her to the bed. "You know there was a second or two when you first walked into my office that I thought you might be shy." He placed her in the middle of the bed, stepped back, and started unbuttoning his shirt.

Ginger got to her knees and replaced his fingers with her own. "I am." She undid the final button. "Until I make up my mind what I want." She rested her hands on his taut, narrow waist and looked up at him. "And I've decided"—she tugged his shirt from his jeans and undid his belt—"I want you."

She pressed a hand against the bulge in his jeans, boldly traced it with a finger, then looked up at him. "You're hard," she stroked him again. "And big." *Very big. Maybe those rumors in the tabloids were true.* Lucky girl, she was going to find out.

"I get by."

She smiled up at him. "I bet you do." She unzipped him and caressed him through his briefs: marble, long, thick, perfectly carved. "And you should know"—she ran her finger from his base to his tip—"that my swearing off sex for two years doesn't mean I don't like it. I do. A lot. And this"—she parted his unzipped jeans, leaned forward, and kissed his cotton-shrouded erection—"is the stuff of my dreams."

"Fuck!" He raised his chin, closed his eyes. She felt tension jack through his body, heard him swallow when he dug his fingers into her shoulders.

"Okay," she mumbled. "We'll start there." She inched closer, braced herself by putting both her hands on his chest. His skin was hot. Burning. She made circles on his chest with her open palms, grazed his flat nipples, then played with one, twitching it with a nail until it stiffened. When she took it between her teeth, stroked it with her tongue, Cal growled and shuddered.

His heart pumped rapidly against the hand she held against his chest, and he brought his head down. "You're hot, Cameron." His low voice rumbled over her lips and his eyes narrowed to meet hers. "I like that. I like you."

He took her mouth, fast and hard. No more butterfly kisses, soft brushings, or whispers. Ginger felt his muscles clench and harden, heard the clamor behind his rib cage. "So let's get you out of whatever the hell it is you're wearing and get started." He lifted her, and she came off the bed to stand facing him, her heart crazy, her lungs straining for air. "Take it off, Cameron. Take it all off." A smile hovered briefly over his lips before he added. "I've been wanting to say that since the day we met."

She grabbed the bottom of her sweater, pulled it over her head, and started to undo the zipper on her slacks.

"Stop," Cal said. "Stop right there." He cupped her breasts, ran a finger along the fine lace of her scarlet demi bra. "You been wearing this kind of stuff under those clothes of yours all along, Cameron?"

"Uh-huh."

He pulled the bra down to expose her nipples, took each of them between thumb and forefinger and tugged gently. When he looked at her, his expression was half annoyed, half amused. "Damn good thing I didn't know that, or we'd have been here long before this." He bent to take one aching, needy tip into his mouth. "Definitely sugar," he murmured, licking her with long slow strokes of his tongue before pulling back. He nodded at her wool slacks. "Off."

She stripped to her G-string panties.

Cal, his shirt off, his zipper lying open, the ridge of him jutting high and heavy between his thighs, didn't move. His tone was deep, rough, and low when he said, "Hell, I could come just looking at you."

She shivered, not with the chill of the cool air hitting newly exposed skin, but because of the way he looked at her. Appreciation, desire—and raw, stomach-churning hunger.

"Turn around. I want a tour of Wyoming. And take it slow. Real slow."

"What's next? A lap dance?" She tilted her head, lowered her lashes, and gave him a quizzical look.

He grinned, shucked out of his jeans, and peeled off his briefs.

She stared, licked her lips. Clean, lean, hard, and waiting. For her. He was beyond magnificent. The last thing she wanted was to turn her back to him. But when he smiled at her and made a circle with his hand, she raised her hands, joined them above her head, and began a slow rotation.

When her back was to him, he came up behind her and put his hands on her waist. He kissed her nape, her shoulder, his breath hot and steamy against her sensitized skin.

He slipped down her panties, placed his hand over her pubis, cupped her, and pressed his stone-hard length against her buttocks.

"Perfect," he whispered into her hair, his voice low and ragged. "You're perfect, Ginger." He held her for a long moment, his mouth wild and heated against her skin, his chest burning against her back.

He drew circles around a nipple with one hand and ran the index finger of the other through the slick folds between her thighs. She gasped, rapt by the dual assault, burned into place, her body stiff with anticipation.

"Spread your legs, sweetheart. Let me touch you. Feel you. Inside."

Ginger's stomach clenched, the shock and promise of his words sizzling along her nerves to the apex of her thighs. She raised her arms, clasped him behind the neck, and gave him open access to her. He shifted the hand playing with her breasts to her tummy, pressed her back against him. He held her there, while his other hand slid a warm path down, first to simply enfold her, then to boldly explore her cleaved sex.

Deeply.

Then to find her clitoris, its peak a hard, anxious nub, shuddering and moist.

Ginger, her breathing nothing more than gasps and pants, moved her hips in the tempo set by his hand, let her body make love to his probing touch, every bone and muscle coming meltingly alive under the slip and glide of his deft fingers.

"I want to taste you," he whispered. "I want my mouth on these lips"—he stroked her labia with one finger . . . richly, languorously, then used two to separate her, enter and tease—"this drenched flesh. Can't even describe it." His voice was midnight dark, uneven when he added, "You want that, too, don't you?"

Ginger's body arched and her mind leaped to the vision of Cal's fingers spreading her wide for his mouth to take and taste. She shuddered, desire a torch on her skin. But . . .

No. No. Not yet.

If Cal Beaumann gave her that, she'd die from it. Then he'd be gone.

Cal nipped her shoulder, spun her to face him, and took her face in his hands. He kissed, devoured her, his hot mouth and tongue taking her to a place the fierce, often too-rash-for-her-own-good Ginger Cameron had never been, and as close to sexual paradise as she'd ever be.

They fell on the bed in a tangle of need and overheated limbs, and Cal claimed a nipple to suckle with surprising gentleness.

When he started to move down, Ginger grasped his taut buttocks, slipped a hand under him and clasped his powerful erection. He was rock hard and ready. "I want this," she demanded
and made a sheath of her hand, fitting it to his engorged width,
then alternately tightening and easing the pressure.

Cal lifted himself above her, his breathing stopped, and he
went stone still. He closed his eyes, his whole body plank hard,
his neck muscles corded tight to his shoulder blades. She stroked
him. He opened his eyes to look down at her, his gaze opaque,
ebony black. "Ginger, I need to fuck you. Now."

She tightened her fingers around him, the delicate skin over his
rock-hard penis petal-soft in her hand, its tip oozing life into her
palm.

She squeezed and pumped him, her own hunger shifting to
critical. She opened her mouth. No words. He took a nipple into
his mouth, sucked, rasped it with his tongue. The sensation
knifed down, down; moisture seeped between her thighs. He
lifted his head, and his dark eyes settled on hers even as his sex
thrust and bucked, painfully deterred, in her hand.

She drew him to her, rubbed the slick head of his penis along
her labia. Released him. He quickly replaced the sheath of her
hand with a condom.

She opened her legs wide—in the invitation women have
given a heated male from time's beginning—and offered herself.
All of herself.

Cal loomed over her, centered himself, and plunged deep, his
moan, as he entered her, pure male satisfaction.

She lifted her hips, rocked into him, her mind drugged by the
fullness of him, the burn of him. The absolute rightness of him
inside her.

"You're like velvet," he murmured, his voice husky. "Crazy
beautiful." He groaned, pulled out, came back to go deeper.
Again.

And again. His slow easy moves, the weight and length of
him, broke her apart. Her breath shortened, then stopped when
her body clenched around his, desperate to hold him, claim
him.

"And you feel amaz—oh, no . . ." The orgasm, sudden and

tumultuous, blindsided her. Her body folded into itself, flaming hot. She struggled to breathe, bring air to her lungs.

Cal thrust again, pounding his hard shaft, slick with her moisture, to her deepest inner reaches.

And taking her on another wild, nerve-spiking, heart-stopping ride to a place where her breathing was the last thing on her mind.

Chapter Five

Cal shook his head in an effort to rattle his brains back in place.

What the hell had just happened?

He heard Ginger moan, and a couple of his synapses fired, strong enough to make him realize he was crushing her. Taking his weight on his elbows, he looked at the woman beneath him. Her eyes were closed, and damp hair lay across her forehead, across her cheek. He shoved it back, then blew a stray curl from her ear. His chest was so constricted, he could barely draw in breath enough to replace the air it took to do that. Blood roared through his veins, but he shivered, the sheen of sweat over his shoulders and down his back icing up under the cool night air. Or was he just trembling like a goddamn adolescent after his first mind-bending fuck?

He rolled off to his side and tucked Ginger close to his shoulder. He waited for his body to return to something resembling normal, concentrated on figuring out how he and Ginger had gotten from her front door to a riptide climax in a time he was pretty sure would beat any and all world records. For him, a new, and damned dubious, distinction.

Ginger propped her forearms on his chest, met him eye to eye. "Not bad, Beaumann. On the recreational sex scale, damn near a ten." Her tone was light, but Cal saw something darker in her eyes. Sadness? Regret? He'd hate that.

"You make it sound like a game of touch football."

"Isn't that the idea?" She pulled her eyes from his, as if it were hard for her to meet his gaze. She rested her cheek on his chest, and her hair, catching the light from the low wattage bedside lamp, looked as if it were streaked with fire.

He cradled her head in one hand, ran the other down to the sensual curve where buttocks and back dipped to form her waist. Her hair was soft and springy to the touch, and her skin, still dewy from their lovemaking, was warm gold. "Want to know what I thought?" Hell, he didn't know what he thought, but he figured it had something to do with life-altering coitus, bone-deep curiosity, and wanting a lot more of what they'd just had.

"Uh-huh, but only if it's good. Otherwise I'd prefer a nap."

Cal decided to take a second or two to get his thoughts in order. For him, post-fuck conversation was uncharted territory.

Her head popped up; she looked spooked. "You're not saying anything."

"No."

"Not as good for you as it was for me?" she asked, her tone flat, one eyebrow raised in question—or threat.

Not that there was a chance of it, but he wondered briefly what she'd do if he said no—tear his face off, castrate him? He decided this was not the time to tease. "Ginger, sex with you is spectacular"—he kissed her—"and I plan to assault your delicious body again—the second I'm operational again. But—" He rolled, positioned her under him. He liked her there. A lot.

"But? You've got a but?" She ran her hand over his ass, squeezed it before slipping those taunting fingers of hers between their bodies to test his current status. A little more of that, and being operational—real fast—wouldn't be a problem.

He closed his eyes when she cupped his balls, played with them. "Uh-huh. And I'll remember what it is any second now." He had to hand it to her, Ginger sure knew how to avoid conversation. He stopped her hand from wringing out his thoughts completely. "Not a but exactly, more one of those 'aha' things."

"'Aha' things?" She shimmied out from under him and sat up on the bed, a blanket jumbled around her midsection. She didn't bother to cover her breasts, for which he was sincerely grateful. Her breasts were definitely A-list, and he loved the way her nipples jutted, small and fierce, into the cool room. "And what exactly is an aha?" she asked, looking curious but wary.

"An insight, a revelation." He pulled on the blanket, and it came away from her to expose her diamond studded navel. "This was one." He touched the glittering stone, circled it with an exploratory finger. She gasped and yanked up the blanket, and Cal couldn't tell if she was annoyed at him or herself for that give-away intake of breath. "I felt that—on the way down." He pulled the blanket away again and leaned over to kiss her navel. "Pretty."

This time she let the blanket lie pooled and rumpled across her knees. "Thank you," she said, sounding oddly prim. "Now, can we get back to that aha thing of yours?"

He sat up, rested his back against the headboard. "You're definitely afraid of me."

Her eyes flashed. "You think so."

"You took the lead from the get-go and you hung on—literally—until the end." He organized the pillow more comfortably behind his back. "Not that I'm complaining, but you did seduce me, Cameron."

"I seduced—"

"You did. And while I loved every minute of it, a man knows that when a woman commandeers his best friend, she's after control, which usually means she's afraid of losing it"—he watched her face—"with him."

"Dear goddess, I've just slept with Dr. Ruth."

He laughed, lifted her chin so their eyes could meet. "Admit it. You're scared."

She started to say something, he guessed a denial, then stopped and looked away for a minute before turning her gaze back to his. "All right, I'm scared. Okay?" She still looked defiant, but she also looked as if she might cry.

Cal's gut clenched. "I'm not in this bed to hurt you, Ginger."

"Men!" She shook her head, looked at him as if he were the village idiot. "You just don't get it, do you?"

"Get what? And drop the 'men!' thing, okay. You make us sound like a box of cheap panty hose."

"Not a bad analogy, considering they all run—sooner or later."

"Yeah? Well I'm not going anywhere. Not until you tell me why you're so determined not to ease up around me."

"I don't want to 'ease up' around you"—she stopped, looked away, then back at him—"because I do not want to fall for another guy who won't be bringing me flowers on our golden anniversary."

"Which takes us back to your virginity promise, aluminum suits, leather underwear, and crepe shoes."

"I never wore crepe shoes!" That denial out, she hesitated, scrunched up her brow. "I dressed like that because I didn't want to lead anybody on, attract the wrong kind of attention."

"Then you failed. Badly." He smiled at her discomfort. "You've been attracting my attention twenty-four-seven since you walked into Cinema Neo."

"And you've attracted mine." She puffed out a loud breath, and mirroring his position, sat up and leaned against the headboard. "Show me a pretty face, and I'm a goner."

Cal didn't much like the pretty face comment, but he let it go. He'd known his share of women who were out for the hunk-of-the-month award, but his gut told him Ginger wasn't one of them. He nudged her chin until she was looking at him. "Maybe not. Maybe you just recognize real potential when you see it."

She gave him a wicked smile. "Somehow I don't think we're talking about the same kind of potential, Beaumann. I'm talking roast beef Sundays, minivans, and report cards. I think you're thinking more along the lines of this." She ran her hand up his sheet-covered thigh and over a part of him that didn't think logically at the best of times, let alone while being stroked toward oblivion.

He gripped her hand, sucked in some air. "You're doing it again."

"What?"

"Taking control." He lifted her hand to his mouth, turned it and kissed her palm. "And proving my point, about your being scared of letting go with me."

She looked mulish. "Didn't anyone ever tell you that guys don't like talking after sex?"

He gave her a half smile and his breath faltered. "Unless they've had the best sex of their life and are imagining how deep, wet, and hot it's going to be the next time. When they make love." He reached for her. "Because that's what I'm going to do now, Ginger. I'm going to make love to you until you beg for more."

"Beg, huh?" She slanted him a disbelieving look.

"Beg," he promised.

When she came—just the tiniest bit reluctantly—into his arms, he kissed her until that snag in his throat grew to the size of a balloon, and the ache in his gut threatened to damn near unman him. God, what a beautiful mouth; what fantastically soft skin. Cal deepened the kiss, knew for certain he could be in serious trouble with this special woman, but couldn't make himself care. Because he had the dim thought she was exactly the kind of trouble he'd been looking for all his life.

He stretched her out beneath him, tossed the blanket aside, and started to kiss his way down to the begging zone. Ginger's studded navel had been his first surprise, but the tattoo he now discovered on her inner thigh brought his head up: a simulated postal sticker, black, red, and blue, stating boldly, *Fragile, Handle With Care.*

When he touched it, traced it with his middle finger, he heard a raspy grumble from the headboard, "Don't laugh, Beaumann, or I'll have to kill you."

He smiled, bent his head, and licked the sticker. When he raised his head to look at her again, his smile slipped. Suddenly, Ginger Cameron was serious business.

He ran his hands between her thighs. Hot. Smooth . . . unyielding. He applied more pressure, and slipped one hand toward the slick curls at the apex of her thighs. He drew his finger lightly, pencil straight across her opening. "Let me see you, Ginger. Open for me." Another stroke, slower. His finger prowling for her hard tight nub.

Her sharp intake of air told him he'd found it, and she opened her legs. He looked up to see her eyes drift close, her tongue sneak out to moisten her lips.

Easy, Beaumann, take it slow and easy.

"I'm going to open you up, sweetheart. Spread you wide. Then I'm going to look at you. Just look." He parted her, dropped his gaze to her swollen, moist sex. Shades of peach and pink, glistening, ready. He was so hard, so tight, he was breakable. "You're incredible. All velvet and honey. Absolutely incredible."

He touched her clitoris, softly. Plucked it, gently.

Ginger fisted her hands in the sheets, arched herself up, offered him heaven, and he took.

He covered her with his mouth, licked her with easy, expert strokes, lazily encircling her moist plump tip with the tip of his tongue. Then sucking it remorselessly.

She thrashed above his head, tearing the fitted sheet from its mooring. "Cal . . . I can't hold on. I shouldn't—"

"Oh, yes, you should, lover. And you will." He wasn't sure if he said it aloud or just to himself; he only knew his control was washing away with every dewy drop Ginger gave him.

He pressed his thumb on her sensitized tip—and his aching, throbbing erection to her wildly rocking pelvis. When he found her rhythm, he went in on liquid silk, sank deep into her heat.

Ginger raked her nails across his back, dug them into his shoulders, while her vaginal walls clenched and unclenched along the length of him in a mind-bending internal massage. He used the last of his willpower to pull himself out, rest the head of his clamoring cock in the folds of her opening.

"You want this?" He nudged her clit, rubbed her seam. "You'll have to tell me."

Her eyes bright with sex, opened to bore into his. "I want you, Cal." She arched high and shuddered, a shudder he felt to his bones—and every nerve ending in his hammering cock. "But if I have to tell you that, maybe you should go back and take Sex 101." She rocked up, caught the first steeled inch of him, then more.

Halfway in, his brain went hollow, and his world shrunk to the bridge of hard hot flesh joining him to Ginger.

Her body was boiling, steaming quicksand pulling him in, sucking him, nursing on him. He lifted himself, grabbed her buttocks, and buried himself to where her muscle and sinew stopped him.

"Oh, Cal. Oh . . ." She thrust her pelvis up, hard against him, but his looming release deafened him. He strained to hold back. Wait.

Pay attention!

Wait.

She moaned, long and low, and convulsed around him—her insides tightening, even her juices eddying inward. Every restraint gave way and Cal exploded, his aching throbbing body depleting itself, exhausting itself in tandem with hers.

A synchronous orgasm. A damned miracle!

If the universe had torn itself apart in that same second, it would have come in a far second.

Ginger forced her eyelids to open, then quickly sealed them shut again. She should have closed the blinds; the sunrise, all perky and promising, was more than she could handle without a cup of coffee in her shaking hand. Maybe a jolt of caffeine would quiet her wild mix of morning-after emotion, an unruly, riotous crowd of fear, satisfaction, anticipation, and unbridled delight. Unfortunately, fear stood the tallest. Not that she'd admit to it, of course.

Last night . . .

She turned to see Cal's dark head burrowed deep into her pillow, and her heart swelled to her throat. She looked into the sun streaming in her window, decided to blame the light for the misty bit of tears gathering in her eyes. She took a deep breath and reached to gently smooth his tousled hair, careful not to wake him.

Something grabbed her heart and squeezed. It felt suspiciously like love. Cal was right, she did lead with her heart. *She was such a sap.*

She looked again at the darkly handsome man in her bed and stopped breathing. Oh, she'd fallen all right. Too late for denials. And from where she sat—or lay as the case may be—there was nothing to do but strap on a parachute. Because she wasn't about to swear off Cal Beaumann.

Maybe this was it, maybe she and Cal . . .

No! No wishful thinking. No plans for the future. She was going to do what the guys did, live in the sexual moment and enjoy it.

And, as the High Goddess of single, searching females everywhere knew, Cal could supply plenty of enjoyment.

Because when he stopped talking about sex and actually got down to the doing of it, he was a giant among men. She smiled, stretched in satisfaction. She briefly considered waking him, but decided he'd earned his sleep—and a pot of fresh coffee to wake up to. But she couldn't resist leaning over to feather kiss his ear before carefully turning back the covers and getting out of the bed.

She threw on a short purple velour robe and stood looking down at him a moment longer, sighed, and headed for the shower.

She was rinsing her hair when he stepped into the steam-filled bathroom and opened the shower door. His dark hair was rumpled and spiked, his face dark with a night's growth of beard. He was fully, magnificently, erect. "Hell," he said. "You're even more beautiful in the morning."

She touched his stubbled jaw. "I'd like to say the same, Beaumann, but . . ." She smiled. She wasn't about to tell him he looked like every woman's dream, because she figured he'd probably heard it a million times. And she definitely didn't plan on telling him he took her breath away. What she might do was show him.

He laughed. "You abandoned me in a strange bed," he accused, his eyes raking over the whole of her wet, naked body.

She pushed her tangled hair from her face. "That the first time a woman's done that?"

He appeared to consider that, then smiled. "Damn. I think it was."

"Then you'd best get in here, so I can show you how sorry I am." She reached for him and pulled him under the hot streaming water.

He took her in his arms, kissed her thoroughly, then lifted his face to the rushing water. Now as wet as she was, he shook his head, and water flew from his thick sodden hair. He pushed her back against the shower stall, looked down at her. "This 'showing me you're sorry.' Will it take long?"

"That depends"—she ran a hand from his chest to his morning erection and grasped him in her hand—"how long you can hold on to this." Ginger loved holding him, caressing him, feeling his shudder, sensing his open pleasure at her slightest touch. This morning she planned to do more than touch.

She heard him suck in a breath and his hand wrapped around hers. "Not long if you keep up that kind of pressure."

"And if the pressure builds?" She sank to her knees, let her hands glide up his strong calves to his thighs—to his lean buttocks. His skin quivered at her touch. She wanted to taste him, as he'd tasted her. She circled his testicles with her fingertips, weighed them in her palms before pressing her face against his erect penis.

He cursed, tensed, and put his hands on her head. "You're going to kill me, you know that."

"I'm going to try." She ran her tongue up his rigid length and his grip tightened in her sodden hair. When she took him in her mouth, he rolled his hips, bucked. Again she slipped her hands to his buttocks, the back of his thighs. It was like stroking polished oak.

She took him in her mouth, savored a drop of him, before he pulled her to his feet and into his arms. "Another time, baby, or I'm afraid I'll give you more than you bargained for."

She was going to argue that would be okay with her, when he slid his hand to cup her mound, trail a finger along the folds of her opening. The perfect distraction.

He kissed her mouth softly, and she heard the ragged edges of his breathing. He entered her with his finger, played while whispering, "You're wet, Ginger. All slippery and damp." He slid his finger out, in again. She gasped. He looked into her eyes, smiled. "Think we'll break our necks if we do some shower gymnastics?"

She met his gaze, licked her lips, and tried to ignore what he was doing between her legs. "I'm willing to chance it if you are."

"Back up, then, and press your beautiful ass against the glass, sweetheart, and we'll see who starts to hurt first."

"Ass against the glass? Good thing you used the adjective, Beaumann." She did as she was told, and he nudged her legs apart.

He splayed his own muscular legs, braced himself, and lifted her to take her buttocks in his hands.

"Cal, I'm not light."

"You're perfect, and right now my hard-on makes me a bona fide superhero." He grinned into her eyes, arched a brow. "Trust me."

"You have insurance?" Her own lips quirked as she locked herself to him. He pinioned her firmly against the shower's glass wall and entered her fast and deep. Ginger shuddered, closed her eyes when the hard length of him filled her. Water rushed over them, a cascade of heat and energy, and she lifted her face to it, felt it waterfall across her shoulders, detour around her breasts now flush against the straining muscles of Cal's chest.

She couldn't fall, because she was flying, and with every thrust of Cal's pelvis, every inch of him taken in, every plunge that went deeper than his last, she rose higher. But it wasn't stars she touched, it was the light in her own heart.

She opened her eyes and they met his, now dark and crazily feral. When her eyes drifted closed again, he said, in a voice dark and rumbling with tension, "No. Look at me. I want to see you come."

A moment later, gazes locked wide and attentive, she gave him what he wanted, coming apart in his arms on a low aching moan.

"You're beautiful, Ginger . . . so damned beautiful." The words spilled into her ears before the surge and pounding of his own shuddering release.

It was Ginger's turn to shudder as her body tightened around him. She let her head rest against the glass wall, breathed deep of the steam—above and below—and finally closed her eyes to savor, imprint forever, the feeling of Cal's body merged with hers. Not that there was a chance she'd ever forget.

Cal released his tight embrace, eased her legs gently back to a straight position; they felt like warm putty. "That was—at the risk of bursting what is probably your already oversize ego—truly spectacular," she said, her voice weak and breathy.

When she opened her eyes, she expected to see the usual cocksure smile on his face, but instead found him looking seriously stunned. "And maybe a lot more."

"More?"

He stroked her wet hair back off her forehead. "I don't think I can ever let you go, Cameron." He said the words softly, almost to himself, as if even he couldn't quite believe them. "I think love has entered, stage left." His eyes were mysterious and marvelously misty, looking at her in a way she had never been looked at before.

Ginger stared at him, grappled with his words, while trying to shout down her own dangerous needs. Hopes sprouted in her gray matter like so many daffodils . . . or weeds. But, no, this was too much, too soon—all the signs of another mistake in the making.

"Don't," she said, reaching around him to turn off the rapidly cooling water. "Words like that after sex are . . . scary."

In the leftover steam from the shower, he grasped her chin in his cupped hand, forced her to meet his determined gaze. "Definitely scary. Definitely true."

She pulled her face from his hand and stepped out of the shower. When she was three feet from his physical presence, she filled her lungs with air and pasted a smile on her face. "I don't believe in love at first sex, Beaumann." She took a towel from the rack, tossed it at him. "Now, how about that coffee I promised you."

She grabbed a robe and marched out of the bathroom, head high, heart in overdrive.

The coffee was three seconds from ready when Ginger heard Tracy's key in the lock.

She braced herself against the counter and dropped her head. Darn, she'd completely forgotten Tracy was coming home this morning. And considering this was the first man in the house since they'd started sharing space, Ginger knew she owed her an explanation. There wasn't much chance of Cal sneaking out her bedroom window. Her lips twisted upward at the thought.

Tracy threw her keys on the table. "Hi, Ginge." She sniffed the coffee-scented air with appreciation. "Have I got timing, or not."

"I'd say not," Cal said, grinning wickedly. He stood dripping in the doorway, with a lilac towel wrapped around his middle, looking like a girl's dream boy toy: big, bad, and ready for anything. His hair was a wet but appealing wreck, his unshaven jaw was touch-me stubbled, and his eyes were full of last night's—and this morning's—sex. Ginger's tummy bottomed out along with Tracy's jaw. Both women stared.

"I need a fan," Tracy said, plopping herself into a chair.

"I need a Prozac," Ginger said,

"I need some clothes," Cal said, his grin widening. He ambled across the room and kissed her softly. "Thanks, Cameron." With that he turned and walked out of the room.

Tracy looked as if she'd been hit by a brick. "You did it, didn't you? You actually did *it* with Cal Beaumann!" Her voice held traces of a little girl shriek.

Ginger darted a glance at the recently vacated doorway. "Shush!" She waved a trembling hand in the direction of her flummoxed friend to shut her up. "He'll hear you."

"I can't believe it. I just can't believe it." She hugged herself.

Ginger rolled her eyes. "Tracy, get a grip and pull your tongue back in your mouth." She poured herself some coffee and cradled the mug. This might be a bizarre scenario, but she'd get through it. When Trace looked up and it seemed as if she was going to open her mouth again, Ginger held up a hand. "Do not, I repeat, do not ask me how it was."

Tracy closed her mouth, opened it again to say, "You've just lived the fantasy of a million women, and you're not going to share. What kind of friend are you?"

"Trace . . ."

Tracy crossed her arms, lifted her nose, and turned away.

Ginger couldn't help the smile tugging at her lips. "It was beyond fantastic. Okay?"

Tracy spun to face her, eyes overly bright. "I knew it! I knew it would be." She looked down the hall where Cal had walked to Ginger's room. "And he's in our house, probably naked on the other side of that wall!" She stared at the wall, rapt in whatever vision of a naked Cal she'd dreamed up.

Ginger's mouth dried out and she drank some coffee. She didn't need to imagine. "Trace, will you quit speaking in exclamation points. You're hurting my ears. He's just a guy." Right. *And Buckingham Palace is just a house.*

"He's a guy you brought home. That's a first."

"True."

"So?"

"So, what?" She drained the last of her coffee.

Tracy gave her an annoyed look. "So . . . where does it go from here?"

Ginger started to say something glib, but stopped herself and thought for a minute. "From here, Trace, it goes slowly. Like a snail with a head cold."

"Not too slow, I hope," Cal said from the doorway. He was standing in the doorway, toweling his hair with another of her lilac towels.

Ginger jumped to her feet. Did the man walk on air? "Don't you know how to knock?" she grumped.

"No door," he stated, reminding her of the obvious. He walked into the room, smelling faintly of her lavender soap. His damp hair, after he finger-combed it back, glistened under the kitchen light. He walked to Ginger, draped the towel around his neck, and gestured toward the coffee. "Can I take one to go?" He smiled at her, winked at Trace. "I figure my best move is out of here."

"Smart man." Ginger headed to the counter and poured him a coffee. The kitchen, with her, Tracy, Cal, and last night all taking up space was much too crowded.

He came up beside her, took the coffee from her hand, and leaned to whisper in her ear. "I'll call you in an hour. If you're up for it, we'll walk the beach." His voice lowered a notch and he managed to nip her ear. The bite, along with the blush from his warm breath, shot to her groin. "If we're going to go slow, we'd better get started." He pulled the towel from around his neck and handed it to Ginger.

"I'm not in a hurry, Beaumann," she said, keeping her own voice low.

He just laughed at that, then walked to the kitchen door, stopped, and turned back. "Beyond fantastic, huh?"

She threw the damp towel at him, but he just gave her another of his miserably seductive grins, and ambled out.

Ginger pushed the kitchen curtain aside and watched him get into his Cherokee, her flower patterned mug in his hand. She wondered how many men could handle lavender soap, lilac towels, and flowered mugs and still look so masculine your hormone levels shot to red alert just looking at him. She kept looking until he pulled out of her driveway, then she turned back to Tracy.

Tracy, still grinning like a fool, gave her a thumbs-up. "What I want to do is buy your wardrobe. If sacky suits, XL T-shirts, and Sister Sarah shoes can reel in a catch like Cal Beaumann, you're on to something."

Ginger took a chair at the table. "But that's just it, I don't want a 'catch.' I want a serious guy, a solid guy, ambitious, committed."

"And you're afraid Cal is just another of those pretty faces you've always been suckered by. You're afraid he has no substance, no staying power. That all he wants from you is some easy sex and no ties. Did you ever think you might be judging the book by its cover? That there are no bugs under the blanket, and that Cal is just the clean sheet he seems to be?"

"Which is?" Ginger mulled over the clean sheet analogy, couldn't make it work.

"A decent guy who's working hard at his business and who takes it, but not himself, very seriously."

Ginger hoped so, with all her oft bruised heart, she hoped so, but she didn't want to say it aloud—tempt those givers of bad luck. "He makes me laugh," she said, veering off the subject.

"And that's a bad thing?"

Ginger shook her head. "No. It's just . . . new, like everything else about Cal." Ginger got to her feet. "I'm going to get dressed." She walked to the door, stopped, straightened her shoulders but didn't turn to face her friend when she said, "I swear, if I've made another mistake, if Cal isn't the man I think he is, I'll be the first woman in the twenty-first century to be welded into a stainless steel chastity belt!"

Cal stepped into his rented condo in time to hear the phone ring. He headed straight to it.

It was Ian, and after leaving the heat of Ginger's shower, his brother's voice was a cold wind. "How's it going, Cal?" he asked. "Business still okay?"

Cal groaned inwardly. He should have known Ian's call would be about business. "Better than okay," he said, adding, "I'll be taking you out in a year, Ian, as we agreed." Cal loved his brother, but as a *brother*, not a business partner. His lack of enthusiasm for the core business and obsession with numbers drove Cal nuts. He was counting the days until he could pay Ian what he owed him and own Cinema Neo outright.

The silence on the phone was thick.

"I don't think so. I need the money now, bro."

"Now?" Cal's brain imploded. "You're kidding."

"No. I've got this deal—"

"You've always got a deal."

"Not like this one, and I'm not about to pass it up. I've got the buyer lined up. He'll pay top dollar—a little for you and a lot for me." He laughed.

"You can't do this."

"Yes, I can. Unless you can come up with enough cash to buy me out. You do that, we're both happy."

Not a snowball's chance in hell Cal could come up with that kind of cash. In a few months, maybe, but not now. Still, he bluffed. "I'll need some time."

"Don't have any. The buyer's ready and he's got the money. I'm not going to mess with it while you poll every bank in Washington State. I'll be bringing him up in a couple of days." He paused. "Hell, I'm doing you a favor."

"You're an asshole, Ian."

He chuckled into the phone. "Yeah, but I'm an asshole who drives a new Jag. See you in a couple of days." He hung up.

Cal stared at the dead phone in his hand. He was about to lose Cinema Neo and there wasn't a damn thing he could do about it. This sideswipe of Ian's would cost him everything.

Hell, he must have been planning this all along. He'd been suckered. He knew Cal couldn't come up with the money.

He had to figure out a way to make things work. If it were only him—

A thought bolted through him, damn near stopped his heart. This mess wasn't just about him and what he could lose, it was about Ginger. Last night his body had entered hers. That should have been the end of it. It always had been before, but not with Ginger, because in some mysterious way, she'd been the one to enter him.

And she'd become entwined in his life, in his decision making.

He wanted to offer her more than the chance to follow an unenthusiastic itinerant actor make the rounds of casting offices.

There had to be a way.

He went to his bedroom, started to pace.

It was three-fifteen, long after he'd trampled a major rut into his carpet, that his brain offered up the germ of an idea.

Chapter Six

Two days later, Ginger raced into the house, hit her bedroom running, flung herself on the bed, and let loose enough tears to irrigate Nevada. When the flood abated, she sat up, grabbed a wad of tissue, and pulled her knees to her heaving chest. After some ugly gasping gulps for air, she settled herself down.

Stoopid!!

First Cal had disappeared. There'd been no walk on the beach, no flowers, no E-mails—and no damned phone call. He was *so* gone it was as if he'd never existed. And a half hour ago, it got worse. She'd talked to Ellie and found out that Cal was selling Cinema Neo, that he'd left for L.A. to find a buyer. Obviously the man had never intended to stay in Waveside, proving a change in wardrobe did nothing to fire up the neurons necessary for reliable character judgment.

She blew her nose, got off the bed, and stripped off her dress to replace it with a ratty old tee and cotton shorts. In the mirror over the bathroom sink, she stared at the mess her tears had made, felt her skin tighten where the salt had dried on her cheeks. She splashed some water on her face, drank some to stave off dehydration, and headed back to her bedroom.

Cal might make her laugh in bed—among a lot of other wondrous things he did there—but it didn't change the fact she'd made the same tired mistake.

So . . . what now, Ginger Cameron?

Run away. Get her act together. Get a grip on a life without Cal Beaumann in it. Figure out what to do next.

Those ideas firmly in mind, she went to her closet, and opened it—to a sea of beige. She frowned. What had she been thinking? She was not a beige person, never was, never would be.

She went into the kitchen, grabbed a couple of lawn trash

bags. In less than half an hour the offending clothes, ranging from vanilla to dark tan, were ready for Goodwill.

It was time for a new Ginger—and past time for some overdue vacation. A road trip. Yes! Exactly what she needed. Some shopping in Seattle, then north to Canada. A few hours and she'd be in another country. Perfect.

No way was she going to hang around doing the pathetic woman-scorned routine, getting all pasty white and tear-streaked. She was leaving, and there was no time like the present.

She leaped to her feet just as Tracy came in bearing a pack of Girl Scout cookies—one cookie held between her teeth.

Ginger rummaged around in her closet.

"What are you doing?" Tracy asked.

"Getting dressed."

"You are dressed."

"So?"

Tracy looked at the bulging garbage bags. "And what are those?"

"Old clothes."

Tracy donned what Ginger could only describe as her resigned-to-anything look and plopped down on the bed. "Rats! You and Cal had a fight."

Ginger scowled at her. "Please do not mention that name. A woman does not like to revisit her mistakes."

"Some mistake. The guy's crazy about you."

"Ah! Now that's where you're wrong. Cal Beaumann is crazy about Cal Beaumann." She pulled out a pair of black slacks, tugged them up, zippered them closed, and headed for her bureau. There she pulled out a red T-shirt, atrocious with her hair, and a handful of lingerie, which she tossed on the bed. She went back to her nearly empty closet and pulled out a suitcase.

"Where are you going?"

"First? Seattle."

Tracy took the cookie from her mouth. "Why don't you just cool it. Wait for him to call and give the man a chance to grovel."

"Cal. Grovel?" Ginger looked at her friend as if her brain were leaking. "Never happen." She crammed the underwear into the case, followed it with an armful of shirts, pants, and shoes, then sat on it to zipper it up.

"What are you going to do in Seattle, anyway?"

"Shop."

Tracy looked alarmed. "Oh, no. Not another reincarnation!"

"Could do worse things." She pulled a brush through her hair, and it tangled so bad she needed both hands to set it free. Maybe she'd get a haircut. One of those Marine style crewcuts over a dyed blue scalp. Very futuristic. Perfect!

"Don't do it, Ginge. He'll call. You'll work things out. You know what they say, patience makes the heart grow fonder."

"That's distance, Trace. And that's exactly what I intend to put between me and Waveside." *And Cal Beaumann,* she added to herself. "Cal is selling Cinema Neo and moving on." She squared her shoulders. "He didn't factor me into that event. More fool him." She leaned over and kissed Tracy on the forehead. "After Seattle, I'm going to up to Canada. I'll call you from there."

"Canada!" Tracy made it sound as if she were heading for Siberia, rather than a friendly border crossing less than two hours away. "How long are you going to be gone?"

"I'll call you," she said again, and with that she picked up her bag, her injured pride, and headed for the door. She intended to take all the time she could afford. It wasn't every day a woman had to get over a man like Cal Beaumann.

Cal called Ginger the following morning. He had a lot to say and was impatient to say it.

"She's where?" he said to Tracy, not sure he'd heard right.

"Someplace in British Columbia."

Canada. What the hell had taken her there? "Okay, I'll try her cell phone."

"She's not answering it, just took it with her in case of emergency."

"Damn!" Cal's stomach tightened, and he rubbed his jaw. "Did she say when she was coming back?"

"She said she was coming back when she was completely and irrevocably over you." He heard Tracy munch on something. The woman was always munching. "Those were her words, not mine."

"Damn." If it hadn't been Tracy on the other end of the phone, Cal would have used a more fitting expletive. Okay, he should have called, but hell, his business troubles weren't Ginger's.

"I just hope she doesn't do something crazy."

"Like what?" he asked.

"Like coming back with purple hair and a nose ring." Now that sounded like Ginger, but he didn't care if she came back as the tattooed lady, just so long as she came back.

After he hung up the phone, he cursed. There was nothing he could do but wait. And if there was one thing in the world he was lousy at, it was waiting.

Eight days later, Ellie dropped the mail on his desk, and he muttered his thanks. She headed for the door, then stopped. "Cal?" she asked.

"Uh-huh."

"Would you mind if I took off an hour early this afternoon?"

"No problem." He didn't lift his head from the posters he had spread over his desk.

"Great. I'm meeting Ginger at the thrift shop. She's going to help me get a new image."

Cal's brain locked on one word, and when he lifted his hands from the posters, they snapped back into roll mode and hit the floor. "Did you say Ginger?"

He must have raised his voice, because Ellie took a step back. "Hmm."

Cal came out from behind his desk. "Ellie, you can have the whole damn week off if you tell me exactly where and at what time you're supposed to meet Ginger."

"A week? Really?"

"Really."

Ginger, half in and half out of a copper colored sweater, stopped tugging long enough to stare into the angriest pair of green eyes she'd ever seen. Cal! She gave the sweater a yank to pull it over her head, but only succeeded in snagging her hair on one of its decorative buttons.

Without a word he stepped forward and freed her hair. Her head surfaced, and one of the metal buttons clinked to the tile floor, rolling under the rack she'd been foraging through for the last fifteen minutes while she waited for Ellie. Now she'd have to buy the darn thing.

"What are you doing, Cameron?"

She coughed to calm the swell of butterflies and dingbats rising in her belly. She'd been gone for days, but still, just looking at him turned her brain to aspic. "I'm shopping."

He gave her a quizzical scan. "And what in hell is that?" He nodded at her mesh encased torso, silver spandexed legs, and metal-studded calf-hugging boots. "You look like a piece of space junk."

"Really," she said, her voice nicely icy. "Thank you. I like it, too."

"I didn't say I liked it."

"No, you didn't, but that doesn't necessarily mean you don't, does it? Seems to me you have a talent for saying one thing and doing another." She stepped to the other side of the rack, careful to keep it between them. She needed all the protection she could get. If he touched her she was a goner. As added insurance she took a hanger from the rack, held it up and made a pretense of considering it. It was a dress, puce with cabbage roses.

Cal closed his eyes, and she could see him pulling in a long breath. "We need to talk."

She studied the ugly garment. "So talk. I've got all the time in the world to listen. I'm not the one who's leaving town."

"Neither am I."

He said it so softly, the words were registering just as she added, "I'm not the one who sold a business—a life—I loved because somebody opened a wallet and"—she lifted her eyes to meet his—"you're not?"

"No, I'm not." He walked around the rack to stand facing her.

"Not what?"

"I'm not leaving and I'm definitely not selling Cinema Neo."

"You aren't?"

An indiscernible emotion shadowed Cal's face. Hurt? Grief? "No. Selling was Ian's idea, and when I heard about it I had to move fast or lose everything. Which meant getting to L.A. pronto." He paused. "The good news is that I've got a new partner. Hud."

"Hudson Blaine?"

"Uh-huh. He took Ian's position, and he's given me three years to buy him out. It's a good deal for him and a good deal for me." He took the dress from her and hung it back on the rack, then took her hands to his mouth and kissed her knuckles. "But not calling you was a mistake. I'm sorry." He lifted his eyes to hers. "Really."

Ginger wasn't quite ready to concede. "I'm not getting this sudden change of heart, Beaumann." She tried to back off, but her boot-encased feet refused to move.

He shook his dark head. "There's been no change of heart, Ginger. Mine's belonged to you since you walked into my office wearing a burlap suit and nun's shoes."

She couldn't take her eyes off him. And that soft buttery sensation in the middle of her chest told her she was falling again, toppling like one of those duck silhouettes in a shooting gallery. "I'm not sure I believe you," she said.

"Yes, you do," he said, putting his hands on her shoulders and dipping his head to look into her eyes. "I'm in love with you, Ginger. Always will be."

"You will?" Oh, goddess, she was squeaking like a mouse trapped in a cornflake box. Cal loved her.

"Which means I want this relationship to go exclusive." His voice was quiet. "You okay with that?"

The world stopped and Ginger's lungs imploded. Fortunately, she managed a tiny intake of breath and a bit of oxygen filtered into her numbed brain. She hoped he didn't see her swallow. "I should say no," she mumbled.

He grinned. "Any sane woman would."

"I'm still mad at you."

"I figured that."

"You have a lot of explaining to do."

"Probably take a lifetime to do it." His grin was devilish.

She put her hands on her hips, and gave him as level a gaze as she could summon up, given the crashing and thudding of her heart. Obviously hearts tended to do that kind of thing when the object of their desire dangled in front of them, lush fruit for the picking. "Then again, I could spend the rest of my days making you as miserable as I've been these past few days." She ran her index finger along his jaw. "That could be fun."

He pulled her hard to his chest, and she could feel his heart—its beat as erratic and unpredictable as her own. "Then, let the fun begin." He kissed her, a deep lingering kiss so mystical and soul stirring, she couldn't believe it could ever be topped.

Until he kissed her again.

She kissed him back, a kiss from her soul to his. It was the kind of kiss a woman could only give the man she wanted to share her life with. A kiss of fulfillment.

"Is that a yes to the exclusive idea?" he asked, his lips against her throat.

She ran her hands through his thick hair, pulled his head up to look into his eyes. "That's a definite maybe," she said, giving him her own version of a devil's grin. "I want you to start suffering as soon as possible."

He threw his head back and laughed. "I think I've made the biggest mistake of my life."

Ginger smiled. "Better you than me."

Here is an excerpt from
a contemporary sensual treat—
SMART MOUTH
by Erin McCarthy—
coming from Brava in April 2004.

"Reese Hampton?"

Not good. He knew who she was. "Maybe," she said, clearing her throat.

He smiled. A slow, wide, "women adore me" kind of smile.

Reese was suddenly way too aware of the fact that she wasn't wearing underwear.

"You're not sure?" he asked.

"Can I help you?" Striving for professional, she came off sounding more like a sullen McDonald's clerk.

He took another step forward, forcing her back instinctively. He moved clear of the door and closed it behind him.

That wasn't good. "Hey, I didn't ask you in."

"I don't care." He smiled, reminding her that he was crazy. No matter that he was as cute as a kitten and built like every woman's fantasy. He was still wacky and in her hotel room.

"Do I have to call security?" She yanked tighter on her robe as if tugging would suddenly cause undergarments to materialize on her body.

He laughed and reached into his pocket. He opened his wallet and stuck his badge in front of her. "They can't touch me. But I'll leave as soon as you give me what I want."

In another time and another place, that might have had a nice ring to it. But now it just annoyed her. This guy was starting to tick her off with his creepy smile and hot body.

Ripping the wallet out of his hands, she studied the FBI badge. She still wasn't convinced it wasn't fake.

"So, Agent Knight, what is it that you want?" Besides the Tyvek envelope, because she wasn't giving that up. Not when her first and probably last chance to do a real, newsworthy story resided in that envelope.

"Call me Derek."

Oh, ho, ho. Mr. Smooth. She narrowed her eyes at him and wondered just how he could manage to make jeans and a navy sweatshirt look so sexy. He was moving into her room, glancing around with no attempt at discretion.

Reese stayed by the door, hoping he'd get the hint. Of course, the guy had chased her into a deli, so it was likely he wasn't going to be satisfied with a brush-off. Now she knew why he was so tenacious about his envelope. Given only the quick glimpse she'd had, that evidence looked very incriminating. Probably earned Agent Knight here a gold star, or whatever the hell the FBI gave out. Maybe a class at Quantico named after him.

Scaring the Pee out of Unsuspecting Reporters, 101.

"What do you want, *Derek?*" She emphasized his name to show him she was annoyed, if he couldn't tell by her violent scowl. "That is, besides shaving ten years off my life from fright by chasing me half across Chicago."

"Sorry about that," he said, running his hand along the dresser in her room as he turned and walked toward the window.

Reese barely heard him. My God, she'd gotten the first glimpse at his backside. His butt was amazing. She felt inspired to write poetry. To sculpt. To overlook his professional insanity . . . uh, intensity and do a little investigating of her own.

Exhibit A. The finest ass in the lower forty-eight states.

"Where's the envelope, Reese?"

He turned around abruptly and she was left staring at his front side. That wasn't so bad either. Her body agreed. She realized with utter mortification that she was aroused, as in no-need-for-lubricants-here wet. Since she was naked but for the robe, it was disturbing and uncomfortable.

"What envelope?" she said, sticking her chin out at him. Jerk. Clearly he was used to getting his way, even if he had to run innocent investigative reporters off the road.

And make them horny.

And please turn the page for a tantalizing peek at
Good With His Hands
by Lori Foster
from
BAD BOYS IN BLACK TIE,
coming from Brava in May 2004.

Pete was up with the sun. After hearing that disturbing moan—disturbing on too many levels—he'd tried turning in early. But sleep had been impossible and he'd spent hours tossing and turning, thinking of Cassidy over there with someone else while his muscles cramped and protested. He'd tried to block the awful images from his mind, but they remained, prodding at him like a sore tooth: Cassidy with some suit-wearing jerk, Cassidy getting excited, Cassidy twisting and moaning.

Cassidy climaxing.

He couldn't stand it.

By seven, he was showered, standing at his closet and staring at the lack of professional clothes. Oh, he had a suit, the one he'd worn for his brothers' marriages. Gil had fussed, trying to insist that he buy a new, more expensive one, but Pete refused. He hated the idea of shopping for the thing, trying them on, getting fitted. Then he'd have to pick out a shirt, and a tie, maybe cufflinks . . . He *hated* suits.

But Cassidy loved them.

Stiff and fuming, Pete jerked on khaki shorts and a navy pullover, then paced until it got late enough to go to her place. She generally slept in on Saturday mornings. He knew her schedule as well as he knew his own. Right now she'd be curled in bed, all warm and soft and . . . He couldn't wait a minute more.

He went out his back door and stomped across the rain-wet grass to her patio. He pressed his nose against the glass doors, but it was dark inside, silent. Daunted, Pete looked around, and discovered that her bedroom window was still open.

Shit. What if the guy was still in there? What if he'd spent the night? What if, right this very moment, he was spooned up against her soft backside?

A feral growl rose from Pete's throat, startling him with the viciousness of it. No woman had ever made him growl. He left that type of behavior to his brother, Sam, who was more animal than man.

Now Gil, he was type of man Cassidy professed to want. A suit, serious, a mover and shaker. A great guy, his brother Gil. So what would Gil do?

He'd be noble for sure, Pete decided. Gil would wait and see if she did have company, and if so, he'd give them privacy.

That thought was so repugnant, Pete started shaking.

To hell with it. His fist rapped sharply on Cassidy's glass door.

A second later, her bedroom curtain moved and Cassidy peered out. "Pete?" she groused in a sleep-froggy voice. "What are you doing?"

"Open up." Pete tried to emulate Gil, to present himself in a calm, civilized manner. "You alone in there?" he snarled.

Her eyes were huge and round in the early morning light. "No, I have the Dallas Cowboys all tucked into my bed. It's a squeeze, but we're managing."

Pete sucked in a breath. *"Cassidy . . ."*

"Of course I'm alone, you idiot." Her frowning gaze darted around the yard in confusion. "What time is it?"

She was alone. The tension eased out of Pete, making his knees weak. "I dunno, seven or so." The chill morning air frosted his breath and prickled his skin into goose bumps. "Time to get up and keep your neighbor company."

"Seven!"

He took five steps and looked at her through the screen. She had a bad case of bedhead and her eyes were puffy, still vague with sleep. She looked tumbled and tired and his heart softened with a strange, deep thump. "Open up, Cassidy."

Still confused, not that he blamed her, she rubbed her eyes, pushed her hair out of her face. "Yeah, all right. Keep your pants on." She started to turn away.

"What fun will that be?"

Her head snapped back around. Seconds ticked by before she said, "Get away from my window, you perv. I have to get dressed."

The thump turned into a hard steady pulse. "Don't bother on my account."